SCARBOROUGH

QUINN'S STORY

MIDWINTER SONATA
BOOK 2

ELLEN L. EKSTROM

Whyte Rose & Violet, Scribes

Scarborough

ISBN: 978-0692219027

Published in the United States of America

Cover design: Whyte Rose & Violet Artists

Images courtesy of iStockPhoto.com

Whyte Rose & Violet, Scribes

www.whyteroseandviolet.net

queries@whyteroseandviolet.net

"The story of life is quicker than the blink of an eye
The story of love is hello and goodbye, until we meet again."
Jimi Hendrix

SCARBOROUGH

QUINN'S STORY

PROLOGUE

The Days After… and Before

FOUR DAYS had passed yet her perfume lingered in the bedroom and in her study. It was more noticeable when I entered after being outside, like this evening. I glanced about, waiting, and then tossed the keys into the majolica bowl we'd bought on our honeymoon in York. I still smile about that. Of the many romantic places I offered, she chose York. When I asked why, she went up on tiptoes to kiss my chin and said that's where it all came together. She knew then.

The bell-like ring of the metal hitting the glass was our signal; tonight it just echoed.

I wanted to hear one of the Orchestra's recordings drifting out of the study she kept off the bedroom, or her happy chatter after she kissed me 'hello' and ask how the rehearsal or tour went.

Her golden retriever loped into the bedroom and nuzzled my hand; he looked about expectantly.

"Soon," I told him, offering a pat.

Jesus, Mary, Joseph, I was lying to a dog now.

"Dad?"

The front door slammed and Richard appeared in the kitchen just as I entered. He could have been my double: above-average in height and looks with the Italian darkness I'd inherited from my mother and he had my physique. Fortunately, my son was everything I wasn't at his age of twenty-one: easy-going, relaxed, and eager for life. From his beautiful mother he received a positive outlook, and her eyes—big, round, green. His mother swore the 'swoon-worthy,' engaging smile and dimples came from me. I beg to differ. One look at her and you fall in love.

"Any news?" Richard asked, offering a hug when I approached, eschewing the usual guy pat his age now dictated.

"Soon," I replied laconically. "Have you eaten?" His mother's line. In times of stress, she fed us with food and reassurance.

"I'll order a pizza," Richard offered, pulling out a cell phone. While he paced the kitchen and called our favorite place, I made a fresh pot of coffee and watched the brewing absently, my attention caught by little things on the bookshelves meant for recipe collections and cookbooks.

"*I can't cook – why waste the space with books I'll never open? Besides, the kitchen is our living room and these things remind me of that*," she said after I'd spent all day putting up the shelves. A copy of her first book—a history of medieval Italy; photographs of us when we were dating in high school; our prom photo from 1970, when she wore the incredible dress; her shawl of soft wool that looked and felt like it was spun of pastel-colored clouds, the one we wrapped round ourselves on early mornings or evening walks from the castle to the sea…

"Dinner'll be here in about twenty minutes," Richard announced, switching off his phone and pocketing it. He reached around me for two cups on the shelf and in doing so tapped my shoulder. A game we'd played since he was in infant. He winked and said, "You're home, so I guess there's been some improvement?"

"A lot, actually," I said and explained as best I could what the doctors told me about her condition. I didn't mention the long conversations his mother and I shared over the past three days.

"*Don't look at me like that!*" she laughed from the hospital bed only this morning.

"Like what, Faery Princess?" I teased, bending down to offer a kiss.

"Like I'm nuts or need medication."

"How about more medication?"

"Quinn, I know it happened! Everything, *everything* was vivid, the sounds, the colors, even the smells. You know how when you dream, everything is disjointed – out of sequence? First you're doing one thing and then another, and somehow it all fits?"

"Yeah, kind of like this conversation?"

"Stop trying to laugh! Okay, laugh at me," She started to laugh then but tears welled in her beautiful eyes. More seriously, "Please, Quinn. I need you to believe me. You were a part of it. You were there at times."

"You didn't tell me that."

"I am now. And it all makes sense. Please, listen to me."

And so I listened as Alice told me again about The Village. The more she spoke, the more animated she became, stopping only when a nurse or doctor came in to check her vital signs and shake their heads in wonder that she had come back from what would have killed a man four times her size. Then she'd pick up where she left off in the recounting of a time and place occupying her thoughts and made her serene and more determined to live…

"Hey! You guys didn't open the presents!"

Richard's exclamation brought me back to the here and now and I carried my cup of coffee to the living room where our son was kneeling beside a pile of birthday and anniversary presents to the left of the gothic fireplace. A Christmas tree would normally stand there by this time of the month—it was the twenty-fourth of December—but I'd not taken the time or even cared about one, not with Alice still in the hospital and still not out of danger. So I'd made a pyramid of the packages and left them on the floor.

There's still time," I said and did something unthinkable: I ruffled his hair like he were still a little boy. Richard smiled and tossed a package at me. "Here. This one's from Mom. For your birthday."

"No, I'll wait 'til she's home, Richard."

"No," he chuckled, "I think she'd want you to have it now."

Without further prompting, I tore at the familiar paper—the wrapping paper from my grandmother's shop—the blue foil with stars. It had always been a favorite of hers. In between the layers of paper was a handmade notebook covered in dark red velvet with gold embroidery on the edges. Something she'd made, I thought, smiling.

Within the beautifully-wrought covers were pages full of our memories. Here were sketches of us over the years and memories written in her perfect, cursive hand. Here were pages of my notes on the *Fantasy on a Theme by Thomas Tallis* and the *Allegretto* from Beethoven's Seventh Symphony, with snapshots of me conducting the Orchestra in rehearsal. The guitar pick I used the night we played the Keystone and she sang *White Rabbit*. The hair ribbon she wore when we first made love. The train tickets from York to Scarborough. The program from the Orchestra's first New York appearance after I was made conductor.

My throat constricted with a lump as I fought back painful emotion and tears.

So many things to say…to do…

"Pizza's here," Richard said when the doorbell rang.

We dined quietly in the living room and watched *A Charlie Brown Christmas* and other holiday shows on TV. There was no rock-scissors-paper for the last slice of mushroom spinach deep dish pizza. We wrapped it in foil and put it in the freezer for the day she came home.

For the rest of the evening I said nothing and listened while Richard practiced his guitar and sang. He left around midnight with a Merry Christmas and a promise to bring his girlfriend around in the morning so we could all visit his mother in the hospital. Bring the Radcliffe Christmas to her and all that that entailed. The University Hospital was in for a big surprise.

I decided not to sleep upstairs in the bedroom where I would smell her perfume and be reminded. It didn't matter. The memories lived with me and as I drifted off on the sofa, my mind could not fathom why a heart as large and full as my beautiful wife's could fail as it did.

I knew why, for I had broken it.

CHAPTER 1

I'D BEEN here before.

It was oh so familiar…

Opening my eyes after what seemed like a rare night of full sleep, I found myself standing on a bridge constructed a millennium ago, the stones smooth and worn with age, deep ruts etched on a pavement where people had walked over centuries. This held my interest momentarily, for I looked down and saw The Village.

The narrow streets were familiar—twisting lanes that intersected clusters of row houses. They reminded me of The Shambles in York where my grandmother had her shop, where I visited during school holidays and those times when I didn't want to go home or be home. Here, reminded me of there, and where I stood now was a pleasant enough place—what was it that Alice said?

Oh yes, I remember…

It was a place out of a Thomas Hardy novel—or the imagination.

Well, no surprise that she and I would have the same village, or vision, wherever or whatever this was. We liked the same things, shared the same joys and sorrows and we fit perfectly—like puzzle pieces. Strange how long it took me to figure that out when everything was right before me at every twist and turn—but there were other things to consider, as if a door stood in the middle of the road and prevented me from going further on the journey. It only took unlocking and throwing it wide open to move forward.

Maybe that's why I found myself in this place Alice called The Village.

I stood for the longest time on that bridge spanning a beck, taking in the sights. Behind me were row houses, cottages and gardens that seemed to go on forever into a horizon that might have led into Wales. I knew it wouldn't, or couldn't. Alice told me as much. Before me was a street lined with shops—the buildings a mix of medieval and Tudor, the stone and slate of the Cotswolds with flower boxes attached to windows. Above red or green doors or swinging on brass posts were cheerful, painted signs and legends done up in medieval italic lettering that claimed proprietorship, goods and services. Behind me stood a Romanesque church at the top of the high street, and at the end lay The Shop—set off from the other buildings by a garden filled with hollyhocks, roses, tulips and Canterbury bells. The same flowers filled the window boxes. If you were a traveler, say, a Londoner coming up for a weekend, you'd think it was a pub for the mullioned windows and soft glow of light coming through them, the music drifting out and occasional laughter, and for the garish purple and gold sign hanging near the door that swayed and creaked in a constant soft breeze.

It was anything but.

How did I know?

Alice, my sweet Faery Princess, told me.

Since I was there I decided to make a go of it, make the best of what certainly had been a raw deal when it came to most of my life. No one but me would think being talented, drop-dead handsome, above-average in height with an athlete's physique, possessed with charm, and coming from wealth and privilege would be a raw deal, especially when I considered all Alice had been dealt.

She saved me.

"She's in a mood."

The voice startled me so that I wheeled about and

nearly stumbled into the man, a man in his mid-twenties dressed in sixteenth century doublet and hose, a fur-lined great coat of dark green velvet. He could have been Henry VIII, but I knew better—this man was tall, thin, blond, and had a long, sharp nose and blue eyes that were as round as moons and just as cold. His hand was extended as if to greet me, and having been raised to show my manners, I reached out, noticing first the ink-stained fingers and then the folio tucked in a leather bag slung across his body. It was tied close with frayed ribbons and near to bursting with loose pages. My hand went back into my sport coat pocket when he brushed the hair out of his eyes.

"Nice to meet you, Mr. Shakespeare," I greeted.

"Shakespeare?" he whined. "Do you think so?"

"Well, I thought…"

"I'd laugh if I thought you were jesting," he grumbled, flicking me away as if I were an insect and moving past to get to the other side of the bridge. He paused, and turned back, glaring. "Well? You don't have all day and I tell you from experience she won't wait. She's already had a rough time of it this afternoon, though most was her fault."

"Who's 'she'?"

Now he laughed and a bit unkindly. "The Proprietress, The Shop Mistress, Lucifer's Daughter, the Devil's Whore—take your pick. We've all had a go at trying to figure her out. No one's succeeded to this day— and don't think you'll be the lucky bastard! Everyone believes they've got a chance at that upon arriving. Whatever you decide to call Her Worshipfulness, you don't want to make a bad first impression, Tarquin."

"You know me?" I blurted out.

He sighed. "Why do they always say that? Of course I do. And please tell me why a parent would name their son Tarquin and not expect him to be angry?"

"Pardon? Hey, I'm not angry—at least I wasn't until a

moment ago."

"Never mind. I'm late for mass. Now don't make it worse for all of us. Get a move on." He pointed behind me towards The Shop. "Go. Thou wilt leave me thus. Now. Or else!"

"Thomas Wyatt!"

The Tudor poet's eyes bulged for a moment and then he smiled. "Well that didn't take long. Shall we clap hands and strike a gentleman's bargain, Mr. Radcliffe?" He slanted his head to the right, studying me. "You're an intelligent man; a wager that you'll sort it out by week's end."

"So is this really what I think it is?"

"Depends on what you want it to be." Wyatt jabbed the ink stained finger towards The Shop. "Go. And don't you dare tell her she's not the boss of you. We've all tried that one and failed miserably."

Before I could ask, he waved good-bye and went over the bridge—to nowhere. Frowning at the horizon, I studied all before me but couldn't find Thomas Wyatt. After another skeptical moment, I turned round in the blink of an eye to see if I could catch him off guard—annnnnd...*nothing!*

No one was there save a tall young man dressed in navy blue from scarf to boots. He was across the street near a milliner's and just stood there with arms crossed against his overcoat, watching me. When I started off the bridge he raised a tentative hand and waved, going in the opposite direction. The encounter left me uncomfortable; I felt his eyes on me as I walked towards The Shop, sure that I saw his shadow and piercing yet deep blue eyes when I glanced up at the early morning sunlight trying to break through the trees.

"Morning."

Looking down, I received a smile from Janis Joplin. She was leaving The Shop with a mug of coffee in hand, the aroma tantalizing.

I did a double take.

Coffee? Really?

That wasn't her style.

I nodded, a little star struck, noticing that she really did look like her photographs.

"What makes you think it's coffee? Picked a bad day to show up, Quinn Radcliffe," Janis called over her shoulder as she went into a hat shop across the street.

I would have responded but as I gripped the brass door latch, I caught my reflection in a window's polished glass and felt an icy chill run down my spine and grab me. The salt and pepper hair was gone, as were the bags under the eyes, the lines and softening of my once chiseled jaw line, which was chiseled again. The hair that couldn't decide whether to curl or fall in waves was black with the reddish brown streaks that always came out when I was in the sun—and I looked about sixteen, maybe seventeen.

I had celebrated my fifty-eighth birthday only last week.

The bell above the door jangled as I pushed the latch and was hit with the wonderful scents of coffee and bakery goods—and a watering can in the hands of a pretty woman in her late thirties.

"So sorry!" she apologized, trying to blot the water that spilled onto my shirt, her smooth unlined hand delicate as she pressed a handkerchief into the fabric. Upon closer inspection I saw that she was possessed of tranquility; the eyes were vaguely familiar in light color and shine; her hair was covered by a wimple and veil; and the beige and ivory tones of the fabric made her youthful, or rather, ageless. She wore a medieval nun's habit. As she worked, she hummed *O Quam Mirabilis Est* and I knew her at once. She was one of the greatest musicians and women of her day. Hildegard von Bingen was blushing scarlet with embarrassment as she sighed, "Your pardon, sir; in all my years here, I've only done that once before and it had to be Thomas Becket of all people."

"Aren't saints supposed to be kind and forgiving?" I

asked, smiling.

"Hah! Such a noise he made! I've never heard the end of it; he can hold a grudge and for a silly reason. Stupid man; he aspired to sainthood and got it—though what he got he didn't deserve, and I know the Augustinian brothers had it out for him. He caught a break…" she chatted while dosing the flowers with streams of water. Now she turned and smiled, winked. "Well? How is it with you, young man?"

"Uh, fine, fine. And you?"

She winked again and set to carefully plucking dead leaves and dried petals from the boxes. They came back to life as new plants in her hands and were potted with the rest. "Every plant is either hot or cold, and grows thus, since the heat of the herbs signifies the spirit, and the cold, the body. Hearts can be the same, don't you think? There! Another day or two…" Turning, she gestured into The Shop with the teaspoon she was using as a spade. "Mind how you go, Quinn—I suppose you know how it all works?"

"Alice told me, but you know, I honestly thought it was just a dream she kept having over and over, one of those reoccurring dreams that bug the Hell out of you…"

"Isn't that the worst? Well, it's different for everyone, and there are caveats and conditions. You get do-overs, if you want. It's entirely up to you, and the situation. Certain things have to be played out, Quinn. You'll catch on. It's more about changing you than anything or anyone. Oh, and a good thing to remember is that as soon as you think of something, it is there before you—you are in the midst of it, and everything connects—though how that works, I don't know. Ah! A ladybug!"

Hildegard moved slowly towards me, the ladybug in the palm of her hand. It might have been the sunlight, but the little red insect glowed brighter and exuded warmth and contentment that washed over me. Hildegard let it slip into one of the flower boxes and we watched it scurry off under a hollyhock. She straightened up and patted my arm. "Now. Back to the business at hand. Mind how you go—she's in a mood."

Good Lord, what was I in for?

The door slammed shut behind me and my entrance failed to catch the attention of an eclectic if not unusual group of patrons: Charles Darwin and the painter Raphael were sharing a *crème brûlée* while skimming over a portfolio of the artist's work; Ludwig von Beethoven stood over a young Queen Victoria at a piano and tapped out the measures from the *Allegretto* of his Seventh Symphony while she labored through it—swearing like a longshoreman, I might add—and Jimi Hendrix sat alone in a corner reading Proust. The Shop really did look like one of those Disneyland-slash-Las Vegas restaurants or shops, with the bright yellow curtains and café tables and chairs, the whitewashed walls decorated with Woodhouse and Burne-Jones paintings in gothic frames. Stacked on neatly arranged shelves were parquetry wood chests arranged like the shoeboxes piled almost to the ceiling in the old Huston's Shoe Store on Shattuck Avenue. A rolling ladder gave one access to the topmost boxes. What grabbed my attention though was the glass and walnut Victorian case displaying books of different sizes and colors like museum artifacts. A red book the size of a breviary caught my eye—it was difficult to ignore the brilliant color, the light made it ruby at one moment, burgundy the next. I edged up to the case to get a better look. The cover was leather with a gold border tooled on the edges like the Celtic designs Alice used to doodle on her notebook pages and homework...

"There's no maître d'."

A woman appeared behind the counter and flipped open the antique ledger lying on top of it. The book thudded softly and gave off a cloud of dust as pages were turned rapidly. She glanced down her nose and over the top of her cat-eye glasses. It was Helen Mirren in a really bad suit straight out of the fifties. Come to think of it, she did look like Queen Elizabeth II as portrayed in *The Queen*.

"Staring? That's quite rude," she hissed now.

No doubt about it, I was in the right place.

"I'm sorry, pardon?" I stammered when our eyes met, my smug expression disintegrating with my self-esteem. This woman probably had ice water in her veins. She definitely sent a chill through mine.

"I said: there's no maître d'. Take a seat anywhere."

"I'm not here to eat. I'm interested in that book—"

"I didn't offer and you shouldn't ask. Take a seat."

I scrambled for the table furthest from her, one against a window with a view of the high street and where sunlight shot giant beams across the floor and walls.

"That's not surprising," she sniffed.

Boy howdy yes, was I in the right place.

I slipped off my sport coat and draped it on the back of the chair then glanced around.

"Looking for someone?"

The Proprietress looked pleased with herself when I jumped. She was standing inches away from me.

"Yeah! I don't suppose Alice…"

"I wouldn't count on it. What are you doing?"

I was staring at the Young Man in Blue, who now stood in the middle of the road, smiling and waving, trying to get my attention. He disturbed me—no, he creeped me out and I avoided any further eye contact by studying my reflection in the window. I knew, or thought I knew, the why and wherefore of this place but it was still disconcerting to see myself as I had looked at seventeen.

The year I discovered Alice loved me…

"I don't think you've sprouted a wart."

"Look, are you always this disagreeable?" I demanded, wheeling back so that I was in her face. That must have startled her, for she inched away and her pupils dilated for a second.

"You have no idea…" She took off her glasses and

batted her eyelashes.

She was quite beautiful in a young Queen Elizabeth II kind of way, and then briefly, for another moment, I thought I was looking at Alice. But no, the Proprietress was glaring back at me. "Well?" she hissed. "I haven't got all day and neither do you!"

As I kicked the chair aside, a flash of metal on the seat caught my attention. A pendant of some sort, I guessed, and for a moment I felt that surge of adrenalin that hits when a memory surfaces. It was the silver rose from my grandmother Ellie's shop.

The rose I'd given Alice.

"What - did - I - just - tell - you?"

I ignored the glacial tone and words picked out of ice and scooped up the pendant on its heavy silver rope. The polished metal caught the sun and flashed blinding sparks so that I winced and closed my eyes. It seemed like an eternity until I felt I could open them.

"Sonofabitch!"

I was standing in my grandmother's shop in York and it was Christmas of 1968.

"*Sonofabitch!*"

CHAPTER 2

"SWEETHEART! NOW *that* is exactly what I said to your father when he called."

I jumped, startled by Ellie's voice and my surroundings.

"Get used to it, Radcliffe," Janis Joplin whispered in my ear. *"Prepare for a dark ride."*

"Wha—what's that?" I demanded and gasped for air while I tried to get over the shock of last few moments. "You said he called?"

"Oh dear, that must have been some flight across the pond. Yes, he called a few times, actually, and said you might be on your way here rather than meeting him in New York. This is probably one hell of a good story!"

I finally trained my eyes on my grandmother Ellie who stood behind the main sales counter, hands folded on the ancient oak smoothed to a patina by years of transactions. Her fat orange tomcat was curled up on its pillow next to the cash register and looked quite at home in this eclectic, true curiosity shop from another era.

It was a jumble of Victorian charm and clutter, like something out of a Dickens novel. Here were dark cherry wood shelves and lattice-windowed cupboards piled high with antique toys and fine, handmade papers with matching envelopes; curiosities such as a full suit of armor around which was draped strings of Mardi Gras beads and Christmas lights, and from the tip of the broadsword fastened to a gauntlet was a silver cage in which a mechanical bird twittered and chirruped. On the floor next to it was a sword shoved into a stone. On top of the heavy gothic tables were wicker baskets full of sachet bundles she'd made while watching *Top of the Pops* on Thursday nights, each tied up in silk and linen squares with ribbon and handmade labels: little pillows and pouches fragrant with the potpourri of roses, vanilla, lavender, freesias and jasmine, some with woodland, spice-heavy scents and cedar. Next to the baskets were neatly folded scarves and shawls of Italian silk or English wool in bright paisleys with gold metallic fringes and embroideries, and some with conservative Victorian flower patterns. There were drawers of kid gloves, rows of hats suitable for The Ascot, and the most incredible collection of miniature knights and tin soldiers loaded on the shelves with antique roadsters and volumes of classic children's faery tales. The entire Andrew Lang rainbow and Grimm collections competed for space. Beside the cash register – other than the cat - were old-fashioned candy jars stuffed with gumdrops, peppermints, chocolate kisses, gingersnaps and gingerbread boys and girls, all displayed on tartan squares or tea towels decorated with the white rose of York. Off on a corner shelf behind the counter were stacks of Ellie's latest novel that she'd autograph if asked. Hanging from a dowel was a roll of her trademark dark blue wrapping paper with gold starbursts and roses.

You could feed the imagination or run away from life in this incredible shop and Eloise Radcliffe made it happen. For Eloise Radcliffe refused to conform and aged gracefully on her own terms. When she stepped round the counter you didn't get the archetypical grandmother with silver hair tied back in a scalp-stretching knot, one who wore calico and muslin shirt-waist dresses with a single strand of pearls and sensible heels, who smelled of Pears soap and gingerbread, but a woman who enjoyed the Beat Generation and lived it. Did I say Bohemian? That would sum up Ellie.

Today she discarded her usual black and gray and was wearing a dress with purple-colored tights—and a pair of ankle-high boots to match. Over the dress was a long vest in black wool that grazed the knees of her still shapely legs. The dress was a harlequin patterned light show of psychedelic colors: pink, purple, blue and fuchsia were predominant. You needed sunglasses to shield your eyes from the glare.

"Well? Give us a kiss, Quinn, and tell us all about it!" Ellie chirruped. "My you are *the* handsome boy!

"So you always say," I gasped coming out of a Chanel Number 5 clouded hug.

"How was the ride up from London, then? Get some sleep?" She sounded hopeful and I nodded. "Good! We shall have a talk. I sensed something was up, and your call was cryptic. And then your father and mother...let's lock up for the day and go upstairs for some tea and biscuits—and we can order some take away if you'd like."

In one movement she scooped the cat off its cushion and plopped it on the floor as she threw sheets over the displays and counters. I followed in the evening ritual and waited by the light switch until she'd bolted the door and pulled the shades. Moments later we were upstairs in her flat above the store, waiting for the kettle to whistle. The scent of potpourri and incense she carried up from the shop was soothing and the way the late afternoon sunlight spilled from the windows in dusky shafts made everything glow and seem warmer than the winter day. The cat sniffed at my knee and flicked its tail when I refused to give up the chair it obviously thought was his. The standoff ended when Becket took a swipe at me with its forepaw and claimed the blanket surrounding the Christmas tree stand. The bottom tier of glass ornaments danced and swayed when the cat started to sharpen its claws on the trunk. I could have sworn I saw my father's grimacing face reflected in the various shaped orbs. It was fatigue. It had to be.

"Are you sure this a good idea?" I asked as I tried to pull the cat away. "Cats usually have a search and destroy mission where it concerns Christmas trees."

"Never mind Becket," Ellie replied. "I'm wondering what you're doing in England over the Christmas holiday without your parents."

The shriek from the tea kettle saved me for only a moment. When my grandmother returned with a tea tray I was still rubbing my palms on the knees of my corduroy pants and trying to think of something. A teacup was handed off and then a plate of my favorite treats. She nodded and I lost myself in shortbread and Earl Grey, happy to inhale the flowery scent of the tea and swallow the rich and buttery squares that reminded me of better times, of why I was there.

Swallowing carefully and once again rubbing my palms against my knees, I glanced over at her. Her brows were raised, waiting.

"Ellie, have you ever just wanted to die?"

The question came out more calmly and quietly than I expected. Her gasp was a sharp intake and she set down her cup, her hand trembling.

"Quinn, your age isn't the easiest—"

"Not that, Ellie! God, no; I haven't given a damn about what people think for a while—I can't afford to, but there are times I wish I were eighteen or an orphan."

"Oh dear," Ellie sighed. "Let me guess—your father?"

I nodded, reached for another chunk of shortbread and stuffed it in my mouth so I wouldn't have to respond immediately. Finally, "He wanted me to audition for the New York Philharmonic. I told him I wasn't ready, but he insisted. Christ! That's with Bernstein—with Bernstein! I wasn't fucking ready for that."

"What happened?"

"Not now," I grumbled. "Can I have a bath and then go to bed—I've got jetlag."

"You don't have to ask, darling. This has always been your home—and will be yours when my time comes."

"Please don't say things like that. You're the only constant in my life right now!"

"I won't live forever, Quinn."

"Dammit! Don't!" I started up, and then fell back into the chair again, head against the padded wings. "Sorry; I promised myself I wouldn't blow. It's not your fault; none of this is. I've had to keep it in for so long."

"I guess talking to him is out of the question."

"Do you really think he'd listen, Ellie? I don't know why he thinks I'm ready when I know I'm not."

"Neither of you are wrong. You think you're not ready—maybe you're not. Obviously, your father, who is very, very, talented himself and unfortunately knows it, and lets everyone he meets know it, sees the same in you and believes you are. He wants only the best, which is natural when your child is as gifted, handsome and charming as you. He was more than a handful growing up—his father and brothers didn't have the patience you have with him, though." Ellie now leaned over and brushed the hair out of my face, lifting my chin so that she could look in my eyes. When my parents did that, I was always on the defense, but with Ellie it meant a sounding board for my grievances and disappointments, understanding and absolution. "I suppose, too, if I were your father, I'd be worried sick about where you'd gone. Tell me how you did it."

"My British passport," I muttered, avoiding her eyes. "I'm still a British subject. I have my majority here. The letters of introduction from Muir Mattheson of the Royal Philharmonic and the one from the Conservatory helped a bit at customs on both sides. That and lying a bit. I told the authorities I was supposed to meet Dad in London."

She clucked in exasperation but I could see how desperately she wanted to laugh. "Used the birthday and Christmas money I sent, did you?"

"No—exchanged one ticket for another. I may need the money for another quick getaway, seeing how Dad refuses to give me an allowance and when I ask for money for anything you'd think we were arguing at the United Nations for a nuclear ban treaty or something."

Now Ellie laughed and it should have made me feel victorious or vindicated, but it didn't. "Well, that's a trick he learned from his father. Good to know he was paying attention at least part of the time."

"I don't think it's funny."

"Sorry, darling. Now confess; what well-made plans of yours did he ruin this time?"

I took a deep breath. "I wanted to spend Christmas with a friend—not in New York City at another audition or concert tour. I wanted to be...a guy for a change, not some damn prodigy with a cello."

Where that came from, I didn't know.

Ellie took off her glasses and smiled. "A friend? A friend, is it?"

"Yeah…" I answered, flustered, but with a grin on my face.

"You'll have to tell me more about her after your bath—it is a girl, I suppose?"

"What do you think?" I laughed.

"Obviously, I don't. See you in a trice."

I was considerably relaxed after soaking in a hot bath and even though Ellie coaxed and pleaded, I didn't tell her much about Alice. I went to bed that night warm and contented for the first time in weeks. I could stay with my grandmother and live above her incredible shop for the rest of my life—but with Alice.

The smell of coffee brewing and breakfast frying up woke me after sunrise the following day and for only a second I panicked, thinking I was still at home. But no, the overstuffed mattress, the overstuffed quilts and comforters, the overstuffed cat reminded me I was in York. I turned over and grabbed one of the marshmallow-like pillows, ready to tuck in for some more sleep when the overstuffed cat jumped onto the bed and purred its way up to my head where it sniffed and batted at my hair, purred like a lawnmower in my ear.

"Go away, Becket. . ." I yawned.

The cat was making a stand. If I hadn't been so worried about spraining my hand or getting a hernia throwing him, I would have hurled Becket across the attic bedroom and enjoyed listening to the thump or plop when he landed. He got a reprieve when the phone rang downstairs and I held my breath, waiting.

"Quinn! Tar-*quin*!"

There it was—my death sentence.

Cocky self-assurance, smugness and pride at my actions fell to the wayside as I dug out the bathrobe from my suitcase and went downstairs. Ellie had her hand to the receiver when I entered the kitchen. "It's your mother," she whispered.

Nodding, I took the receiver and exhaled, waited a moment before saying, "Mother, how are you?"

"You're supposed to be in New York, darling..." she sighed.

"Well, I'm in old York. Got in last night—but that's no surprise to you, seeing how Dad figured everything out. Glad to know he actually cares about me and not just my talent."

"Don't be ridiculous! What do you think we've been doing all this time? We've been looking for you. We thought something happened to you. What were you thinking, Quinn? Honestly!" She paused, and then, "Your father had to smooth some ruffled feathers when you didn't show. He put himself out on the line for this, and he waited for hours at Lincoln Center."

"If Dad wants a chair in the New York Philharmonic let him audition."

"You blew a chance of a lifetime; it may never happen again. Is this what you want? To keep disappointing your father?"

"I told him and now I'll tell you. I'm not ready for something that big. Every single musician on that stage would be at least ten years my senior in both age and experience. I'd blow the audition just on nerves and I'm not ready to make an ass of myself just because one person thinks I'm good enough. I know I'm not ready and I don't want to do it now—not yet, at least."

"Then you need to come home and tell that to your father. I asked your grandmother to put you on the next flight she can book to the States—"

I threw a frown at my grandmother, who blew a kiss while she turned bangers, mashed potatoes, eggs, and American hash browns in various pans. "Thanks, but I need a vacation. I'll be home after Christmas."

"Christmas? You'll be home tomorrow if I have anything to say about it!"

"Well, that's just it—you don't. I have my majority here in England and I've got my passport. I'm turning seventeen in three days, and—"

"Stop right there, young man! You forget who pays for the lessons, the auditions, the travel, the work that goes into the concert bookings."

"Here comes the threat…" I sighed.

"Not a threat, but the truth. We will cut you off in a minute. Don't think we haven't already thought about it."

"Cut me off from what? Take away the nothing I get for an allowance and I'll still have nothing."

"You know what I mean."

"You can't touch the Salimbieni trust so that's a hollow threat."

"And just who do you think is the executor of your grandfather's trust?"

I paused, glancing around the kitchen at the speckled morning sunlight on the wooden floor planks, the large and round backside of Becket as he leaned over his bowl for the first of many meals that day. My grandmother noticed the silence and turned to silently inquire about what was going on. I turned my back on her and said to mother a thousand miles away, "Rather than threaten me, Mother, why don't you listen for once?"

"I'm listening."

"It's simple. I needed some time to myself and I knew I wouldn't get it at home, not in the mood he's been in for months now."

"You both share the blame for that," Mother said.

"Really? Do you think so? You don't know what it's been like! Geezus, Mom, there are days when I just don't want to get out of bed. And when I do, I just want to throw myself out the window—"

"Quinn! My God!"

"—I'm okay; I'm okay! Now I am, because I'm with Ellie." I turned and winked at my grandmother, who shook her head slowly. "I'm with Ellie and she'll keep me in line. Let me have Christmas vacation just once? Is it so much to ask?"

The pause and silence was my answer. Of course it was too much to ask.

"What do I say to our friends? And what about your birthday? We made plans," Mother started.

"Your plans. Not mine. Not what I want. What guy my age wants a party with the Cal music department? Consider this birthday and Christmas gifts to me. All I've done for the past two years is spend my vacations and free time at auditions or in concerts and doing what I'm told— and before you ask, it hasn't been a waste of time. Yes, I love music, and I love being a musician, but there's more that I want. I want a life. I want to spend my birthday with my friends, not booked for concerts and auditions." Again, there was a long and telling silence on the line so that I had to ask, "Mother . . . Mom? Are you alright?"

The sigh sounded like a hurricane in the receiver. "Yes...I'm fine—no, I'm not. I don't like what's happening. You and your father are constantly at each other's throats these days." Again there was a pause. And then, "What friends?"

"I've got a few. Does it surprise you?"

"You've never said a thing."

"Would you have listened? Dad thinks I don't have time for a life. Every, single, damn, hour of the day has to be packed with lessons, auditions, interviews, rehearsals. He won't listen."

"Quinn, this arguing. It has to stop."

I took a deep breath and then said, "Well, you know what the remedy is, don't you? Don't worry. I promise you, I'll be home before New Year's. Ellie will make sure I'm on a plane to California."

Mother sighed and then said in her rare 'parent voice,' "Don't think you've gotten away with anything, young man! You gave away your hand."

"Then I'll have to play a different game next time."

"If there is a next time—oh dear, your father's home. I don't want to continue this argument. Call me Christmas Day, would you?"

"Sure. Mother—Mom, I love you—"

A click and a hum.

I handed the receiver to Ellie and slumped down into a chair at the table, staring at the flower design on the plate. "Love you too, Quinn," I sighed under my breath.

"Where did that come from?" Ellie mused as she dished up bangers and eggs, scoops of hash browns, and poured cups of Earl Grey and coffee. "All that self-assurance and speaking up for what you want? You sounded like your grandfather Richard for a moment."

"I have no idea," I admitted and dug in like a starving man.

"Don't look so pleased with yourself, Quinn Radcliffe," Ellie chided, but not unkindly. "It's only a stay of execution."

"Let a condemned man have his breakfast before driving him to the airport," I said.

"Airport?" Ellie laughed. "Oh no; it's been years since I had my grandson over for Christmas! Let me be a part of this rebellion. Finish your breakfast and then we'll go for a walk."

I suddenly felt better, our morning walks were special times together, our tradition. It began with Morning Prayer at St. Peter's Cathedral, the Minster. Ellie may have been non-traditional in her lifestyle and views, but when it came to religion she was dyed-in-the-wool Anglican. This was comforting, for my parents had no religion but the faith borne of self-love and ever since I could remember, the quiet beauty and mystery of a church made me feel loved and safe.

We went directly to the crossing under the lantern and stood there for a moment, praying for the great-grandfather I never knew: an Anglican priest named Harold Faithwaite killed in the so-called 'Baedecker Raids' on April 29, 1942. Then we slipped into stalls in the quire and handed each other a prayer book. Forty minutes later, we strolled through the nave and whispered to one another about what we thought of readings, the sermon, the chanting by the Minister choir. Then it was up to the Walls.

A 2.5-mile perimeter of ancient stones and towers protected York, and as we started our up the Bootham Bar steps, I touched one of the stones for luck. Ellie saw and smiled, letting a gloved finger trace the outline of the rectangular stone.

"You remembered," she said.

"If the stones have been here since the eleventh century, may I have the same luck," I recited.

"Your grandfather touched that part of the wall every day for as long as I could remember – certainly since his childhood. A superstitious thing,"

"And silly."

"No. Something full of hope, don't you think?" Ellie said and linked her arm through mine. "Come on then, we have several bars to hit." She laughed at her little joke and after a moment I got it.

"The "bars" were defensive gatehouses and Bootham was the oldest. Here my grandfather, a lesser-known poet, musician and historian from the Beat Generation, Richard Radcliffe, would hold me in his arms and show me the city of York from these heights and tell me wonderful stories of its history. Today I wanted to pick up Ellie and swing her around in my arms and tell her how happy I was to be there, to be with her.

"Other than your father, all is right in your world?" asked Ellie when we paused at Monk Bar. We smiled back at tourists and locals as they squeezed past us.

"I'm enjoying school more. I've got a reputation for being the mysterious Brit thanks to the accent that won't seem to go away. The girls seem to like it," I answered.

"One girl in particular?"

"Well, I wouldn't know. It's not something you ask a girl. 'I say, jolly and sexy good voice, don't you think?'"

"You're not going home until you've told me all about this young lady who's got you in a spell," teased Ellie.

"Then I won't be going anytime soon," I teased back.

"I would love to have you all year 'round, and having you at work in the shop would be fabulous for sales— all the girls from Saint Barbara's School coming over to have a look at the dishy sales boy…" Ellie sighed in mock exasperation as we continued our walk, now moving towards Mickelgate Bar.

We strolled silently for a bit, and then I said, "If I wanted to, I could stay with you, right? Not just for Christmas, but if I need to get away, if I decide to leave home."

"Quinn, you're almost finished with school and then you have university. It's only one more year, sweetheart."

"It's a hypothetical. I don't want to leave Berkeley right at this moment, right now, because I'm in love with a girl. I know I couldn't tell this to Mom and Dad; it would defy all reason, but you, Ellie —you remember being in love?"

"I still am, Quinn," she answered softly. "There isn't a day of the year I don't miss Richard."

"That's why you never remarried after Grandpa died?"

"Now who would be able to put up with me and that fabulous shop?" Her laughter was brittle and she squeezed my arm. "You have to tell me and there's no wiggling out of it. Who is this mysterious lady?"

"Her name is Alice Martin."

"And what is she interested in, other than you—or is this unrequited love?"

"Pretty much, for now, at least. I know there's a guy...she's a costume and set designer for the drama department at school; she also loves medieval history." I gushed once over the initial embarrassment of saying what I was thinking—something I did when nervous. "She would fit. She would fit incredibly into my life."

"You'll have to bring her here, won't you?"

"I think she'd like York."

"She's pretty?"

"Large green eyes, dimples, incredible smile, and light brown hair—sometimes it looks blonde—and fantastic legs. She's tiny, like a ballerina, but with all the right curves," I laughed self-consciously.

"What do Jane and Andrew think of her?"

"They don't. Haven't met her, but they'd find everything I think interesting and disapprove."

"Such as?"

"From what I've heard, her father disappeared and her mother is dying of some sort of cancer, that her only brother is a homosexual and he gave up Dartmouth to take care of the both of them—well, Missus Martin at least. Alice can take care of herself; she works two jobs to help support the family."

"And you want to ride up on your snowy white charger and save her?"

"Chestnut—the horse would be chestnut. And she'd be the knight in shining armor."

"She'd save you?"

"I wouldn't be surprised."

I didn't remember saying that. It must have been the right answer because the sun started to break through the clouds and I half-expected to find an angel choir when I glanced up. Ellie's smile was the truest confirmation of a step in the right direction.

"Seems like she only needs to be saved from poverty."

"She's not poor; maybe in the sense everyone takes it, she is. When you consider everything that's happened in her life—well, I sound like a spoiled brat complaining about my comfortable lot."

"You are a spoiled boy," Ellie mused and she gave my forearm a squeeze. "But never a brat. Your grandfather would be proud and delighted to know you've finally grown a pair!"

There was nothing I could say in response to that. But I did laugh and Ellie laughed with me. And I did pick up my diminutive grandmother and twirl her about. When we stopped spinning, the stones of the York walls swirled and melded into each other and when the dizziness subsided, I found myself smiling down at the Proprietress and not Ellie.

She glared back, effectively wiping the grin off my face.

"Oh, dear. Someone doesn't like the gifts others would kill for. You're quick; I'll say that for you." A key came out of the handbag slung across her wrist and opened the display case separating us. "That in itself deserves a reward."

A book covered in purple suede and decorated with large yellow and orange cabochons was thumped onto the counter.

Tappa-tappa-tap-tap-tappa-tappa…

The fingernails kept a rhythm on the glass top. I reached out and took her hand, stopped the impatient drumming meant to annoy. "That isn't the book. I'd like *that* one, please."

I pointed to the ruby-colored book with gold arabesques and findings. The Proprietress' eyes narrowed and reminded me of Becket cornering a mouse. "Aren't you the clever young fox?" She hissed. "Don't count on it—yet!" The purple book was locked back up in the case and the key disappeared into the handbag. "Go find something to do while you're here. It's going to be a while in spite of your cleverness and what a certain young miss told you."

She snapped her fingers and pointed to the corner.

"Can I at least have a cup of coffee?"

"Take a seat!"

"Look, all I want is a bloody cup of coffee—oh."

The table in the corner was set for one, a cup of coffee steaming in a pottery mug and just as I wondered what I was going to do to pass the time, a notebook of music manuscript paper and a pen appeared before me.

"It's different for everyone, Quinn. Take Doctor Martin, for instance. She came with a laptop computer; used to tap away on that contraption especially when angry, and that was a lot…"

I looked up at the sound of the man's voice—deep, melodious, a touch of weariness. He was seated at a table across from me and had *The New York Times* before him and opened to the crossword. The late-fifteenth century clothes were a giveaway as to his identity, as was his face: angular and handsome, the weariness in his voice reflected in slate-gray eyes that missed nothing as customers arrived and went about their business quietly. He seemed particularly interested in the Proprietress as she made entries in her great ledger, and noted my own curiosity.

"It's not an attendance record she's keeping," the gentleman said as he applied a Mont Blanc pen to the crossword. "We all assume it's a catalogue of sins."

"If she's writing about me she's going to need a bigger book," I muttered and puffing a sigh out of my cheeks, rubbed my hands on my knees, looked around for something to do.

"I'd at least make a pretense of industry," he said. When I didn't respond, he added, "Look busy."

I opened the notebook and gasped to find a page I'd written from memory. Every one of the pages were full of musical notation and my boyish scrawl in the margins.

"You started that when you were, what? Ten? Let me guess. You wanted to impress your father?"

"There's no pleasing some people," I commented. I glanced at him, and he smiled back, the corners of his eyes rising. The ruby-red doublet winked with diamonds and golden embroidery, caught the light and threw color into his wan complexion.

"I learned that too late. Now, if I had known then what I've learned since the spring of 1483, history would have been written differently."

"And history would have been kinder, or some historians kinder, Richard Plantagenet."

I leaned over to shake his hand and was not surprised in the least that he had a powerful grip. It was also no surprise that his presence didn't frighten me. Sitting in the Curiosity Shop seemed natural.

"Guilty of being Richard, but not other things, no matter what gossip is being thrown about in The Toad in the Hole." Richard III said and then winked, a shy, crooked smile crossing his thin mouth.

"I guess you'd know something about trying to please parents?"

"And everyone else." Richard saluted me with a cup of coffee and reached behind him to the bar where an antique toaster sat. "Three...two...one!" He grabbed at two Pop Tarts as they appeared with the ring of a tinny bell, and then looked at me. "Marvelous inventions, these! I don't suppose…?" he queried, offering the toaster pastries.

"I don't eat them."

"Who doesn't like a subtlety? Come, I insist."

I took one to be polite and just as Richard started to take a bite of the other it was snatched out of his hand by a tweedy old gentleman who suddenly appeared and hurried past us like the March Hare, muttering about being late. I laughed and caught myself when the Proprietress shot a look at me and Richard threw a warning glance. What was the problem? How could one be late to a place where time seemed to stand still or move at leisure and by circumstance?

"He'll be your problem," Richard said and before I could ask what he meant, the tweedy gentleman circled back towards the front of The Shop, dropped the Pop Tart on a Wedgwood plate from the bar and whispered, "Marvelous! Marvelous!" as he worked his way around tables. His eyebrows seemed to have lives of their own and undulated like caterpillars as he puffed on a Chesterfield and hummed a song. I couldn't place him; one thing was definite: he was like the strange uncle that stank of Old Spice; the one no one wanted to sit beside at the Christmas dinner table.

Good God; he was coming towards me…

"Rafe! What did I tell you?" the Proprietress snapped. "Put that vile thing out!"

The cigarette was extinguished in a planter, which set Hildegard von Bingen into a state. She fished it out while muttering German invectives under her breath, taking the offensive butt and tossing it into a trash bin just past Richard, who frowned as it missed his head and plunked into the can. Ignoring both the nun and the king, and patting the pockets of his early twentieth century suit coat, this Victorian throwback called Rafe pulled out a chair at

Richard's table, brows raised in hopes of permission.

"Not like I have a say in the matter, do I?" Richard groused.

The Pop Tart on its plate was shoved toward him. "You've been told to use a plate, Your Grace," the gentleman chided. He looked at me and winked. "No one likes to clean up after a person, be it kingdoms or crumbs."

Richard cleared his throat and asked, "What's an eight letter word for 'Disney film with classical score'?" He looked up. "Anyone?"

"*Fantasia*," Rafe and I said in unison.

"Of course you would know that!" Rafe laughed, and tapped the music manuscript. "It was one of your favorite films, wasn't it? Though a bit simplistic for you even as a boy, given your prodigious ability." When I scowled at him rather than respond, he added, "I'm Ralph Vaughan Williams, Maestro Radcliffe. Pronounced 'Rafe' as in safe. Pleased to finally make your acquaintance, sir."

His hand came out of a pocket and pumped mine vigorously. I must have looked a fool, for all I could do was jump to my feet and gape with mouth open. I was shaking hands with one of my musical idols, one of the greatest composers of the early twentieth century, and I all I could do was stare at his dancing eyebrows.

He leaned down and glanced at the manuscript. "Let's see what's here—why, this is the viola solo from the *Tallis Fantasia* I composed in 1909! At letter…I. Yes, yes, well this is a job well done, Maestro!"

"I always wished you'd written this part for cello and not viola," I said, trying to wrest the manuscript from him for I was embarrassed by my childhood hobby of copying down others' masterpieces. Rafe was interested, however, and hummed along as he read the music.

"What was this for? A school exercise?" he wanted to know, brows finally still as they arched.

"No," I admitted, flushing bright red. "Just wrote

down what I heard."

Rafe frowned and looked at the notation again.

I continued, "Let me explain—my grandmother gave me a recording of the *Fantasia on a Theme by Thomas Tallis* for my ninth birthday. I listened to it and then started writing down what I remembered. I wanted to show my father...it was going to be a Christmas present..." my voice trailed as I remembered. "Doesn't matter now."

"You've captured the *poco piu animato* of the viola almost perfectly—how many times had you listened to it?"

"Only once. No, maybe twice or three times."

"*Thrice?* Three times you say?" Rafe sputtered, and looked at the juvenile scrawl of notation even more closely. "And what did your father say?"

"Why wasn't it my own composition. And then went to pour himself another whiskey neat."

"Bastard," Richard said. When he saw us glaring at him, he added "Seven-letter word for spurious or disingenuous," and buried himself in the crossword, avoiding further eye contact.

"This is fine work and should be commended," Rafe said, patting my shoulder sympathetically.

"My music teacher was impressed," I said, closing the notebook.

"There was another piece of music, wasn't there?" the Proprietress spoke up, though she kept her eyes on the ledger entries she made.

"There were lots of scores I transcribed," I chuckled.

"But there was one in par-tic-u-lar," The Proprietress sing-songed.

Richard glared at the Proprietress. "Really, Madame, would it hurt once in a while to say what you mean?"

"Or mean what you say?" Rafe added, winking at me.

"That's not the point of the exercise," she growled. "They're given free will and boatloads of chances to figure things out, and yet they end up here anyway. I am expected to sort them all out like apples!"

"Poor you…"

Richard's sarcasm was not appreciated, judging by the silence that fell over The Shop.

"Well, Your Grace?" the Proprietress addressed Richard after a very long, almost too long, moment of reflection during which I could hear Richard's pen scudding across the crossword puzzle. "Since you've taken it upon yourself to champion certain lodgers in the village, perhaps you'd like to take on the responsibility for The Shop and all that it entails?"

"Don't pull me into it; you know what happens every time," Richard said.

I leaned over and slapped my hand on top of Richard's crossword. "What?" I whispered, "What happens?"

"Maestro, your taxi is waiting."

The Proprietress crooked her finger at me and then pointed out the door.

Rafe gave me a gentle, playful nudge and winked, saying, "Go along with it, Quinn. See you in a bit?"

I shuffled unwillingly to the door, but as I was leaving, the Proprietress cleared her throat and pointed toward a brochure rack. Looking at me from over the glasses, she narrowed her brows and I grabbed one of the pamphlets, which wasn't a pamphlet at all, but a hall pass from my high school. As I opened The Shop door I walked through to the first floor of Berkeley High School out of the Principal's office.

CHAPTER 3

I SLAMMED to a halt, surprised, and the door hit me in the back, which made two football players snigger as they passed by; I could have sworn one of them said that I liked getting it from behind. I was used to hearing stuff like that but jumping the idiot bastard and punching out his lights would land me in detention, so I waited a moment before making a sharp right towards the lockers on the third floor.

The lack of students and noise confirmed it was somewhere during a mid-morning period. My loafers squeaked and groaned on newly-waxed floors, footsteps echoing as I turned another corner and just as I expected, I remembered, I saw her. She was standing in front of her locker at the end of the corridor near the stairwell.

Alice Martin.

This was our very first conversation—the one personal encounter that mattered the most to me for so many reasons. From the cool September morning in 1968 and the play of light, the scent of autumn, and her look. The look of her. The way she looked at me.

She was going through notebooks and books, searching for something. I noted first the crease in her brow and how her eyes were red-rimmed—she'd been crying. This time, however, I knew the cause of her anxiety and even though she was muttering and snuffling back tears, I once again was captivated by how pretty she was.

No, she was beautiful.

Her light brown hair that was sometimes the color of honey and sometimes the shade of walnuts, depending on the season, was falling out of a knitted cap (one, I would learn, that she made during a bout of angry knitting—a hobby of which I would become too familiar), locks tumbling in sexy array onto her cheeks and forehead. She wore a pair of boots that had seen better days and over a midi-skirt of fake suede was a long sweater, also hand knit. A scarf made of the same yarn as the hat was coiled around her neck.

Debussy's *The Girl with the Flaxen Hair* came to mind, especially the way the late morning sun played on her hair and streaked it with gold.

Her eyes were incredible, like two perfectly round peridots on a face that was equally round and perfectly symmetrical. And her mouth—all I could think about doing at that moment was kissing that mouth, those incredibly pink lips that now puckered and puffed out a sigh.

Steeling my courage, taking a deep breath, I approached. I knew what would happen but the perspiration started on my hands and I could almost hear the thud of my heartbeat in my ears. That delightful, sickening sensation of joy and wanting to throw up took hold just as it had so many years before.

"I'd ask if you were okay, but clearly you're not, and you'd probably tell me to go to Hell anyway," I spoke up.

Nope. I never had the courage to do that!

She wheeled, eyes wide, and took a step back.

"Hi." After my introduction I figured something simple would be best.

"Hi…" It was tentative, forced. Her voice had the same effect on me as her eyes and mouth – who was I kidding? All of her. I wanted all of her.

We stared at each other for a moment. She resumed whatever it was she was doing with angry purpose:

organizing, searching.

"Hi, I'm Tarquin—Quinn. Quinn Radcliffe. I just transferred from Bishop O'Dowd. I remember you when I first came here. We were in the same grammar and junior high schools..."

"Yes, I know who you are." The door to the locker closed quietly, almost thoughtfully, and Alice turned, a sketchbook held against her like a shield. She looked up at me and I thought I was going to melt. *That mouth...*

"Look, I'm not prying. It's just I've never seen you so upset. You usually have a smile for everyone." There was genuine concern in my voice.

"I just got some bad news. My mom..."

"She's not dead?"

"No, no, but..."

I took another step closer; fortunately, she didn't back away, but I resisted the urge to tuck the strands of hair falling across her brow and into her eyes off that face that I wanted to stare at forever. Her mouth, however, was so tempting. I shoved my hands into my coat pockets to hide their trembling, but more importantly, to keep them out of trouble.

"Anything I can do to help?" I finally queried.

"No, but thanks. I have to go—drama class." She pointed in the opposite direction.

"Sure; but if you just want to talk, or you need anything?"

Most assuredly and most definitely not what I had said in September of 1968, or remembered saying. Besides, what could I give her other than what I obviously had in mind and wanted?

"Sure. Well, bye. Quinn."

She nodded when she said my name, glanced at me shyly. I was going to melt, that's all there was to it. I was going to die in a puddle right there in the corridor. A very happy puddle.

I watched Alice start off and halfway down the hall she looked back and I was blessed with a smile. I held on to that image for the rest of the day, and when my father's driver came by to pick me up after school it was engraved in my memory for all time.

"You're in a good mood, Mister Radcliffe," Andersen commented, glancing back at me in the Bentley's rear-view mirror.

"Relatively," I answered and winked before slipping on my father's expensive sunglasses that were lying on the seat. "How do I look?"

"Like a rock star, sir."

"You always know what to say, Andersen."

"Your parents pay me a tidy sum; do you expect less?"

"Enough that you'd let me take this car if I got a date? Or borrow some cash?"

"Something you'd like to share, sir?"

"Not until I know for sure, but thanks for asking."

We pulled into traffic and I rolled down the window as we passed kids from the high school, smiling at some girls who gawked and giggled. Another block and we were at the corner of Addison and Shattuck where students were converging on the intersection. I was ready to charm a group of cheerleaders when I saw the clutch of unpopular girls following a few feet back—this was the braces-and-glasses crowd, the girls who struggled with the latest fashions but no matter what they did always came up short, staying home on Friday and Saturday nights, on prom night. What I didn't understand was Alice in their midst.

The sunglasses came off as we glided up. All heads turned and there were giggles, some whispering. All heads but one. Alice seemed more interested in a shop display.

"Alice!" I called.

"Judas priest, it's *him!*" a tall girl squealed after she popped bubble gum all over her face.

"Who?" a chubby girl wearing a Beatles sweatshirt demanded, craning to get a better look. "Damn! It's that handsome rich guy from the castle!"

"Who?" another girl demanded.

"You know? The musician? The English boy?" the tall girl giggled. "His parents are like millionaires and his mother is supposed to be related to some Italian prince."

"Cute, huh?" the girl next to Alice remarked, nudging her conspiratorially.

"Alice, d'you need a ride?" I asked.

"Go on!"

"What're you waiting for? I'd jump at the chance!"

"See you tomorrow, Alice!"

"Call me! I want to hear all about it!"

Hissing and whispering at the girls while they continued to giggle and offer encouragement, Alice was gently pushed in my direction. She was clutching her notebooks defensively when I slid over to unlock the car door and let her in.

"Thanks," she whispered and ducked to avoid the stares and calls as Andersen switched gears and we headed east towards the Berkeley Hills.

"Where to?" I asked nonchalantly, as if I gave a beautiful girl a ride home from school every day. She didn't have to know that was never.

"Rose, right below Grove Street—a few blocks from Garfield, actually."

"Thank you, Miss," Andersen replied.

"I wasn't interrupting anything, I hope?" I began. "I didn't think you hung out with the math and chess club girls."

"Well, they're stage crew, actually, but they're all right."

"That's right—you're the designer for the drama club, I've seen you working backstage when I rehearse with the orchestra or chamber group."

"Kids say you're some prodigy, that you play the violin with famous orchestras and tour Europe," she said glibly and I noticed a strain of disbelief in her voice.

"Cello. I play cello. It's a bit larger than a violin."

"And do you really own a castle?"

"The house here in Berkeley or in Dorset? Yorkshire, maybe?"

"Geezus," she sighed. "And you're from England. You were born in England."

"All true. I spend a lot of the year there."

"So that's why you still have the accent, I guess."

"Again, true."

"And why you're not in school for part the year," she said, nodding.

She noticed? She noticed my absence?

"The music, you see. I have concerts. There's always a tutor around to make me do schoolwork. Or Ellie."

"Ellie?"

"My grandmum – grandmother. Sometimes I stay with her in between gigs."

"Oh. Yeah, yeah."

We rode in silence and I pretended interest in the squat little houses we passed along the block after Garfield Junior High.

"Here. This'll do," Alice spoke up suddenly.

Andersen nodded and smiled in the mirror at Alice while he eased into the curb. Before he could get out and get the door she was already on the sidewalk.

"Well, this's me," she announced. "Thanks for the ride."

We were outside a brown shingled house with a neat lawn and flower boxes, one of those arts-and-crafts houses that looked like it was straight out of a storybook, something an artist would live in.

"This is it, huh?" I ventured, hoping for an invitation.

"Well, bye. Thanks again."

"See you tomorrow, Alice?"

She waved and stood on the walk until we drove off. I looked in the rear view mirror and saw her go up the block to the broken stairs of a shabby Mediterranean-style house with a tiled roof and gothic windows. The yard was protected by a low wall that wrapped around the property. The yard itself needed work; it was patches of weeds and overgrown lawn. The stucco face of the house was blotched with moss stains and dirt, the whitewash peeling. The screen door needed a new screen. Alice was a bright flower midst the shabbiness.

"What do you think?" I asked Andersen. "She's amazing, isn't she?"

"Glad to see the house makes no difference," Andersen mentioned as we circled the block and began the climb home.

"I'm more my grandmother's child than my father's. My grandmother's said as much."

"Thank the saints for small miracles," Andersen said and that was the end of the conversation until we reached the steep driveway of our house on Buena Vista Way, high above the city.

"Thanks. For caring, that is," I said, sliding out as he opened the door for me and I shook his hand.

"Well sir, someone has to care, don't you think?"

I glanced up at the house. "Is he home?"

"Returned from Paris this morning. You'll want to take the Late Night Out Door."

Andersen handed off the pile of textbooks and binders and nodded with his chin towards a gate obscured by camellia bushes further up the drive. I thanked him and caught a flash of light from the third story window in the main part of the house. One of the living room drapes moved—for a moment I thought it was The Omnipresent Silhouette; no, it was Magda, the maid, vacuuming the drapes. Skirting past the main entrance, I sprinted to the back gate and was careful not to let it slam for that would give me away. I scooped up a key hidden in a flower pot, and unlocked a seldom-used door by the garage, the one obscured by shrubs and vines - the door Andersen showed me after my unsuccessful attempt to sneak into the house after curfew last winter. My parents would never come down here to the basement rooms. The cat in the pantry and the Cook barely glanced up as I took the back stairs to my suite of rooms in the tower.

Yes, I lived in a castle.

It was an avant-garde mansion, really, built in the 1920s on a hill called "Captain Thomas' Lookout" where a retired sea captain originally placed a cannon, flagpole and telescope. It took years of planning and it resembled a monastery from Toulouse, but to anyone driving up from Berkeley it might have looked like a castle, sitting on a bluff eight hundred feet above the city with a tower that overlooked San Francisco Bay, especially if they could see the courtyard cloister and all the gothic architectural styles—it was called "The Cloister." There were times I wished we had trebuchets and arbalests on the roof, but not to keep away the tourists. I would train them on a particular room inside the house.

I was never happier than when reached the top of the stairs and entered the study, walked through to my bedroom and slammed that heavy oak door, relishing the deep echo. Today I stood in the middle of the huge room with its fireplace and window seats and wondered if I should make an attempt at cleaning. It would certainly make Magda happy, and would scare the hell out of my mother. I glanced at the trail of clothes, clean and otherwise, leading from the bathroom to the closet, the books, magazines and records, the folios of music, the boots, shoes, the tuxedo, and toiletries on the table, desk and floors and thought, why bother?

Throwing myself on the enormous bed, I stared at the ceiling. Today I counted twenty-seven gilded stars set in twenty-seven trefoils that were bordered and set in squares painted blue and gold. Was the ceiling in Alice's bedroom painted with faeries and unicorns, or was it peeling, showing patches of wood? I didn't think of Alice staring at the ceiling; well, she would if she had been there with me, curled up in my arms, her hair on the pillow, her beautiful green eyes soft, the corners creased as she smiled and leaned over to kiss me…

Damn! There it was again.

I flew off the bed and started to clean to drain the energy and frustration. Maybe I'd take a shower, too. A cold one.

Her room was probably full of pink stuff and frills, probably smelled like vanilla and white flowers, just like she did. I imagined what she looked like asleep with the long, curly eyelashes and that mouth, maybe her hand tucked under her cheek and the rise and fall of her breasts.

I started pushing the furniture around.

"What the hell is going on up there?" my father shouted from the floor below.

"Looking for the new box of cello strings!" I yelled back.

"Well stop it! You're going to break something!"

"Too bad it's not your damn head."

After an hour of putting things where they belonged, I stepped back and admired my progress. At least there was a path to the bathroom. A door slam below made me glance out the window. I saw the Bentley leave the driveway and breathed easier. Moments later I heard Magda's transistor radio playing Motown favorites. The vacuum revved up and she started to sing along with Aretha Franklin. It was contagious. I skipped downstairs to the kitchen in search of something to eat for dinner harmonizing the melody line to *Respect*.

Mother was in the kitchen, cooking.

I did a double-take as if I had dropped into one of the Proprietress' twisted parallel universes.

She was *cooking*.

My mother stood tall, straight, a slim frame as she peeled carrots onto a sheet of newspaper, then carefully diced them into a sauce that bubbled on the stove. Meals in our household were catch-as-catch-can due first to conflicting schedules and second to a lack of interest; family conversations were grunts of acknowledgment as we passed each other in the hall with a sandwich or bowl of cereal in hand.

"What're you doing?" I ventured.

"What does it look like, sweetheart?"

"You never cook."

"Your father is out tonight—department meeting—so I thought I'd make dinner for just the two of us. I told Cook to take the night off."

"Can I do anything?"

"Keep me company."

I began opening cupboards and drawers for placemats, cutlery, and dishes, and set the table, humming Beethoven's *Allegretto* from his Seventh Symphony, which segued to *Here Comes the Sun*.

"That's interesting," my mother laughed.

"Maybe I should use it for the next audition, along with *Purple Haze*."

"This is how I like you, Tarquin. Happy. This is how it should be."

I considered the pattern of roses on the fork I placed on the table and drew a breath. "When he goes to Ravenna for the music festival this summer maybe we could stay home?"

Where the hell did THAT come from?

Mother now attended a salad, arranging lettuce, tomatoes and avocado slices with bits of bacon. Without turning she said, "I thought you enjoyed the festival."

"Used to. I'm hoping for something different this summer. Maybe stay home, or go to York, but I'd rather stay home and just hang out."

Mother took her place at the kitchen table facing the window to the backyard and pulled the bread basket I'd just placed between us towards her, taking a dinner roll and picking off a morsel. "Do tell," she said, winking, and passed the roll to me.

"There's a girl…"

"*A* girl? I could have sworn the last time we were in public together you had a following like a pop star," Mother teased.

"Yes, well, I had to make a choice from all those fine women, didn't I?"

"Had to break some hearts, I suppose?"

"The price you pay for all this," I said and gestured with a breadstick at my torso and then leaning in with a dazzling smile and wink of my big brown eye. "I just hope mine won't be broken—damn, that's selfish…"

When she smiled and reached for my hand, the cardigan sleeve rode up and I saw the ugly bruises on her arm. Mother tried to pull away, but I held her fast and pushed the other sleeve back to reveal more discoloration and healing scratches.

"Again?" I demanded quietly.

She pulled away, and in a dismissive, anxious tone said, "One of my patients at the hospital; it's nothing."

"Bullshit!"

"Watch your mouth, young man!"

"I heard the argument. I heard your sobbing."

"Let's talk about this girl—"

"The hell we will! When will it stop, Mother?"

"It really isn't what you think, and it certainly isn't your business. No, do not interrupt! In time you'll discover how difficult relationships really are. You don't understand—and honestly, with everything going on in your life, you wouldn't understand, or want to."

In a fashion typical of most adults I knew, Mother avoided the subject with busy work, or in this case, serving up portions of spaghetti and meatballs, baked zucchini, and salad. The family paradigm hadn't shifted after all, for we ate silently, the angry scraping of forks, knives and spoons the only communication.

"I'm not six years old," I said all of a sudden. "You can't buy my silence with a comic book or toy. I'll go to the police."

"You won't." Her voice was like steel, matching her eyes. "You can't afford the press. Your career doesn't need it."

"I can deal with it."

"Can you? When everything is said and done?"

I stared at her for a moment and then backed down. Pushing the food around on my plate gave me something to do. Finally, I shoved away from the table. Before I left the kitchen I placed a hand on her shoulder and said quietly, "One thing's for certain; I would never harm Alice. And if he touches you again, Mother, I'll take responsibility for my actions if only to keep the bastard away from you."

"Darling...!"

I waved her off and went back up to the tower and slammed the door shut so violently that the entire wing rattled and the echo went on for what seemed like a minute.

A good sulk was what I needed but I needed to work off the anger more. I reached under the bed and pulled out the guitar case from under a pile of socks and Playboy magazines and dusted off the case after a quick glance at Miss July 1968. A soft, tentative Clapton riff, followed by a Hendrix, and then a passionate rendition of *Something*, calmed me some. I paused for a moment and then glanced at Petula, my cello, sitting in the corner. Putting the guitar down, I pulled the cello to the window seat and began to play *The Girl with the Flaxen Hair*. Slowly relaxation took over, replacing anger and frustration with tranquility. I sensed a shift or a change and felt the familiar heat of stage arc lamps, the soft glow of spotlights above me. I was sitting center stage in the high school auditorium and it must have been the spring of 1969 for the Easter decorations someone had fixed on the scrim.

I sensed movement behind me and to the left but continued to play until I let Debussy's notes fade into nothing. As it always happened, the exercise was emotionally and physically draining and I sat staring at the bow in my hands, waiting for my heart to stop pounding.

"Don't stop—that was lovely."

Alice's voice surprised me, and set my heart pounding again. Turning, I watched her come from downstage, a box of costumes and props in her arms.

"Hi!"

Damn, I hope that didn't come out like a squeak.

"I didn't want to interrupt you. I was marking the sets for the play next week," she said, and put the box down on the stool beside me.

"No, no, that was it." A moment, then, "So tell me, what's the play?"

"*The Crucible.*"

"Miller? Good choice."

I made a big deal out of noticing a smudge on the neck of the cello and slowly wiped it down with my thumb. I was waiting. After a time I said, "Well, better go. Andersen's outside probably looking at his watch."

"I didn't mean to chase you off. You can stay while I work."

Was it me, or did she sound a little disappointed that I was leaving? The girlfriend of the most popular jock in high school?

"I could use a bit more practice," I said nonchalantly and then picked up the acoustic guitar I'd brought. I started to play a folk song that I loved and one taught to me by my grandfather. Alice spun about, her eyes wide; her face lit up in a smile.

"I know that song! My mother used to sing it to us, my brother and me."

I stopped and flashed what I thought was my most seductive smile. "*Crossing the Stone?*"

"Well, I heard it as *Tros y Garreg.*" She took a step forward and I caught a scent of vanilla, white flowers and tempera paint. "It's the story of a warrior, a knight, coming home to his lady love after a battle."

I wanted to say that it made perfect sense—Alice and medieval history fit. Looking at her now, she seemed otherworldly. The round eyes and round face framed by her hair that refused to stay up in her knit cap—and that mouth. *Oh, that mouth.*

The contents of the box were her focus while I did an encore of *Tros y Garreg*. I half-closed my eyes to concentrate, but more to watch what Alice was doing. She was labeling props and when that was done a sketchbook and pencil came from the bottom of the box. While I continued to play, she sketched and sang along—in Welsh. Her voice was clear, trained, and had color from high to low notes, a touch of vibrato. Enough to give the sound richness, but not so much the lyrics were obscured by a tremble.

"You have a beautiful voice, Alice," I complimented after a moment of silence when we'd done. "That was lovely."

"Thanks," she sputtered, pushing her hair behind an ear and looking away—she was blushing.

"I didn't know Mr. Collins taught Welsh folk songs."

"No, I don't think he does. My mother taught us."

"Your mother's Welsh?"

"Well, her father—my grandfather. She was born here; my mother, that is."

"From…?"

"San Francisco. My father, too."

"I'm from York originally, then London, now here," I babbled. We stared at one another a moment and I was the first to look away. "Well, I bet you know this song," I said and started playing *Y Blodyn Gwyn*, one of the numbers from *Post Card*, Mary Hopkin's first album, which had been released in February that year.

Alice sat at my feet to listen while I played. When I finished, I glanced down and she was smiling at me. Again my heart started to pound.

"Play *Crossing the Stone*, again, please?"

How could I refuse?

I closed my eyes and played the folk tune again, pouring all of my heart and soul into it and when I drew the last notes from the strings and opened my eyes, I was back in my tower bedroom.

CHAPTER 4

THE DISAPPOINTMENT WAS palpable and had Rafe not been in the room, I would have cried like a three-year-old girl. Instead, I wiped down the guitar with a rag, paying attention to the finish more than was warranted.

Rafe shifted forward in my ancient recliner by the fireplace to pat my shoulder. "You show a remarkable, extraordinary talent, young man," he said softly and winked. "Why your father does not appreciate it…"

"I suppose that's the purpose of this exercise, or whatever Her Worshipfulness calls it. Let's get inside Quinn's mind and soul—figure out the War of the Radcliffes," I said as I put the guitar back in its case and shoved it under the bed. When I sat up, Rafe was still in my chair. "That's my spot." I pointed to the recliner.

"Where you spend time dreaming about the perfect snog! Maybe in this very chair!" Rafe laughed.

He was right. As if he couldn't tell by the angry red flush running up my neck to my face.

"So? I'm a guy. What do you expect? What are you doing here anyway?"

"The real question is what are you doing here?"

"This is home, isn't it?"

"Is it?"

"Shit, more questions…"

I threw myself into the desk chair and spun it about. When I stopped, I was in The Shop at my table and Rafe was seated beside me, enjoying a Pop Tart and a cup of coffee. We were alone save for the Proprietress.

"Just once I'd like to land on a tropical island or the south of France or—"

"—or Alice Martin's bed? Please, dear boy," the Proprietress sighed. "You should be used to it by now and if not, why?"

"Where is everyone?" I ventured.

"Doing whatever they're supposed to do, which is what you should be doing." She commented as she organized the mysterious books and boxes.

"I could do with some silence. Hint, hint," I said and stretched back in my chair. In doing so, I glanced out the window and saw The Man in Blue with Alice. They were animated and laughing like two best friends and when he touched her cheek in a romantic, affectionate manner, my curiosity got the better of me. Blue Boy wasn't going to ruin my plans even if I hadn't figured things out yet. I sort of knew what I wanted.

"There he goes…" the Proprietress sighed as I went out the door.

The high street had never been busier since my arrival. It was like a village fair in the summer: lots of happy and busy people going about their business whatever it was and stopping to chat. It wasn't anything I hadn't seen or experienced before except that Henry II of England and Thomas Becket were arguing in the middle of the street as a bright red double-decker bus came at them. The bus driver managed to stop when Henry held out his hand. For his part the King with the bad temper didn't miss a single heated adjective in his quarrel with that 'miserable' priest, the Archbishop of Canterbury. When they cleared the street General Patton, the last Anglo-Saxon king of England Harold Godwinson, and the Empress Theodora came off the bus and paused only a moment to decide where to find lunch. They didn't settle on The Shop, but a pub between a hat shop and perfumery across the road. *The Toad in the Hole.* I decided to check it out when I saw

Alice and Blue Boy head in that direction.

It was a popular place—an English village pub with all the traditional amenities like warm beer, dart game, dusky light and dark wood booths that stank of cigarettes, wet wood and beer. Lenny Welch's rendition of *Since I Fell For You* played on the jukebox while patrons stood shoulder to shoulder at the bar or crowded around tables or in booths.

The Proprietress stood behind the bar and gestured to the only available seat in the house, a place at the counter.

"The usual?" she sniped.

"Sure, why not?"

"Ah, the maestro plays along! Do you know what the usual is?"

My brows creased, then, "Cheeseburger, well-done, bacon, avocado, and a side of French fries."

A bowl of split pea soup in which bits of diced sausages and bacon floated was put before me with a glass of beer.

"The usual," the Proprietress sniffed. "Two and six."

"I hate split pea soup."

"Then why are you here?"

"Why does everyone keep asking me that?"

Alice's soft laughter distracted me and I glared at the Proprietress before turning to see Alice and Blue Boy seated at a corner table, enjoying conversation and coffee. I stared for the longest time, hoping that was all she'd enjoy or that she'd notice me.

"It only takes a second to get up and say hello or ask someone out," said the Proprietress as she wiped down the counter.

"You're not me," I sighed, and pushed away the bowl. "You can have the soup back. Not hungry."

"You're an odd duck," sniffed the cleric seated to my left. He whispered something in Latin before he attacked the bowl before him with a spoon and smacked his lips. "You have to speak up and make your voice heard, let your opinion be known. It will work to your advantage," he said between bites.

Richard entered during the cleric's soliloquy and nodded hello to me. To the cleric he said, "Worked well for you, did it, Tom?"

"Thomas of London to you, sir," he sniffed. When Richard just grinned he put his spoon down and walked away muttering to himself.

"Becket's always been a sore loser. Oh, my favorite!" Richard chortled when he slid onto the stool beside mine. "Madam, this is the best soup I've had in years." The Proprietress simpered and put another bread roll on his plate, narrowing her eyes towards me. "You must be fair to the boy. I'm sure if Quinn knew of a better way to say hello or get someone's attention he'd think of it," Richard continued. "You can't measure a man's worth by what he likes to eat."

"How much thought does one need to explain oneself?" The Proprietress asked. "To ask a girl for a date? Analysis is good in psychotherapy; if you do it too much in life, you forget to live, or worse, you become afraid to live."

"That's the kindest thing I've ever heard you say," I said to her and smiled. She actually smiled back.

"There's no salt," Richard spoke up. "Quinn, would you mind getting that salt shaker on the table?"

I glanced where Richard pointed with his spoon and nodded. "Sure." When I swung off the stool, I was at LaVal's Pizza at Northside in Berkeley in the early January of 1969 and walking towards the booth where Alice sat doing homework. She glanced up and blushed when she saw me hovering.

"Chemistry?" I opened, balancing a pizza box on one hand while I fumbled for my sunglasses, taking them off and ditching them in a pocket.

"Worse—biology." She looked down at her notes and placed a hand over them as if embarrassed and then avoided my obvious staring by flipping through the book in search of something.

"I've always wondered how learning the names of all the bones and muscles will help a person in life, unless they were going to be a doctor," I yammered. "But you're an artist, so I guess...sorry, I must be bothering you."

"No, no; you're actually a welcome distraction."

We both laughed and after a tense minute of over-analyzing what I'd said and what she'd said, I realized I was holding a hot pizza box in my hands.

"I've got to get this pizza home, and I guess you're waiting for someone," I started.

"For Will, yes."

"Maybe I shouldn't be here then."

"I can't have friends?" she said, smiling.

"I'm a friend?"

Damn, that sounded desperate!

"Well, I don't have many," she answered with a shrug. A pause, then, "My brother said he heard you play at the opera house last weekend."

I just stared at her mouth.

"He said you were amazing."

No, you're amazing, Alice Martin...

"Did he? Thanks."

"It must be hard, all the touring, and I've heard about your parents," she went on, now closing the biology textbook and binder of notes. Inwardly I cringed. *Oh God, what had she heard?* "Your parents are petty nobility and your mother—well, I've seen her. She's really beautiful, an Elizabeth Taylor-Grace Kelly beautiful."

I wish you could read my mind, Alice, because I think you're more beautiful...

"Looks aren't everything," I laughed self-consciously. "You'd think differently if she were lecturing you every night about the state of your sock drawer and white tie and tails, or how long you practiced the Bach suites."

"The grass is always greener on the other side of the moat?"

"Ouch—I sounded like a spoiled, privileged bastard, didn't I?"

"Spoiled and privileged, yes; I wouldn't know about the other."

We laughed again and she looked at me—I could tell she was studying my face for something and I looked away out of self-consciousness only to see Will Parmenter, captain of the football team and Alice's boyfriend, enter the restaurant with his usual cohort of team members. Watching his approach, I blurted out, "Well, pizza's getting cold. Gotta go. Look, Alice, maybe I'm out of line here, but maybe we could go out to a movie or something? I know you're with Parmenter, but as friends, maybe, so, there it is."

She didn't answer for as Parmenter grew closer and was shouting Alice's name, I ducked out before he could see me and walked home.

The Bentley parked in the driveway was the first indication that it would not be the tranquil Sunday evening I was hoping for. After dinner I was going to work on a song I was composing for Alice – I wanted to surprise her with it – but knew that wouldn't happen.

I entered through the main door for a change because I knew where'd *he'd* be – out in the garden killing the roses along with the weeds - and skirted past my mother's study to the kitchen where Cook was cleaning up what looked like the remains of a dinner not eaten. She was angrier than usual and slammed pots and pans, banged cupboard doors and merely glanced in my direction as I took a plate from the cupboard and sat at the table, throwing back the lid and inhaling the scent of a pepperoni and sausage pizza with extra mushrooms and tomatoes.

"And for this am I truly grateful," I said before digging in.

"Where did you get that?" Cook demanded, but in kind way.

"Dad wasn't home, so I used my mother's credit card

when she told me she didn't have change for a twenty. I just needed a five. This is our secret, right?"

"One of many. They're piling up. Other than a contraband pizza from a borrowed credit card, how was your day, sir?" Cook asked as she moved empty plates, cutlery and glasses from the table and handed me a napkin, fork and knife.

"Fine, went to a movie," I mumbled with my mouth full of pizza.

"See anything good?" she asked, now wiping down counters and moving canisters of flour, sugar and salt, tea and coffee around to clean the already spotless counter space beneath them.

The Lion in Winter. Plantagenets, twelfth century. That was one messed up family," I said, and holding up the box, offered a slice, which she took with thanks. "King Henry didn't give his sons money when they asked either."

"...This has to stop, do you hear me? I can't take much more! It's gone on long enough!"

My mother was shouting—she never raised her voice above a whisper. She was in the seldom-using dining room off the kitchen, having come downstairs from wherever the argument had started this time. I went to the door with a slice in hand.

"I don't answer to you, Jane! You'd be wise to keep that temper and your comments to yourself!" Father bellowed back. "No one would take your word, anyway. That's the way it is. You just might as well close your eyes and your mouth like my first wife and be thankful you and the boy have a place to live. It's been my work and sacrifice that's paid for everything you both have. Do you ever think about that, you stupid cow?"

The clink of glass told me he was pouring a drink. The crash of that glass was a good indication that Mother had knocked it out of his hand or he had thrown it.

"Doctor Radcliffe isn't the only one in this house

who's had enough," Cook muttered and when she saw my frown, added, "Sir, come away. You know how he gets when he's been drinking or when things go badly at the opera house," she murmured.

I shook my head, waiting.

"Both of you are ungrateful and selfish! You sit back while I take the criticism and get to hear the rejections," Father growled. "He needs to be taught gratitude, he needs to know his place!"

"I am warning you again, Andrew," Mother was saying.

"What will you do? Whatever you say or do will find its way into the wrong circles; you can kiss your career goodbye, then! And his!" Father laughed. "That's what you want, isn't it? To be the victims—where the hell do you think you're going? Come back here!"

The running footsteps and slamming doors gave me a chance to take the back stairs up to my tower rooms.

I finished my supper in my bedroom and turned up the stereo loud enough so I couldn't hear the yelling and the thump of furniture, the usual noise that went with their quarrelling. When I stuffed the last piece into my mouth, I crawled into bed, burrowing deep under the comforter and blankets so that everything was dark and sounds were muffled. Eventually, I drifted into a fitful sleep only to be roused by the light coming in from the study as the bedroom door opened. The scent of cigar smoke and scotch did what it always did: brought the fear out. I lay quietly, even slowing my breathing so that maybe he would think I wasn't there, that it was just a jumble of blankets and books on my usually-messy bed.

The comforter slid off and the shock of the cold air made me gasp, but I didn't move when I felt the pressure against me, my father lying down on my bed and spooning me. Still, I refused to move.

"I know you're awake, Tarquin," he whispered in my ear, the stench of his breath sickening. "Your mother's been so disagreeable tonight; what do I do with her, I wonder? Tell me, what should I do? What should I do to a wife and a son who show no gratitude and won't do as they're told? What shall I do?"

Oh God, oh no, it was starting—the waves of dizziness and confusion. I felt like I was riding waves in a small boat or on a roller coaster. As much as I wanted to cry out when I felt the pressure and the fire, when the sobs began to choke me and tears soaked the pillow, I didn't, but I opened my eyes and saw the Man in Blue standing by the balcony door. He watched and did nothing.

But there were tears streaming down his face.

CHAPTER 5

NO SOONER did morning break than I rose and gave my battered psyche and body a shower, took my time dressing and paid more attention than usual to my appearance. If anyone asked, I'd had a late night at the opera house or in rehearsal with the symphony. They didn't need to know the truth or that I'd been crying.

Andersen was lifting the iron to a griddle as I entered the kitchen, saying, "Cook called in sick, Sir. I'm making waffles if you're interested."

"Thanks all the same; not hungry," I replied, taking a drink of orange juice out of the carton.

"You shouldn't do that," Andersen commented, pointing with a fork to the carton I was putting back in the refrigerator.

"Not that anyone would care," I said and added with a laugh, "but if it was an audition all hell would break loose, wouldn't it?"

"Going to school now?"

"I don't need a ride, Andersen. I can walk."

"Where's your lunch?"

I opened the refrigerator and took out a half-empty jar of peanut butter, the dregs of strawberry preserves and slapped spoonfuls of them between two pieces of bread, which was squashed together and thrown into a waxed-paper bag, then tossed into my schoolbag.

"That is not a meal. What about some of this asparagus and this pate foi gras?" Andersen suggested as he started to remove aluminum-foil wrapped dishes from the bottom shelf.

"It's hard enough at school without bringing something like that. I'll either get beaten up or held down and forced to eat it front of the entire school. I can go off campus."

Andersen now took a ten dollar bill from his pocket and passed it to me. "Treat yourself."

If I had refused the loan he would have found an opportunity to slip it into one of my schoolbooks or the cello case, so I fumbled for thanks and grabbed an orange out of the fruit bowl and waved goodbye.

My route to school was down Rose Street, the two blocks past Garfield Junior High and it was my good fortune that Alice was leaving her house as I was at the corner. The crossing guard smiled and waved me through the intersection.

"You can only let it go for so long, Quinn; you have to stop acting like there's nothing wrong," the guard said as I passed and it was then I recognized her as Janis Joplin.

"It's none of your business, but thanks for your consideration," I answered, glancing around in the hopes that no one saw us.

"Isn't it?" Janis asked, waving a milk truck through the intersection. "Isn't that the point of this whole exercise or whatever you want to call it? Someone has to care and make it their business or get you to really make it yours."

"Like I said, your concern is touching. What can you do about it?"

"What will you do about it?"

"You need to go away and stop bothering me!" I snapped.

"I beg your pardon?"

It wasn't Janis now, but old Missus Terry, the guard that had to be at least ninety and talked to herself about cats.

Now I sprinted to catch up with Alice but when she

turned the corner Parmenter was there. He tossed away the cigarette he'd had in his mouth and kissed Alice, then draped one of his gorilla arms around her as they set off for school together. The day could only get worse.

It did.

The guidance counselor called me out of Advanced English to his office where I found my mother. She was poised and cool, charming every man within a foot with her patrician beauty and manners. And all because she sat in a chair opposite the counselor with a handbag in her lap and impeccable gloves that rested lightly on it. She was royalty to them.

"Quinn, darling. Sorry to take you out of class," Mother said as she rose and kissed my cheek. "I was telling Mister Jenkins that I have to go out of town for a conference—a last minute call, you see. And your father left for Madrid—again, a last minute thing. He's singing in *Der Rosenkavalier*."

"Rosenkavalier? Dad hates that opera. You could have told me this when I got home," I said, looking at the skeptical Mr. Jenkins.

"That's just it; my flight is in an hour—I didn't want to leave a note or do this in a phone call."

"How is this any better?" I wanted to know.

"Darling…" Mother was fidgeting with the clasp on her expensive handbag. "You know how our lives are. Some things can't be prevented—like this trip. As I was saying to Mr. Jenkins, you're not going to be left on your own. Andersen, Magda, and the Cook will be home to look after things. Your father will be back in a week."

"Lucky me," I said and before I could let my mother or Mr. Jenkins reprimand me for the sarcasm I opened the office door and gestured towards Mother. "I'll walk you to your car. We can say goodbye there."

This was what I hated. All eyes were on us as we walked to the parking lot. Whispering, stares, comments about the stunningly beautiful Doctor Radcliffe, catcalls and hoots, some whistles even. There were times when I wished my Mother was fat and ugly.

"I'll call when I get to Chicago," Mother said as she slid into the back seat of the waiting taxi. I closed the door and leaned down on the doorframe to accept another kiss on the cheek. When she moved away, I grabbed her hand.

"Lying to Mr. Jenkins is one thing. Lying to me—well that's just cruel. Safe trip, Mother."

I didn't bother watching the taxi drive off but walked back towards the school and entered *The Toad in the Hole* back in the Village.

The same crowd as before was there, including the Man in Blue. He looked up and offered a sympathetic smile. A dark memory came back and I scowled; it would take a while to get used to my secrets not being my own any longer. Shamefaced, I avoided eye contact, but did look around for Alice, who'd disappeared somewhere. I worked through the crowd to the counter, looking for a spot. My space beside Richard was still open and I climbed onto the stool to be amazed: waiting for me were a cheeseburger with bacon and avocado, and fries, served up fresh.

"What's this?" I asked the Proprietress.

"What do you think? Your usual, sir."

"But that's…"

"When one does something unusual, one gets their usual. Enjoy."

I dug in as soon as she went off to annoy someone else. Richard watched, amused, as I devoured every bit.

"What?" I asked, wiping my face. "You've never seen a guy eat?"

"Just proud of you, that's all. It's a small step, to be sure, but you'll have a gold star in your book. Perhaps two."

"I don't think being a smart ass to my mother in front of Mr. Jenkins justifies a reward," I scoffed. "Nor does making a peanut butter and jelly sandwich."

"You placed things in perspective and that will help you later."

"Will it?"

"You know it will."

"Maybe I don't," I sighed and traced a trail of catsup with a fry around the plate before popping the fry in my mouth. "What if I didn't have to deal with that stuff?"

"What stuff?" the Proprietress demanded.

"I don't have to spell it out. If you don't mind, I'd like to concentrate on the big mistakes, like those I made with Alice, and not the ones I'm not responsible for."

The Proprietress laughed as she took away my plate as I was in mid-trail. "Aren't you silly? Haven't you figured out that they are all connected in some way, like a puzzle? One piece fits with another and another."

"My life at home has no bearing on Alice."

"Doesn't it?" a chorus of voices asked.

"Why should it? I learn from my parents' mistakes like everyone else and I know it will somehow be better if we, I mean, when we, get together at last."

"You sound confused," Richard said.

"I'm not confused," I groused. "Not about her. There are rules, you know; you don't make a move on another guy's girl."

"Is she?" Richard asked, scraping his bowl in an irritating manner. "Her so-called sweetheart pummels other boys for the sport of it and walks around like a king and treats her as if she were his goods and chattel—he hasn't come far from the middle ages. Now, you; I think you know how to bring some clarity to that issue. You're the type of fellow that makes grand gestures to show your affection."

The musical instruments on a stage off in a corner caught my attention when someone opened the door and sunlight flashed on the drum kit. With the guitars, a keyboard, and the drums, was my cello.

Then it hit me.

"Her favorite song," I whispered to myself and went to the stage.

No one paid attention as I took a chair and carried it up, took one of the acoustic guitars and started to play *Stairway to Heaven*. One by one, heads turned and soon the pub was silent but for the sound I plucked from the guitar strings. I had finished the introduction when Richard joined me and took the guitar while I drew out the melody on my cello. Soon we were joined by Jimi Hendrix, who grabbed the electric guitar and improvised a riff as only he could. By then I was so wrapped up in the music I thought nothing of the medieval-looking faery tale prince that appeared out of the bright reflections and shafts of sun bouncing off the walls. He took up the drum at the bridge and kept up with me so that I thought the late, great John Bonham had joined the session, his performance pure artistry. The customers in the pub started to sing along and keep time as I continued in a trance through every measure until the last note died away and I was left drenched in sweat, exhausted, but happy.

The applause and cheering didn't mean a thing. Alice had reappeared and was standing beside the Man in Blue and I pushed through the crowd now congratulating me to reach her. He stepped away as if to present Alice and said in a melodious, rich, voice, "Well done, Radcliffe!"

Only when I was there in front of her bending down to kiss that mouth turned up to mine and just inches away, the light changed suddenly and it grew dark outside; a rumble of thunder echoed off in the distance.

"Tarquin!"

It was my father's voice and I was in my room again. The heavy footsteps pounding on the hardwood stairs warned exactly how close that thunder truly was. I'd avoid the coming battle with a shower I really needed; stripping down in record time, the cold taps on full force, I jumped into the shower stream. I sang in time to his pounding on my bedroom door. Halfway through the second verse of

Here Comes the Sun in *largo voce più fortissimo* the beats were on the bathroom door.

"Quinn? Are you in there? Answer me! Quinn!"

"Who the hell else would it be?" I growled back.

"What did I say? What did I say about the music?"

Practice?

The door wrenched open and the shower door slid back.

"Fuck! Dad! A little privacy and some consideration, please?" I shouted. I grabbed for one of the towels behind him and my father reached around me and twisted the taps off until I thought they'd snap under the pressure.

I knew *I* was that close.

"What the hell was that?" My father demanded. "You should be working on the Bach solos! God knows if you'd practiced those more often than your rock 'n' roll and folk crap, you would have been given the internship with the Symphony! How many times do I have to put myself on the line for you?"

"Maybe I don't need you to. Maybe I don't want a fucking internship."

"Watch your mouth with me, young man; you're not backstage at Carnegie now!"

"What's the matter? Are you still sore that the director of the Carnegie pretty much told you to back off and let me do what I wanted?"

Didn't remember saying that and definitely I had no memory of what I blurted out next!

"Y'know, Dad, the world doesn't turn on Bach, Beethoven or Brahms. Or your fucking, fragile, ego."

"Don't use that tone with me, boy! If you don't start taking your musical career seriously there'll be no car, no allowance, no privileges—"

"What privileges? I don't have any!"

Grabbing another towel, I wiped my face and dried my hair, using the violent movement to gather my thoughts and defense, reveling in the sudden sensation of warmth and contentment, but when I pulled the towel off my face, expecting to glare at my father, I was looking down the nave of a Romanesque chapel filled with soft, butter-colored light, and not just any chapel, but Saint John the Evangelist in the Tower of London.

This was not the chapel I remembered visiting as a child before we moved to America. The tunnel-vaulted ceiling was painted blue and speckled with stars; the columns were painted with chevron and striped patterns in subdued shades of blue, pink, green and red and yellow up to the *triforium* where the walls were frescoed with shades of pink, purple and orange blending together like a sunset. Taking all this in I was reminded of a Disney cartoon, dreading an impossibly-proportioned heroine to come waltzing in with singing mice or, since this was the Tower, ravens. There was music off in the background, but they were chords strummed on lutes. Seated in a window embrasure were Richard and a man in late fifteenth century garb: a tall, powerfully-built man with the chiseled blond good looks of a faery tale prince and dressed for the part in velvet and brocade. The drummer from my Village jam session.

They were playing a ballad from the twelfth century in two-part harmony, Richard singing the melody in a French dialect. The faery tale prince ended the song with a flourish and glanced up at me, his smile almost seductive.

"Was that a ballad by Richard the Lionheart?" I asked, taking a few steps forward to study the lutes. They were not replicas, but the real instruments and I had to see them.

"Just so. Please," Richard offered, holding the lute. My hands were trembling when I felt the smooth wood of the neck, felt the strings and tentatively plucked out the melody I'd just heard. "What did I tell you? He's a musical prodigy, Ned," Richard said to his companion, and then, "Quinn, may I introduce my brother, Edward." The pride was evident in his voice and when King Edward IV, victor of the Wars of the Roses, Round One, ruffled Richard's straight black hair with a massive hand, he was pushed off playfully. Two brothers couldn't be any more affectionate but different.

"'No prisoner can tell his honest thought unless he speaks as one who suffers wrong; but for his comfort as he may make a song,'" I recited the verses they'd just sung in English, strumming chords.

"I forgot to mention that he's a bit puffed up," Richard said, winking. "In the realm of music, it's said he has no peers. Read it in the *New York Times*. He doesn't fare so well in other realms."

"What about these other realms?" Edward queried.

"A quarrel for another day," Richard answered.

"What makes you think it'll be a quarrel?" I asked.

"The realm of womanhood always raises questions and hackles," said Richard as he tightened one of the strings and it snapped with a jarring note.

"Discord, to be sure," Edward spoke up, a deep mellifluous voice similar to Richard's. "People are never what you expect—people have shades and color, light and dark, like this chapel. Even women, if you dare to believe it."

"I don't remember the colors or the warmth," I murmured, looking around at the Norman decoration.

"There was never real discord, Your Grace. Even when we did quarrel, he knew how to seduce me into agreement."

We all turned at the sound of her soft, low, voice. Alice was a few feet away at the end of the *triforium*. An open sketchbook dangled from a hand as she leaned against one of the multi-patterned, multi-colored pillars. The sunlight was shining off her hair, a hint of a smile crossing her lips. The flower-print dress and simple cardigan were the same as those she wore on our trip to Scarborough, georgette silk crepe skimming her curves with light and shadows.

"Really?" I laughed. "I always thought you were a captive audience."

"By choice. Your voice was, is, your reasoning at times, as seductive as one of your kisses," Alice said.

I strolled around the *triforium*, never taking my eyes from her face. "And yet it ended so badly."

"Did it?" she asked, tilting her head, crossing arms across her body.

"Your silence was a clue."

"You had other things on your mind, if I remember correctly," Alice responded as she took a step forward.

"And some things needed to be sorted out."

I was less than a foot away from where Alice stood and would have taken her hands, drawn her away to a place more private when a bird suddenly flew in from the window over the altar below and hovered, flapping its wings in my face. When I managed to bat it away I was back at the high school, in the corridor near Alice's locker.

She wasn't alone. Will Parmenter was leaning in and brushing locks of hair off her face. He towered over her and had playfully snatched the knit beret off her head. Alice squealed with laughter and demanded it back.

"How much is it worth to you?" Will teased, holding it over her head so that she had to jump against him to retrieve it. "Worth a kiss, maybe? Maybe something to remember me by, huh, Alice?"

"What do you mean—to remember you by?" Alice giggled, hopping on her toes to reach the cap. "Will! C'mon, stop playing games."

"I think you just might be nicer to me when I tell you my news."

"What? Now give me my hat!"

"I enlisted. I'm going to Vietnam. Eventually," Will said, tossing the beret into the stairwell.

She gasped; one of those exasperated sounds girls make when they're pissed and you know you're in for it. Will clearly had no idea of the trouble he was in, or he didn't care.

"What?" Alice demanded. "Did you say you're going to Vietnam?" Alice took a step back with arms folded across her breasts. I knew the look of steel in those beautiful eyes and that fierce stance—God help him, was he in for it.

"Yeah, you heard right." Will's tone was a bit defensive.

"Why the hell did you do that?"

He paused, staring her down, towering over her. Good Lord, if he was going to hurt her in any way…

"Cal doesn't want me—I got the letter yesterday. And as for the other football scholarships, it's a good guess they won't come through. I mean, if Cal doesn't want me…"

"But Vietnam? You could die over there, you idiot! You stupid idiot! Forget about dying somewhere in the jungle. I'll kill you now if your parents don't!"

"Calm down! I take my chances where they fall, Alice. What about you?" He bent closer. "Are you willing to give me something before I go?"

"Will, we talked about this,"

"Yeah, and all we do is talk. What about it?"

My throat was dry and the pounding in my chest was a good indication to walk away, but Alice saw me and I decided to hang back for a moment. She smiled that shy, pretty smile that melted me to my core, and started fussing with her hair. Why did girls always do that when you looked at them? Will turned to see what distracted her and jerked his chin in my direction.

"Radcliffe. This is a private conversation."

"Alice looks upset," I spoke up, moving closer. I wouldn't show my trepidation. I was taller, but he was bigger and could pulverize me with one of his ham hock fists. Will was looking up at me but I held Alice's gaze.

"Yeah? And it's none of your damn business, Maestro."

I tilted my chin in the smart-ass manner my father

always hated, waiting a dramatic moment before I said with a smile, "Your insults are getting better. That was helluva more creative one than what you called me yesterday. What was that? Faggot? Queer?"

Alice stifled a laugh and I winked at her. Will clenched his fist as if he were going to throw a punch and I steadied myself, waiting. I'd never been expelled or suspended from school for fighting—this would be a memorable first and worth it.

Imagine my surprise when Will backed down, swore, and pushed past me towards the other end of the hall.

He turned around and flipped me off; I winked and pointed a finger at him—but not the middle one. I was in the presence of a lady.

I took a step into the stairwell and retrieved the beret. It was soft, made of blue wool and looked like something she'd made. It also was scented with her perfume. I silently held the out the beret and a moment passed before she took it.

"It's my favorite—why he does that I don't know...thanks, Quinn."

The fourth period bell rang and Alice ducked past me to go down the stairs. I smiled when she looked back. That was the second time she'd said my name, and it was spoken in the softest, saddest voice...

CHAPTER 6

THE PROPRIETRESS was waiting at the top of the stairs with my binder and stack of textbooks, which were handed off as she shifted the omnipresent bag dangling in the crook of her arm to push open the door to the landing. When we stepped through, we were back in The Shop.

"You really are a sad little puppy," she sighed, taking her place behind the counter. Pages in her great ledger were slapped angrily as she searched for something. "Here you have talent, devastating good looks, to say nothing of intelligence, charm and sensitivity. I think Edward would agree you'd be worthy competition, wouldn't you, Your Grace?" She winked at Edward IV who was sitting with Richard. Edward winked back and I could have sworn there was a gleam or spark of light in the movement. The Proprietress blushed and simpered like a school girl and when she saw me staring, continued, "Add to that a penchant for hopeless romantic gestures that women tend to love. Clearly more than a match for that footballer, and yet what did you do, Quinn? Hmmm?"

"Used my wit?"

"Should have used your fist. Your popularity would have taken a lift out of the basement," Janis Joplin said as she passed by to get a slice of cheesecake.

"How would that solve anything? I'd be no better than Parmenter."

"It would be defending your lady's honor. How is that not proof of your own honor and affection? Am I not correct, Your Grace?"

Again, Edward IV winked.

"Of course she is. I need a cup of coffee," I said and took the cup offered by Hildegard von Bingen as I went to my corner table. Janis Joplin and Rafe had taken the other seats and were poring over my transcription of the *Fantasia*, humming the various themes as they went along with Janis throwing in a bluesy riff every now and then.

"Want to try this strange brew?" Janis held out her mug.

I waved her off, saying, "Not this early in the day, thank you."

"Suit yourself. What have you got against a strong cup of Sanka?"

"The fifty percent Southern Comfort in it?" I guessed.

"How do you know until you've tried it?" Janis put the edge of the mug to my lips and knocked it back so that I had to gulp down a mouthful. Surprisingly, it wasn't bad and the combination of the bitter coffee and smooth liquor spread warmth over me like a blanket and I savored the taste. It was one drink, but I felt as if I'd emptied a fifth in one swallow. "Time to earn your stars and bars, little prince," I heard Janis whisper as I drifted off to sleep…

"…Hey! How many of those have you had?"

Jordan Gregson's question didn't faze me, nor did the fact I was sitting on the kitchen floor of an apartment on Durant Street in Berkeley in the spring of 1975. He slid down off the sink counter and handed me the joint he'd fired up.

"Second, maybe third," I said, sucking on the ice in my glass after I toked.

Jordan reached for the bottle beside me and turned it upside down, watching drops slide down the glass. "Shit! It's empty. That scotch cost me a fortune, Radcliffe!"

"So I'll buy you more when I go back to England," I giggled drunkenly.

"Yeah, like you're going back."

"Don't use that tone…"

I sounded so much like my father that we both burst into laughter and ignored the girls who stepped over us to get to the refrigerator. They gave us look backs, though, on the way out to the living room or wherever with a replenished ice bucket. Jordan nudged me, angling his chin towards them. "The blonde was foxy; she was checking you out."

"Nah, she was checking you out."

"No you, Radcliffe—okay, me."

"Probably thinks we're an item," I laughed.

"By the way, where's your date?" Jordan asked, looking around.

"God knows where; with her tongue down someone's throat, probably. Hit me."

Jordan handed over the joint and I dragged off it, sucked on the scotch-coated ice and banged my head softly on the cupboard door in time to the Creedence song playing in the living room.

"I shouldn't have come back," I mumbled; "I should have stayed in London, y'know?"

"How would you live? No job, no money, no home— Buckingham Palace and 10 Downing Street on your ass."

"I told you, that shit wasn't true."

"So you continue to say, and so I continue not to believe," Jordan scoffed. "There are too many people telling the same tales."

"Should have gone to Ellie's and figured something out."

Jordan passed a bag of corn chips and I dove in, then handed it back. "And then what would you have done?" he asked, blood-shot blue eyes rolling.

"Move in with her until I figured out Plan B."

"Moving back in with your parents was Plan A?" He snorted in derision. Had it come from anyone else, I would have tried to get up and stagger away, but I was wasted and to the point of oblivion.

"Fuck you," I said playfully. "At least I have somewhere to go, no matter how fucked up my career and my fucking life are."

"See, if you hadn't fucked that princess at the hotel,"

"You're fucking jealous of something that didn't happen," I laughed.

"Says the liar. Gotta hand it to you, Radcliffe, there are worse ways of getting thrown out of an orchestra. Your talent wasn't a factor. Just your inability to think things through and keep it in your pants."

We both burst into laughter at this and Jordan leaned over and grabbing me by the scruff of the neck, planted a wet one on my lips, which caused more laughter and gave us some curious looks. I shoved him off me and scooted as far away as I could get without having to give up the joint or the corn chips.

Jordan had become my best friend since our meeting at Oxford. A talented musician with a tenor voice, dimpled smile and baby blues that made the women drool and pant, he didn't give a rat's ass about the rumors circling around us, but then, when weren't there rumors about classical musicians that hung out together and were always seen at the same clubs and bars without women on their arms? Truth be told, Jordan and I were the other's 'wing man,' or hoped to be—we hadn't been flying of late and it didn't seem possible until that night.

I would be the lucky one.

"You want to get out of here?" Jordan yawned, glancing around. "I could get us into the Playboy Club— just need a taxi cab and some breath mints."

"You've got a key," I stated.

"I've got a key."

"How in hell did you manage that?"

"When I signed with Angel Records they thought it would be good for the image. International playboy and all that shit."

"And has it worked?"

"No. But I haven't been to the club in San Francisco. Let's go."

"Sure, let me find Candace." Glancing at the crowd, I scanned the couples either dancing or making out and nodded. My date had definitely found someone more interesting than me. "On second thought, she won't miss me," I said. "Wait while I get my coat—"

"Fuck me! Who is *that?*"

I craned my neck around the counter to see who had caught Jordan's high-end tastes. Looking past the Cal History Department TAs and grad students crowding the path into the living room, I saw her.

Tanned, sun-streaked hair, a bit of makeup, especially around the eyes that made them stand out, and wearing lots of chunky jewelry made of silver and turquoise with a floaty, sheer, peasant-type dress and gold sandals. My heart started to pound and my hands sweat.

I felt that familiar, wonderful jolt of desire looking at Alice Martin for the first time in three years.

"Coffee, I need coffee," I said, dragging myself up off the floor and looking at the cluttered counter tops and range. There was a Mr. Coffee machine and the pot was full and warm. I poured some into a wine glass near at hand and gulped it down, then drank another glassful.

"Time to ooze the London charm, accent and all," Jordan said as he smoothed back his hair and popped a mint into his mouth.

"Hands off," I growled, brushing past him. "That's Alice!"

"Blimey!" was all he could say as I pushed my way into the living room. "I'll get myself back to your mum's…Quinn? Right then, see you later."

"Radcliffe! You're back?" a guy from my Berkeley High graduating class called out as I walked past him to get to Alice. "Thought you moved to England. We're going over to Larry Blake's after this if you want to join us."

"Sorry—got plans," I said.

That is, I hoped I had plans.

She was alone. Good!

The scent of her perfume brought a wave of nostalgia. I tapped her lightly on the shoulder and when she spun about, the questioning stare was replaced by a smile.

"Fancy meeting you here, Alice," I greeted.

"Hello!" she exclaimed. The deepening dimples and the light touch of her hand brushing my arm was proof that she was glad to see me. Then she studied me for the longest time. In the background I heard The Moody Blues—*Never Comes the Day*—and wondered what to say next.

It wasn't the best of openings; in fact, it was pretty lame, but as I smoothed back unruly curls and ran a hand over the five o'clock stubble I said self-consciously, "If I'd known there were fine looking women here I would have cleaned up a bit. You however, are just, well, mighty fine, Miss Alice. Mighty fine!"

"*You're* fine," she gushed over the music. "You look great; really great."

"Do I? I feel overdressed for this crowd," I said, flicking some bread crumbs off my suit jacket lapel, ditching the glasses I'd been wearing into a pocket. "The history department uber intellects go for corduroy and Roots, Birkenstocks, I guess, and have an adversion to soap and deodorant…"

"Ah, you noticed. Welcome to my world. It won't be so boring now that we've got a classical musician to put a refined edge on things."

"I'm not the only one, though." I looked back into the kitchen saying, "Let me introduce you to my classmate from Oxford, Jordan Gregson—brilliant voice, he's got a recording contract with Angel records—oh hell, that's right; he left. Christ, guess I am the only one!"

"Don't worry. All the rumors about history professors biting are just rumors. They actually like musicians."

"Depends on who in the department's doing the biting," I teased back.

"Trust me, you wouldn't enjoy it," Alice said and then it dawned on her. "Oh. *Ohhhhhh*. Yeah. Geez," she added and drained her glass in one quick swallow. If the room was brighter I bet I would have seen a blush.

I pointed at her drink. "What was that?"

"Gin and ginger on the rocks."

"Don't go anywhere."

Then I was back with two drinks. I handed one off and then raised mine with the toast, "To the most beautiful girl I know. To the most beautiful girl ever."

Alice giggled and tipped her glass to mine. "You once did say I was beautiful—but that was before you needed glasses, so you're either crazy, or drunk. Wait, let me rephrase that. You'd have to be drunk to show up at a department party. So you're crazy drunk."

"Crazy glad to see a friend—and such a beautiful friend—after being gone so long."

"Three years, right? When did you get back?"

"Last week."

"*Wrong answer*," Edward whispered in my head. I turned in the direction of his voice ready with a bugger off when everything shifted like a car in traffic and you had to slam on the brakes. Alice wasn't standing in a dark corner of a history professor's apartment but on her front porch.

No; not that mistake. Of all the low points in my life, not that bitter February day three years before!

I'd walked down from the Cloisters and was sweating but not from the exertion. Who was I kidding?

She took a few steps down until we were eye level. I gave her a tentative kiss, hoping for some warmth and was chilled by the indifference. Oh God, my mother. My mother must have called her...

"Last week—and you're just now coming by?" Alice demanded in her frighteningly quiet voice.

"Things happened, Alice, I meant to call you after I got the news."

"What news?"

"We have to talk."

Alice gestured with eyes and hands and I started to sit below her on the steps, but thought better of it and began to pace.

"Look—Alice, I know we made promises, but I've changed, I mean, my life has changed."

I couldn't believe that had come out of my mouth, because it surely wasn't what I was thinking at the time. I sounded like all the boys Alice complained about—the guys who found excuses to break up no matter how phony and ridiculous, the kind that got what they wanted and then got the hell out. Now she was staring at the ground, or my shoes, or whatever, but she wasn't looking at me. Finally she sighed and nodded.

"I guessed as much when you didn't show up at the library. I guessed then you were going to break up with me, that I wouldn't see you again," Alice said.

"Alice! It's not what you're thinking. I love you!"

"Don't suppose you know what I'm thinking. Remember? But you do know what's in my heart."

"You have to understand. I was given a provisional chair with the Royal Philharmonic. The letter came the day after Christmas."

"And that's why you didn't show up despite the promise."

"I didn't sleep that night—I knew what it meant. It's like an internship, but actually, it's a real chair in the section. And there's a lot of traveling. Alice, I'm twenty and they've never had a cellist as young as me. If I give this up…"

"I guess we both know what this means."

Again, the soft, controlled voice. Damn her! Why couldn't she be like those girls who screamed and threw things? Why didn't she just kick me in the balls? That pain

I knew I could endure. Not this heavy pressure mounting in my chest, nor the grief I was already feeling just looking at her. She just sat there with her arms linked around her knees and stared at something far away.

"Alice? Alice, say something."

"When? When do you leave?"

"I have to go back tonight. I had to pick up the rest of my things, take care of some stuff."

"Well, at least I'm stuff and not an afterthought," she said.

Now she looked up me and the tears started to well in my eyes. It was a look I'd never forget; the look that haunted my sleep years later and now, in this moment in time that I'd fallen into, saw on her face at the party.

That stricken look was all I needed to see to know I'd blundered. She took a pull from her glass and started skimming the room.

"Looking for someone in particular?" I ventured. "Someone without a foot in his mouth, maybe?"

Alice glanced up at me and then away, brushing her air off her face and behind her ears. "That obvious?"

"I shouldn't have said that—sorry, I remember that afternoon."

She moved away and I followed. We were standing by one of the speakers and the lyrics to *Never Comes the Day* were painfully true for the situation; they were screaming inside my head.

You wouldn't want to know me somehow...

"I'm sorry, Alice. That was just bad. I'm wasted."

"What? I can't hear you; the music!"

"What'd you say?"

"The music, Quinn!"

"Fucking bloody hell...hang on!"

I drew her outside to the front yard where we sat on the porch and faced each other while resting against the support beams, stared as if putting to memory every change that age and regret had put on our faces. After a time, I said, "That was bloody stupid of me. I'm sorry."

Alice's brows raised a bit, then she frowned. "I don't remember…"

"What?"

"Hunh? Oh, nothing, nothing. Ever get that sense of déjà vu?"

"Yeah, the whole night's been like that."

She shrugged and took a drink. I knew she was angry; she decided to look out into the yard or street, whatever happened to catch her interest, rather than look at me. Some things never changed, did they?

Alice finally set her drink down and stared me straight in the eyes.

"Why are you here? You don't know anyone in the history department. Did Denny tell you where I was?"

Her angry attack wasn't what I remembered and I had no desire to beat a retreat, so I kept my cool and said, "My father is a friend of one of the department heads. He sings in the chorus at the Opera once in a while, you know, a spear-carrier role. That friend has a daughter; it's a blind date. She knows quite a few people here, went to grammar school and high school with them."

"Oh."

No, I didn't think she'd have an argument for that.

"Where is she?"

"Hell if I know. Look, if you want me to leave—"

One…two…three…

Alice didn't say a thing and I took that as a cue. I'd gotten better at reading signs where it concerned women and so I managed to get to my feet and started back inside.

"Hang on."

Or at least I thought I did.

She gestured towards the porch and I slid down.

"Sorry. It was one ugly bitch of a day; I shouldn't have taken it out on you," she apologized. "That wasn't fair. It was wrong. I was wrong."

Again she looked away and drank quietly. She knew I

was studying her, watching, wondering.

"How've you been, Alice Rose? How are you really? Everything okay in your charmed world?" I asked softly and seriously.

"Yes; as a matter fact, I just got back from Italy, if you want to know."

"I do."

Of course I did—all I could think about at that moment was who she had been with in Verona and Florence...

"It's where all the faery princesses go to get away from it all."

"And what would you need to run from?"

"Strange, that you of all people would have to ask."

We stared at one another, waiting. I blinked first and looked away. "I deserved that." I drained my glass and set it down, moving to her side of the porch, but not too close. "How was it?"

"Italy, or the afterlife, or life after?"

"Italy. Donovan—Donovan? Is that his name?"

"Who?" The tone was sharp, almost mocking. "Who are you talking about?" she wanted to know.

I was distracted momentarily by a flash of lightning and the requisite clap of thunder, gazing up in anticipation of a sudden storm.

"Yes, who *are* you talking about, Quinn?"

The Proprietress was scowling at me, arms crossed and fingers tapping impatiently on the staff of an umbrella. She was standing on the porch and it was raining—on the porch.

The umbrella protecting her had swirls of color in motion like one of my light shows. I was entranced, watching and marveling at the sequence of hue and motion, the light.

"How drunk are you?" the Proprietress demanded. When she repeated the question and I failed to answer, she slapped me across the face to bring me out of the trance.

"Hey! What'd you do with Alice? Enough with the rain!"

"Do us all a favor dear boy, and not bring up people and matters that have no business in your messed up life."

"All things considered, Donovan Trist did a pretty good job of messing it up, Your Worshipfulness."

"Wrong!"

"Right!"

"I don't think so, my darling. Wrap your brain around it. Do you want to scare her away? Not now, my pet. Not here. Not yet. You should use the mind in that handsome head of yours to better purpose, like arithmetic."

"What's that got to do with anything?"

"She didn't meet Donovan in that first visit to Italy; that came later."

"I didn't...I didn't think, okay? I've had so much to drink..."

"Do you know what works better than coffee to cure a hangover?" she asked. "A good dose of reality."

She was gone with a snap of her fingers and Alice was back on the porch, staring at me, brows arched and waiting for a reply.

"Hello? Anybody home?" Alice asked, and leaned over to nudge me.

"I heard Donovan was touring Italy; thought that maybe you'd been to one of his concerts," I said, reaching for her glass.

"Never liked Donovan. Thought you knew that," she laughed.

"Now I do."

Alice regarded me with a smile and held my gaze as she took a drink. "Well, Tarquin Oliver Laurence Radcliffe."

"Shit, not the full name. Means I'm in trouble up to my hips or worse."

Another drink and she said, glancing at the drink and then at me, "If you scramble the first initials of all of your names, know what it spells?"

"I have no idea."

"T-R-O-L. Or, troll. And that's what I thought of you for a long while…until now. Until tonight."

"What changed your mind?"

"Seeing you after all this time and realizing you weren't entirely to blame for everything that happened. So that's an apology for what I was thinking."

The glass passed between us several times before I had enough alcohol floating in me and the courage to lean over and brush her lips with a clumsy kiss that made her giggle.

"Am I forgiven, or still in trouble?"

"I'm thinking…"

I waited, hoping…

"Do I call you Maestro?"

Not what I was hoping.

"*That.* Didn't work out as I'd hoped," I sighed and started taking pulls from the glass. Now I was avoiding her curious study. "I learned that being arrogant and talented works for English guys here in America, but when you're American, and they think you're an arrogant bastard with talent—well, doesn't work so well across the pond."

"Were you?"

"Pardon?"

"Were you a bastard? I already know you can be arrogant," she commented and nudged me playfully.

"Define bastard, excluding medieval terms of parentage."

"Did you go over there acting like the Professor?"

I shook my head. "He didn't help matters, though. But that's water under London Bridge now. I've got some auditions coming up. Until I've locked up a chair, I'm teaching guitar and piano at the night school, and—here's the worst part—I'm back living at home until there's a job in sight. My mother didn't like the idea of me starving in a garret somewhere."

"Consumptive girlfriend wasn't too appealing, I

guess."

"Your health has always been excellent. And you just got your degree in history,"

"Aces straight up, Mr. Radcliffe."

"And I bet you're working on a scholarly paper about kings whose names start with AE,"

"You forgot my interest in medieval Italy."

"Whoops. Okay, D minus for that pop quiz."

"B plus because you remembered."

"I can live with that. Are you teaching?"

She shook her head and sighed. "Not yet, didn't get my credentials. I'm taking some time off before grad school. In fact, that's what put me in a foul mood this evening. Dennis and I fought over it tonight. He wants me to finish but can't afford to pay for it. I've put in the scores of loan applications. And I took a job."

"And I bet that's what he got pissed about."

"I'm working as an appraiser and doing book restoration for an antiquarian bookseller in San Francisco. Post Street, near Union Square. Denny would rather I teach third graders or do some serious scholarship. He thinks if I stray off the track I'll lose sight of my goal."

"You? Impossible," I commented, raising her glass to my lips and then to hers. I couldn't help but notice that her eyes never strayed from my face.

"There's nothing I can do with a history degree except write until I have my doctorate," she continued as the glass passed back and forth. "Your passion is music, and mine has always been history. Well, that and theater design—I was talked into the history degree being more practical. But is it? I don't know. I want to go to England and hunker down in some serious research on the Italian merchants and bankers in London and Bruges who pretty much bankrolled the English monarchy before and during the Wars of the Roses, then there's Anglo Saxon England and the Norman Conquest, or what happened after the Bastard invaded. Do you know he really was a Bastard?

Shit, your eyes just glazed over – a bit much? I'm sorry. I forget that not everyone likes history."

"Wow, ambitious. I thought maybe you'd get a gig with the Starship or Fleetwood Mac," I teased and she screwed up her face in an 'I-can't-believe-you-said-that' look and then burst out laughing.

"Thank God you didn't mention ABBA!"

"They called and left a message—loved your rendition of *White Rabbit*..."

We laughed easily. How many years had it been since our last date, our last kiss? Our last anything? Circumstance and obligation had made decisions for us.

"Geez, it took weeks for Denny to get over that," Alice giggled, shaking her head. "He even forbade me to sing around the house."

"I remember the first time I heard you sing."

Alice nodded, then turned her head so that it was almost resting on my shoulder. "I was finishing up on the sets and you were on stage practicing. You were always practicing there. You played *Tros y Garreg—Crossing the Stone*."

"And you sang. I think I fell in love with you then—no, it was long before."

Oh hell, where did that come from?

"Quinn," she sighed, laughing softly, a nervous laugh.

"I won't apologize for that," I confessed. "I think it was a long time coming. And I think you'd agree." We sat in silence, a numbing silence, and then I spoke up again. "My mother wishes you would come by the house, just stop by for coffee, just say hello and not be a stranger."

"Given the history, I didn't think she'd want to see me." She paused. "Or that you'd want to see me."

"I'm here; you're here. I'm sorry for so much...so."

"So?"

Not what I had said, I'm sure of it!

I drew her close, our lips ready to touch when I whispered, "I'm ready to make amends; all I need is your absolution."

"Given."

The touch was cool, sweet, but that was all I got for the moment.

"Am I interrupting something, Tarquin?"

Alice moved away first and scrambled to her feet, making an effort to distance herself, but she stumbled and I caught her before she fell off the porch. We both stared up at my date who looked as if she'd been shagged a few too many times. Clothing in disarray, lipstick gone, mascara smudged into raccoon-like rings. She stank of whiskey and men's aftershave and teetered back and forth like one of those 'Bobo' punching clowns. Years later we'd call it the 'walk of shame.'

"Have a good time tonight, Candace?" I asked.

"I've had better, or expected better," she said and started to giggle.

"Oh good, a happy drunk," Alice whispered.

"What was that?" Candace demanded, coming closer. "What was that? Who's your friend, Tarquin?"

"A friend," I said, pulling Alice out of her way. "Need a ride home, Candace?"

"If you wouldn't mind," she sniffed, giving Alice a once over with bloodshot eyes.

"I'll need an address."

I was speaking to Candace, but looking straight at Alice. Candace let her eyes slide from me to Alice and back again before she pivoted on a heel and said over her shoulder, "I'll just get my things."

So there we were on the porch. I could have followed through with the kiss but the carriage of Alice's shoulders and how she fiddled with her handbag was evidence enough that it would be a huge mistake. Whenever she was upset, Alice rummaged through whatever bag she was carrying at the time as if looking for the solution.

"Look, I know my timing is off as usual, but Alice, I really meant—"

The screen door banged and Candace was there, and barked "Okay, let's go."

"Alice," I started again as I dug for my keys and Candace started down the sidewalk to my father's Bentley at the corner.

"Good to see you again, Quinn."

"It's not what it looks like, I swear."

"It looks like she's mad."

"Alice, would you just listen to me, please?"

She started digging through her bag and pulled out a crumpled electric company bill. It was shoved into my hand. "If it isn't what I think it is, and you're sober, come by. The address is on the bill—it's not far." And she was gone, the angry clip of her sandals echoing until she turned the corner and was gone.

The walk to the Bentley seemed like the longest in my life. Candace glared at me when I threw myself into the driver's seat, slammed the door and sat staring at the street.

"I'll have to thank your father another time."

"Wha...?" I looked at the stunning brunette as if seeing her for the first time.

"Well, your father and mine thought..."

"Never count on anything Andrew Radcliffe puts together as a done deal—or that it's even welcome," I grumbled as we finally drove off.

"He led me to believe that you were available, if you want the truth."

"Sorry—I don't. And no, I'm not."

Candace started fidgeting with the hem of her skirt, shifting so that her long, shapely legs up to the thigh were exposed. "So I guess the stories about you aren't just tabloid gossip?"

"Pretty much. Do I make a right or left here?"

"Right. My parents are in the city with yours if you want to come in for a bit?" A leg was crossed slowly over a knee, executed in such a way that I'd notice. I noticed. I wasn't interested—but I wasn't dead.

"I don't think that would be a good idea."

"Why not? The night's still young—unless you and the other girl really are together."

"She's part of the past," I lied.

"Didn't look like it to me."

"Well she is."

"Maybe I could change your mind about things, you know, the tabloid gossip."

I almost pulled the emergency brake out of the floor board when she placed her hand inside my thigh and moved her fingers upwards. We almost went into the yard of one the larger homes on Santa Barbara Road but I managed to pull the car over. Turning to face her, I snapped, "First, I don't see how you'd still have the energy after being so busy tonight. Second, and most important Candace, I'm not queer, not involved with anyone; I'm just not interested."

She made a strangled sound and flew out of the car, not even closing the door so that the warning bell chimed until I leaned over for the handle and the cheery note of A Sharp lengthened to a chirrup-chirrup of the telephone in my studio and office in London on Kensington Road.

CHAPTER 7

THE JOLT OF ADRENALIN and surprise that accompanied these visits was particularly strong on this stop of The Journey of What-the-Hell. I stared at the phone with its flashing button and happy chirrup as if it would answer itself. Fortunately my secretary took the call. I spun about in my desk chair and looked at the stacks of books and scores piled on the credenza where the tea tray brought three hours ago still sat untouched; the dark blue wallpaper and walnut moldings along the walls and ceiling; the overstuffed sofa of velvet and brocade—the worst in faux Victorian, Ellie sniffed when I bought it—still draped with a blanket and two pillows stacked at one end after last night's late rehearsals. My eyes settled on the personal effects I'd brought from home. Things that meant something: the sweater Alice made. Frodo the teddy bear, also made by Alice. A striped scarf Denny knit and gave as a present on Christmas in '71, never mind how ugly it was. We all received one. There was a photograph of Harry, Denny, Alice and me sitting on their back porch on Christmas Day to record the momentous occasion. I used the scarf as a coaster for a coffee cup from Harry. The oversized mug was decorated with the phrase *Whatta Guy!* and a picture of Brahms in Ray Bans. Never mind that I really didn't like Brahms. Then there was the bouquet of silk flowers purchased in York.

Plants die when you breathe the same air, or live in the same room, Quinn, Alice had laughed when she saw the sorry state of my gardening efforts. I remembered that one afternoon while visiting Ellie and she suggested the silk flowers, which I gathered one by one, a flower for every letter in Alice's name. Alice Rose Martin.

Glancing at the carefully arranged clutter midst reports, scores, cubes of rosin and the overflowing in and out boxes, the awards and certificates, I suddenly realized that everything important to me did not come from my parents and everything I loved was here in my office.

I reached for Frodo, running a hand over the silky white fake fur and smiling at the little guy. Alice confessed that if you looked under the bow tie around the neck at the seam, there was a rust-colored stain. The drops of blood drawn by the needle as she stitched Frodo together during her first winter break from college, the Christmas she gave him to me.

The Christmas I proposed.

I glanced at the calendar to get my bearings, to see if the melancholia I was suffering was justified.

June of 1978.

I'd been conductor of the Royal Philharmonic for almost two years.

I knew what was coming, but how to set things right...I was as clueless in that moment as when it first happened.

The knock startled me. I tossed the bear guiltily on the desk and looked up at Graham Sudley, concert master for the orchestra, when he poked his head around the door.

"Do you have a moment, Maestro? Unless you have to meet with Sir William."

"I chased him out an hour ago, and the name is Quinn," I sighed, leaning back in my chair and waving him forward.

Graham threw himself into the chair that wasn't piled with scores and articles of laundry. He dropped the score he was holding onto the desk, setting one of the Matchbox cars I used as a paperweight crashing into another that held down phone messages.

"You can't be serious, Maestro—Quinn."

I took the score and fanned it, handed it back. "I am. Let me guess—the brass section is complaining?"

"It's light. It's fluff. It's not what we're used to, if you want the truth."

"We did Brahms, Berlioz, Mozart, Rachmaninoff; I think this would be…fun."

"I'm not so sure. I thought Beethoven was the program for the American tour? It's what they're used to, isn't it?"

"That came out full of snobbery, didn't it?" I said, and took the cigarette he was about to light out of his mouth and handed it to him. "Don't like smoking in here, Graham. Look, this program is something I've wanted to do for a while. For once I'm side-stepping what's usually done and what our biggest donors want, and I want to do a Ralph Vaughan Williams program for the opening night in New York. It's marketing for the recording with Decca. Everyone knows Beethoven, Tchaikovsky—how many people know Vaughan Williams? If our audience likes what they hear in New York, they'll buy the album."

"The Board is starting to grumble, if you must know."

"Let them," I sighed. "Jesus Himself could be up on that podium playing all of the Bach Suites on my cello or conducting Mahler's Second and they'd complain about something."

"You haven't been conductor for very long and with all the stories of your nightlife in the tabloids, and so many changes already; well, you said we'd take things slow so people would adjust."

"This isn't the Church of England. We don't need a committee to discuss every move I make; don't need a weekly forum. Don't need to hear how much better it used to be. If I waited until everyone was comfortable—well, the seven words of death for any organization are 'That's the way we've always done it.' And as for my nightlife and the tabloids…"

"Yes?"

"Never mind. Don't worry. I have no intention making the orchestra suffer through an all-disco program or kiss-and-tell in the Tattler. I know that's what they're thinking."

"Nothing gets by you, does it?" Graham said, trying to suppress a grin.

"You'd be surprised at what I miss and what gets away. I do have something different in mind—something unexpected."

"Oh God help us, Bee Gees!"

"No, but it goes in hand with the Vaughan Williams planned for the opening night in New York. In its own way. Relax; we're doing Beethoven's Seventh, too."

"And?" He leaned forward, waiting.

"And I hate disco."

He kept leaning forward and when I shook my head, Graham sighed and heaved himself to his feet, putting back the cars where he found them. "Are you coming with us tonight?" he ventured, not looking at me.

"I've already told you, it's not my scene. Thanks for the offer, though."

"Sorry—the blokes and I thought..."

"Don't think. Play the violin. See you tomorrow?"

He flooded with bright color and moved towards the door. "You let me off light, Maestro. Thanks."

"Graham!"

"Sir?"

"It's Quinn. Don't believe everything you read in the tabloids."

"Right. Night, then." Graham wheeled back, another grin creeping over his face. "So the story about you in the bath at the Savoy?"

"I've got a girl back home. See you in the morning at eight-thirty sharp. We'll be working with the strings on *Lark Ascending*. I've got you down for the solo."

"What happened to Pavel? The *Times* Sunday supplement's been screaming his praises for weeks."

"Broke his hand—don't ask."

"Thanks! See you."

He flashed a real smile this time and I considered it a victory. Most of the orchestra avoided me by keeping their distance; once in a while I got a smile with the requisite 'Maestro' or 'sir.' I was starting not to worry about such things because it meant to the Board of Governors and President that I was garnering respect as the Artistic Director and Principal Conductor. That part of my life was becoming easier.

When Graham was gone I switched off the desk lamp and went to draw the blinds, staring down at the rush hour traffic on Kensington Road.

A young woman in a light summer dress caught my attention. Her light brown hair was falling out of its clips, and the fabric of her dress pressed against every curve as a breeze came at her while she was pulled through the crosswalk by a little dog. The dog's exuberance made her laugh. All of this reminded me of Alice. Maybe that's why I felt jealous when the dog managed to entangle itself in the leash of a basset hound being led by a man about my height and coloring, about my age. A cloying, stereotypical meeting with laughter and apologies. All it needed was the background music of John Denver or The Captain & Tennille. Too bad the orchestra had gone home for the day; we could have offered *Moon River* or *The Shadow of Your Smile* while the newly-discovered lovers strolled arm in arm to whoever's flat was closest.

"Get a grip," I sighed to myself.

I've got a girl back home.

Why did I keep lying to myself? Who was I fooling?

"Only yourself," I heard Janis' voice in my ear.

The clock chiming the hour distracted me for only a moment and I stared down at my watch. It was eleven in the morning in California.

I started to dial the number and while it rang remembered that Alice was in the east now. Just when

Harry answered, I paused and then hung up. The sigh I exhaled moved the papers around on my desk.

Call it a night, Radcliffe…call it a life.

There was a pub not far from the Royal Albert Hall where I had my studio and office—The One Note. It was a haunt of mine, like The Bitter End in York, and my appearance never caused excitement; I was the youngest orchestra conductor in the classical world then, the youngest ever for the Royal Philharmonic, not a rock star. I was another musician coming in for a drink and supper. It was a place I could call my refuge and leave it at that.

"Evening, Quinn," a waitress named Judy greeted, tossing down a menu and a coaster. It was force of habit, for her next words were, "The usual, sir?"

I nodded and took the *Times* out of my briefcase, bypassing the entertainment pages for the sports to look at the scores. Out of the corner of my eye I saw Judy hovering, looking nervous. "What's wrong?" I queried. "No cod or chips tonight?"

"Sir, Professor Radcliffe is here—again. I told him what you said."

"It's alright, Judy. Not your fault." I sighed, gathering up my things. "Look, stall him; tell him I had to take a call."

"But he's standing there—right by the telephone."

"Damn! I just don't want the bother…sorry about the inconvenience. Make it up to you tomorrow night, okay?" I put two pound coins on the table and skirted around a cluster of students from the Royal Academy waiting for their drinks at the bar. They recognized me and began to whisper and greet me, but I waved them off and headed for the bathrooms in the back. There was a door leading out into Prince Albert Court for the staff and I pushed it open and escaped into the London Streets, my walk taking only a few feet, for I paused and glanced around.

I was back in Berkeley on that spring night of 1975.

Alice's utility bill was wrapped around a sack of

Chinese takeout that I'd picked up on the way. I juggled the sack as I unfolded the bill to check the address of the apartment house I now stood before.

Up a flight of stairs and to the right, another right. I smoothed back my hair and then remembered how she liked it messy, then raked my fingers through it. Waited a second and then pressed the doorbell. And again. Jesus, what if she wasn't home or worse, met up with some guy, or . . .

She was backlit, incredibly beautiful and smiling.

It took me a moment to respond. "Hello," I opened and then held up the sack of cartons. "I'm not drunk, just hungry."

"Chicken chow mein and broccoli beef, mmmm! You remembered," she said and stepped aside to let me in.

"Nice place," I said, following her into the kitchen and setting the cartons on the dinette table, gently shoving to one side fashion magazines, sketchbooks, watercolors and pencils. "Hey! I remember this sketch. Wasn't this for the Scottish Play?"

Alice turned to see what had caught my attention and smiled, for I was tapping a sketch of a medieval costume design. The prince was my seventeen-year old self.

"Now it's for the Danish Play, it's a new rendition of something I had in mind then," she answered.

"But the model is still me," I teased.

"I traced the original." She glanced up at me and winked.

"You were always drawing when you weren't knitting."

"You called it angry knitting, I think. Here. You might like these. This is for a repertory theater," she continued and shuffling through a stack of watercolor sketches in a portfolio, held up a few more. "These are for a ballet troupe, believe it or not."

"Good Lord, Lord of the Rings!" I said and then chuckled. Our first serious conversation had been about

Tolkien. "Good to know some things haven't changed," I remarked and closed the portfolio reverently.

"We'll eat in the living room. More space and less chance of you spilling stuff on my work," Alice teased as she went past me with a stack of plates, silverware and a bottle of wine.

Everything was set on the coffee table and I dragged a bean bag chair over and plopped down, watching Alice serve up equal portions.

"What happened to the blind date?" she asked, half-seriously, kneeling on the carpet beside me. "Wait; you don't need to tell me. It's not my business and besides, I've been on enough of those to know better than to ask."

"All you need to know is that my father set it up."

Alice nodded and then threw me The Pathetic Look. The Poor You Gaze. I didn't have to offer further explanation.

After a few minutes of dining in silence I glanced around the living room and saw familiar treasures like the paper flowers Denny made, the snow globe I'd brought from York, photographs of her mother and brother and Harry, the collection of medieval knights that now did battle on the second shelf of the bookcase. Her dog Sammie's puppy collar. There were no photographs of us, or me. "I guess there's somebody?" I asked.

"Not anymore."

"Funny; I thought that in Italy . . ." my voice trailed off as an incredible pressure in my chest took over. Was I going to die now?

No. I saw The Proprietress in the mirror over the fireplace mantle and she was glaring, shaking her head. Yes, I'd done it again – divulge information that I knew before time.

"Quinn? Quinn, are you okay?"

"What? Just a sudden attack of heartburn," I lied. I glanced at Alice and she blushed and looked away, as if she knew that I knew, that she was deliberately keeping something back, or lying. We both ended the awkward moment by concentrating inordinately on fried rice, chicken chow mein and broccoli beef.

"I forgot that you inhale your food," Alice said and nudged me playfully with her elbow.

"It's been so long," I said.

"Since you had dinner with a beautiful girl?"

"Well that, and being with a friend."

"From what I heard, you weren't wasting any time making friends who were beautiful."

"Depends on what you mean by 'friends.'

"The Pink Section of the Chronicle had some pretty interesting stories about your dating models and actresses and driving the company directors crazy with your coming in late and hung over, or not showing up at all – real diva stuff. Local boy makes good and goes really, really bad sort of storyline, y'know?"

I knocked back a glass of wine, poured another.

"I didn't believe it, because I think I know you pretty well."

Another glass was emptied.

"Whoa, cowboy," Alice laughed. "Where'd you learn to drink?"

"Back stage at the Royal Albert – it helped get my mind off things and gave an excuse to be alone."

"*You weren't supposed to bring that up!*" the Proprietress hissed, and tapped her wristwatch before dissolving into the soft diffused light from the lamps reflected in the mirror.

"So . . . it's true then? About the wild parties?" Alice ventured taking a sip of wine from my glass.

I was ready to take another drink but thought better of it and set my glass down. I actually looked directly in those lovely eyes – something I hadn't done all night. "Where did you hear this stuff?" I asked softly. "More newspaper crap?"

"Actually, I heard those stories from some of your

high school orchestra and jazz band mates."

"First, whoever they are, they're not my friends. Second, I went to a party in London and The Who showed up for all of five minutes. They weren't there long enough to break up a toothpick let alone a Stratocaster."

"So you didn't try to flush a photographer's head down the toilet and you weren't caught making out with Princess Anne in a bathtub at the Savoy?"

"Uh, no."

"But you did mess with that photographer?"

"He insulted my mother."

"And you didn't trash a hotel room coming down off of LSD."

"Again, no."

"And there weren't orgies of any kind."

"I'd be a happier man if . . . never mind. Classical musicians are always trying to be bad boys." We both started laughing and I leaned in, feeding Alice chow mein. "I'm amazed at all the reasons people come up with to explain to themselves why I left the orchestra and disappointed them," I sighed. "Why it's their problem, I don't know."

"You'd tell me, right?"

"Rumors started. Ugly stuff and business about my life, how I got the job, my mother – I don't want to go into it right now, but I'll tell you it didn't help when my father showed up in London. So you can imagine what that did to my credibility as a musician and that being the only criterial for being with the orchestra."

"Oh, geez, Quinn! Didn't you once tell me that Jane made him promise to stay away?"

"He always managed to find an excuse. Mostly on the pretext of publicity for the university or the opera company, or both. He followed us to several venues and started coming backstage and making demands, arguing with the wrong people. He said he was there to do damage control, for what, I sure as hell didn't know. Wasn't long after that the director asked me to leave. I guess they made up their mind that I was bad news."

I paused there and stared at my hands, saw Alice's beautiful, long and tapered fingers rest on mine as I gathered my thoughts.

"I wasn't bad news," I continued. "Sure, I'd done some things that raised an eyebrow or two, but no one got hurt. Still they made it look like it was my behavior that got me fired when in reality I hadn't done anything at all except behave and be professional: show up for rehearsals, performances, always on time, and take master classes and extra practice."

"Now that was one *hell* of a lie or an artful embroidery of the truth."

Rafe was seated beside me now, not Alice. He reached for one of the cartons and sampled the broccoli beef, then looked at me inquiringly, his caterpillar brows undulating.

"It's enough of the truth, isn't it?" I demanded.

"To quote Pontius Pilate, 'what is truth?'" he said and set aside the carton. Smiling, he added, "Or to be more precise, what is *your* truth? The truth as you see it? I'm sure you'll know how to get out of this pickle. I must say, though, you do know how to make life interesting. Carry on."

He was gone and Alice was there again, spooning the rest of the broccoli beef onto our plates. She always shared, I mused; if it had been me, I'd have emptied the carton on to my plate and asked later if she'd wanted any of it.

"Funny, whenever I ran into Jane at the Co-Op or Hink's she always said things couldn't be better for you," Alice said.

"If I were your son, or you had a son like me, would you want the world to know he was a royal fuck up?"

Her hair had fallen like a curtain around her face as she leaned in to use the chopsticks on the food but I could tell she was smiling. "Quinn," she said softly, "If you were my son, there'd be no problem of screwing up, because you'd be loved and I'd never let you fail. And even if it seemed like you might I would be there to help in any way I can. Because I loved you."

We finished the food in silence, listening to the music Alice put on the stereo, something sad and medieval. She was getting ready to clear away our late night supper when I said, "Alice, do you ever wonder what it would been like if we'd gotten married?"

She stopped and looked at me, surprised, but without the wounded look I'd seen too many times that night. "We'd be living in an apartment in Greenwich Village while you were teaching music at School of the Performing Arts. I'd be working in a book shop while I finished grad school. You'd be first chair in a chamber orchestra barely getting by but with good reviews, of course. You'd spend your afternoons at auditions for that perfect chair in the perfect orchestra. And we'd have some incredibly beautiful children. Two, maybe three."

"So you have given it thought," I laughed.

"Sure, who wouldn't? I mean, you always wonder about the one who got away, the one you knew you couldn't have, right?" She said this smiling over her shoulder as she carried the remnants of supper into the kitchen.

I followed and when she turned with a look of surprise on her face to find me there, I pulled her close.

"What if he was right here? Right in front of you?"

I kissed her then and was glad she didn't back away. I leaned against the wall for support as the kisses grew hotter and the need became urgent. Alice broke away first and nodded her chin towards a door at the end of the hall. "The bedroom's that way. I'll only be a moment," she whispered and gave me another warm and loving kiss.

Alice slipped away and into the bathroom. I tried not to run to the bedroom, anticipating the warmth, the excitement, most importantly to have beautiful Alice in my arms again.

When I opened the door and inhaled the familiar, nostalgic scents that reminded me of her, of our days and nights together, I found myself back in the Village on the bridge.

CHAPTER 8

"Sonofa . . . are you kidding me?!"

I stared up the high street to the church and down to the Shop. I turned, hoping to be transported back to the late spring of 1975.

"Quinn!"

Rafe was leaving The Shop and hailed me, almost jogging to catch up. He paused a moment to catch his breath, leaning on my shoulder for support. "I know that look," he gasped; we've all worn it at one time or another. Just when you think you've got matters in hand..."

"I was going to make things right," I whined, adding, "What does she do? She brings me back here. Damn her soul!"

"She? Our Lady of Sorrows? Does she have one?"

"What?"

"Does she have one? A soul?"

"Who else would set things up so perfectly for happiness and then pull it away," I answered.

Rafe shook his head and reached for a cigarette in his pocket. "Are you sure it was her? Are you sure about making things right? You had the opportunity presented to you on a silver platter and you didn't make the best of it. What exactly were you going to do, Quinn?"

"I just want a straight answer. Why does everyone here answer questions with questions?"

"All right then. You're here to find the answers."

"Not funny." I shoved my hands into my pockets and

stared him. "Okay, I'm game. I want answers."

"Don't we all; well, we have to decide which questions need our attention."

"Jesus, you're kidding…"

"Tell me what you're looking for."

I started pacing now, kicking the pebbles on the walk, watching the leaves scatter under my boots. "I wasn't looking for anything when all of a sudden I'm here. And where is here exactly? Can you tell me?" I snapped. "I was taking a nap with the dog on the sofa, taking a break from arranging the numbers for the next concert, and on top of that worrying about Alice every waking minute, and then, I'm here. I have a sense of what I'm supposed to do, but I don't know what I want to do because I'm afraid I'll lose what I already have. I don't know what to do."

"Do what you want." Rafe looked up at me and nodded, taking a drag on the cigarette. "Oh, I see now— do you think this is about atonement? Yes, I suppose one might, given the circumstance and what you've been told."

I stared at the pavement, watching a column of ants march past my toes, the precision and dedication of their movement and purpose. "I've done what I think have been some pretty ugly things in my life, especially when it amounted to hurting Alice," I said. "Tell me if I'm right. I can make it up to her."

"Well, that's up to you, Quinn. And didn't you already? Let me posit this: what made you do those things? What was the motivation? Find the reasons and you've got a purpose—if you want it."

"My father…"

Rafe chuckled and then coughed, tossing the cigarette to the ground and then stamping on it. "She's right, you know; I should give up this nasty habit. Quinn, you and I and everyone knows that your father is the big villain, but there's got to be something else."

I blinked at him, frowning, and when I didn't respond, Rafe patted my shoulder.

"I'm not a religious man, but I find that sitting in a church sometimes reveals answers of a most surprising kind." He pointed behind me to the Romanesque church at the end of the high street. The sunlight played off the slate roof shingles and affected a halo.

Of course it would, I thought, and glanced skeptically.

"All sorts of answers, I think."

Rafe nudged his chin in the direction he wanted me to go.

I took the stairs to the porch two at a time and then paused before entering the church, just in case there was a service in progress. Sure enough, when I passed through the narthex to the nave, a soft blue cloud of incense hung in the air and motes followed the draft from the door as I approached the altar. This church resembled the Norman chapel in the Tower and St. Bartholomew the Great in London, a crescent of pillars stood behind the rood screen and table. There were flowers in every vase and stand. Pale blush, pink, yellow, mauve and the palest of blues – the colors of clouds in the late afternoon at Scarborough.

I thought I was alone until I saw her kneeling at the communion rail. She turned at the sound of my footsteps and rose slowly, smiling, as if expecting me.

"I was hoping to see you today of all days," Alice greeted, going up on tiptoe to kiss my cheek. She stepped back and smiled again. "You look well, but then, I always thought you were your most handsome after twenty-five. No. Sixty-five. You improved with age, as they say."

When I didn't respond for staring at her incredulously, for taking in the wonderful sight of her in a form-fitting medieval-styled gown of ivory lace and pearls, she took a white freesia from the bouquet in her hands and held it out for me to take.

"It's all too much, isn't it?" she said.

"You," I paused and took a breath, swallowed, "You look amazing. You're so beautiful. You've always been so."

Alice took a turn, the train following her and whispering on the pavement. "A bride is supposed to be beautiful on her wedding day."

"I remember when you designed that; I always wondered if it was for our wedding."

"That's because you said you pictured me in a white lace dress as I stood on a cliff looking out to sea. It never left my imagination, you know," Alice whispered, stepping close.

"And yet you wore it for your wedding to him."

"Yes. I lost faith and hope. I thought if I wore the dress, I could imagine you were beside me at the altar, and that at least I would have kept my promise—well, it doesn't matter now, does it?"

She kissed me and once again I felt a lightness and warmth, a reality I had searched for and now found here, in this chapel and with Alice now in my arms. When she finally broke away, I opened my eyes and was relieved that she had not been taken from me. Alice was still in my arms, but it was August of 1969 and she was wearing the red velvet dress; it was the night of our first date.

We were stretched out on the overstuffed sofa in the study off my bedroom, the *Fantasia on a Theme by Thomas Tallis* playing on the stereo turntable. I had gently pulled her into my arms and she was looking at me with the most lovely, gentle eyes as she brushed my unruly hair off my face, keeping her hand on my cheek. I would always think of this night at the darkest moments of my life; it was one of the few, truly happy times.

"Do you know how long I've dreamt of this?" I whispered.

"I couldn't guess—I've never thought—I mean, had I known that you wanted me of all people, and to kiss me, that is," Alice stammered nervously.

"If you want to test that statement, I won't object."

"Let's see."

I closed my eyes and felt her lips on mine, tentative at

first and then warm, passionate; it was all I could do to keep from carrying her into the bedroom and locking the door behind us, and yet my need for Alice was greater than the physical. As we kissed again and again and she let me kiss her neck and the hollow between her breasts, I gathered strength from her, a strength born of happiness and love. I sensed her need, too, and pulled her even closer and held her tighter until she gasped that she couldn't breathe, and laughing, we separated for a moment.

We smiled at one another. Alice's face was shadowed by the soft lamplight and the wavy curtain of hair that fell around her shoulders and spilled on to my neck and chest. I imagined what it might feel like on my naked skin.

"Who would have guessed?" I laughed softly.

"I can't imagine," was her reply and she looked as happy I did.

"You don't mind that I'm not in the popular crowd, or a jock, or drive a GTO or Mustang? Or that I have a chauffeur?"

Alice sat up on her knees and brushed her hair off her face. She offered a beguiling smile before taking my hands playfully. "Well, I hope you won't be too disappointed when I tell you that I think it's brilliant you're a musical prodigy, that you're tall and handsome, taller than most boys, and that you live in a castle. How many faery princesses get their prince and a castle?" She leaned closer, her lips almost touching and it made my heart pound like crazy, as if it would burst out of my chest. Then she said in a sultry voice, "Of course, if you need further proof…"

"I think I'll need some serious convincing, Alice!"

She gave me sufficient evidence, and I was in heaven. Then the clock struck one and Alice broke away, her delectable lips in a pout. "Shit! It's past my curfew!" she sighed and sat up, retrieving her gold sandals from the carpet. "I'm sorry; I have to go. I had a wonderful time, Quinn."

"Then stay just for a while longer—until the record ends."

"Denny will kill me."

"What if I have Mother drive you home?" I gently pulled Alice back into my arms. "So, let's just wait a bit; stay here with me."

She relaxed in my arms and I stroked her silky hair and kissed her forehead. Closing my eyes, I imagined us in bed, wrapped in soft and warm blankets and each another's arms, a full moon shining on us from an open window. Now that window was in Alice's bedroom on that night of our reunion.

The soft, silvery light played off shadows and made Alice even more lovely and desirable. I slid my hand down her shoulder and arm, to her waist and thigh, feeling the silky skin and pulled her close for a kiss.

"Alice," I whispered; "I wasn't completely honest with you."

"Hmm…." She murmured drowsily and I hoped contentedly.

"There's more to the story."

"Isn't that how it always is?"

"I still care. I still love you. I never stopped loving you. But I'm one fucked up person, and we have to talk, because I knew when I saw you tonight that I couldn't let you go again and now I know I can't. I just can't."

Alice turned in my arms and drew the sheet and blankets around us, snuggled even closer. "We'll talk in the morning then, because now I just want to sleep in your arms and be with you," she said softly between kisses.

"But—"

"Hush. Stay with me tonight. Tomorrow we'll talk."

"Damn! I forgot - I have an audition in the city at nine-thirty,"

"I'll make you breakfast, and you can shower here; have your mother bring your cello over or meet you at the Berkeley BART Station. Meanwhile, here's something for luck," Alice whispered and gave me a kiss I'd never forget – in fact, I thought of it when I woke, or thought I'd wakened with the morning sun in my eyes.

But it wasn't the sun shining on us, or rather, me.

I was standing in the glare of a white-hot arc lamp backstage at Lincoln Center in New York, loosening my tie and accepting a bottle of Coca Cola that one of the stage hands brought. I thanked him and took a pull, almost emptying the bottle down my throat in one gulp. Out front, people were still applauding and the stage manager waved me over, saying, "Give them one more, son," and held the curtain open for me to go upstage. I took a bow and waved to the audience, stepped into the dusky light of backstage again and without thinking wiped my mouth on the sleeve of my tux just as the Director of Lincoln Center appeared.

"Mr. Radcliffe! What a performance!" he said, a hand extended while a grin spread across his face so that his eyes were lost in rosy, Kris Kringle cheeks.

"Sir - ! Sorry, I was so thirsty."

"I'd be too if I'd just performed the most technically demanding of the Bach cello suites, and you did it proud, young man!"

"Thank you—it was a gamble; a last minute decision," I said, feeling a trickle of sweat sliding from my brow to my chin. I searched for my handkerchief and realized it was in the dressing room. As much as I wanted to wipe down my face, I didn't; I was sure the funny look on the Director's face was due to the drops falling on my tux lapels.

It was a freezing mid-December night and here I was sweating. Performing was a physical workout and took everything I had. Usually I went to the dressing room or green room, or to the car and had a lie-down just to recover, but there was no way I could or would avoid the Director, especially if he was going to continue the Radcliffe Love In. Here was someone whose opinion mattered and could help my career out from my father's oppressive shadow.

"A stroke of brilliance is what it was. I'll tell you something else: the critic from the Times was here tonight and thrilled with your rendition of *The Girl with the Flaxen Hair*. Not many cellists have that in their repertoire," the Director continued to gush. "Where did you learn your technique? The Conservatory?"

"Con—oh no, sir. I'm still in high school. I was hoping to apply for next fall, though."

"You should. I can put in a word for you if that will smooth over the application process."

"I wouldn't want or expect special treatment. But a letter of reference or a recommendation from you, now that you've heard me—"

"Conservatory?"

My father's voice was like a cannon and all heads turned when Andrew Radcliffe, M.A., Ph.D., former principal tenor of the Metropolitan and Royal Operas, entered the circle forming around us. People stepped back respectfully, for my father was a legend in the classical music world and he made sure it stayed that way and everyone knew it.

"Maestro Radcliffe, this son of yours is amazing. A young man, an artist, any father would be proud of," the Director said, patting my shoulder. "I haven't heard Bach's Fourth Suite played with such passion and so flawlessly in years. I couldn't believe it when he said he was still in high school."

"Conservatory, is it? What did I tell you, Quinn? When will you get that nonsense out of your head?" the Professor snapped.

And there it was: the enormous pin that burst the bubble of my happiness and achievement.

The Director smiled nervously and looked relieved when a stage hand called him away. I hefted the cello case in one hand and the bottle of Coca Cola in the other and walked off stage and out into the New York City winter night.

"If you think, young man, that you're going to turn down the scholarship to Oxford and the Royal Academy," my father was growling behind me, his breath rising in noxious clouds as he continued to rant.

I turned on him as the hotel limousine pulled up. "What makes you think I want to go to school in Oxford? Or London? My chances are better here in New York!" I hissed.

"They were until you botched that audition for the Philharmonic!"

"Oh for Chrissakes, get over it. Dad, I told you I didn't want to audition for that chair. I'm not ready—I know that. You should have known it, too."

"So now you know better than me?"

I took a gulp of freezing night air and waited before saying quietly, "I'm the best judge of me and what I can do."

The driver opened the doors for us and I intentionally threw the cello on the seat so my father wouldn't be able to sit with me. The whites of his saucer-like eyes were turning red with rage, as was his face. He sat up front with the driver and tapped on the glove box, a 2/3 meter, all the way to the hotel and kept his silence until almost midnight, coming out to the sitting room of the Plaza suite.

"Would you mind turning that off?" he asked quietly, pointing at the television. That he had asked shocked me; that it was a quiet request had me worried. I leaned over and switched off The Tonight Show with Johnny Carson and leaned back against the sofa, waiting for the worst. My father took a pipe from his dressing gown pocket, tamped down the tobacco and after a moment lit the bowl so that an aroma of cherry wafted through the suite.

"You never argued before, Tarquin. I'd like to know what's going on."

"Why does anything have to be going on?" I wanted to know. "Maybe this isn't right for me."

"Right for you?" His eyes started to bulge again. "Did I hear you correctly?"

"Yes; maybe I should take a break, you know? Take a few months off."

"No, I don't! All your life this has been the dream, *the* dream!"

"It's been *your* dream, Dad. Sure, I love music—"

"You will not squander all I've done!"

"That's right; all you've done." I pushed myself off the sofa and tried to brush past him. When I felt his hand on my shoulder I was sure he was going to throw a punch and I braced myself, clenched my fists to defend myself and hoped I wouldn't bruise my right hand like last time.

"Quinn, I didn't mean it like that."

*Well, **that** came out of nowhere!*

"You did. Let go of me. Please."

"Let's discuss this as adults. Man to man. I'll make us drinks."

"Dad, you know I don't—"

"An eighteen-year-old who doesn't want to drink?" he laughed. "That's news to me!"

"I'm serious. Nothing for me; I took some medicine for my sore throat."

"Tonic, no gin." My father laughed as he came from the wet bar and sat beside me. I was handed a tumbler with ice and fizzy water. We drank in silence. Slowly I began to relax; the tension abating as if I'd taken a pill. I barely noticed my father's arm draped around my shoulders. He pressed my head against his shoulder as if I were a small boy.

"We have to compromise where it concerns life and what we want, son."

"I don't agree with you." I said, yawning, my words slurred by fatigue. All I could think about was hitting the pillows and dreaming about Alice, grabbing a pillow and holding it close, wishing it was Alice beside me as I slept. I wanted to make love to her and not just grope and snuggle half-dressed on the sofa in my study. We would be in my bed or hers, and there'd be no rushing, no fear, and afterwards we'd talk about the future, our future, and we'd laugh and tease one another about little things that made the other smile. One kiss would lead to another and we'd make love all over again, and it would be as exciting and passionate as the first time that night. . .

"You know making sacrifices is important. It's always a give and take compromise if you want to succeed. Are you willing to give up a brilliant career that other musicians dream about for this girl you're infatuated with? Because that's all it is. Take her to bed and get it out of your system. Then you'll discover that it's nothing to lose sleep over. You have work to do."

"I won't compromise where it concerns Alice. I love her. It's as simple as that. She's opened my eyes…"

"Dating, what, four months and you think you're in love?" My father chuckled and clattered the ice in his cup, made it ring like a bell to the point of irritation so that I shook head and took it away.

"I think I should go to bed; man, am I tired." I yawned again, and tried to stand, but my father gently shoved me back down.

"Let's talk about this love, Tarquin. I'm interested to hear what you have to say."

I laughed—no, it was a guffaw and he failed to see what amused me.

"What do you and Mother know about love?" I demanded. "Sure, you know about sex because you use it like a weapon to hurt and control but what about caring for the woman you married?"

"This from your vast experience, eh, Quinn?" he laughed in turn, but it was full of menace.

"I've had the experience of unconditional love, of being accepted for who I am. I've been embraced by a family that isn't like any other, but yet, it's a true family. They're what we should be: loving, protecting, a sanctuary. And you don't know about that. Any of it."

"So wise," my father chuckled, tousling my hair playfully. "So hopeful. Your mother and I do love you…"

That was all I remembered of the conversation, except for the Man in Blue, who again stood in a corner and wept silently. I must have slipped into unconsciousness for when I woke I was sitting at my table in The Shop, leaning back in a chair and my legs propped up on another. Edward IV glanced up from strumming Jimi Hendrix's Stratocaster and smiled, reached over to tousle my hair in a brotherly manner.

"He's back," Edward said. "Well met, friend! You fought a fair battle and came away victorious."

"I did? What'd I miss?" I yawned, stretching. And then sitting upright when I recognized the surroundings added, "Damn! I'm still here!"

"You'll have to do something about that, won't you?" the Proprietress sniffed, crooking her finger at me.

"I'm in no mood for word games," I growled, crossing my arms across my chest in the universal sign of defiance.

"That's as may be, Maestro. If you please?"

"What's in it for me?"

I knew that was the wrong answer; there was another silence punctuated by crickets chirruping. Hildegard came in and glanced around nervously and in the same state began tending the plants and singing.

"If—you—please!"

I shoved myself out of the chair and knocked it over as I moved towards the counter. Once there, I glared down at the Proprietress, who glared black.

"Haven't seen a standoff like this since Richard the Lionheart and his father back in the day," Jimi commented as he gently pried the guitar out of Edward's hands. He strummed Dylan's *The Times They Are a-Changin'* and ended the phrase with a blues lick.

The Proprietress opened the case without taking her eyes from mine and withdrew and set upon the counter the burgundy leather book. Still glaring, she took a key out of her bag and handed it over.

I unlocked the book and didn't try to mask my satisfaction as I read the notations on the first page—a commentary on my birth in York in the winter of 1951:

A promising young man with lungs to match his stamina. Won't sleep, but will eat. Smiles a lot. Becomes tranquil and happy when he hears music. Music will save him.

No, I thought. It will be love. It will be Alice.

I hope.

As I started to leaf through the subsequent pages and find them blank, the Proprietress pulled the book away from me none too gently and towards herself. She took an envelope out of her bag and from that pulled out a sheet of gold stars. A minuscule star, a speck of a star, was pressed onto the first blank page.

"Hey, that's not fair—didn't I just try to explain things to Alice?"

"You'll have to do better than that!" she sniped, tapping the speck of gold.

"Perhaps if you found a means not so physical?" Hildegard said to me in passing.

"Some would say a physical dialogue speaks volumes and is beyond words," said Edward IV.

"Some being most men," the Proprietress countered.

"What's wrong with that?" I wanted to know.

I felt a gentle pressure on my shoulder and turned to my right, looking down at an extraordinarily beautiful young woman with blonde hair and sloe eyes, a small rosebud of a mouth and rosy cheeks. Her mode of dress was a revealing Regency gown in a dark red. The color of my book.

"Your pardon, sir, the King of England sits at my table," she said in a low, quiet voice and pointed in the direction of my corner and table where Edward was now enjoying a cup of coffee and PopTarts. "Since I would never presume to address the king with familiarity, and since he is your acquaintance, perhaps you would speak with him?"

"But that's where Alice and I sit," I corrected, smiling.

"However shall I remedy this predicament?" she sighed. "I was expressly instructed to come here and help but to do that I must have a place to write."

"And I must have a place to compose. You may join me—I insist. Be my guest." I waved her forward and Edward lit up when this young woman flitted by and took the chair next to mine. She retrieved a notebook and pencil from a pocket and with a great sigh started to write, take a moment to ponder, and write again.

Edward leaned in and said, "Why did you never write a story about me, my fairest Jane?"

The woman shot a glance at him. "Pardon, your majesty," she began, nodding deferentially. "Do I have leave to speak?"

"There are no rules of courtly etiquette here, as you know," Edward replied, winking.

"And may I speak boldly and with honesty, sir?"

"I would have it no other way, Jane."

"There are hundreds of novelists who've written romantic tales about you, Your Grace, true or not," she sighed. "As to their quality, they go from horrid to horribly bad. Just like you."

I choked on a laugh and reached for a glass of water from the coffee bar. Jimi played a three-note *wah-wah-wahhh* on the Stratocaster.

"You can be such a snob, Jane Austen," the Proprietress laughed.

"Be that as it may," Hildegard spoke up as she moved to water the pots of freesias and lilies in my corner, "if any woman can tell you about what women in love want, Quinn, Miss Austen is your best resource."

"But I know what a girl wants," I laughed nervously.

Again, that annoying silence.

And the damned crickets.

Jane Austen looked up from her writing, assessing me with critical eyes that were narrowed as the scrutiny continued for a painfully long time. She did not blink and neither would I. Finally, she sucked on the blunt end of the pencil and resumed her work. I made a pretense of reviewing my music transcription but I watched her out of the corner of my eye and waited.

"If you truly know, and if you speak truly, Maestro, you'd know you were wrong; especially about the use of sexual coupling to placate or please a woman—"

A protest of male voices went up in unison at that remark, my own included.

"—and that particular Christmas which finds itself locked in your memory; the one to which you refuse to be reconciled, or even part with…"

Her voice trailing, I went cold. They waited for my response, every pair of eyes fixed on me. I responded by slamming the door on my way out of The Shop.

CHAPTER 9

THERE WAS NO air to breathe outside; it felt like it had been sucked out of my lungs and must have been at least a hundred degrees as I walked up the high street. Wasn't there a day or time when the sun didn't shine here? I'd landed in a perverse little corner of Camelot, where the rain never fell until after sundown, leaves got whisked away by breezes at night, and snow—where the hell was the snow? Wasn't it supposed to be December?

As I trudged along in no particular direction with no particular purpose the street came alive; cars and buses trundled up and down, back and forth. These were vehicles from every era, including horses decked out for tournaments with an occasional knight riding past and saluting me. I noted one peculiarity: every crest and insignia was the *Rosa Alba*—the white rose of York. In fact, I started noticing silver roses and the rose design everywhere I went.

"Roses are the most beautiful flower," Hildegard von Bingen commented when she appeared next to me. She was carrying a basket of white flowers: roses, freesias, lilies, and paper whites. Slipping her arm through mine and smiling up, added, "Let's walk together for a bit."

We walked in silence as Hildegard passed flowers to villagers as we approached them. Their faces lit as if it was Christmas and the smiles were radiant, so much so that even I felt like smiling. I did feel warm and content.

"Am I dead, Hildegard?" I suddenly asked.

"Do you want to be? Ah no, don't worry; I'm not going to ask more questions. Let me say this: I think you were already past it when you arrived."

"How about a man drowning?" I said.

"Very good."

"I'm getting it—at least I think I am. The whole purpose of the Village. Like right now, I've been noticing white roses and silver ones. For me, that's Alice. It's a symbol of Alice. Maybe life."

"If you think I'm going to tell you something maudlin like roses being a metaphor for life and love, with the opening of the bloom, the bloom maturing, the bloom dying, you're sadly mistaken."

"You just did."

We laughed as we came to a corner and waited as traffic moved effortlessly through the intersection despite pedestrians coming out into the street and crossing however they wished, with cars, buses, vans and bicycles going through them—literally. Hildegard shook her head.

"I think they do that on purpose, letting the vehicles proceed. It slows everything down and the newbies are always shocked."

"Newbies?" I asked, chuckling.

"Isn't that what you call them? They just stand there, staring at their hands and feet, their torsos…some people have a great laugh, though it's not amusing at all. Not in the least. They wouldn't dare do that in downtown Manhattan at rush hour, though I suppose that's how a few got here. Ah! Here we are. You'll want to catch the number 7." Hildegard pointed at two York double-decker buses coming at us.

"This was a set up."

"We call it that in every era."

"I don't suppose I should I ask why."

"Just go my dear. Oh. And remember what you said about knowing what a woman wants. You'll find you have lots to think about and you might find yourself in an untenable situation."

"Can't wait."

"I'm not one of those who like to say 'I told you so,' but I know someone who is. See you in a trice?"

I was nudged towards the bus stop. The brightly-painted buses glided effortlessly to the curb despite and doors opened with a hiss. Checking the sign on the first, I mounted the steps and then fumbled in a pocket for exact change. The driver smiled and I did a double take, for he was Denny Martin, Alice's brother.

"Step on back, Quinn!" he said cheerfully and nudged his chin in the direction behind us. I slid onto a seat near the back. We pulled from the curb and set off down the high street and past The Shop, riding into an English countryside peppered with villages and farms, meadowlands that gave way to hills like those in the Lake District and flattened to moors and a coastline.

"Have you a map, sir?"

A bus conductor of all people, and one that looked like the great Sir Thomas Beecham, the musical director and conductor of the Royal Philharmonic Orchestra, was smiling down at me. Once again I fumbled in a pocket.

"Sorry…I wasn't expecting…how much?" I queried.

"Ten pence, sir, for where you're going."

"All I have is…" The English currency in my hand was a surprise and I picked through pounds, tuppence, and pennies, finding a ten pence coin. I exchanged it for a bland-looking ticket and an equally dull brochure.

"No Disneyland ticket book?" I chanced, looking up hopefully. "Alice said,"

"This isn't the train, sir. I hope you're not too disappointed," Beecham apologized.

"Uh, no," I said and held the brochure up, smiling and adding thanks as he moved on.

"Be sure to read the itinerary before your stop, Maestro," he said over his shoulder.

The brochure opened like a map; each unfolding revealed a scene from my life that connected with another scene. Pictures of my house in Scarborough, laid out with frothy descriptions like, 'charming breakfast nook full of sunlight under the spell of medieval castle ruins,' and, 'romantic attic bedroom with skylight and fireplace' held my interest for the longest time, as did the photos of the bay at Scarborough—tranquil, misty, the water the same color of blue as the sky so that it was hard to tell where one began and one ended. The waves in the picture were suddenly gliding back and forth as a tide pulled. It only took moments to travel from the bus on a Yorkshire road to sitting on a beach with Alice. It wasn't Scarborough, but a beach somewhere on the northern Pacific coastline where fantastic rock formations jutted out of the water and gulls swooped and dove around them.

It was December of 1969.

We, or rather, I, had escaped Berkeley and my parents' idea of birthday and holiday cheer by driving up the coast. Alice was a willing accomplice. The day was blustery, cold, and every color of gray imaginable was in the landscape before me—except Alice. She was all pinks, mauves, blues browns, and lightness.

"We'll visit Scarborough someday," I said, draping my arm around her shoulders. "My grandparents used to take me there for holidays and vacations."

"Your parents didn't?"

"Once in a while—when there was time. We used to take the train down to London for concerts, the usual stuff. When my father wasn't performing, or my mother teaching, or I wasn't taking class with some virtuoso that owed my father."

"I love trains."

I love you.

"I liked sitting in the compartment and watching the scenery fly past, thinking, 'I'm this far away now,' and when we pulled into a station I wanted the train to start up again so I could be that far away—but I never was."

"From what?" she asked.

"From them."

I pulled Alice to her feet, though it was no effort, for she was ethereal, a wisp. She wrapped us in her giant shawl of blues, mauves and pinks, of browns with touches of gold that reminded me of sunsets in Yorkshire and we kissed for the longest time, clung to one another. I felt a desperate need to keep holding, to never let go.

"C'mon," I whispered. "We should be getting back. Andersen will want his car."

"You drive; I like snuggling."

So we drove back down to the East Bay, to Berkeley, and Alice did snuggle close to me as we drove in silence. I was happy to just feel her warmth beside me, take in her scent and listen to her snore. Yes, my faery princess snored. Not ugly troll-like belches and gasps, but kittenish sounds.

"Hey love," I whispered in her hair as I kissed her brow. "We're here."

Alice sat up and looked around, then stretched. "Already? Do you want to come in for a little bit, stay for dinner? Your parents won't mind?"

I glanced at my watch and knew they'd be back, but I looked up and smiled, saying, "Sure, as long as Denny won't."

"Of course he won't, silly," Alice laughed, leaning over to kiss me, and I pulled her close for a more passionate exchange.

"Maybe after dinner…?" I hinted.

She just smiled.

The house was warm and smelled like Christmas—of gingerbread, spice, pine and a roast—though Christmas was thirteen days away. As soon as the door closed, Alice shrieked "Denny! Denny, I'm home! Miss me?"

I tried not to laugh, and then a lump rose in my throat, for that was something I'd never dare do at home: slam the front door and shout my arrival. Actually glad to be there and think anyone would notice if I wasn't.

"Denny, I brought someone home for dinner, hope it's okay," she called out as we walked through the dining room that looked more like an office or studio with its homey clutter and state of chaos. I smiled at one of Alice's drawings in a sketchbook: it was me. Alice noticed my preoccupation and closed the book hastily as we passed. "You're not supposed to see that," she giggled.

Dennis met us halfway to the kitchen with a bowl of mashed potatoes in hands, Harry in his shadow. "Oh. I was hoping Sidney Poitier," he sighed.

"Or at least Paul McCartney," Harry added.

"Long time no see, Quinn," Dennis said as he returned to his work in the kitchen. "Wasn't it just this morning? Harry, set another place. You two, find the glasses and uncork the wine. Dinner's in a few minutes."

Alice reached for a cupboard door and Denny tickled her, his unexpected actions making her shriek with laughter. "Dennis, stop! You're embarrassing us!"

"Nothing embarrasses me anymore," I commented in passing as I carried dishes out to the table.

"Well that's another thing we have in common other than our love of your father's singing," Dennis said. Alice threw me a look and I winked to let her know it didn't bother me. "It takes a lot to make me blush nowadays."

"Don't believe him, Quinn," Harry scoffed. "Just last night he drank more than his share of Courvoisier and gave me a rousing chorus of *I Enjoy Being a Girl*, complete with dance number."

"Harry! What happens behind closed doors," Dennis warned. His face went apple red.

"Wish I could have seen it—especially with those chicken legs," Alice snorted and ducked when Dennis tossed a dinner roll.

"Figures," I said. "He throws like a girl."

"Okay, you've had your fun," Dennis sighed in mock

annoyance. He threw a roll in my direction, which I deftly caught and lobbed on to a salad plate. The cheers went up and I took a bow. Another roll was pitched and that landed in the salad.

"What d'you think? Think I could have helped the Orioles this year?" I asked, laughing.

"Don't know," Harry said. "That looked more like the Mets before their miracle."

"More like Jim Palmer in game three," I answered.

"Not only is the boy a virtuoso musician, but he knows his baseball."

"I'm a man of many talents and passions."

"We'd rather not hear about the passion," Harry said and glanced warily at Alice, who shrugged.

"Where'd you kids sneak off to?" Dennis asked after plates and glasses were fully charged and loaded.

"We didn't sneak off anywhere, Dennis," Alice replied, taking a forkful of Italian flat beans off his plate. "We needed an adventure."

"Doctor Radcliffe didn't call it an adventure. She called, by the way, looking for *you*." Dennis pointed his fork at Quinn.

"Dennis," Harry sighed.

"We had a difference of opinion," I said as I helped myself to more of the pork loin roast. "They wanted to invite the Cal music department over to celebrate my birthday. I didn't want another black tie cocktail party. I just wanted to hang out with you guys and Alice."

Dennis lit up in another smile and one that mirrored Alice. "When's your birthday?"

"Today. Today's my birthday."

I wasn't expecting the silence, or the painful glance from Alice. Harry remedied what I sensed was awkwardness by jumping up and saying, "Hang on; I've got just the thing."

"I'm sorry; I never told them," Alice whispered as she took my hands under the table.

What was there to say? How could I tell her that the best present anyone could give me was right there? That sitting at a table as part of a family that had so much love for all within that it made my heart break from envy?

There was a lot of clattering in the kitchen – cupboard doors opening and slamming shut. "What are you doing?" Dennis called.

"Hang on, hang on," Harry answered and moments later he reappeared with a tray of Hostess Cupcakes, a half-dozen of the orange-flavored ones I loved, with an impossible number of candles burning on top of them.

"Hap-py birth-day to you…" Dennis began and Alice and Harry joined in, Alice harmonizing on the last few notes.

"Okay, Prince Charming, make a wish and blow out the candles before they burn the house down," Harry instructed.

I already had my wish but I did as I was told and passed around the cupcakes.

"How'd you guys know about the cupcakes?" I wanted to know but Alice's tearful smile was my answer.

"I mentioned it one day when we were at the grocery store," Alice said as we went upstairs to her room. "There they were on the shelf and I said, 'Quinn loves these.' Harry grabbed almost the entire display and dumped it in the cart."

"Wow," was all I could say.

"I know it was silly,"

"No, no; it was fine. Perfect, actually. We never really celebrate my birthday," I mentioned casually as I threw myself on the window seat in Alice's bedroom.

"What do you mean? I thought the music department…?" Alice asked as she took a brush off the dresser and started running it over and under hair.

"Yes, well, that's for the child prodigy whose parents hope he will land some prestigious gig to validate all their hard work. It's never a birthday for me, for Quinn."

After a few thoughtful strokes, she put the brush down and slid into my arms so that we fell backwards against a menagerie of stuffed koalas and giraffes.

"I think we gave you a party tonight," she whispered, kissing me.

"The best yet."

"Tell me something," Alice whispered sometime after, as we lay on the bed wrapped in a soft, cloud-like bedspread with a winter moon shining on us.

"Anything."

"What is it about Scarborough? You talk about it so much, it's like a special place, a sanctuary."

"When I'm on my own it will be my refuge; where I go to get away."

"No girls allowed?"

"All but one. Would you come with me someday?" I dared to ask.

"I'd love to."

"I know Ellie would love to meet you."

"Would she? I wouldn't have to pass muster like with the Professor?"

"Hardly," I laughed. "Ellie thinks my father is a changeling—wait until you meet her. She'll take off her glasses like Holly Golightly and look you up and down with her eyes narrowed and her lips pursed, like this." Here I did my best to imitate my grandmother, which had Alice in giggles. "Then she'd say, 'Well then! Give us a kiss and a hug. You'll do well enough, Alice Martin!'"

"Will I? Would I? I can't wait," Alice sighed happily. "Wouldn't it be nice to spend Christmas in York?"

"I know we will, but not this year, unfortunately. I'm going to be in New York for auditions."

"On Christmas? Quinn!"

"The day after."

"I wish the Professor could see what he was doing," said Alice as she snuggled closer, putting her head in the crook of my shoulder and arm, using my chest as a pillow like I'd imagined so many times. She was playing with a row of cable on my sweater, riding a finger in the grooves and bobbles up to my chin and lips. I kissed the finger every time it arrived at my mouth and the game continued until I leaned in for a kiss, rolling Alice gently on to her back.

"I wish I could just tell him no more, no more of anything, just once," I said between kisses.

NOT what I had said in December of 1969!

"You will, but not right now. Tell more about Scarborough."

And so I told Alice of the South Bay, of the ancient castle ruins, of the houses clustered under and on the cliffs, the views, the sound of the gulls, the winter sky and the summer sunset between kisses and caresses, as she let me unbutton her sweater and kiss the perfumed skin of her neck and throat, the cleft between her breasts.

I fell asleep in her arms; my dreams were of walking in the castle ruins and the town of Scarborough where discovering the house—my house.

Our house. I walked through each of the rooms paying attention to the details and remembering what it would look like not long after I purchased it, when Alice came to York and changed my life yet again. When I woke, I was staring at the brochure as the Yorkshire bus lumbered to a destination as yet unknown.

Or maybe I knew and just didn't want to know.

"A nice summer home, I think." Rafe was sitting beside me. "All that it lacked was a muse."

"Oh, the muse was there," I commented, smiling, turning over the brochure again, as if searching for something in particular.

"A muse?" the Proprietress sniped as she turned to face me from the forward seat. "A little bon-bon, a little piece of cake, perhaps." Her cat-eye/harlequin sunglasses made her look like an alien from Roswell.

"Is she talking about what I think she's talking about?"

I murmured to Rafe.

"Scarborough!" Denny shouted from the driver's seat and with a hiss, the doors opened.

"See you in a trice." Rafe patted my shoulder as I squeezed past him to the aisle and then walked off the bus.

The descent seemed to take forever, with the stairwell leading not out of a double-decker bus but the Flying Scotsman, the train we'd caught from London. Our bags slung over my shoulder, she followed me off the train and stood there, bewildered in the bright rays of the sunset. An advertisement for the latest James Bond movie, *The Spy Who Loved Me*, screamed from the fence near the car park and the headlines on the *Times* were of the a serial killer in Yorkshire and a tremendous, paralyzing blackout in New York City.

It was July of 1977.

"This isn't Edinburgh," Briony Atwell sighed, glancing about. "Quinn? Quinn, are you alright? *Hellow!*"

"Hunh?" I glared at her, disappointed.

No, this wasn't the weekend I'd hoped to re-live...

CHAPTER 10

"WE'RE IN SCARBOROUGH," I said brightly, hailing a taxi that had cruised up to the stand. Briony took a pose, the stance that meant an argument and no sex. After dating a year, you'd think I'd learn the cues, or just learn, but Briony Atwell was still a mystery. My record with women wasn't anything to brag about. The few encounters I'd enjoyed at clubs, those oh-so-brief encounters with women who were earthy, unassuming, and didn't expect much gave me a false reading of my sexual prowess. Briony managed to keep me humble about that. She was the daughter of a peer of the realm—a minor peerage— and her father's patronage kept the orchestra afloat.

At least that's what Briony kept telling me and why we were still dating.

Not really—I was sure I was in love with her and was willing to wait until she was ready. I wanted to settle. Not just settle down, just settle. Maybe she was of like mind since she was always around and never turned down my invitations.

At least, I hoped...

"When you said we were going to a concert, I thought you meant the music festival in Edinburgh," Briony said, taking her handbag from me and sliding into the back seat of the taxi. "Let me guess: the orchestra is touring and this is one of the venues?"

"I told you; at least I'm sure I did," I said, dropping down beside her in an exhausted heap. As the taxi moved into traffic, I leaned over the front seat and said "Grand Hotel, please."

"The Rolling Stones will be at Edinburgh," she moaned. "I don't suppose you could ask them to come here for a show?"

"If you're nice," I whispered seductively into her neck, and she squealed as I nuzzled her with my five-o'clock shadow and then nibbled until there was a hickey just under her ear, my hand sliding along her thigh under the skirt. She giggled and pushed the hand away.

"I am nice and you know it."

"Maybe I could do something about that tonight."

She held me off and looked at me with steely gray eyes that could freeze an iceberg twice over. "Are we ever going to have a real vacation, Quinn?" she asked. "A real vacation where you and I spend time alone, go to suppers at those exclusive restaurants you're always being invited to? Or to a club you're always making an appearance at with rock musicians? Can we sit in the audience together at the cinema and not get hounded by the press? A proper date shouldn't be you on a pedestal, whilst I gaze adoringly from a box orchestra center as you wave that baton and take curtain calls."

"I suppose you'd rather be on the pedestal?" I murmured to myself, but she heard it and glared. "We're closing the Summer Festival here, Bree," I said, taking her hand in mine. "That's like being the closing act at the Fillmore or Winterland. The Board made it clear if we're successful this week, pick up respectable reviews, they'll approve the American tour I've been asking about and give me a raise. I'd love it if you came with us—don't tell me you don't want a weekend in New York or Los Angeles. You've got to see San Francisco. I can show you all my adolescent haunts, especially the notorious ones."

"You might have said something earlier," Briony grumbled, pulling away. "I turned down a trip to Paris with my mother and sisters."

"Okay—there's another reason. I found a house. When I was here last month about the festival arrangements and festival master classes, I found a place. It looks out over South Bay and from the main bedroom balcony you can see the castle," I gushed, my enthusiasm growing about this find I thought was so spectacular.

Why didn't it surprise me when Briony turned slowly and said, "*I* live in a castle."

"Yes, well, and so did I. In California. It was a big, eccentric mansion in the hills above Berkeley…" my voice trailed off as her gaze became stonier. "The house here will be my vacation home and a place to work. Somewhere to get away from city distractions," I ended.

"Master classes? We're not going to see each other the entire week, I suppose."

At moment it didn't sound like a bad thing.

The ride to our hotel on St. Nicholas Cliff was silent after this, as were the next two hours. Briony sulked in a bubble-infused tub and I settled in go over the week's work, to read the scores for tomorrow night's first concert of the festival and review the master class notes.

There were advantages to being the youngest conductor in the classical music world and of an internationally-renowned orchestra. I was considered as famous and press-worthy as a rock star to the British tabloids because I was seen with beautiful women like Briony and kept company with rock stars and royalty. Yet here I was on a Friday night going over scores and class plans. The image the public and most notably, the press, had of me was of a bad boy musician from California by way of York, screwing anything that moved at drug-and-alcohol-driven parties held at exclusive discotheques and night clubs, on wealthy debutantes' yachts off the coast of Monaco, or the penthouse at the Savoy. I apparently had slept my way through Debrett's Peerage and the orchestra's success was due to my keeping rich, landed, women happy. Sometimes I wished it was true but most of the time I relished the idea that my father was hearing the rumors and believing them, that I was ruining his well-laid plans. I had the advantage because I knew the truth.

"Darling, I'm calling it a night," Briony called from the bedroom.

"Not surprised in the least," I sighed to myself.

"You don't mind? I thought you said something about a reception for the orchestra at Tapping's."

"Just a bunch of tweedy, boring, classical musicians — the Stones and The Who won't be there."

"What's that?"

"Nothing."

"Are you going to take the other suite?"

"If I promise to behave can I sleep in there?"

"Silly boy! Good night, darling — see you in the morning."

"'Night…"

There were certain bridges I'd not been able to cross with Briony. There had been plenty of suggestions about taking our relationship, such as it was, to another plateau—teasing was a better word for it—but the lovely Lady Briony of Kensington and Oxford made it clear that her parents wanted an honorable match and no damaged goods.

What was this, the twelfth century?

I had learned to perfect the cold shower.

Flipping off the cap to a bottle of Guinness with a church key, I settled in for a long night.

I skimmed the notes and measures with my fingers as if reading Braille or playing a piano, hearing the music in my mind, going over every note with meticulous care. Soon the quarrel with Briony was in another universe, the anxiety-and-career-driven fatigue I'd suffered in the last months dissipating like fog when the sun burns through clouds. All I heard were the cadences of the *Allegretto* from the Seventh Symphony as I watched a sunrise of rays of pink and gold light coursing through my sitting room window on a July morning in 1978.

It was a different weekend in Scarborough.

"That's not the Tallis *Fantasia*," I heard her teasing murmur in my ear.

I shifted to my left on the sofa and smiled down at Alice, curled up beside me. She was in decidedly fetching disarray with hair tumbling out of the knot she'd pulled it into when we shared a bath sometime after midnight. Dressed in my bathrobe and a pair of thick, wooly socks that'd she made, still scented with bath products and perfume, Alice was delectable.

"It's Beethoven," I said, leaning over for a kiss.

"Doesn't matter; I like to hear your voice; singing, or humming. Especially when you're happy and working as you are now," she said, offering the steaming mug of coffee she'd brought to the sitting room.

"And you made coffee again," I said, daring to take a sip.

"It's fresh, and so are you," Alice squealed, feigning offense, swatting my shoulder playfully. She yawned then and looked out over the view of South Bay. "We've been up all night—but I loved it. It's been so long…"

"Remember my Senior Prom?"

"We sat up in the tower in your house and watched the sun come up."

"And then caught hell from my parents who thought we were having sex all night long," I laughed, remembering.

"Not far from the truth," she said, winking.

"And then there was that time right before I left for England."

"That. Not as romantic as this. We were in the waiting room at Alta Bates while Denny was being checked out." Alice paused, resting her chin in her palm while studying her socks, the toes wriggling back and forth. "Poor Denny. He's sick again."

"Does he know you're here with me?"

Alice shook her head. "What could I say?"

I took another sip of her awful coffee. "Starting with the truth is usually a good idea."

"We've been over this, Quinn. You've got your reasons for what you're doing, and I've got my reasons."

"Deception, denial, fear? Roshambo to see who gets what."

"I thought we weren't going to do this."

Alice flung herself off the sofa and scuffing into a pair of clogs, stomped upstairs. I didn't bother calling after her, but I did sit there quietly and drink the rest of the coffee, and when I put down the cup I was back in The Shop and everyone was glaring at me. No surprise. When didn't they? The Proprietress at her station behind the counter crooked a finger at me and for once I didn't balk but obeyed.

"Well, it's obvious whose charm doesn't win over the fairer sex," Edward IV said as I walked by. "Pray, what is roschambo?"

"Rock scissors paper. A game," the Proprietress sniffed. "Which-is-what-you're-playing-at-young-man." She jabbed a finger into my shoulder with every word.

The burgundy journal came out of the case and sat before me on the velvet cushion. A sheet of gold stars came out of the handbag and this time, the Proprietress placed a star half the size of the journal on the page.

"I must be doing something right." I pointed at the difference between the last star and this new one.

"That depends on your definition of 'right.'" She then took a wooden box from the shelf, which was placed reverently beside the journal. The Proprietress waved a hand at it, raising her eyes to mine.

"Ah, the boxes."

"Just so."

"Alice told me about these. They hold dreams, don't they?"

"For some. For Alice it was heartache. And for you,

dear little prince—well, we'll just have to see."

Without further prompting, I opened the lid carefully—who knew if a springy snake or a hideous jack-in-the-box would leap out at me—and stared at a shiny black pebble and the silver rose I'd given to Alice. The pebble held my interest for a second; it reminded me of a coffee bean.

"I shouldn't have been so unkind about her coffee," I said. "It wasn't half-bad. Not good, but tolerable. All she ever does is try to please and she does, she really does."

"How charitable of you," the Proprietress said. She started tapping her fingers on the velvet interior of the box and let one of those impeccably-manicured figures point at the rose.

"This was the very first important thing."

The Proprietress crooked her head to the right.

"I gave her the record albums, but this rose was special. I wanted to link her to the best of me and be a part of that, to be a family with Ellie and me."

I took the rose and held it in my hands, watching the light spark off of it and paying attention to the craftsmanship that went into its creation. The petals were textured as if in various stages of growth – some smooth, others lined and showing age, each crafted individually and soldered at a central point that was decorated with stamens. Each stamen in the center of the rose glowed with a different color as a ray of sun touched it, their hues reminding me of winters in York, the soft diffused light coming in through the lace curtains in Ellie's living room, how the sunrise looked when you stood on the walls near Bootham Bar—orange, pink and gold sometimes, sometimes silvery gray.

The rose was placed reverently in the box and closed the lid to a small jeweler's case that I now held. I was standing at the counter in Ellie's shop and my grandmother's cat, Becket, batted and sniffed at the ancient, rubbed velvet-covered wood and padded away when he realized it wasn't something he could devour in one bite. Ellie chuckled as she finished an Easter display at the window in her shop and unlocked the door for the day's first customers.

"He's an old kitten, that's what my Becks is—good morning, Missus Fairchild, how are you? Miss Hathaway! How's your mother's back doing; better I hope?"

"Where'd you find this?" I asked Ellie when she came round the counter and started to tidy up the candy jars. Ellie glanced at the box and nodded, opened it up.

"*That*. I found it in a basket of old trinkets at Chamberlain's Antique Shop down The Shambles. He didn't want it; didn't think it was worth anything. I thought it was pretty enough—you certainly do."

"How much do you want for it?" I asked, mesmerized by the simplicity and beauty of the petals and stamens worked in silver, the patina of age that made it even more precious in my sight.

"Take it, sweetheart. Give it to your Alice. If you want the truth, I thought of her immediately when I saw it. Belated Christmas gift from Quinn's Gram."

I chuckled and slipped the rose into my jeans pocket. "It's almost Easter, Ellie."

"Yes, I noticed. And shouldn't you be going home soon? You've been here, what, a month? Like I said when you did this in the winter of sixty-eight, I know you don't care what your parents think, but you can't make this a habit every time you have a quarrel with your father. Running away from problems never offers a solution, does it? And what about Alice?"

"Alice and I have been writing, and I've been calling her."

"Calling her? Lord in heaven--oh, Quinn…that's not something I can afford."

"Relax; I go down to The Bitter End and use the pay-phone. Won't cost you a dime or a farthing."

She calmed down and frowning, patted my cheek

none-too-gently. "Still, darling boy, you have to face the facts. You're avoiding something serious that for the life of me you won't share. If you won't ask for my help then you need to steel your resolve and do something."

Her parental moment dissolved as soon as it appeared as we started waiting on customers, taking our turns at the register, each of us greeting and smiling, exchanging trinkets for legal tender. Ellie was especially amused when the girls from Saint Barbara's School came by at the lunch hour and giggled and simpered their way through queries and purchases. One of them brazenly slipped me her phone number with a five pound note. She was pretty and reminded me of Alice with her light brown hair and big eyes. I watched her leave, especially the flip of her pleated school uniform skirt as it brushed back and forth against her thighs and bottom as she walked out with her friends. She looked back and waved; I ducked my head and felt my cheeks burn. Ellie nudged me.

"People don't get burned at the stake for adultery or cast into a circle of Hell for looking," Ellie teased. "She's pretty, that one."

"She looks like Alice."

"I remember looking for Richard in every man I met at university."

"This is torture."

"Then go back to California."

"Look, Ellie, I know you don't want me here," I said and she cut me off.

"I never said that. You do need to mend fences and face reality. I can think of ten more similes if it will help you to understand."

Later that day we continued the conversation while locking up the shop.

"I've never said I don't understand. I'm not ready tell Alice some things. I couldn't bear it if she walked away once she knew about me -- all of me." I admitted, counting notes and coins in the cash register. "There will come a time – I'm promising you, Ellie. I'll tell Alice everything."

"What exactly is everything?" she wanted to know. It was asked in her serious voice – the one I dreaded most: controlled, low, sounding almost like my father.

"Dad and I – we've come to blows a few times. Over the usual stuff – the auditions, practice, master class, spending too much time with Alice."

"I see." Ellie paused while she arranged the counter display of bunnies and eggs. "Has he hurt you? Did you hurt him?"

Now was the chance to open my soul and share something of my pain. Ellie turned my face to hers and our eyes met. *Now is the time*, I heard my mentors whisper. *Now is the time.*

"No," I lied. "It's nothing I can't handle."

"I'm curious as to what you'll tell Alice about the last few weeks."

I shrugged sheepishly and grinned. "She'll forgive me if she thinks I've done something that needs an apology."

"Yes," Ellie sighed, "I think that rose and some pretty spectacular groveling might set things right with Alice. But I wouldn't count on it."

"There's nothing gone wrong," I laughed, following her upstairs.

"How do you know your parents aren't calling her, asking if she'd heard from you? And what excuse did you give her for your absence?" Ellie went on. "I know if I were Alice, I'd want some answers, and more particularly the truth."

"I'm giving her as much of the truth as I can and want – for now. I don't want to lose her, Ellie. Can't you see?"

Ellie turned so sharply on the narrow staircase that I almost lost my grip on Becket and the stupid cat squealed when I grabbed him tighter. I got a scratch on my hand for my attempt to save him.

"I don't, Quinn." She glanced at my hand. "I'll get some antiseptic cream."

It was Thursday night and *Top of the Pops* was on. I stared at the acts, not paying particular attention to any of them, not even to Petula Clark, while Ellie hummed and sang along as she made that week's batch of potpourri and stitched the hems in silk squares for sale in the shop. One of the squares, a mix of pale colors in a paisley pattern with little flowers, reminded me of one of Alice's dresses, and excusing myself, I grabbed my jacket and headed for the door. Ellie was singing along with Petula Clark's *Don't Sleep in the Subway* as I went out.

I loved the city of York, and I loved it even more in the evening, when the lamps of The Shambles glowed and the medieval and Tudor buildings that made it looked like something out of one of Alice's faery tales. I half expected knights in shining armor and damsels to come out of the shops and secret away to a lover's rendezvous. Instead, I was met up by shopkeepers and neighbors who nodded politely and asked how I was getting on, how my parents were, was I staying in York now.

The proprietor of the public house winked when I came in and slid a bottle of Coca Cola at me, nodded at the telephone booth at the back of the room. Coins were exchanged and I took the cola into the booth, pulling a long drink and checking my watch before dialing the number. She'd be home; it was Saturday morning in Berkeley and she'd be curled up on the day bed in her sanctuary with the puppy, sketch books and balls of yarn surrounding her, one minute drawing a costume, the next minute knitting—or maybe homework.

"Hi, it's me."

"Quinn! I was just thinking about you!" Alice laughed softly.

"So was I—thinking about you. I always think about you, Faery Princess."

"Are you okay? You sound...different."

No. I wouldn't tell her. Not everything that I knew, that I wanted to forget; it wasn't time yet.

"Tired. Homesick. These auditions can sap the life out of a guy. Listen. I'll be home probably the day after tomorrow, maybe the next day after. Do you think Denny could pick me up at the airport? Would you be with him?"

"Sure. Wait, what about your parents? Aren't they…"

"Out of town again. I want to surprise them."

Lying to Alice was not good.

"Okay, sure. Yeah, I don't think Denny will mind. He's been asking about you. What time?"

"I'll call you in an hour, no, two. I have to figure out the flights."

"I've missed you, Quinn. Can't wait to see you again," she said softly in the voice that melted my insides.

"I'm sorry, Alice. I didn't think I'd be away this long— I promise to make it up to you." The pause at the California end of the line made me wish I hadn't called. "Alice?"

"Is there something I should know about that would make you promise amends?" The voice was still soft, incredibly sensual, but there was an edge to it. One that warned.

"Well, today there was a girl in the shop, and you won't believe this, but she gave me her phone number."

"A girl? You're seeing someone there?"

Her voice was sharp, but the quietness was unnerving.

"No, no! It's just that she reminded me of you, she looked and acted like you, and for a moment I wanted to talk to her, and I knew I wouldn't. I couldn't."

"Well, if it's just to talk," she said, but the edge was still there.

"I wouldn't. In that moment I knew I loved you more than anything. Why would I ruin or lose something so important to me?"

"But there's something you're not telling me, Quinn. I can sense there's something wrong."

"Nothing to do with you—with us. It's my father."

The sigh could be felt in York. "Oh. *Him*. Well, would

it help to know that I've avoided his calls? I even ditched a basket of groceries at the Co-Op to avoid your parents. Denny says I'm a rude little bitch."

"Yeah, I wanted to talk to you about that. Could you take care of some guys in my P.E. class?" I teased.

"Quinn…" she groaned and then laughed.

"I have to go. Call you later. Love you!"

I hung up and grabbed the bottle of Coca Cola, holding it aloft in thanks as I sauntered out of the pub and back to my grandmother's shop.

She was still in front of the television, working on another batch of potpourri. I threw myself into the recliner and drank the rest of my soda and more importantly, avoided her smiles of inquiry and regard. When I couldn't stand it any longer I thumped the empty bottle on the table, sat back and glared at her.

"Now that would make an interesting bud vase," Ellie chirruped.

"I know you want to know."

"I know."

"No you don't."

"I do. And you know I do."

She continued to hum and tie up little bundles of herbs and spices, smiling at me all the while.

"Fine. Take me down to Woolsington, then?"

"You know it's a good decision," Ellie said as she slid Becket off her lap and tumbled him on to the sofa before pushing herself out of the rocking chair.

"I know."

Our goodbyes were said the following Thursday at Woolsington Aerodrome, the airport in Newcastle, where she pressed a package into my hands. "Something special for Alice. The rose—and something else. If what I know about her is right, it will be right. And they're from you. Take my meaning?"

We waved until the plane rolled down the tarmac and lifted off, until I was airborne and England became a greenish-gray speck on the globe. Settling in for the long flight was no problem, for my anxiety about returning home brought a physical and mental exhaustion that allowed me to sleep. The banker from Newcastle sitting on my right woke me as we landed at LaGuardia in New York and the realization that I was going home to Alice, the rush of excitement when I boarded the plane for California, replaced all other concerns.

And I was oh so glad to be home when Alice rushed into my arms as I came out of the tunnel from customs. For the first time since my childhood, I didn't mind the public display of affection or that we blocked foot traffic as we kissed and Harry and Dennis offered cat-calls and whistles.

I was home.

"Where to?" Harry asked, looking over his shoulder at us while we piled into his VW van.

"Home!" Alice giggled.

"Well, maybe Quinn wants to see his mom and dad," Dennis said and looking at my face, added, "Or maybe not."

"They're probably not home anyway," I spoke up.

"Do they know you're home?"

"Dennis…" Alice used the warning voice and I decided to help him out by lying.

I expelled a sigh and shrugged, saying, "I seriously doubt it, since they didn't know I left England."

"C'mon, Denny," Alice pleaded. "You can talk opera with Quinn and you've got a willing victim to try out your new shirts and ties — Quinn'll be a sensational model. Harry can whip up something to eat, right, Harry?"

"Or we could live on the edge and have Alice cook something," I teased. As expected she playfully socked my shoulder and I kissed the fist, then pulled her close.

"Someday I'll make you eat those words," she said.

"Which will probably be more tasty and nutritious than the beef stroganoff she served up last night," Harry chimed in.

We laughed while Alice squealed in protest and then joined in. After this I said, "I've missed all of you so much."

"I hate it when you go away," Alice sighed. "Promise you'll always be here and be a part of us."

"I will be, Faery Princess. I am. Always and forever."

"Still lying to Alice?" Janis Joplin whispered.

I turned at the sound of her voice and took the coffee mug of Southern Comfort out of her hands and set it on my table in the Shop. Jimi Hendrix and Jane Austen threw warning glances at me.

"Not your concern, Temperance Tarquin," Janis snapped, taking it back and taking a pull.

"I saw what it did to my father. Look what it did to you."

"Bad choice of words," Richard III mumbled.

"And I know what it'll do to you." Janis lobbed that over the table and then sat back with hands folded behind her head. "Now pay attention to what I'm about to say, Pretty Boy. Your concern is honesty and I don't want to stay here any longer than I have to. Get a move on."

"I could not have said it better," the Proprietress chirped. "On your way, Quinn."

The thump of her rubber stamp in one of the books became the slam of the Volkswagen bus door and I was back in Berkeley in the spring of 1970.

"I'd sleep better tonight if you at least call your parents after dinner," Dennis said as we all piled out and grabbed at my bags and belongings.

"You can be such an old man, Dennis Martin," hissed Alice as she walked past him to the front porch.

"Too bad, Faery Princess," Dennis sniped. "And don't go sneaking off upstairs or down to the Sanctuary. Even if you can't boil an egg you can help with dinner."

"Yes, sir…"

Yet after my luggage and cello were set in the front

hall, Alice disappeared upstairs and gestured with looks that I should follow but Dennis intercepted my play and I was left with the men in the kitchen.

Harry handed me a paring knife and a bowl of potatoes, saying, "Who cooks in your house?"

"We have a cook, but she prepares the food and puts it in the freezer, disappears until morning and then starts the process all over again. She says good morning or good afternoon occasionally," I said, pulling up a chair to the counter.

"I'm jealous. I can only imagine what the menu is like at the Radcliffe house," Dennis said.

"Thank you very much," Harry chuckled.

"It's not all Waterford crystal and silver place settings. When anybody is home it's catch-as-catch-can, I guess. There isn't much to do if all I want is a bowl of Cheerios and a banana."

I shrugged when Harry and Dennis exchanged glances and I started making little cubes out of the potatoes as if I'd been doing it all my life.

"Not your mother?" Harry asked. "She doesn't cook?"

"This isn't going to be twenty questions, is it?"

"No, just trying to crack the mystery that is Quinn," Dennis said, winking.

"Our girl just giggles and blushes when we ask," Harry piped in. "I know you're a promising concert cellist and come from money."

"Nothing like stating the obvious," Dennis sighed. "Forgive his bad manners, Quinn; Harry's misspent youth was and still is wasted on Cape Cod and Long Island."

"And in the company of second-rate designers."

"You can't stand to be out my sight for a minute and you know it." Dennis turned to me now. "Did you always have it in mind to be a musician?"

"No. Hockey player—or a pitcher. Or if we stayed in England, batman at cricket," I admitted nonchalantly as I continued slicing and dicing the potatoes.

"What made you change your mind?" Harry asked.

"It was made for me, and my favorite color is red. Are we done with the questions now? How many of these do you want?" I shoved the half-full bowl of potatoes towards Harry who pointed at the celery and broccoli next, the kidney beans and steak. "Shepherd's pie," I said, nodding. "Anything to keep me down here, I suppose."

"Quick study," Harry said to Dennis, and then to me: "Seductions are best done where we, and I mean, Denny, doesn't have to hear his sister in the throes of passion."

"What makes you think I'm the one doing the seducing?" I asked as I slit a celery stalk down the middle and took a bite.

"About that," Dennis said. "How much are you willing to tell us?"

"A guy doesn't kiss and tell, especially if he respects the woman he loves."

"So…"

"So you have nothing to worry about."

"Good," Dennis sighed. "Good, because you're like a brother to me, to us," here Dennis made a circle with a hand around Harry and himself, "and friends and brothers are hard to come by."

"Thanks," I whispered.

"Now, call your lady love for dinner and let's hope she can spare a moment from her bubble bath to grace us with her presence," Dennis said. As I nodded and walked away to do as requested, he called, "You'll do, Prince Charming!"

I counted that as affirmation but the real affirmation came with what happened later that night.

CHAPTER 11

"HEY, ALICE! DINNER!"

I stood at the bottom of the stairs and shouted again, smiled when I heard the slam of a door and caught a whiff of perfume, and maybe bath products, as Alice showed up on the landing.

She skipped down into my arms for a kiss. "Mmmm, smells good—Shepherd's Pie?"

"*You* smell good," I said as we walked hand in hand to the kitchen.

Dennis glanced up as we came in. "I'm surprised you don't melt from all the baths you take," he said to Alice and pointed with a wooden spoon at the table. "Sit. Harry, your turn."

Once we were seated, Harry crossed himself and said, "We thank you Lord, for the food thou hast given us, for the preparation of our meal and the fellowship given at this table."

"Amen," Alice, Harry and Dennis intoned, and then started serving up portions.

"Wow," I whispered.

"I know," Alice said, smiling. "It surprises even us sometimes. Mom had a great influence on us."

"Well, I'd like to think it was Jesus, but Mom can take the credit," Dennis added.

There we were, crowded around a kitchen table that nearly took up the entire room with the food set out on the counters surrounding us. If something was needed, one of us reached behind to take a dish or spoon or bottle. When Dennis nearly spilled a gravy boat in Harry's lap Alice started to giggle.

"You know, if we cleaned up the dining room and used it we wouldn't have these problems," she said.

"I need work space and room to spread out," Dennis replied.

"Use my sanctuary. I don't mind."

"No. I made a promise that you'd have a place of your own, with privacy and it's going to stay like that. Besides, that place is like a drag queen's nightmare."

"Okay, then take my bedroom. I've grown out of the little girl ruffles but you haven't," she teased her brother, which caused him to launch a dinner roll in her direction.

"Hah, ha," Dennis replied. "Can I borrow that shirt?"

It looked like he was pointing at my Izod polo shirt. "This?" I asked.

"No, I'm talking about the low neck, high-waisted number Alice's got on."

"Sure; I took it out of your closet," Alice fired back and gave Dennis a kiss.

"Not the typical dinner conversation at the Radcliffe house, I guess," Harry ventured. "And I guess you don't have to worry about space in the dining room."

"Harry, if you want to ask me what it's like living in a mansion, just ask," I laughed.

"You should see the dining room at Quinn's," Alice spoke up. "Carved, beamed, ceiling, heraldic banners,"

"Not real family devices," I interjected. "My father had them designed after families in his favorite operas."

"But your mother's got a crest, right? From the medieval Salimbieni family, from Siena," Alice said.

"Yeah, that's where the money comes from," I shrugged. "Pass the pie, Denny?"

"That house is something else," Alice went on. "Anyway, the dining room has a table you could skate across. And his study has a fireplace and window seats, there are book shelves in a loft over the window seats and his bedroom—"

"Bedroom?" Harry and Dennis asked in unison and glanced at me.

"It's a room in a house where a person sleeps," I said.

"Don't change the subject," Dennis said.

"I'm not. You should see the place. *Better Homes and Gardens, Architectural Digest* and a couple of other art magazines have done stories on it. They came in and took a lot of pictures, some of them of my bedroom, which is in the tower. The house has a tower, like a castle. That's my sanctuary—my fortress of solitude."

Dennis glared at me for a second and then took the basket of bread I passed his way.

"The Cloisters, right? The big place at the top of Buena Vista, on the ridge?" Harry asked, piling more Shepherd's Pie on to my plate.

"Yep."

"I've always wanted to see that house. It's pretty famous, you know," Dennis added.

"Maybe when my parents are away I could have you over for dinner."

"It's a date," Harry said. "Just let us know when and what time."

"Pretty much whenever; they're gone a lot these days."

"You're okay with that?" asked Dennis.

"I've got my fortress of solitude, my music. I'm okay."

Alice smiled. I also had my faery princess.

By the end of the meal, when the ice cream had been licked off the spoons and cups of coffee circulated, I ceased to be the poor little rich boy in Harry and Dennis' minds and by Alice's estimation was accepted into their close circle due to the amount of good-natured ribbing I received from Harry and Dennis' sharing of family secrets that made her blush and feign embarrassment. I was also the evening's after supper theatre. I didn't play the cello or sing; instead I modeled Dennis' latest creations to the delight of my girlfriend and her family. I took expert turns and glowered on cue when I burst through the curtain that separated the living room from the dining-room-turned-studio. I received the accolades and applause with nonchalance. Finally, Harry and Dennis decided they wanted to go out for a drink and left us alone. On the flight over I had fantasized about my time alone with Alice and was glad that Dennis and Harry slipped out—but not before giving me the evil eye—yet I wasn't disappointed in the least when we started clearing up after dinner and doing the dishes instead of each other, and it was just as well, for that would have upset the balance. That moment in our relationship hadn't happened—it was weeks away. I was sure I'd finally done something right.

"Imagine their faces when they come back three sheets to the wind and find the place clean," Alice giggled as she soaped up the plates and scrubbed each rose and petal on each with delicacy, rinsed them with the same care and passed them one at a time to me to dry with a towel.

"You don't do housework?" I laughed.

"I received a dispensation from housework due to homework, extra-curricular activities, and part-time jobs."

"Am I homework or an extra-curricular activity?"

"Dessert," Alice purred, tiptoeing up for a kiss.

"Mmmm, as much as I would love to be a chocolate soufflé, I think your brother and Harry would have other ideas on what to do with the Quinn and it might have something to do with a meat grinder."

"Funny you should mention meat; put this in the fridge, would you?"

Alice held up a rope of homemade sausage links.

I don't remember laughing so much or having so much fun doing simple things like housework. When the dishes were done and put away, we brewed a fresh pot of coffee and took our mugs and plates of Alice's sad-looking homemade cookies to the living room where we turned on the radio to KFRC and shared a very long and passionate kiss while The Doors' *Light My Fire*, the long version, played in the background.

"How did the auditions go?" Alice asked when we at last came up for air.

"What? Hmm?" I asked, reaching for her again.

"The auditions in London and Cambridge? The trip to Oxford?"

"More of the same – you wear a tux, you wait, you go on stage, you play and you get thanked," I said, still trying to claim those lips again.

"You didn't have auditions in England," she commented. Alice moved away and carefully selected cookies for her plate. Then she glanced at me, brows raised.

"I went to see my grandmother," I confessed. "You knew all along?"

"Unh uh." Alice shook her head. She bit the head off a gingerbread man. "No; I guessed and I guessed right, I guess. From what I know of you, and what you've told me, I knew you'd never go to an audition without your shadow. So tell me; what did the Professor do to make you run away?"

I hedged and avoided her gaze and the question with a tried and true maneuver. I took a sip of coffee and savored it a bit too long, helped myself to the cookies. "It wasn't what he did," I lied. "It was more what he doesn't do. Listen. Offer encouragement, a few words of praise every now and then. I thought it was time for a little rebellion."

"It must have worked, because he called, or your mother called, every day for a month. Well, practically a month. I didn't say a thing. It wasn't my place."

"Thank you; I should have told you the truth."

A reflection of light in the mirror over the fireplace and the appearance of Richard III and the Proprietress holding up placards with the words "WELL DONE!"

affirmed that I had done something right.

"I'm not angry, Quinn," Alice said. "I wasn't then—but I was worried about you. I wondered how many more times would you run away until the time came when you didn't return?"

Run away from her, she meant to say, I was sure of it.

Then the doorbell rang followed the opening of the screen and by heavy raps on the solid door.

"Now who could that be? Maybe Denny left his wallet in the kitchen. He'd forget his head if it wasn't attached," Alice sighed, moving off the sofa.

I knew. I'd been dreading this moment; if only I could propel myself back to the Village...

The knocking became more frantic.

A worried expression was tossed in my direction as she stepped around the coffee table and my legs. I held my breath and waited, my hands shaking as I grabbed for the coffee.

"Sammie! Oh, Missus Alves, did he get into your yard again? I'm so sorry!"

It was wrong of me to feel relief while the neighbor berated Alice and her dog, but I couldn't help it.

I knew what was coming.

The front door slammed and Alice reappeared clutching a grateful Pomeranian in her arms. After scolding the dog in a baby voice, she released him in the kitchen and shut the door making her way back to the living room when the doorbell rang again.

"It's always just one more thing with Missus Alves; usually a scolding," Alice said as she circled back to the door. The doorbell rang once more, twice. "What did I do—"

It was quiet and when Alice didn't come back in, I got up to make sure she was all right.

My parents were standing on the porch. Alice turned at the sound of my footfall, that bemused expression on her face dissolving to fear—or maybe guilt. I didn't want to think the latter.

"It's been a while, Quinn." There was no emotion in my father's voice. He must have been sober. Wait, it was past seven on a Friday night. Impossible.

My mother, the consummate politician, stepped forward in the next wave of awkward silence and brushed my cheek with her lips. "Darling! Welcome home. We've missed you. And look at you! I think the sabbatical did you some good – or maybe it's seeing your lovely Alice again!" she gushed in a nervous staccato.

"Let's not stand here letting moths through; please, come in," Alice chirped, waving us into the living room, which was a five step walk in normal circumstances but that evening seemed like a death march. "Make yourselves comfortable while I get more coffee and snacks." And while she went back to the kitchen, I threw myself back on to my spot on the sofa and my parents glanced around at the shabby, comfortable, well-loved furnishings. They were still rudely staring at the copies of *Vogue* and *National Geographic*, Alice's art supplies and the knitted and crocheted throws covering threadbare spots on the chairs and sofa when Alice returned with an over-flowing, over-ambitious tray of food and drink. They stared as if it were sprinkled with arsenic.

"How long have you been here?" my father demanded.

He was never one to beat around bushes.

"Just this afternoon," I replied.

"Eventually you would have made your way home, though?"

"Eventually."

"You've lost weight," Mother sighed, touching my face. "We'll have to send your tuxedo for alterations."

"No I haven't and no we don't."

"Judas Priest!"

We turned to Alice, whose outburst took us by surprise. She folded her arms across her chest defensively.

"He's been gone out of your lives for weeks and you worry about a suit and how long he's been here? I know Denny would suffocate me with a hug if I'd been away that long," she said quietly but with anger that I'd learned to dread. Then she did the unthinkable. She turned on my father. "And if I were in your shoes," Alice sniped at him, "I'd be wondering what I did that chased him away."

"But you're not, are you?" my father asked.

The sneer in his voice would have warned anyone else to back down. "You're on my turf, Professor," she answered quietly.

"It's always nice to see you, Alice; I never know what's going to come out of that mouth of yours. Proust or *National Enquirer*," he responded in an oily, obsequious voice.

"Hey! That was uncalled for," I growled at my father.

"Quinn, we should go; I'm sure you're exhausted from the flight. Alice can come by tomorrow if she wants," Mother interrupted and pulled me away from Father so that there was a bit more than six inches between us.

The front door slammed yet again and now Harry and Dennis were back, bags of groceries in their arms. They both stopped short in the doorway and looked at me, then Alice, and finally my parents.

"My goodness, more company? Quinn, are these your parents? Jane and Andrew?" Dennis spoke up, setting his bags down so that he could shake my father's hand, which he did. "Dennis Martin, Mister Radcliffe. I've seen your staging of *La Traviata* at least six times. This is such a pleasure! I'm a real fan. And this is my friend, Harry."

My father let his icy stare fall on both and said nothing.

It was Harry's turn to chip away the frost and he said, "Does this mean you're not coming with us to the coast tomorrow, Quinn?"

Alice slipped her arm casually through my mother's. "Dr. Radcliffe, you don't mind if Quinn comes with us?

I've wanted him to see the Ranch for a long while and this is the first chance we've had, since he's not touring or booked with auditions."

Mother glanced at me for only a moment and then I saw her give Alice's hand a squeeze.

"I know this means a lot to you Alice, but," she began.

"You could join us next month, right Quinn?" Harry suggested.

"We have this monthly trip up to The Sea Ranch. Harry's folks have a place up there," Dennis explained now. "We were going tomorrow and when Quinn called for a ride home from the airport, I thought why not bring him along? We invited him to sleep over so we could get an early start." A pause then, suddenly, "He'd be sleeping on the sofa here—strictly honorable, despite what the kids want."

"Dennis!" Alice hissed.

"Maybe next month," I said, staring down at my boots.

Another wave of tension blew through the living room. I was avoiding Alice's curious, pleading, glance, not to mention my father's glare. Again, it was my mother who braved the waters. "I suppose one more day won't make a difference, Andrew," she said to my father. She kissed my cheek again. "Have fun. I'm sure you'd rather spend time with your girlfriend and I don't blame you a bit. We'll see you tomorrow evening, then?"

"We should be back by ten, depends on the traffic," Harry volunteered.

"Well, you have a good time. Alice, you just get prettier every time I see you, and you're already stunning, isn't she Andrew? You're a star! It just isn't fair for the rest of us girls."

"A real supernova," my father offered with a disingenuous smile that fooled no one. "We'll say good night. A pleasure meeting you all."

They were gone without hugs or kisses, but I saw my

mother's tears.

No one said a word until we heard the car drive off. Alice looked at her brother and offered a strangled "I love you!" before hugging him. He shoved her off playfully, spinning her around in my direction.

"You should be hugging him. Never let it be said I got in the way of true love."

"Looks like we arrived just in time," Harry said as he handed over one of the bags and nudged me towards the kitchen.

"In time for what, I really don't want to know," added Dennis.

"Patricide, maybe?" I suggested.

Alice followed us into the kitchen and we started to put away the groceries. For once there was no playful banter or laughter. Only silence. A silence that bound us together. Alice disappeared and reappeared with the plates, mugs and trays of her failed attempt at hospitality, barely looking at me as she passed.

"Whatever you're thinking, Quinn, she had no idea they were coming," Dennis said as she'd come through a third time, another pass where she kept her head down, eyes averted.

"There's no such thing as a coincidence," I stated.

"I saw her face. If you know her as well as you think you do, you'll know I'm right."

"You didn't have to lie on my behalf, Dennis."

"I think I didn't have a choice. We can turn it into the truth, if you want. Come up to Sea Ranch with us or not. It's up to you."

I followed them to the living room, expecting to see Alice bent over a sketch book or knitting furiously. Since we started dating, I learned that whenever Alice was really angry she got quiet. She was also a furious knitter. I had an afghan for my bed and six pairs of socks already; I wondered how much of it was because of me. Alice was nowhere in sight.

"She's upstairs?" I asked, nodding towards the stairs.

"Or in the sanctuary."

I stood there with hands in pockets, rocking on my heels while I contemplated my next move.

"Summon your courage," Dennis said as I finally left the room. "But leave the door open!"

My courage had been summoned, but it was gone when I knocked on the bedroom door and received silence, opened it just a bit expecting to be struck by a lamp or stuffed animal. I stopped sweating and relaxed when I realized no one was there. I went to the back porch steps and sat in the chill winter night. While I did that, a light appeared in the window of the basement apartment they called the Sanctuary.

I remembered the first time I'd been here. It was a place she made her own and it was where she sought refuge and quiet. She'd taken a large cluttered space and made it her own with throw rugs and tapestries from Cost Plus, a day bed that Dennis and Harry refinished as a birthday present and set on a carved wooden platform decorated with gothic trefoils in lozenges and strewn with overstuffed pillows that were covered in medieval and renaissance patterned brocades. Gauze curtains decorated with stars surrounded and separated the bed from a work area consisting of a drafting table, stool, workbench and bookshelves and her father's old recliner. The walls were covered in trompe l'oeil skies that went from sunset to dawn on three of the walls, complete with clouds, planets and stars, the sun and the moon. Dennis had set three mirrors into gold-leafed panels like a triptych and placed it on the wall beside a five-panel screen decorated with medieval ladies. The screen gave her privacy from the open stairwell up to the kitchen and laundry room.

I hadn't been here since that afternoon when we made the light show for that disastrous audition for the Fillmore and Bill Graham. She never doubted me and gave such encouragement. All I seemed to do was put up barriers to my own happiness and success, or blame others, just like I'd done that evening.

"Alice?" I called.

"You can come in," she answered.

Alice was curled up in her father's recliner doing homework. She looked up and gave a half smile, one of those stupid grins meant for brush-offs. Sure enough, it disappeared and she returned to whatever it was she was reading, then pushed her hair behind her ear and started taking notes. I stood by the door and wondered if I should make a retreat and was just about ready to say goodnight when I heard the book slam shut. Alice picked up her knitting and started work on what looked like a bedspread but what I would later discover was a shawl and one I would come to love.

"I suppose you're not looking forward to classes on Monday. All the questions and the staring." she said.

"It couldn't be any worse than what happened tonight," I said, sitting on the floor and leaning my head against the platform of the day bed. "What exactly did happen?" I finally asked.

"Let's see," Alice sighed. *Knit one, purl three, knit one, purl two.* "We drove to San Francisco to pick you up at the airport and we were glad, all of us, that you were finally home." *Knit one, purl three, knit one, purl two.* "We came home, had a wonderful dinner and one of the greatest kisses of all time and then your parents showed up." *Knit one, knit one, knit one.* "It looked like your parents wanted to see you but didn't seem all too happy about it." *Knit one, knit one, knit one, knit one...*

"You looked like you were enjoying playing the hostess, maybe even glad to see them?"

Oh holy shit, where did that come from? Oh no....

"I was being polite. It's what people do when guests drop in." *Knit one, knit one, knit one, knit one.* That was going to be one very large shawl. "I was just being polite, which is more than can be said for your parents." *Purl, purl, purl, knit.* "I wasn't exactly thrilled when they showed up. I hadn't seen my boyfriend for over a month and didn't want him taken away under house arrest."

"That's more than what I was thinking..."

"What were you thinking?"

"I thought..." I paused, playing with the stuffed koala that had fallen off the bed. "I thought maybe you invited them over."

"You thought what?" she demanded. "For a bloodbath? For a vase launching contest? Damn you, Quinn!"

Knit, purl, knit, purl, knit, knit, knit, purl, purl, purl. That went on for several minutes with an irritating click of the metal needles as they touched and slid against one another.

"Listen," I began, not knowing if she did or would. "It looked all too convenient, carefully planned—to have my parents show up like that."

She finally spoke, putting down the needles and yarn. "Knowing your parents, and knowing me, why would you ever think that?" she demanded quietly.

"You seemed so friendly with my mother."

"Again, I was being polite and you know I like your mother. That you wouldn't trust me, or think that I would betray you, Quinn...you know what? Just go. I don't want to argue."

"Alice, you have to see it from my point of view!"

"Do I? I think you should trust me and believe me. Now go. Come back when you're ready to apologize."

The knitting needles and yarn were in her hands again. *Purl, purl, knit one, purl, purl, knit one.* I decided retreat was a better alternative than fighting, so I went back into the house to watch TV with the men. Harry passed his beer to me and I shook my head.

"No thanks," I said, taking my place on the sofa.

"You *are* a good boy," Dennis replied, taking a drink from Harry's bottle.

"What are we watching?"

"*Green Acres*," Harry and Dennis answered in one voice.

I supposed watching a show with a ditzy New York socialite and a pig that seemed to be smarter than the socialite and everyone else in Hooterville and Pixley was better than chipping away at the wall of ice Alice had managed to put up in record time. Halfway through the show, Dennis nudged me.

"Yeah?" I responded.

"You don't seem like a guy who actually enjoys watching *Green Acres*," Dennis answered.

"If they hadn't taken *Star Trek* off the air I'd be watching that." I grabbed one of the sodas on the coffee table and took a pull, then settled in to the sofa. The cushions held Alice's perfume. "I'm working on my apology," I said when I noticed they were both staring at me.

"I'm not usually the one to say 'I told you so,' because I leave that to Harry, but tonight is an exception. Alice really had nothing to do with your parents coming over," Dennis said.

I nodded to accept his explanation and continued to stare at the television screen.

"I know it's none of our business, Quinn, but how bad is it? At home?"

Harry's question was familiar and usually one asked by guidance counselors and doctors, well-meaning teachers and chamber orchestra musicians. Rather than dance around it and charm them with wit, change the subject or walk out, I said to Harry and Dennis, "There are times when I wish they were dead. Or I was dead."

"You," Dennis began. He placed a hand on my shoulder. "You'd never act on that, right?"

"And have Alice pissed off at me for all eternity? That's not one argument I'd want in heaven or hell," I jested, but it was the truth. More quietly and seriously, "I think every guy thinks that of his parents, don't you?"

"I did," Harry said, shrugging shoulders. "More than once."

"You know you can come to us if you ever want or need to," Dennis offered.

"I hope that time never comes," I whispered.

"DAMN!"

Jimi Hendrix's exclamation exploded in my left ear and I turned to face him in the Shop.

"That was the closest the Maestro's come to the truth," the Proprietress said.

"Was it enough?" Richard III wanted to know.

"What do you think?" asked Jimi as he started playing the introduction to *Purple Haze*.

"Not even close," Richard answered. "Tarquin, if you want to go home, if that's what you call that hellish life of yours, you'll need to do better than that."

"Surprise us," the Proprietress said and when she stamped the ledger before her it was the sound of my feet stumbling against the coffee table as I rose from Dennis' sofa.

"*Green Acres* too much, I take it?" Harry asked.

"If you'll excuse me, I have to stand outside Alice's door and beg." Dennis glared for a moment and I added, "I'll be the perfect gentleman." Taking the back stairs at the end of the hallway, I went down to Alice's sanctuary and tapped on the screen to announce myself. When she didn't answer, I slipped around it and was met by her puppy, Sammie, who wagged its tail upon recognizing a friend, and then wandered off.

Alice was asleep on the day bed.

Drawing the curtains back around the bed, I gazed down at my sleeping beauty. She had her hands tucked under her cheek, a cheek still wet with tears. Very gently I sat down and with a finger and then my lips, I traced them. Alice stirred and her eyelashes fluttered. The brows went up and then pinched in a frown.

"Hey, Faery Princess," I whispered. "I'm sorry. I

really am."

She studied me, or focused on my face, while she woke up. Finally Alice smiled and welcomed me into her arms. I kicked off my shoes and slid under the bedspread and blankets that were warm and scented with Alice. No sooner had we kissed than we fell to sleep and I woke just as the sky was turning. I heard the slam of a door and bolted out of bed, not wanting to be found in Alice's bed or accused of something I hadn't done, we hadn't done. I grabbed my shoes and slipped out, only I found myself coming out of the *Toad in the Hole* and heading down the to the church.

Thomas Wyatt was sitting on the bottom step with a quill pen and parchment, writing, and as I tried to step over him to get to the church, he grabbed my ankle.

"Not so fast," Wyatt said. "You may live to walk away, but there's always tomorrow and the next day."

"Not your best rhyme, Mister Wyatt. Now, let go? I'm tired."

"Tired? No one is tired here! Sit."

I obeyed and drew up my elbow on my knees as I watched the daily parade of historical personalities and nobodies as they went about whatever business they had in the village. As usual, Hildegard was lovingly attending her flowers and bidding a good day to the patrons of The Curiosity Shop, offering roses and lilies to each as they came and went, some pithy advice; Edward came out with Richard—something I'd never seen in my time there—and they headed towards us.

"Good morrow, Quinn," Edward greeted when he joined us and threw himself on the step beside Wyatt. "Excellent day, isn't?"

"Every day seems to be excellent," I commented, glancing up at the cloudless, brilliant blue sky.

"Some more excellent than others," Richard added, leaning on the gate.

"Some days are excellent for telling people the truth,"

Edward continued. He turned and looked at me, saying, "Eventually you'll have to tell her about the abuse and anger, the threats."

"I'm pretty certain that she knew even then," Wyatt said.

Richard nodded. "Oh I know she did."

"It's not something we talked about then," I growled. "I don't need pity, least of all from Alice."

"It never occurred to you that being honest about your life would have been beneficial to your love for each other?" Richard asked.

"We didn't talk about it then. Who would have believed me? The stigma, the whispering—there were already so many lies about me. It cost me two jobs; almost killed my career. I didn't want to lose the one person I loved."

I had their attention and for the first time I didn't see pity or disdain registering in their faces but empathy, perhaps understanding.

"It's not time; not yet," I said softly.

Edward clapped me on the shoulder. "As long as you know it. Haven't we all suffered as you?"

"Your queen Bess deserved more than an occasional 'Sorry about that, you know how boys can be' and the expensive bauble," Richard III said to his brother. "Who really suffered there?"

"Brother, you know my wife's temper only a little. If you knew the whole of it…"

"So you know what I'm up against," I said.

There was a murmur of assent and I was clapped on the back in turn by each of the three men, offered somber looks and told to be of good cheer.

"Funny how everything is disconnected, yet it falls into place," Wyatt said as I got up with the weariness of an old man and slowly mounted the steps to the church.

It took forever, this climb; the light changing from late afternoon to early morning as if with time-lapse photography. I had gone forward to that particular and important weekend I could never forget or shake off, and found myself climbing the stairs to my bedroom in the house at Scarborough in late July 1978. There was an unfinished conversation I had to pick up. I would have to listen whether I wanted to or not.

Alice was wrapped in one of her fluffy shawls and standing on the balcony. The sun had been obscured by morning and mist and fog but pale yellow rays shot through chinks in the clouds and gave the morning a dream-like appearance.

She didn't turn when I opened the door and joined her. We stood quietly, near enough to touch but aware of a static tension that kept us apart. I was ready to beg her forgiveness when she turned and smiled.

"So this is Scarborough. Now I know why you love it."

"All my life's happier moments have been either at York or here, or with you. There was one false step," I said, and stopped, for that step hadn't been taken yet. Glancing up at the sky, I was relieved that nothing had changed. It had been a smart move. I moved tentatively to take her hand and fortunately she didn't pull away.

"Not this morning, Quinn," Alice whispered, touching my cheek with the other hand and then went on tiptoe to kiss my mouth. "Nothing false about what you said. You reminded me that sometimes I want more than I am allowed to have. Having to learn patience and making do with what life hands me and what I've chosen is worse than hearing the word 'no.'"

"I didn't say no. With what I've been through and what you've decided in your life, it's the best course to take right now. I need help. I don't want to become my father. If all I ever have with you is this, then it will be more than my parents have and more than I deserve. And who knows what may be ahead? Besides, Faery Princess, who has all the patience of saints to put up with me all these years?"

"I just,"

"Yeah?"

"I just think that after all I went through as a girl, with my father, my mother, Denny and me living alone, you'd think someone would give me a break."

"Is this Alice Martin being selfish?" I teased.

She turned and smiled, clutched the shawl to her as a morning breeze chilled us. "Yes, dammit! Yes, it is. I can't have you so I'll settle."

"It's not a bad thing, settling, I guess. Is it?"

"Quinn," Alice whispered and embraced me. The woman in my arms was all I cared about. We kissed and clung and didn't let go when tears started to fall. But those tears were replaced by laughter when Alice started to sing.

"'Are you going to Scarborough fayre? Parsley, sage, rosemary, and thyme. Remember me to one who lives there. He once was a true love of mine.'"

I loved her all the more for her honesty. Being used to sycophants and hangers-on, people who thought their stars would ascend by hitching up to mine, Alice Martin was the only person other than her brother Dennis who more often than not served up the truth. Whether I wanted to swallow it was my problem.

"You know where I'll be," I whispered.

Her kiss was soft and full of yearning. The warmth of her lips on mine was still with me as the whiteness of the mist surrounding us melded into a cohesive shape and became the moon over North Yorkshire, shining into the hotel suite living room and propelling me to that other bittersweet weekend.

I sensed another person in the room and hoped it was Briony, my beautiful, enigmatic, girlfriend for all the wrong reasons Briony, deciding she wouldn't call it a night after all but invite me to share a bath. But no, it was Thomas Wyatt leaning against the frame of the doorway and sipping a scotch on the rocks.

"Great. More unwanted advice," I sighed as I put away the music and hoped when I finished he'd be gone. But no...

"Let me ask you something, if I may," Wyatt spoke up.

"Why ask? You'd tell me anyway."

"You've got one of the most beautiful women in England in your bed right now, and at one time you not only had a beautiful woman in love with you but she was intelligent, witty, and compassionate."

"I know, I know."

"I don't understand why it's been such a struggle to make a choice."

A door closed and Richard came in with a London Times tucked under his arm and three bottles of Guinness. "Let me respond to that, if I may. Where in our time, Master Wyatt, everything was called black or white. Men did what they did and women did what they were told. What our parents did or didn't do to us was of no consequence. We blamed it all on God if we turned out less than stellar in our peers' eyes, or said it was God's curse."

"Such as your hunchback, the withered arm and slobber?" I teased.

"The back, the arm, yes—I don't slobber," came Richard's reply as he handed off one of the bottles of Guinness. "Let me finish, if you please? Quinn lives in a different time with different mores—I believe he struggled to make a choice because he had to get his shit together." Richard took a sip from his bottle and looked at us, anticipating a response, which he received from Wyatt.

"That which is adverse and unkind gives us character," Wyatt said.

"Yes, the buck-up-and-be-a-man argument. Many six-year-olds on the playground understand that," I added.

Richard looked like he wanted more of an explanation and so I thought a moment and sighed, saying quietly, "In my life and time we eventually came to seek justice in payment of the abuse done to some of us. We sought our remedy in law. Most of us did. Some found payment with violence that only brought more retribution. But for the longest time we hid our ugly secrets and pretended they didn't exist. Learning to just live with it, forget it and move on, and yet…"

When Wyatt frowned and looked as if he was going to respond, Richard shook his head in warning.

"And yet?" Richard asked in a gentle voice.

"We're still the guilty parties. To ourselves at least. We're convinced it's our fault, we try to forget about it and move on and live what others have: a normal life. But we wind up inflicting pain on others without even knowing what we're doing. Or we find someone who is as damaged as we are and continue inflicting pain."

"Which is Alice?" Wyatt queried.

"She's a rose. The white rose that I plucked petals off one by one until there was nothing left. And I wondered why she became so distant, why she settled instead of choosing what she really wanted. I knew. Just didn't want to admit it."

"You didn't really have a choice, did you?"

I glanced over at Wyatt and for the first time saw kinship in the expression on his handsome face.

"Time to earn my stars," I said. "One heartbreak at a time, one mistake after another."

"Master Wyatt, shall we on?" Richard asked and hoisting the poet by the sleeve, they disappeared through the fireplace.

I was alone again and still staring at the full moon. Well, time to set things in motion; better to get it over with—it made the final act that much closer.

I crossed the suite and tried the bedroom door. It wasn't locked.

Briony was curled up in the fetal position on a corner of the king-sized bed and she stirred, stretched like a cat and smiled when I kissed her.

"Sorry about earlier," she yawned, wrapping arms around my neck.

"I should learn to think before I speak," I jested.

That came out easier than I thought. And it was what Briony always wanted: to have her constant state of perfection validated in thought, word and deed.

"Well, I guess it's to be expected; with prodigious talent there's bound to be a hiccup or two, don't you think?"

She smiled and leaned in for a deep, long and passionate kiss and I took the bait, expecting a giggle and a 'Not now, darling boy!' when I tried a path of kisses from brow to breasts. She had turned to liquid, her body lithe and relaxed for a change. Not even my hand slipping inside her nightgown started the usual ice flow and worry over losing her virginity before marriage, or worse, getting pregnant.

"I suppose I don't need to extend an invitation, Quinn?" she laughed softly.

The nightgown went over her head and to the floor.

It had been so long that I prayed I wouldn't seem too eager, or worse, not able. I played the playboy, the man of the world, someone who took a different lover to his bed every night. My moves were detached and subtle as if the whole idea bored me. Another debutante in my bed? Must be Tuesday. I took my time getting her worked up, and then she suggested turning out the lights and locking the doors. So I took my time turning out the lights, locking the doors and getting out of my clothes. I made sure I didn't stare too obviously at her perfect breasts or the shapely long legs, the flat and toned abdomen as she pulled off the sheet. Okay, I was staring.

Then it all fell apart.

Briony Atwell, the most photographed, most beautiful woman in *Tattler*, *British Vogue* and *Majesty*, the most beautiful woman in the world some said, was naked and in my arms, and I found myself indifferent and limp.

The curves of her body were angles hewn from a love of dieting and cigarettes, cocaine. There was nothing soft about her. As we kissed and explored each other's bodies, I tried to imagine any number of women in my arms—that art student from King's Lynn who kept me awake all night and into the next morning, the nurse from London, the philosophy major, the reporter for the *Times* who kissed and told and put me on a list of Britain's one hundred most desirable bachelors, and Alice...

I willed the sinews and muscles to be the warm curves and excitement of Alice Martin, the sharp, spicy notes of Estee Lauder's *Youth Dew* that Briony and her mother both wore, to the fresh heady scent of white flowers and vanilla. When I ran my hands down Briony's torso and legs, I didn't feel the softness of flesh, but bone and taut skin that had been baked in the sun, dry and too perfect, and it put me off. Again I tried to be in the moment, as we would say in my later years, but it was no use. I fell away, angry, exhausted, disillusioned.

"We're both tired, love," Briony yawned.

She didn't notice when I rolled over and took most of the blankets with me, or later, when I went into the living room and slept on the sofa. I woke the next morning to find she had already showered and was ready for an outing. Proper dress, hat, shoes and gloves. Perfectly applied lipstick and arched brows. Not a hair out of place.

She was sipping a cup of coffee and reading the *Times*.

"What do you think, love?" she greeted, and poured a cup of coffee that was shoved towards me when I joined her at the table. "You're number one in the *Times'* Arts Page Poll. Ten classical musicians to watch. I suppose with that kind of press you could dance naked on the walls of the Tower of London and the Board of Directors wouldn't say 'boo' to you. You'd still get your American tour."

It was supposed to be a jest and I smiled politely. "I

think there are a few women who wouldn't mind the show," I jibed, and then, "Are you in the mood for—"

"Oh, darling! I think after last night—"

"—for a trip to see my new house?"

She blushed and put her cup down gently, unfolding her napkin and delicately tapping the corners of her mouth with it, being careful not to smudge Number Whatever of Chanel lipstick.

"Why not?" she sighed brightly.

The house looked less impressive and shabbier than the last time I'd seen it—the imagination does that. You remember things as being brighter, lovelier, and bigger than they really were. I suppose that would account for people, too.

Eight steps of flint and set at an almost forty-five degree angle led the way up to a door with red, peeling paint. I had hoped to make a grand presentation but instead I fumbled for the keys in my pocket, and after retrieving a handkerchief, guitar pick, and half of a roll of Lifesavers, I found them and turned the largest of them in the lock. The door pushed open slowly with a creak and the smell of new whitewash greeted us. The painters and refinishers had only just cleared out an hour before.

The narrow hall from the door led past a kitchen and bathroom to a living room divided by pillars and low partitions of stone. The walls were a bright white and the trim was blue. The sitting room area had masculine blue-striped paper on the walls and the fireplace was capped by a mantle that ran the length of the room. The windows were deeply recessed with shelves.

"I thought to put my smaller piano here, facing the windows—a great place to compose with the view and all; here, the bookshelves—seems a good place for them, seeing how the walls are recessed, and a sofa and chair beside the fireplace with a table. My recliner here."

"Oh dear, that old thing you brought from California?"

"Yes, what's wrong with it? It's big, comfortable."

"Ugly."

I ignored the comment and continued, leading the way. "Upstairs there are two rooms and an attic—the attic I was thinking for an office, and the master bedroom, well, come and have a look." I turned hopefully to see if she followed. "But, I guess you don't care."

Briony was standing in the middle of the room, handbag clutched between gloved hands, the sunglasses hiding her appearance but not her disapproval.

"It's pretty," she finally acceded.

"But not a country home—not Chatsworth or Haddon Hall."

"Oh Quinn, why do you try so hard?" The giggle was derisive.

"Maybe because I want you to approve of something, anything, I do, however small and unimportant it seems."

"Why must you think I don't, Quinn?"

The tone of voice, for one. The steely, on-edge clip of the words for another. The way her head turned to the left and held there. Defiant.

"Look, I know classical musicians don't make a lot of money, and in my case, I've had a rough go of it because of my youth, my history, and I suppose those are strikes against me considering what you're used to having. Even so, Bree, I get an idea that you do care for me."

"I wouldn't have let you sleep with me if I didn't," she snapped.

"But what type of care?" My voice was quiet, soft. "Do you care about us? Or is it all about the image? Oh and thank you for the rare privilege of sharing your bed, by the way."

"You're not being fair—and you do this every time something doesn't go your way! Oh why is it that classical musicians are such divas?"

When she made that mocking, perturbed sound, her lips pursing together and then clicking, sighing loudly, I took a step closer and said, "Briony, despite all of our missteps and the differences, I want to marry you. I think, I know, I want this to work." I waved a hand towards the living room. "This is a wedding gift. This little house where we can escape from the world and be ourselves. Just us."

She struck a pose, the one of her at The Ascot that filled the front page of *The Sun*. Only now the headline would scream: *Lady Briony's Huge Anglo-American Disappointment!*

"Well?" I asked when the silence started to kill me. "Say something."

"I took something for my headache last night, Quinn. I don't know what happened."

"Nothing, I promise you."

"And it's just as well."

"I guess that means you never wanted it happen?" I asked quietly, using the controlled delivery borrowed from my mother.

"I didn't say that, Quinn."

"You're on the defensive, though. I've made my feelings clear more than once, and I've been patient about everything. It's your turn. Briony, for once would you just tell me the truth?"

"I resent that," she hissed, her face turning a tell-tale pink.

"Who is he?"

Not what I remembered saying that summer of '77!

"Why do you think there's someone else? There's no one else. There doesn't have to be anyone!"

"For you, yes, there always has to be someone. It doesn't look good on the tabloid pages or the eleven o'clock news to be seen alone at a pricey nightclub or at an opening night."

"I have never once while we've been dating!"

There it was, the sound of disapproval escaping from those perfect lips. The hiss of the snake from my lady Eve.

"Are you certain?"

"I'll see you later."

The slam of a door seemed more final in an empty house, the echoes carrying. I waited, listening for the clip of heels on the steps—maybe she'd come back and apologize. Who was I kidding? The day Briony Atwell apologized for anything the ravens would leave the Tower of London. When she didn't I strolled upstairs to look at the work in the master bedroom, the largest of the bedrooms, the one with the alcove and the bay windows, the balcony facing the castle. It was a place where I could sleep and dream for at that time I realized that that was all I had.

A spark of light caught my eye and I noticed someone had left a prism dangling from a cord in front of the window. The slivers of colored, bright sunlight danced and made a kaleidoscope that caught me in a trance until I was standing on stage at the Royal Albert Hall in the middle of an After Party with members of the orchestra and the board of trustees and our friends and some family. The light crew for the Hall had rigged something up so that the stage was like a disco—we had a deejay and Top of the Pops and disco hits for dancing, getting high, or whatever happened to float our fleet that night in 1976. I had found a bottle of the most expensive scotch the bar had to offer and settled on the steps to the catwalk to watch my new mates enjoy themselves and let their hair down, long hair that it was.

"Drinking alone?"

Chloe Carlisle, a violinist, had found me and dropped herself on the step below me. Her pretty face was flushed from the heat on the stage and no small quantity of alcohol.

"I thought anonymity was best tonight, Carlisle. You remember the last time out?" I queried, pouring another glass for myself. Chloe waved me off when I offered to top her glass.

"Don't see any royals here, fortunately for you," she chuckled. "Good of the old men to give you a second chance."

"Didn't think I needed a second one."

"That's opinion of many," she said into her glass. She was ready to take a drink when she pointed towards backstage. "Look, we got the petty nobility tonight. Those who've got the money—and they're coming this way."

Chloe was right and Sir William, the chairman of the board, was with them. Sir Hector Atwell, Member of Parliament and earl of Swansea, approached, listening attentively to William and nodding in appreciation while he rattled off the usual orchestra propaganda. With them was a striking young woman I'd seen on television, in the news, and just about on every tabloid front page. Lady Briony, his jet-setting, society daughter. The last I heard she was dating one of The Rolling Stones and causing quite a stir in Monaco for late night fun and games.

Chloe shoved me off with a wink. I ditched the bottle and straightened my tie, smoothed my hair back as they stopped short of the stairs. Lady Briony locked me in her sight and smiled demurely. Of course demurely—how else would a daughter of nobility smile?

"Quinn Radcliffe, may I present to you Sir Hector Atwell, member of the board of trustees for the orchestra, and his daughter Lady Briony Atwell. My lord, this is the young musician we've been celebrating all evening."

"Mister Radcliffe, a pleasure—and may I tell you what a pleasure your performance was this evening. Never have I experienced such passion in Debussy! I've always thought Debussy was lightweight, but your artistry has changed my opinion considerably."

"Thank you, my lord." I let my eyes slide to Briony. "Do you listen to Debussy along with The Who and the Stones, Lady Briony?"

"I make a good show of it, especially if it gets me introduced to handsome musicians," she purred.

We held a gaze and she was the first to look away. After a few minutes of pleasantries they were lured away for introductions to other rising stars and potential income for the orchestra. Briony gave me a smile and a look back.

I went back into the midst of the party, accepting congratulations and toasting the orchestra's successful opening night. An hour later I would be thinking of Briony while ramming my tongue down the throat of a socialite and groping her in a dark corner backstage, getting all the green lights because I was Tarquin Radcliffe, the new darling and sensation of the Royal Philharmonic Orchestra and handsome to boot. That was only the first indiscretion in several hours and by morning I would be leaving another girl's flat near Kensington Palace, shagged out and hung over, feeling guilty as I walked to my own place in Raphael Street. A walk of shame, I guess. Why, I didn't know—it was the '70s and no one questioned a young man's libido. Maybe it was that while I made love to three women that night, I thought of Alice, and hoped to find something of what I had with her. I was certainly feeling that as I walked home and Big Ben announced seven-thirty in the morning; London was already awake. I definitely was feeling that as the stroll through Kensington became the walk from my house in Scarborough to the hotel on St. Nicholas Cliff several years later.

Briony was in the sitting room on the telephone with someone and I suppose she hung up when she heard my key in the lock for her movements were quick and anxious. She smiled with the brittleness of someone used to the lens. In this case, it was a lens straight into the heart.

"Come to apologize?" she demanded.

"I don't think I need to."

"Tarquin, why is it—"

"Look, it doesn't matter at this point because we both can't admit something's wrong and we don't want to fix it. Maybe we don't want to settle, because that's what we'd be doing. Last night, this entire weekend made me realize I don't want to settle. Even if it means I'm alone the rest of my life."

She stood and grabbed her handbag and sunglasses, looked up at me; I was surprised to see tears in her eyes. She raised her hands and dropped them to the sides of her summer dress so that the material at her thighs danced and shuddered at the impact.

"What was I supposed to do when I found out this was all arranged? When were you going to tell me that my father blackmailed you?" Briony asked.

"He suggested that it might be good for my image if I was I seen with a beautiful woman who supported the arts and said he knew just the girl. I didn't think at the time that he meant his own daughter—and I wouldn't call it blackmail," I laughed uneasily. I carefully avoided her glance.

"Isn't it when someone says, 'date my daughter, be seen in public with her and you'll get to keep your job and we'll make you conductor? You'll get all the money you need for the orchestra? Do it or we'll confirm the rumors and stories going around about you'?"

"It's nothing I haven't heard before and nothing I can't handle,"

"And then I hear from Father that you're a damn sight better than the rock 'n' roll singers and race car drivers I was usually screwing and caught in bed…I didn't mean…"

Her face had gone gray and she diverted her eyes, hands fidgeting with the magnetic clasp on the handbag, snapping it open and shut, open and shut until I reached out and stopped her, tried to take her hand, which was withdrawn and clenched in a fist by her thigh.

"Screwing, huh?" I asked quietly. She didn't answer. Well that little secret was out! So much for twelfth century politics and matrimonial alliances, of keeping the goods undamaged and intact for the wedding night.

She took a step towards me and stopped. "Quinn, I never meant to hurt you, but Father made it clear,"

"And so have you. Looks like we don't have to settle. Doesn't make it hurt less."

We stared at each other for one of those gut-wrenching, painful moments when we both wanted the other to say something or make a move.

Briony sighed. "This isn't working out as we expected."

No it wasn't.

Imagine my relief when she boarded a train for London an hour later. In retrospect, I knew it was coming even then, but I was always in a state of denial, especially where it concerned women.

CHAPTER 12

"YOU'RE NOT SULKING. That's odd."

I had ceased to be annoyed or startled whenever they showed up. No one ever seemed to notice them, or thought that I was talking to myself—at least, not that anyone said anything. So there was Rafe standing at the elevator bay when I left the hotel room in search of breakfast and some air to clear my head. He followed me out of the hotel, and no surprise, to The Shop. Rafe was fidgeting with a pack of Chesterfields and I held the door for him, listened to the mutters about 'bad choices' and 'worse women' as I threaded past tables to reach mine.

When I sat down the sight of a bright red double-decker bus passing by the window caught my attention and I recognized the silver roses on the advertisements. Rafe snapped his copy of *The Evening News*, the page turned to local events. There was a listing for the Royal Philharmonic Orchestra's appearance at the festival and I winced at the photo of Briony and me at a happier time. Then I saw it in the corner: an announcement for a summer course in 1978, the next year, at The College of Ripon and York St John.

"It would have been nice to have been dropped into *that* weekend and the week after," I groused. Rafe frowned and turned the page to see what I had tapped.

"Oh, so you feel short-changed? Put out? I don't blame you. Let me see if I have this right. By the time that summer came round she'd already published several articles and papers, and had a book in the works, and when the original professor dropped out to join Donovan Trist's dig at Petra, she was a perfect choice to replace him. Did you expect her to sit on a shelf until you made up your mind and decided you were no threat?"

"I would never hurt Alice."

"Then why were you so afraid? She goes from strength to strength these days."

"What exactly are these days?" I wanted to know, taking the manuscript pages from him.

"Whatever you want them to be, dear boy. Do you want them to be wine and roses, great passion, artistic success?"

"I want sanity and peace. I want Alice."

"If you insist," Rafe sighed and made a production of turning the pages of the newspaper spread out before him, snapping it yet again, and when he put the paper down, The Shop filled with the usual crowd: Richard III with his crossword puzzle, Jane Austen writing and mumbling to herself, Jimi Hendrix and Edward IV playing a duet, this time *Since I Fell for You*, with Janis on vocals. Hildegard was watering the flowers and making bouquets for customers; the Proprietress was arranging parquetry casks on shelves and in display cases.

Rafe poured two cups of coffee and brought over a cheesecake and Pop Tarts, which he offered to the others, and then pulled my music manuscript over to begin another review, turning the pages carefully.

"When did you know, Quinn?" Rafe asked, using a pen to count notes on the page. When he saw that I was more interested in what he was doing than the question, he nudged me playfully. "When did you know you loved Alice? That she was The One?"

"When I gave her the cap," I replied without hesitation. "When her jerk of a boyfriend tossed her little cap into the stairwell, I picked it up and gave it to her. The look she gave me…"

"What would we, each of us, give for that?" said Jimi, and Edward nodded.

"More to the point," the Proprietress spoke up, "Why would you give it up?"

"I didn't."

"Didn't you?" Jane sighed, scratching out what she'd just written.

"Okay, I didn't want to. It wasn't an easy decision, and when you come down to it—"

"What is it?"

"Let me finish,"

"No, what is it you come down to?"

"Oh good Lord, really?" I sighed. "Okay; it comes down to having decisions made for you, being forced on you, and all you want to do is just walk away."

"Which is why you need to go back to Scarborough," the Proprietress commanded.

"What? No!"

"Such a sad little puppy," the Proprietress sighed and slammed her palm down on a bell at the counter. "Shouldn't you know by now who it is that's in control?"

"I think we're done here. Just show me the way out of wherever I am," I demanded, and looked around for another exit, or some support from the others. I found neither. Richard looked apologetic, and was ready to speak.

"Richard! You know the rules. You know how it works," Edward snapped.

"Oh, for God's sake, Ned, he knows! At least, I think he does," Richard grumbled.

"Know what?"

"Quinn!" the Proprietress barked. "You have five minutes to make your train."

"It's a hard road back, Quinn," Hildegard spoke up as she passed by, and handed me a nosegay of white flowers. "And you have to take a side trip."

"I said…"

"We heard what you said," Jane sighed, making another entry in her journal, and then pointed with the pen. "There's the door. There's the way."

"The train, Maestro Radcliffe?"

Hildegard was opening the door for me, the sweet jangle of the bell annoying as she turned the latch and let in a bright stream of sunlight. Grabbing my coat I shuffled out, ignoring the advice from the Proprietress to mind the hour and remember that I only had a week.

Being outside and alone reminded me of all the times I escaped to Indian Rock Park—the times when my father got to be too much, or my mother's passive-aggressiveness and her complaisance made me want to throw myself from the Campanile at Cal. The transatlantic flights to Ellie's house in York were like this. I had stepped out of a toxic cloud into fresh air.

As usual, it was a bright, spring day and villagers were out and about, the shops bustling with commerce and everyone seemed to be someone from my history books, the imagination or random thought, for why else would Thomas Hardy be strolling up the high street carrying a basket of groceries for Bathsheba Everdene? Or Abraham Lincoln arguing with Winston Churchill while Queen Victoria tried to get a word in edgewise?

Sitting by the mill pond was Thomas Wyatt, his brows knitted together perhaps from the bright sunlight, or in concentration as he wrote in his folio.

"I should have listened to you," I called in greeting as I approached.

Wyatt glanced up, frowning, and then he grimaced. "Oh thank you kindly, master musician," he sighed, "Now I can go home and sleep tonight, knowing I have your approval!"

"Sorry to have offended. See you 'round."

As I did an about-face, he caught my jacket sleeve. "Noted. But am I the person to whom an apology should be offered?"

Wyatt jerked his chin towards the bookshop across the street.

"Why can't people just say what they mean?" I

grumbled, starting off.

"What would be the fun in that?" Wyatt called.

"I could show you some fun," I muttered as I entered the bookshop and collided with Charles Dickens, who was carrying a stack of books that crashed to the pavement. "Why is it that no one watches where they're going in this Godforsaken place?" I demanded now.

"I wouldn't say it's Godforsaken; maybe you are," Dickens responded.

"Oh shut up."

"Some people think they're above the rules; some people want the attention but not the work that goes into it; some people want the love but don't know how to respond to it," Dickens said under his breath, but I heard it as soon as it was uttered and knew it was meant for me, especially when I saw Alice standing at a shelf. She was wearing that damned white lace wedding dress as she perused the collection, taking books from the shelf, opening them, skimming, and then carefully placing them back.

"Hello," I greeted, deciding simplicity would be best.

"Hi. Oh dear; you've been losing sleep again." Her hand was warm on my cheek.

"I'm sorry."

Alice laughed and her smile warmed me. "Why is it men think that's what we want to hear?"

"I thought you wanted us to admit when we were wrong."

"About what?" she asked, and her hand moved from my cheek to a book on the shelf. "Oh, don't listen to them, Quinn. They've been wrong more than once, twice, three times. Knowing why is more important."

"I thought you knew why, Alice."

"Well, now I do," she said easily and without bitterness or malice. "But then?"

Off in the distance I caught the shrill of a train whistle.

"There's your train; you shouldn't miss it."

I hesitated only for a moment, and took off running only to be back in the book shop for a lingering kiss.

"What do you think you're doing? You're going about it in all the wrong ways!" Wyatt shouted at me as I sprinted back down to the railway station, the shiny green engine catching the sun and a plume coming from the stack. It was the Green Arrow, a London Northeastern Railway Class V2 4771 locomotive, a favorite from my childhood. I paused only for a moment to admire her and when the conductor shouted, "All aboard!" I jumped onto the stairway of the teak-paneled first class car and hurried down the passage looking for an empty cabin.

There was one left and I took it. I had barely thrown myself down on the upholstery seat when the train chugged and steamed its way out of the station—a little out of the way place, nothing exciting or impressive. Though I noticed Ludwig Beethoven directing a small concert band on the platform, the type that played in parks at the turn of the last century. It would have been nice to know what century I was in.

"Your ticket, Mr. Radcliffe?"

Jack Lemmon was standing over me, punch ready, eyes twinkling and smile genuine. He gestured with the punch to my right coat pocket and I pulled out a booklet of tickets made of bright stock paper with the letters A to E stamped upon them.

"'A' ride?" I ventured, more to make conversation if anything.

"Oh no, sir! 'E' at least. This will be a dark ride."

As soon as the ticket was punched he pushed a button on the wall by the sliding door and an ear-splitting squeal of brakes as the train lurched to a halt made my heart leap in my throat. I braced myself for a crash but when I opened my eyes I was in a taxi outside the hotel in Scarborough on the opening night of the festival.

"Here you are sir; need help?"

The driver saw me fumbling for the door and my

wallet, and was out of the cab and holding the door as I staggered out. The clocks were chiming midnight when I arrived back after the wildly successful opening of the festival. I was a little drunk and feeling smug, unconcerned about the break up that finally made it to the six o'clock news. Eighteen curtain calls can make the worst pain seem trivial. I was ready to continue the celebration with a fifth of scotch, maybe a bottle of Guinness and a hot shower, but those plans fell to the wayside when a second taxi cab pulled up and my father got out.

"Sonofa—you followed me?" I hissed, avoiding the paparazzi that materialized out of the hotel façade. "How many times do we need to have this conversation?"

He came forward arms outstretched for a hug while I stood on the top step wondering if I should push him down the stairs.

"No word of welcome, son?" he laughed.

I winced as I was captured in his embrace and the flashbulbs exploded. "What did I tell you, Dad?" I sighed.

"My God, that was a program, wasn't it? Who would have thought? I'll have to ring up William Kemp in the morning and congratulate him for that stroke of genius. All Vaughan Williams program! I suppose that made your day!"

"It did; considering it was all my idea and Sir William wanted nothing to do with it at first."

It came slowly at first, the low grumble from the belly and the spasms as my father let loose a chuckle that was nervous and tinged with anger. Something that happened when he was proven wrong. Then we stared at one another before he said, "Well, aren't you going to invite me in?"

"Could you leave us?" I barked at the photographers and press starting to circle.

"Do you have any remarks about Lady Briony's allegations?" one guy with balls shouted.

"Want her number?" I shouted back. "You can find

out what it's like getting screwed by the most gorgeous woman in Europe, and I don't mean that in a good or literal sense," Laughter followed and I waved them off, grabbing my father by the arm—but not before he used the contact for another photo op—and pulled him into the lobby where I ducked away for the elevators.

"Is it like this all the time?" Father laughed happily.

"Mostly."

"There's the lounge. How about that drink you've been promising?"

I didn't hesitate. "Under any other circumstances, yes, but I've had one of the worst days of my life."

"Impossible! With that program and all those curtain calls?"

"I broke it off with Briony. I've been fending off reporters and her attacks in the press all day."

"Excellent decision, Quinn."

He didn't hesitate either. Not surprising.

"You may think that now, but by the end of the festival the money and my charmed status will be gone. Briony's father was the life support for the orchestra; her absence from my side and her tirade on the news was the talk of the after party," I rambled as I punched the button for the elevator car a little too violently. A couple waiting nearby threw glances at one another and whispered and I glared back. When the elevators at last slid open my father pulled me back, and smiled at the couple as they hurried past us. The doors closed before I could jump in and escape.

"And so you make a fool of yourself in public?" Father hissed, following me as I paced.

"It'll be great publicity for the orchestra. Who knows? Maybe it'll land me a spot on Tony Edwards' show, or better still, Johnny Carson. Wait, no. Only rock stars get the call from Johnny."

"Lower your voice!"

"Why are you still here?" I demanded, punching the

call button again. "I didn't ask you to show up. You're like a cockroach—can't get rid of you."

I stumbled into the elevator car when it arrived and couldn't hit the button for my floor fast enough. Unfortunately, Father was quicker than I hoped and we were alone in the car.

"I get it! You were hoping to get in good with Bree's dad," I laughed.

"You think I care about that vapid little girl?" Father laughed. "I came to see you."

"You came to do what you do best. Tell me how great you are and what a loser I am."

"Can we have one night without arguing, son? Let's put the day behind us and raise a glass to your blossoming career."

He was right behind me when I opened the suite door, once again managing to squeeze through before I slammed it shut.

"The bar is in there," I said, pointing to the living room as I went towards the bathroom. "Let's make this quick."

"C'mon, Quinn; I have to be back in California tomorrow—I was hoping we could discuss some ideas I've been thinking about," my father called from the living room.

I flushed the toilet and zipped up, glanced at my reflection in the mirror, which was blurry—wow, were my eyes really that shade of bright red—and took my time washing up so I wouldn't have to be with Father for too long. For the first time that evening I regretted the amount of champagne I'd consumed and not getting the telephone number of the pretty brown-eyed woman from Gatwick who giggled and blushed when I signed her program.

"Quinn?"

I flushed a second time, waited, and then went out into the living room. My father had found a classical music station on the radio and was sipping a scotch neat while

Rachmaninoff played in the background.

"I think another drink would do me in," I sighed, taking the easy chair across from him, and waving away the gin and tonic he offered. "My God, that was the longest, best After Party I've been to in a while."

"Still all parties and sex, Quinn?"

"If it were that, I'd have a delicious brunette in my bed and I wouldn't have to be staring at you, Father. So what are these ideas? Give me the short version." The low rumbling started and my father got up and went to the bar. "I said, nothing to drink."

"Alka-Seltzer, that's all."

He dropped two tablets from a packet into a glass and water and held it up as if watching the metamorphosis of salicylic acid and bromides for the first time and handed the drink over. I watched the tablet fizzing at the bottom of the tumbler and then shot it back, almost gagging at the salty taste.

This was a familiar scene, one played out several times over the past six years: a drink after an audition or concert. I was painfully cordial, my father putting on a façade of parental pride and love, chatting and joking, glad-handing me as if we'd always been the best of friends and it never occurred to him that I left America not only to pursue a career in music, but to get away from him. He never got it into his head that no one would ever miss him if he were gone because he never went away.

"What would you think of teaching a master class at the university?" Father was asking now. It seemed to me that he'd been talking for a long while, and I was just hearing his voice. I felt as if I had just come up from water and couldn't get my bearings. Christ, the hangover in the morning was going to be lethal.

"I'm booked with concerts and recording sessions through next May," I dismissed him.

"What about the American tour?"

"That may not happen, now that things have changed.

The orchestra has to find—I've got to find an alternative source of backing, or grovel. Or another Sloan Ranger to screw."

"When you come to California,"

"Dad…"

"When you come to California, whenever the orchestra is performing in the Bay Area, you can teach a class at the university, and maybe be guest conductor for the Symphony or even the Opera. I'm sure they'd love it."

"Dad, c'mon…"

I was feeling dizzy now and was sure I was going to throw up. I tried to stand but my father was kneeling before me, pushing me back into the chair.

"Too much champagne, Quinn? Not to worry, things will be fine—they always work out, don't they?" He was whispering in my ear.

The sensation of falling overwhelmed me and I wanted it to stop, wanted to hold on to something. This had happened before…it had happened so many times…

"Take a hold of him!"

It was Hildegard von Bingen barking orders at someone. I felt firm but gentle hands on my arms and the sensation of being lifted, now carried.

"I didn't think he'd weigh this much!" Richard III was grunting.

"He works out!" Rafe was gasping.

Hey! I didn't weigh that much!

"Easily, easily! Now through the door."

I was falling through blinding colors of red and gold, lavender and silver, feeling the sensation of warmth and excitement. When I opened my eyes I was laying on the grass outside the church in the village, the sky above me its usual bright blue, speckled by the leaves of the ancient sycamore I was under. Hildegard, Richard and Rafe were crouching beside me.

"How are you, my boy?" Rafe asked gently.

"Like I need the tail of the dog that bit me. I don't

remember having that much alcohol," I groaned, struggling to sit up.

"What do you remember?" asked Hildegard.

"A very lovely brunette—she reminded me of Alice. Lots of champagne, lots of it. My father ambushing me—his usual nonsense."

"That's all?" Richard wanted to know.

I shrugged. "What else is there?"

Hildegard, Richard and Rafe exchanged wary glances and it was one of those odd-man-out moments in a conversation, where a private joke or significant knowledge is shared between everyone but me through eye contact.

"Just in time," Hildegard sighed and got to her feet, dusting off her habit.

"Let me buy you a slice of cheesecake," Richard offered.

"I think I'll stay here a while," I responded, glancing around. "Just to think through my strategy the next time Her Worshipfulness decides to throw me into the deep end of the pool with my father."

"He's so calm about it," Rafe mused, digging around in a pocket for his cigarettes.

"That's because we got him just in time," Hildegard whispered none-too-quietly, and then, "We'll see you in a bit?"

"In a trice," I teased. She winked, but not before offering a kiss on my brow that felt like the sun.

They were gone and I was left under the tree.

I understood why Alice and so many others loved this village. The tranquility and beauty of it outweighed the strangeness. I always felt a strength and swelling of emotion when I looked around at the peaceful yet bustling place. This was a place I'd known all my life, even though I'd never been here until now. The beauty and symmetry of the houses and shops, the gardens and greenery, they were the comforting part of my life and I would have been content to sit there under the monstrous oak until I heard a familiar clatter by the side of the church facing the beck. Dusting myself off, I strolled over and tried the gate into the close and found it unlatched. When I pushed it gently, it squeaked and groaned with age and slipping through, I found myself in the high school cafeteria, not a church garden, and it was January of 1969.

There was a lunch tray in my hands and a stack of ligature paper and a pen beside the plate of what might have been lasagna—it was covered in tomato sauce and pasta-like—with meatballs, of all things, and a carton of milk.

I took a seat at one of the empty tables in the back of the room, the furthest from the main door, the one close to the exit leading out toward the gym. The usual kids were there. The castoffs and untouchables, the members of the stage crew and the orchestra, the debate and chess clubs. They found strength and friendship in the herd mentality and sat in a clump at the table in front of me, looking up every now and then when there was a squeal of laughter, making sure it wasn't directed at them. I sat by myself. I always sat alone.

The lasagna was half gone when I took one of the manuscript pages and studied my work from last night. I was transcribing *Debussy's The Girl with the Flaxen Hair* and had reached the *poco animato* after measure fifteen, when I heard the argument. No one else seemed to care.

Alice stormed into the cafeteria, pushing past the cheerleaders and debutantes, who were scandalized and showed it by the dirty looks and shouts, followed by Will Parmenter. He pulled her into a corner and they argued until Alice walked away and took a seat at one of the unpopular tables.

I continued my notation, hearing the strains of Debussy in my head while I surreptitiously stared at Alice and always looked away when she glanced over. Then I felt the table shake and glanced over to find Will Parmenter and two goons at the other end. They ignored me and I ignored them until I heard one of them say, "Why do you let her get away with that shit?"

"Let her play the damsel in distress, I don't care," Parmenter growled, making it apparent he did.

I looked over at Alice again. She had opened a sketchbook and was drawing rapidly while with the other hand she opened an ancient grocery bag and placed lunch on a napkin. An apple, a sandwich, and something in a container that looked like carrots and celery cut into sticks. No wonder she was so thin with so little to eat. I couldn't fault her for that, knowing her situation at home. If she was trying to lose weight that would have been a mistake, for she had all the right curves in all the right places. Guys were always doing a 'look back' and making comments about her that I tried to ignore—like right now. Alice had twisted about on the bench and crossed her legs, legs that were damn fine and gorgeous and just about every guy in the room was staring.

"Damn, Parmenter!" the second goon whistled. "Are you going to give up *that*?"

"Who said I'm giving up? I just need to show her that there's more interesting things in life than theater—like seven minutes in heaven with me," Parmenter boasted.

"Yeah, you're what every girl dreams about," I said aloud as I scratched angry notes on the ledger lines.

Oh God, what had I done? I thought I'd kept silent…

The three jocks turned and glared.

"Radcliffe." Parmenter acknowledged me with an upwards jerk of the chin and a glare.

"Writing a symphony, pretty boy?" Goon Number One asked.

"What's it to you?" I wanted to know.

"Didn't you know that Radcliffe is some musical genius with a cello or violin, and travels all over Europe playing concerts?" Parmenter scoffed.

"Yeah, I bet all the girls want to be strummed with

your bow," Goon Number Two said and nudged the first, laughing, or more accurately, braying at his own joke.

It was pretty clever but I didn't lift my head to look at them. Still working on the notes, I said after a time, "Hey Kowalski, I noticed your girl eyeing me in French class. She slipped me her number."

Goon Number Two started up but his friend pulled him back. "Next you'll be saying you slipped her the tongue," he growled. "Or something else and it better not be true."

"Nope. Don't go after other men's girlfriends."

"So you think you're better than me? Better than us?" Goon Number Two demanded.

"You said it, not me. But I suppose when I'm living in Monaco or Paris and partying with The Rolling Stones, or leading an orchestra, you three will be pumping gas for the Union 76 on University Avenue, or selling wing tips at Huston's."

Parmenter was on his feet and standing over me. I ignored him and continued working.

Not something I'd done...

"You've got your fucking nerve!" he said.

"Just calling it like I see it and I don't like what I see."

"What? Like what?"

"She's your girlfriend, isn't she? Alice? Why do you treat her like that? Like she's nothing?"

"What of it, Radcliffe? I told you before to back off!"

"Tell me all you want," I said rising to my feet. Parmenter stepped back as I started gathering up my stuff. "Show her some respect. Don't you owe her that?"

"Hey! She's lucky to have me!"

"Wow. I'm jealous."

Parmenter took a swing but I blocked the punch and caught the attention of the principal, who was heading towards us. There was nothing that needed explaining as far as I was concerned, and I walked out of the cafeteria with all eyes on me, especially the most beautiful eyes of the most beautiful girl in school. . .

CHAPTER 13

I HAD EARNED respect by my actions. Kids who never gave me the time of day now made eye contact and smiled as I went from class to class that afternoon. Yes, I was feeling victorious, walking taller. But I turned to Jell-O when I arrived at my locker at the end of the day and saw Alice talking to some theater department kids as they came out of the art studio not far from where I stood. Fumbling more than usual with the combination lock, I whistled The Doors' *Hello, I Love You* while I tried to look and act cool and eavesdropped on the conversation.

"He did *what*?" a girl squealed.

"He'd rather be with her, and if that's what he wants, fine by me," Alice said.

"But the Winter Ball," another girl interjected.

"Oh screw the Winter Ball," Alice sighed in a tremulous voice. "I'd rather do the decorations than go. Everyone would think I was a freak to be there—I'm not supposed to go to proms, being a theater kid."

"Don't worry, Cinderella," a cheerleader called as she walked past with another member of the squad; "you too shall go to the ball!"

"Someday!" her friend added and they started to giggle as the passing bell rang.

The first cheerleader noticed me staring and added, "Maybe you can get Tarquin to take you!"

The two 'evil stepsisters' burst out into laughter as they walked to the next class in search of their next victim on the day's checklist.

That pretty much ended the conference in front of the art studio and the little group around Alice dispersed, but not before asking in turn if she was okay. They left us alone. I pretended to be more interested in the jumble of textbooks, binders, notebooks and old lunches in my locker, knowing she was behind me.

"That was pretty amazing—what you did in the cafeteria."

I kept stuffing things back into the locker, hoping she couldn't hear my heart pounding or see the sweat beginning to bead on my forehead.

"Not really; I just don't understand why guys like Parmenter have to be such assholes and expect everyone to love them for it," I sighed, taking out a chemistry textbook and my music scores, slamming the locker shut before everything fell out.

"They do it because they know they can get away with it," she said sadly. "They're untouchable."

When I looked down she was inches away, that perfect, beautiful face inclined, and if I'd had the guts I would have kissed her there and then in the hallway.

We just stared at one another for the longest, most incredible time. I saw a tear drop from her lashes and glide down her cheek and not even asking, I wiped it away with the gentle brush of a finger.

"That can't be easy—putting up with their crap."

Her eyes registered surprise at that. They were large, round, even more beautiful. "No. You get used to it, which is sick in its own way." Alice dug into her sweater pocket and pulled out a handkerchief and turned away from me to wipe her eyes. "Thanks for the kindness of not asking if I'm okay. I guess it's obvious I'm not," she said.

"Nobody's really okay. It all depends on what's going on in their life and how they handle it."

"Your own experience?"

"Pretty much. I'm learning to choose the battles I can win."

"Or the ditch to die in?"

"I'm not ready for that battle."

"I think you'd win."

"Why would you say that?" I asked, a self-conscious smile masking my hopefully-not-too-obvious nervousness.

"You always look so . . . confident. You always look like nothing can hurt you. That makes you deserving of victory, I think."

"Really? Why?" I asked again.

"It's like having a poker face. You show the world that nothing and no one can hurt you."

"I wish that was true, Alice. But thank you for the vote of confidence."

When I smiled, I watched the color rise in her face and then slowly subside. The second passing bell rang.

I took out the Debussy piece and handed it to her. "I transcribed this for flute—I know you play. It's one of my favorite pieces, but I thought of you when I listened to it one night, and so…"

The manuscript separated us. Alice held one end, and I the other. Rather than look at her, I focused on the page, and was bemused that it seemed to age before my eyes. In fact, when I released it, it was folded into a neat rectangle and used for a bookmark in a copy of *Far From the Madding Crowd* Alice had been reading. I closed the pages over it, the book replaced on the mantle of my house in Scarborough where she'd left it a week ago.

Strange how the paper retained the scent of her perfume so many days later. Of all the moment in my life I hated, and there were plenty of them, this was one I'd rather forget—August of 1978.

By this time next week, she would be married.

She was back in Rhode Island by now. Glancing at the clock I guessed the plane would be on the tarmac, a driver holding up a sign for her somewhere past the luggage carousel. Throwing my overnight bag on the chair, I unzipped it and pulled out the LP she'd given me at her flat in Gillygate, York. The slipcover was speckled with worn areas and scuffs, the record itself marred by a scratch going through the circumference, all the way to the red and blue stripes around the white label. I frowned, remembering how the scratch was put there; Alice would laugh however, at the memory, and tell me again that it wasn't often a girl was fought over in the streets of Berkeley…

That was the hardest of goodbyes, that day in York when a weekend of conversation still had no conclusion and the answer to the question on both of our minds finally had an answer that was reluctantly accepted because, you know, it was all for the best, all things considered.

After a moment's reflection I glanced at my watch and then picked up the phone and dialed a number I'd already memorized.

One ring… Two… Three…

"Hello?"

Jesus! It was him!

My heart fell into my stomach and I paused, listening to a clock chime on the other side of the Atlantic.

"Hello?" He sounded impatient.

"Hi! Uh, is Bathsheba there?"

"Bathsheba? Who is this?"

"Bathsheba Everdene—I was told to call this number…"

"Nobody here by that name."

"Sorry."

A click and then the hum of the dial tone.

If she had been there, and if he told her about the call, Alice would know. Bathsheba Everdene was her favorite literary heroine from her beloved *Far From the Madding Crowd*.

"Of course she would," Rafe said as he crossed the

living room from the hallway with a tea tray that was placed on the end table near the sofa. "Thought you'd like something to eat before returning to London."

I reached for a square of shortbread and took a bite, savoring the buttery sweetness and recognizing it as Ellie's. "I needed that, thanks," I mumbled, now reaching for the tea.

"I thought you wanted a little honesty with your conversation?" he chortled. "What do you say, Ellie?"

When I turned at the slam of a door, I was back in The Shop and my grandmother was walking through, pulling off her gloves and sunglasses simultaneously in a flighty socialite manner she'd affected for laughs.

"I'll say that I don't understand," she answered sitting down at my table but not before kissing the top of my head.

"But if you're here, then…"

"Of course I'm here. We all stop by eventually. Please, Tarquin, you know the game and the rules. And what was it you asked of Alice after you two went to my store? You wanted the truth, but went for the double-standard instead. It should have been obvious what you needed to do: to talk to her about your father, honestly; your career, honestly; all the sacrifices expected of you, again honestly—and what do you do? You run to London."

"I had a recording session," I defended myself weakly. "I think you know what happened…up at the castle, that is."

"It was a start," Ellie sighed.

"It might have gone a bit farther," Richard III said as he pored over his crossword puzzle.

"After all," Jimi spoke up, "You were thinking about it, weren't you?"

"I believe he was," Jane added.

"Well," sighed Ellie, "There's no other solution."

I would have protested, but Ellie snapped her fingers and I was standing on the podium in the recording studio, snapping out the beat with my fingers, "Seven two three four, eight two three four and...now! Hit me with it, people!"

The orchestra's sound swelled as I encouraged the shape, pulling the notes out of each musician from piano to fortissimo as we entered measure seventy-four of the *Allegretto*, the second movement of Beethoven's Seventh Symphony. The string section was smiling and nodding, watching my direction, following my cues. I was already dancing on the podium. As quickly as the sound grew into a thunderous statement, it slowly and gently softened, like a sun breaking through storm clouds.

"That's your cue, Martin! I need a clarinet here!"

Day three of recording a new album on a hot August afternoon in the Decca studios in Broadhurst Gardens, West Hampstead in North London. It had been smooth so far, with my temper staying in control and the orchestra actually listening to the engineers, and more importantly, me. I felt as if I were playing baseball or running; the physical exertion of conducting was a work out, for I was 'one of those' who conducted with his whole body and got emotional. I didn't just stand there and politely wave a stick. In fact, my baton was somewhere under the tympani, having flown out of my right hand somewhere during this last run-through of the *Allegretto*. Thankfully, no one was injured this time.

I wasn't expecting the applause when an hour later we recorded the piece and the engineers in the booth gave a thumbs up. The orchestra was on its feet and cheering and applauding; the engineers and Sir William were also smiling and applauding.

"I think that's a wrap, don't you?" I teased when the room was quiet again.

Sir William came down and clapped me on the back. "Well done, young maestro!" he chuckled. It was first time I'd seen him smile since my being hired as musical director and chief conductor—and the first time anyone of any importance in the organization called me 'maestro,' a term only used for senior conductors with a proven record. "One take. I think it's something to give the Americans on the U.S. Tour next year, what do you say?"

"The board approved the tour?"

"Unanimously, Quinn. There wasn't even a discussion. When the tour was brought up there wasn't even an argument about funding. We've got backers and well, after the festival performances, the sold out concerts, I think you've earned a trip home, don't you?"

"You sure it wasn't that spread in *People* magazine?" I joked.

"That didn't hurt, though it was difficult to get used to the screaming women at concerts."

"That will stop once I get married."

Sir William's eyes lit. "And when will this happen?"

I shrugged. "There's a girl back home."

"Make the announcement on the tour! Propose to her at the end of a program! We'll have scores of young couples coming to the symphony for a romantic evening and a proposal of marriage after you make it fashionable!" He studied me carefully and then clapped my shoulder in a fatherly manner. "Well, you certainly are a dark horse, Quinn Radcliffe. And here we all thought…doesn't matter now."

It shouldn't have before, I thought; no matter what the latest rumor was.

"I imagine Andrew and Jane are delighted at the prospect," Sir William continued, following as I gathered up scores and a coffee cup from the podium desk, took my baton from one of the engineers.

"What they think is of no importance to me, sir," I admitted, shocking even myself. Sir William merely smiled.

"Ah, Lady Briony."

"No—the young lady in question never had prospects, if there's a good term for it. She had no money, a tragic childhood, and was raised by a brother. No, she doesn't pass muster with my parents' standards, even though she's intelligent, independent, beautiful, and funny."

"Make your move before she gets away!" Sir William laughed.

I grinned apologetically. "I have to make sure she's still available," I admitted.

And that's where it stood when I arrived at my London flat that night. Around eleven, I switched on the television news and was greeted by an item about Briony and a polo player's engagement, which brought a derisive chuckle to my throat. And she thought an orchestra conductor/concert cellist was a sorry bet? There was little else on the news to interest me, other than the weather report that guaranteed another three days of above-average temperatures. I threw open the windows in my bedroom and sat down on the bed, staring out at Piccadilly.

The next thing I knew I was calling California.

He picked up on the first ring; the greeting was impatient. He was struggling for breath as if he'd been climbing the stairs, or running down them. I let him ask, "Who is it?" twice before hanging up on my father. A moment passed, and I called a different number.

"Hello, Denny? It's Quinn."

A pause and then, "Quinn? Quinn, oh my God, what a great surprise! Where are you? How are you?"

"Fine, fine; In London for recording sessions. I suddenly thought of you guys while I was walking home, and just wanted to see how you were doing. How's it going?"

"Oh, the health has been up and down, but I blame being busy—the business is picking up. I don't have to ask how you're doing—you've made quite a splash on both sides of the Atlantic."

"Yeah—but don't believe everything you read." We both expelled chuckles and then I drew in a breath and paused before exhaling. "How's Alice?" That was dumb. I knew how she was. I just wanted to know something I already didn't, something she'd tell her brother and not her lover.

"We're leaving in the morning for New York. Alice is getting married. I guess this is news for you?"

"No, no. We saw each other—by accident; serendipity I guess you'd call it. While she was in York for the summer term, the guest lecture series. I was in town to take care of my grandmother's shop and estate. We just—ran into each other. She told me."

"She didn't say a thing about it when she came home."

"Given the circumstances, would you expect her to— no, that wasn't fair. Sorry."

"No, don't apologize. I can't imagine how the news hit you. It can't be easy for you. Hit us pretty hard. But, we make our choices even if no one else agrees with us."

"The last thing she needs is me riding up on a charger to steal her away from the Black Knight," I laughed nervously. "Well, you're probably busy with the details—I suppose you designed the dress."

"No, she did. You might remember it from her sketches."

"Medieval, no doubt. She was always drawing faery princesses…you know, I hope I wasn't too much trouble, and leaving California when I did and how—I guess being the orphan son of two living parents who don't give a damn has its challenges—teaches you all the wrong lessons where it concerns manners and etiquette, how to treat people you love."

"I'll always think of you as a brother, Quinn. You accepted Harry, and you pulled Alice out of a dark place."

I paused, swallowing a lump in my throat, and waited for Denny to say something else, but I heard an impatient sigh.

"That's impossible—she was the one who saved me. Listen, I better go, it's almost midnight and I have an early call tomorrow," I apologized.

"Don't be a stranger. Stop by when you're home or in

between concerts or talk show appearances."

"Deal. Take care…"

"Quinn?"

"Yeah, Denny?"

"Alice never told us what happened, or why. All I know is that it just didn't seem right at the time."

"We make our choices even if no one else agrees with us. Or they're made for us."

"Hope to see you soon, Prince Charming."

Maybe sooner than you think, Denny…

I dialed another number and waited only through two rings for the pickup.

"Hi…it's me."

"Hi!" Alice squealed, genuinely surprised and pleased, by the sound of her voice.

"Hey! I guess you're pretty busy with dresses and flowers, and all that stuff, but I wanted to see how things were, and to let you to know I was in Scarborough before coming down here to London for the recording sessions and I found your copy of *Far From the Madding Crowd* at the house."

Damn! I was rambling…

"Damn, I'm sorry—I'm rambling."

"And so you call long distance to tell me I left my book at your place," she said in her sweet teasing voice, the one I loved. "Ever the shining knight, Quinn Radcliffe."

"A bit tarnished these days," I joked.

"I find that hard to believe."

"So…how are you?"

"Getting ready for a wedding, but I guess you knew that."

"Yeah; yeah, I glanced at the calendar while straightening up the office, so I thought…"

"Did you call a few days ago? Maybe a week?"

"Guilty."

"Now I know why Donovan mentioned the call for

Bathsheba Everdene."

"Well, I couldn't introduce myself as the guy you'd recently made love to, could I?" I half-jested. The silence on the other side of the Atlantic made me regret that stupid remark. "Alice? Alice, I'm sorry—that was uncalled for. Look, I just wanted to see how you were doing, if you made it home safely, how the new job was going…all that."

"No worries," she said softly in that voice that mesmerized and sent the blood rising, the heart pounding.

"Don't do it."

Not what I had said in August of 1978!

"What? What did you just say?"

"Wait a while; think about it—call it off, postpone it. I think if you really loved this guy and you weren't having second thoughts, we wouldn't have—"

In the background I heard a door slam and a man's voice, the timbre similar to mine, calling Alice.

"Why are you telling me this now? What about what we talked about at the castle? Has something changed…?"

"No; nothing has changed…"

His voice calling Alice was closer and I could hear the scuffing of feet.

"I have to go—bye."

"Alice! Alice, wait…!"

I listened to that hum for the longest time and finally hung up the phone and lay down on the bed, pulling back the comforter and crawling under it. I didn't move until the happy 'chirrup-chirrup' of the telephone woke me around seven the next morning.

"What?" I growled and then yawned into the receiver.

"Morning; it's Graham. You called a seven o'clock rehearsal of the string section for the *Fantasia* before we record. We're here; you're not. Will you be here soon?"

"Shit!" I frowned at the wallpaper across the room, studying the flower patterns while I thought and then I took a deep breath and said into the receiver, "Yeah! Uh, no. No, sorry. Something came up overnight. I've got a family emergency back home; would you take the rehearsal and tell Sir William and Gordon we should have a conference call about the tour. I'll call as soon as I'm settled."

"Is everything okay?" Graham actually sounded concerned, not skeptical.

"No. That's why I have to fly to New York. Family business. I should be back by Friday—ask Thompson to reschedule the studio sessions for Wednesday next, uh, five in the afternoon? Will that work? Yeah, let's make it five."

"If you say so," Graham sighed. "Anything else?"

"A ride to Heathrow, maybe?"

CHAPTER 14

I MANAGED TO get a flight to New York and it wasn't until the Manhattan skyline was below me that I admitted this was a bad idea. It was the worst idea I'd ever thought of. Not even the infamous party at the Savoy the winter of 1975 was as bad as what I intended that August evening, three years later.

Once I got through customs and found my luggage, I brushed through the happy reunions around me and looked for a taxi. It was just my luck that a photographer from the New York Post recognized me and started a cannonade of flashes as he snapped away and got people staring. Now I understood why some people wore sunglasses at night.

"Are you here for the music awards, Mr. Radcliffe?" the photographer shouted at me. "Family business," I grumbled, sweeping past and hailing a cab that glided to the curb. I threw myself into the back seat after the luggage. "Plaza," I yawned at the driver, my body and mind realizing it had been almost twenty-four hours since I last slept.

My sudden appearance at the Plaza Hotel didn't bat a single eyelash on any of the staff, least of all the concierge. A bell hop materialized out of nowhere and the concierge handed over a key to one of the better suites. "Are you in town for the music awards, Maestro?" he queried cheerfully.

"Yes, I suppose I am," I yawned, adding, "Pardon

me."

"Long flight?"

"My arms are tired."

The joke went over him at first and then he chuckled with a soft, "Aha!" as I followed the bell hop to the elevators.

Now what?

I had one day, if I was going to do anything at all. One day.

I fell asleep as soon as my face hit the pillows and my last thought was this is the very worst of ideas...

The wake-up call in the morning had me feeling no different. Through a shower, breakfast and pacing for an elevator, I was truly convinced this was a mistake, and I was risking my career for something and someone I could no longer have.

Then I saw the morning news.

The television in the lobby was switched on by an employee as I walked through and there on the screen was Alice and her fiancé, Doctor Donovan Trist, archeologist. I would meet him a year later almost to the day, but the shock of seeing him would never wear off: a man who looked as if he could be my older brother. Same dark hair and eyes, same chiseled jaw line, same pretty boy handsome looks, though I had a few inches in height on him, and I had what Alice called the 'swimmer's build' of broad chest and shoulders, small waist with the long arms and legs. Trist looked...ordinary. Our differences lie in personality and self-love. He had enough self-love for both of us.

Ordering a cup of coffee, I occupied one of the overstuffed chairs and never took my eyes from the screen.

The morning news anchor was gushing over this 'wedding of the century' for New York and Providence society. After all, the eligible bachelor being taken off the market was the only son and heir of the senate majority leader, a man being groomed for the presidency, and his ex-wife, who was the heiress to a banking fortune and owner of an award winning sports franchise. The bride, the anchor read from her notes, was a history professor from Brown University, and this spectacular wedding would take place at The Cloisters tomorrow, Saturday, the last weekend of August.

Of course . . . The Cloisters.

I knew where the idea had come from.

"Here's your coffee,"

It wasn't the hotel staff member handing me a steaming, fragrant cup of coffee that woke me up, but Alice and we sitting on the back porch steps of her house in Berkeley. It was the morning after my return from England in 1970 and hours after the confrontation with my parents. A glance at the sky told me it was almost sunrise.

"You okay?" Alice was sitting one step below me. She took a sip from her own mug and turned, waiting for a response.

"I was the one who upset you. Are you okay?"

"Maybe I overreacted, Quinn."

"I shouldn't have assumed anything, especially since..."

I took a sip of coffee and let the sentence die as I watched a flock of birds cut through the yard.

"Since?"

"Since I'm the arrogant bastard here."

"Arrogant, sometimes. Bastard never - or maybe you're a changeling or adopted since you're nothing like your parents."

That made us both laugh and I had summoned the courage to lean in for a kiss that fulfilled my hopes of sweetness and redemption.

"We *slept* together!" she giggled.

"I know, and we *slept*!" I laughed. "No one would believe it if they knew."

"Certainly not Dennis."

"God forbid you're not being respectable, Prince Charming," I mimicked Dennis and we both laughed. I knew I'd been shrived of my sin when Alice moved up a step and snuggled against me. "Had an interesting dream, last night," I said then.

"Was Dennis chasing you with a shotgun? That was mine."

"No, but it was strange, though. I dreamt we got together."

Her eyes widened and she turned pink with a blush. "Like doing it? Having sex?"

"Wow! What kind of dreams do you have, and why don't I know about them? No . . . you'd think it was silly."

"C'mon...let me decide that," she whispered, moving in for another kiss.

"Okay, buy don't laugh. Or worse, run away. I dreamed...I dreamt we got married."

First she frowned, and then arched her brows. Her silence was an indication I should have kept my dream to myself. Then she smiled and shook her head. "Wow," she said. "I always thought it was the girl who thought about weddings and stuff. Really, Quinn?"

"Really. Funny thing is, you're in some medieval-looking dress and we're in a medieval chapel in New York City, if there is one."

"There is—the Cloisters. It's a museum with just medieval art and it's a place I've always wanted to visit."

"Well," I said, pulling her closer, "maybe when we're out of school we can get married in a place like that."

"Now you're making fun of me. Don't tease," she groused.

"I'm not. I'm serious. I'm not teasing."

"The Cloisters? Really?"

"The Cloisters. Maybe by the time comes around you'll be a famous history professor and I'll be conducting the New York Philharmonic, or the San Francisco

Symphony and we'll rent out The Cloisters."

"The Cloisters. Wow."

It wasn't my faery princess commenting now, but the morning news anchor as her fast delivery of the news story brought me back to the Plaza and the lounge where I sat in an overstuffed chair and drank my coffee and watched the interview with Dr. Donovan Trist.

To hear my evil twin go on, one would think he had thought of and created everything that this magical weekend would hold, including love and the institution of marriage.

Oh yes, he was mightily pleased with himself, crowing about this obscure young woman from California; he saved her from a life of poverty and encouraged the History Department at Brown to hire her. Worse still, his mother, the senator's plastic ex-wife in designer clothes and pearls with her hair pulled back so tightly she didn't need a face lift, simpered and gazed adoringly at her son and ex-husband like it was a political campaign stump and said her future daughter-in-law was sweet and charming and as far as the young women today were concerned, more than adequate to take the ancient family name of Trist, a name brought over on the Mayflower. As if anyone cared about that any more. Landed gentry they presumed to be, they probably checked Alice's teeth and had a team of midwives examine her for fertility, had the CIA or other national security teams do a background check to root out any leftist leanings that might interfere with their political ambitions.

And where was the bride-to-be during this puff piece?

"Call for Mr. Radcliffe!"

The desk clerk's shout made me pull away and go find out what it was. He smiled and pushed a courtesy telephone at me.

"Hello?" I asked into the receiver after a moment of trepidation. Did I tell the orchestra where'd I be? I couldn't remember. Surely my father didn't know I was in the States…

"What the hell do you think you're doing? This is not part of the greater scheme!"

It was Herself the Proprietress, and she used the same tone as my always disapproving father.

"Aren't I supposed to make amends, change things?" I demanded.

"Leave at once and come back! You are going to jeopardize everything! Do it at once!"

"No."

"What? Did you just say no?"

"You heard me."

"I cannot protect you or her from the consequences if you interfere at this time, Quinn. Just be patient…"

"Again, didn't you want me to make amends?"

"Yes, but…"

"But nothing. You put me here, now deal with it!"

I hung up and went back to my chair and coffee.

The news story continued with a reporter and camera crew at The Cloisters. They showed a beautiful August morning with the sun coming up over the medieval buildings of the museum in northern Manhattan, set on a hill in Fort Tryon Park. Florists and wedding planners had already descended upon the venue; no matter that the wedding was a day away. Trist money made it happen.

I wondered what else their money would buy as I left the hotel and grabbed a taxi that soon was on the George Washington Bridge and heading towards the Henry Hudson Parkway. No one paid attention to yet another Yellow Cab pulling up at the main entrance of a museum. There was too much activity for anyone to care about another curiosity seeker slipping past the perimeter of barricades being set up.

Secret Service agents suddenly appeared, followed by Senator Martin Trist of Rhode Island, a woman in her thirties draped on his arm and wearing an incredible amount of jewelry; next came the senator's ex-wife Arielle and her latest husband who was the president of the governing board for the Providence Opera Company, followed by Himself the Groom waving to the photographers and stopping to chat with gawkers at the barricades as if he was a movie star and this was a premiere, and behind him, Dennis and Harry, who looked lost and uncomfortable by all the attention.

Where was Alice?

Local television crews moved in and the party stopped to honor requests for interviews. The Secret Service men whispered into their sleeve cuffs and took positions around them, making it easy for me to go by undetected.

Again, no one seemed to pay attention to the man who wasn't supposed to be there.

Dodging past florists and caterers, museum personnel directing traffic, I nearly sprinted through the corridors and galleries until I found her.

She was seated alone in the Chapter House, sketching her surroundings while stylists and makeup artists hovered and tried to get her attention for a photo shoot. Hanging off a mannequin was a wedding gown of heavy ivory lace studded with pearls and crystals, and a chaplet of silver flowers and a veil. Dennis was right; I did recognize the dress and the crown, for she spent hours designing it.

It was my dress; the dress she was supposed to wear for me.

"Miss Martin, the television crew will be here in twenty minutes; your fiancé promised an exclusive for the evening news," a makeup artist pled.

"I made no promise. I agreed to an hour of photographs and that hour's up," Alice said wearily. "Would you leave me be now? Please?"

"Would you leave us?"

The groom had appeared as if out of nowhere and everyone but Alice left quickly and quietly.

As much as I wanted to leave, I had to stay; I wanted to learn what held these two together, for Alice and her bridegroom were like oil and water. I knew that from conversations with Alice years later; I knew it from our meeting in New York a year from now.

"Can we talk?" he asked after a time spent pacing the room, following the pattern of floor tiles.

"Will you listen?"

The voice. Calm, controlled, but on edge.

"I thought we agreed—"

"No. What we agreed upon, what you and I agreed upon, was a small family gathering with my rector from St. Alban's, not a Roman Catholic priest from Notre Dame. Not this media circus and every single damn wedding consultant from Bloomingdale's to Saks! I told you, Donovan, this is our wedding, not your mother's."

"It's expected, Angel! And face it; you said you didn't have time for the arrangements."

"But I can listen to suggestions, and give an opinion— or is that not important to you? Since when did I ask for the string section from the New York Philharmonic? What happened to the classical guitarist?"

"We've been over this; something like this is expected of my family—and it certainly will help with the election, and Father can use all the help he can get."

"Rich boy marries poor girl? Pygmalion come to life? Show the world that the Trist family is just like everyone else?"

"If we made it a quiet affair after all the press, the arrangements, people would wonder and talk."

"What's expected tomorrow is that there will be a groom and a bride standing over there." Alice gestured towards the east end of the Chapter House. "I wouldn't place any money on that right now!"

"Running back to California again won't solve anything."

"Who said I was going to California?"

"Mother heard your conversation with Dennis."

"Your mother does a lot of eavesdropping and nosing

about where she doesn't belong."

Alice got up to leave but he caught her in his arms and tried—and finally succeeded—in kissing her.

"Yes, and you gave her reason not to trust you last year while you were in England," he hissed. "Not to mention your bridegroom!"

I felt sick and wanted to leave for the perverse curiosity that brought me here was turning to resentment. As I wheeled, Janis Joplin blocked my exit.

"No; you insisted on coming here. Stay," she ordered quietly.

"I wasn't expecting this," I whispered hoarsely and none too quietly.

"Who's out there?" the groom demanded, uneasy, turning in our direction. "Not more damn photographers!"

"You invited them; what do you expect?" Alice sighed.

I turned to tell Janis to make herself scarce—for how would one explain the presence of a woman dead almost nine years—and tried to slip away myself, but Alice saw me.

I would never forget the look on her face, nor the pain that I both felt and saw.

CHAPTER 15

SOMEHOW I MANAGED to escape The Cloisters without the Secret Service and New York Police Department on my heels. Once out on the street, I grabbed a bus to midtown and my hotel and hid for the rest of the day, drowning my childish misery in gin and tonics, heavy on the gin.

"When did you start drinking?" Jimi Hendrix asked me when he appeared out of the page of a Rolling Stone issue I'd left on the suite's living room coffee table the night before. "You, Little Prince with the perfect morals?"

"Hey, I'm nowhere near perfect."

"No argument with that, except with the music,"

"Well, there's that." I topped off the highball with another inch of gin and went to the bar for more ice. "I started drinking while in England and then and now it seemed like the best first aid for all sorts of wounds, don't you think?" The ice in the glass, I turned to salute the best damn guitarist in the world and found he was gone. Just as well, I liked drinking alone.

There was a knock on the door late and just as I was staggering to bed. I paused for a moment before going to the door. As drunk as I was, I knew Alice didn't know where I was, nor my father—unless that photographer sold his shot of me to the Times or Post. Even so I was hopeful and wary as I carefully opened the door just wide enough to see who was on the other side, and exhaled fumes of alcohol when Edward IV and Janis Joplin entered the room with a restaurant trolley piled with covered dishes.

"Christ's Blood and Bones! What toxic brew are you drinking?" Edward said, wincing.

"Nolet's Reserve Dry Gin. If you're going to die, die happy I say."

"Not yet, Little Prince. You've got unfinished business with just about everyone," Janis said, taking the highball and upending it down her throat. "Tastes like mouthwash."

"All the more for me," I snapped, grabbing my glass.

"We thought you might want something to eat to soak up that mead or whatever it is you're drinking. Besides, drinking alone is never a good idea even in the best of circumstances," Edward said breezily as he pushed the trolley into the living room and stopped it right at the coffee table. "You'll want this here, I suppose?"

"She sent you, didn't she?" I wanted to know, even though I didn't.

"The questions you ask. Of course she did. I didn't want to come, but we all have to do our bit to help each other," Edward chattered as he served up a late night dinner of ravioli and sausages—my favorite. "I don't mind telling you that when it was my turn, Peter Abelard was of no help whatsoever. Here you are."

"Served by a king," I chuckled, slumping down on the sofa with my plate so that the tomato sauce splattered on the white wool like drops of blood. "Why do I have all the luck?"

"You don't, and don't kid yourself, kiddo," Janis commented on her way to the wet bar.

"You were warned," Edward said, handing me a napkin. "You were told not to bother right now and not at this time. Now look what you've done."

"What I–?" I sputtered and more tomato sauce fell on the sofa. "What the hell are you talking about? I didn't want to show up in that village, nor take this scarier-than-hell ride down memory lane. I had no say in it."

"Didn't you?"

"No, I didn't."

Edward sat across from me on the other sofa and sniffed the highball on the coffee table, wrinkled up his nose and shook his head before setting the glass down.

"Yes you did," Janis interjected when she returned with a cup of coffee that she shoved at me. "It's coffee, all right?" she snapped when I looked at it suspiciously and then sniffed, just to be sure.

"You saw what happened. If you had waited another hour, even to the next day...oh well, sometimes there's no hope for it or for people." Edward continued. "Finish your supper; we have to take you back."

"Not going."

Janis sighed. "Ned, I told you this would happen."

"Oh, very well; do what you must," Edward said.

She leaned over me and gave me the most incredible kiss I'd ever experienced. I literally went limp and was sure I was dying from the experience. For I felt weightless as if I were floating and suddenly I was propelled through a tunnel of white and mauve clouds at the end of which was the White Light.

Yes.

The bright white glow that I'd read about or heard in stories of people with near-death experiences. Even Alice.

Alice!

Maybe now was the chance, or time. Wasn't the light supposed to herald a change or new beginning? I began to feel euphoric and I laughed, sensing this was my time and the journey was over. All the things I would say and do, the promises.

And then the glow started changing—to hues and swirls of color like liquid food coloring dropped in water, spattering and splashing as I fell and tumbled, sailed and rolled and finally landed in my own bed at home in Berkeley on that horrible Christmas night of 1971.

"*No!*"

The linens still smelled of Alice's perfume and just as I was ready to give in to remorse and tears the light rap on the door warned me that Mother had come to smooth things over.

"Quinn? Are you awake?"

Pressure on the bed told me she'd crossed the room and sat on Alice's side. I feigned sleep and indifference only until I felt the familiar touch of her hand in my hair. It was no longer comforting.

"I was asleep, thanks," I growled.

"Darling, your father's thinking of the big picture, the future. And can you blame him? Not even he had the opportunities you've had. He doesn't want you to throw them away and neither do I. If Alice and you are meant to be, you'll will withstand the separation necessary while pursuing a career."

"Don't expect pity and don't tell me he's jealous. C'mon, Mother; your lies used to be more creative."

"It's not a pack of lies. Darling, something's come up. We couldn't say anything in front of Alice. Here."

I saw the envelope she was holding out of the corner of my left eye, the flash of gold from the bracelet on her wrist as it caught the nightstand light. Mother waved it impatiently and I sat up, grabbing the envelope.

It was a letter addressed to me from the Royal Philharmonic Orchestra, from the Board of Directors and it had been opened, stained with coffee rings. The letter was three weeks old.

"You opened my mail?" I demanded. "If anything, getting married and moving out will give me some privacy." I grabbed the reading glasses I'd started to wear from the nightstand and unfolded the letter, the news before me overwhelming—and I didn't understand. I held the letter out to her. "What is this? What did you do?"

"Well, an opportunity showed itself and your father wasn't going to let it slip away. We couldn't say anything while Alice was here. We were going to make it a Christmas present. We weren't expecting your news."

I held the letter in front of Mother's face. "Tell me what this is?"

"One of the opera symphony musicians mentioned in passing that there was a chair open with the Royal Philharmonic and your father made some calls, took a meeting or two, and there you have it."

"It says that I have been given a provisional chair with the orchestra. Since when does a musician get a chair handed to him when he doesn't audition?" I demanded quietly.

My mother studied my face for a moment and then touched my cheek running a finger along stubble of my five-o'clock shadow. I moved away, repulsed. "Eventually you'll learn that artistry and talent aren't the only means of getting ahead, Quinn. Really; I thought you'd be happy about this."

I scanned the letter. "It says," I ran a finger down the last paragraph. "It says that I am required to report for work on January fifteenth. 'Failure to do so will revoke the provisional chair and no exceptions will be made.' I am allowed to continue my studies at Oxford and arrangements will be made to accommodate my studies— well, thank you very much for that!"

"You've only one year left in your studies at Oxford. This will give you the edge on the competition," my mother chatted breezily. "And if they decide, you'll be given a contract as long as you fulfill this obligation, and the orchestra will make you a full member, a full salary— but for now, it's the only way in."

"*What?*"

"Another opportunity like this won't come around again. A lot of effort and work have been put into the arrangements."

I couldn't believe my ears. I crumpled the letter into a ball and threw it into the fireplace and walked over to stir the embers and watch it ignite and blaze. "You know how long I've wanted this," I said after a time. "And to put conditions on something I should have been able to work for through normal channels like everyone else is wrong."

"If you hadn't botched the New York audition—"

"Oh to hell with that, Mother! When are you going to let go of my mistakes? This is blackmail."

"This is reality."

I stabbed at the log in the fire to stir up flames, watch different sparks fly. When I threw the poker down embers leapt from the hearth and I now stamped out the ones that had fallen on the throw rug. "So what you're really saying is that I take this provisional chair or I kiss my chances with the Royal goodbye."

"Exactly."

Now I made a theatrical turn to face my mother. She was a few inches away, but the look on my face must have warned her, for she moved away and for effect or avoidance started organizing the items on desk, paying particular attention to a framed photograph of Alice. "Well, let's be honest here. How much of this is a move to get Alice out of the picture?" I wanted to know. She didn't respond. The crackling of the fire, the sound of Brahms coming up from Father's study below, and the sound of items being shuffled on the desk were magnified by her silence. "Mother? I would expect an honest answer from you. Is it because of who she is, what she comes from? Her brother?"

Still no response.

"I guess all of it. Despite your kindness and friendliness, it isn't hard to figure out you don't approve of Alice," I said quietly. "This is a way to get rid of her."

"Consider one against another," she said at last. "What you think is true love and a career you know is possible. That's not a decision your father and I can make for you."

"I thought you just said this was something that could only be offered once? If my career is so sure and possible, why go to such lengths to nail it down? And who are you to tell someone about the right decisions when you've been living a lie for so many years?"

She spun around to the door. "Again, there's a choice between so-called true love and a career you've spent in preparation for most of your life. I won't be the villainess here and make the decision for you."

"I thought you already did!" I called out as she left.

The door thudded quietly as it shut; the whisper of shoes on carpet fading as Mother went down to tell him the deed had been done. How must it feel to be a stoic wife of Sparta? She certainly had the role down.

A gleam of metal on the floor caught my attention while I stood in the middle of the floor pondering my future. I pushed aside the throw rug with my toe and found one of Alice's hairpins—the one with crystals in the shape of a flower on the end. She could never be in this room without leaving something of herself, I thought, smiling, twirling the pin between two fingers so that it caught the firelight.

I would never forget what I did next and I'd always regret it.

"And what was that?"

Glancing up from my study of the hairpin, Richard III had taken a seat at my table in The Shop. He pushed a cup of coffee in my direction and a plate of freshly toasted Pop Tarts.

"There were a lot of things I regret," I answered, looking out the window at the high street, hoping to see Alice there, be anywhere but where I was.

"Your Grace, don't play the therapist," the Proprietress called out. "He knows what he did."

One by one, people in The Shop turned to look at me. Jimi stopped plucking out chords on the Stratocaster and Edward IV gave up trying to flirt with Jane Austen. Hildegard crept closer and placed a single white rose on the table, whispering, "Great love brings an even greater love."

"I didn't have a choice—not then," I said. I looked at Richard and smiled weakly. "Two wrongs make a right – no they don't. Let's call it and let go of me. It ends now."

"No!"

Every voice was against me. The Proprietress crooked her finger and I went to the counter where she took down a box decorated with vines and roses, an ornate 'Q' carved in the middle of the lid. The lid was thrown back and an opal of incredible size and beauty glowed as if taking in the light around it.

"Opals are bad luck," the Proprietress said sweetly. "But that's nothing new for you. Bad luck, that is."

She dropped the opal in my hand and it started to grow warm and glow even brighter, and then something even more strange—though I'd have thought by now that nothing surpassed strange in the village—the opal began to ring like a bell that softly and gradually became the clicking signal of a telephone connection that carried me back to my bedroom on Christmas night in 1971.

It took forever for someone to answer the rings.

"Please, please, please not be home; please be asleep. Please, please, please…!" I whispered fretfully.

"Hello?"

Alice had picked up.

"Hello?" she demanded. "Hello? Who is this?" Her voice was strained and tired, hoarse, as if she'd been crying.

Without saying a word, I hung up the phone.

In the morning I left for England.

CHAPTER 16

I GOT MY wish. I was finally able to live in England away from my parents. Strange how dreams come true and they don't end up the way you thought they might. I'd commuted from London to Oxford and back for the orchestra internship and finished my degree at the university with honors, of course. I settled in London and waited for the meeting with the Music Director that would give me a permanent chair in the string section. Towards that end I attended every class I could, practiced well past the obligatory eight hours, showed up on time and only spoke when prompted by the conductors, concert master, section leads and anyone with any influence in the orchestra organization. The other members of the orchestra stayed away, and I didn't blame them for in their shoes, I'd be suspicious or downright hate someone who showed up and was handed a spot for which others were in competition. Their eyes were on me whenever I entered or left the rehearsal hall, and when the conductor or concert master gave me praise. It never occurred to any of them to say hello or ask me how I was getting on. The few times I tried to socialize were miserable failures and only made matters worse, and it didn't help that I was shy. I learned the hard way that I wasn't the center of the universe no matter what my parents had fed me. I was learning to get by.

I had already given up on hope. Letting go of happiness wasn't too far behind, having made sure of that when I went home in the early winter of 1972 to break it off with Alice. But what choice did I have? No one would believe me if I told them the truth; no one would have listened to what I thought at the time were sound and valid reasons. I was a mess. I didn't want that disease to spread to the one person in the world that I loved. I didn't want her to take care of me, nurse me through life while putting her life on hold indefinitely.

No, no one would have believed my sad existence and what I'd gone through in twenty years. They'd have given me sympathetic stares and shake their heads in pity—and then whisper, avoid me, take something horrible and turn it into gossip or a tabloid headline, *The Tragic Life of Tarquin Radcliffe, the Loss of Promise.*

Within months of arriving in London, life fell into a predictable routine governed by schedules. When I wasn't in orchestra rehearsals I took classes to improve my technique and went to auditions for solo parts, taught music at a local school to supplement a meager income, sent letters of regret to Alice that were never answered and tossed the ones from my parents unopened into the rubbish bin.

Greenwich could adjust their clocks by the life I had chosen to lead.

It took a party at the Savoy to make the paradigm shift that set everything in motion.

"It's the American bloke; the sod from California."

I heard the none-too-subtle comment as I shouldered my way into the pub after a full day of master classes and rehearsal and avoided eye contact with just about everyone I passed to get to a booth at the back of the common room. I knew what they thought; I didn't like myself either in those days. Scores of struggling musicians with better credentials looked over because I had parents who knew people and were owed favors of one kind or another. As soon as the Music Director made his decision and it happened to be me, I had a feeling it would be payback time. Worse yet, I'd sold out. I'd sold my soul to get ahead.

When the waiting was over, I would find Alice and make it up to her.

Oh, wait...

I found an empty booth and shoved my cello case on to one seat and slid over on the opposite. The girl Judy appeared out of nowhere as she always did, always smiling, always nice to me.

"Usual, Quinn?"

"Yeah."

"Radcliffe!"

I looked up from my paper and saw Chloe Carlisle pushing her way through the crowd at the bar, waving, holding her beer over her head. I pushed the cello case aside to make room for her as she plopped down and took a deep drink of her beer.

"Radcliffe, I've been in four pubs looking for you—damned hot in here."

"Hi, Carlisle. Have you eaten?" I offered when Judy brought my dinner.

"Thanks, but yes. Glad I caught you up. I wanted to tell you about the do at the Royal Albert on Friday—the orchestra's throwing a fundraiser and it looks good if the members, especially the new boys and girls, show up," Chloe said between drags off a cigarette.

"This is the first I've heard of it," I said.

"Well, of course it would be; that crowd doesn't go out of its way to make a girl or boy feel welcome." Chloe nodded in the direction of the bar where senior orchestra musicians were laughing and having drinks together, basking in the idolatry of the juniors and classical music fans gathered. "Maybe we could show up together—be the other's courage? It's the kind of event where you are paraded about and sized up. Plainly put, it makes or breaks musicians."

"And here I thought practicing twelve hours a day was a way to get ahead."

"See you then? Eight o'clock at the Royal Albert—

Friday!"

Chloe disappeared into the crowd again and I couldn't help but think that she acted like a girl getting a prom invitation.

Oh God, did she think...?

I avoided her the next day, ignoring cheery greetings and attempts to make eye contact as I went to my chair and set up for the rehearsal. The conductor noticed me and left his conversation with the concert master to come over and say, "You've got it. Congratulations."

The adrenaline rush hit me hard and I swallowed and nodded, whispered my thanks. It couldn't have been more uncomfortable when I noticed the First Chair hadn't shown up for rehearsal and when the orchestra was assembled the announcement was made and met with complete silence. That I was a full member of the orchestra wasn't the only news.

I was First Chair of my section. The concert master turned and smiled and nodded toward the empty chair.

Getting up and walking over a space to the chair and music stand, taking my music and things with me, was the longest walk I'd ever taken.

For the next seven hours I ignored the stares and didn't make eye contact except with the conductor when I launched into the cello solo in the *Adagio*, the second movement of Haydn's Symphony Number Thirty-Six.

I was prepared for this. Only yesterday I'd run through it with the concert master at his request; I'd studied it and went over the adagio for at least three hours last Saturday night.

No one said a word when we finished that night, but as I was leaving the rehearsal studio Chloe scrambled to put out her cigarette, smiled and took a few steps in my direction when I came into the street.

"That was amazing, Radcliffe," she greeted.

"Thanks," I mumbled.

"I bet you think the whole day was pretty amazing,"

she added.

Nodding, I chuckled and felt my face burning. "Not what I expected," I laughed.

"Well, I'll see you tomorrow then," she said starting to go.

"See you around—Chloe."

"Oh, and don't let those bastards in there make your life hell. You earned that chair, that's what I think, and so do others."

She waved and started to fumble in her purse until she found her cigarettes again, heading east up Kensington Road.

"Chloe!" I ran as quickly as I could to catch her up. Carrying a satchel of scores and the cello hindered any chance of it, but fate—or the Proprietress—was kind and the light changed so that she was still waiting at the corner when I finally joined her. "You want to grab a bite to eat?" It came out breathless and needy.

"You and me?" she sounded incredulous.

"Sure—unless you have plans…"

"Uhhhh…"

"Oh. You're with someone."

"Not at present, but I'm interested in someone else and I was going to meet up."

"Julian, in the brass section."

"Anna, pianist."

"Ohhhhh. Man, am I dense."

"No. And for your information, I go where the wind blows. Don't know if it'll be Anna or Julian, or both, Tuesday next and wouldn't that be fun? Now you. You're friendly when you want to be, and sweet. And you have that scent of unrequited love all over you. Puts a girl off."

The light changed and we walked silently across the road. I made ready to go further east, to my flat in Raphael Street when she pulled me back. "Anna will understand," Chloe said. "I think you need to talk and she says that one of my best qualities is that I'm a good listener."

So began my friendship with Chloe Carlisle. We walked over to a pub on Kensington Road, one where we wouldn't run into the Orchestra crowd. Once we had fish and chips and bangers and mash before us, Chloe handed me a napkin and smiled. "Who is she—or is it a he?"

"I get so tired of that question!" I laughed bitterly.

"You're dishy, dreamy, and sexy – you could go both ways. Just ask half the orchestra, especially the woodwind section."

"That conjures up all sorts of disturbing scenarios," I said and pushed the malt vinegar towards her.

"That isn't an answer to my question."

"Her name is Alice Martin and I left her to come here," I said at last. "I put my career first."

There in a noisy, crowded pub, I emptied my heart to a stranger and told my story. We weren't strangers for long.

"Can I just say you're a bastard, Quinn Radcliffe?" Chloe asked as we finished the basket of chips and dug around for the last bits of batter and salt.

"I am, and it's not something Alice isn't thinking right now – if she's thinking about me at all."

"Do you do that all day? Think about her? Wondering what if?"

I hesitated, then lied, "No; I'm finally getting on with my life."

"Throwing your passion into your music – it shows."

"Can't argue there, Carlisle. It's an explosion, a release. I always feel like I've run a marathon or whatever when the piece is done."

"Oh my," Chloe sighed, looking at me with large, oval, spectacularly blue eyes as she leaned her cheek against her palm.

I walked her to the Underground. "See you around, Carlisle," I said, shaking her hand. "Thanks for an interesting evening."

"The evening's over? I was hoping you'd like to

channel that energy and passion," Chloe replied as the train pulled up.

It had been a while and she was intriguing, very pretty, and didn't play games. I jumped into the car with her and stumbling against her as I reached for my balance against a truncheon we kissed.

At her flat it was the usual awkward fumbling to get her out of her clothes and me out of mine, but we eventually landed in bed and it was a sweet experience. Not exactly the explosions and whatever that I was hoping for, but I did think Chloe was pleased, judging by her smile and the way she wrapped her curvy, muscular, body around mine afterwards.

"God, Radcliffe! I don't doubt Alice Martin is thinking about that every night. I know I will."

"Good to know," I laughed and pulled her closer.

Then came the inevitable silence between two people still unknown to one another, when one tried to think of something else to say other than 'This was nice,' the sounds of our breathing, the traffic in London and the ticking of a clock filling a void. I was dozing off when she said, "Stay the night, Quinn, but I hope you don't think that I'll hold you to anything – or this is exclusive."

"Understood. Anna or Julian or Anna and Julian. Don't want to ruin that, do I?"

We laughed and so began a very different relationship and friendship for me. Over the next year we met for coffee, dinners, trips up to York with and without her lover Anna—or Julian, depending on whether it was Tuesday. Never sex. It was as if she knew I was shut down and emotionally unavailable, unapproachable. I was fine with that, for her friendship was more important, hard as that might be to believe of a man in the 1970's. With Chloe Carlisle I could open up if I wanted to, and I at last had a true friend in England.

And then came the New Year's Eve Party at the Savoy.

If we had it to do over, we would has risked disciplinary action or dismissal rather than go to that damn party.

It was a star-studded event that, like the fundraiser earlier that year, made or broke careers and it was a mandatory event. Show up or get fired. We didn't have a say in the matter. And this was one thing I couldn't turn around because it would have altered too many peoples' lives.

Chloe met me at the hotel entrance and nodded in approval when she saw the tux. "They'll be in disco night polyester," she remarked and nodded towards a limousine that rolled up and deposited several orchestra members in their best attempts at Annabel's, Berkeley Square. She had cleaned up nicely herself: the dress had a low, square neckline like one of those Tudor dresses and showed off her amazing figure. The blue of the silk matched her eyes and went well with the short, curly hair that was sprinkled with glitter.

"Shall we?" I invited, offering my arm to Chloe.

As we nodded at the doorman and greeted others on the way to the ballroom, that overwhelming sensation of travel, of being out of my body and floating took over. Yes! I would not have to relive one of the worst nights of my life! I could go home, I could...

I could be feeling the effects of the cold medication I'd taken.

The hat check girl looked suspiciously like Jane Austen and she glared as we passed my overcoat and Chloe's cape across the counter. "Play it through, Mr. Radcliffe. It's the only way," she said under her breath when Chloe stepped away to check her appearance, and before I could respond, Jane had gone into the back of the cloak room and came out as the Proprietress. I knew that was an argument I couldn't win.

"Christ! Looks live every TV presenter and every personality from BBC 2 is here!" Chloe grumbled. She had stopped at the entrance to the ballroom and I almost tripped on the hem of her gown. The dizziness didn't help. Fortunately no one was watching or interested since Penelope Stanhope, Lady Talton, had arrived on the arm of the Music Director and everyone within an inch of her was fawning or at least trying to suck up to the extraordinarily beautiful young woman who was engaged to a royal cousin in line for the throne.

"She's all right," Chloe sniffed, noticing my preoccupation with the delectable Lady Talton.

"All right?" I demanded. "How many chances do you get to meet a goddess?"

"You're the best looking man in the room. A fiver says you go over there and make an ass of yourself trying to charm the Goddess Pen."

"And if I don't?"

Chloe winked at me and got close enough so that I could count the number of freckles across the bridge of her perfect, straight, nose. "That's up to you," she purred.

I was game. "Okay, if I make an impression on her we'll have a good and proper snog."

"You and the future Queen of England?"

"No; you and me. Tonight. I know I've got a chance with you."

The blush spread over her breasts, neck and face. "I get it—trying to get me to change my mind about Anna," she said in a sultry, playful, whisper.

"No, Julian."

"No reason to feel inadequate, Mr. Radcliffe."

"Done."

"Don't spit in your hand, Quinn. A deal's a deal."

I used the hand to smooth back my hair and straighten my tie, blow a puff of air into the palm to check if the mouthwash was still working. Chloe blew a kiss as I marched off.

Whether by luck or by art, the men circling Penelope backed off as the Music Director looked up when I approached and waved me forward. "Lady Talton, may I present our rising star, Tarquin Radcliffe; the soloist for the Haydn this evening." He made the introduction and I smiled at the diminutive, absolutely gorgeous woman standing before me. Her eyes really were the color of violets and everything about her was perfection and exactly how she looked in photographs. I seldom dated blondes but for her I would make an exception.

"Ah," she greeted. "Mr. Radcliffe."

"Lady Talton. This is an honor."

I took the hand offered and was pleased mine was neither timorous nor slick with sweat.

"Is that a northern accent?" she wanted to know, the voice rising as she made a flirtatious tilt to her head.

"I still have it? Then my cover's blown," I teased.

"I'm sorry if I embarrassed you, Mr. Radcliffe, it wasn't my intention. It's just that I've never heard a voice quite like yours – an intriguing accent."

She was flirting and I was glad to have made the bet with Chloe. How lucky could a guy get?

"I live in California. Well, I've been living in California since I was ten," I explained—as if she really cared. But the way she was hanging on to every word and looking at me was encouraging. I continued, "My father and his parents are from York, my mother from Dorset; I was born in York, but like I said, I've lived in California since I was ten."

"Why on Earth would you want to be here if you could live there?" she asked seriously.

Our conversation continued with banter about the differences between California and Yorkshire and the struggles of classical musicians in the pop-dominated music industry. The board members and donors looked pleased that I had attracted her attention. It would be good for business, no doubt, and I was the man of the hour especially when the band started to play and she accepted my offer to dance. We were soon gliding onto the dance floor with a cannonade of flashbulbs in our wake. Reporters were trying to get my attention as we slow-danced to *You've Lost That Lovin' Feeling*. It seemed I was the only orchestra member to have their photograph taken with Lady Talton that night and the woman whose silence was as legendary as Greta Garbo's, the woman who might be Queen of England someday, had been seen flirting and talking to an orchestra nobody.

"Wonderful! Our faces will be all over the *World* and *Tattler* in the morning, and I'll have to spend hours explaining myself. I told them no, but they made me show up," Penelope griped as she closed her eyes to yet another photographer.

"They?"

"The Duke my fiancé and his overbearing family."

"I suppose in time you get used to it and pretend they're not around," I said nonchalantly.

"It comes with the job description," she sighed.

"Then you won't mind if I try some evasive maneuvers, Lady Talton?"

"Call me Penny—it's the least you can do if you succeed in shaking off these jackals," she laughed.

We glided in between other guests, using them as a screen, slowly dancing towards a corner. By that time our maneuver proved successful and Penelope's escort started searching the ballroom.

"Oh dear, the Lady Talton has gone missing!" Penelope giggled.

"I'm not going down to Scotland Yard for this, am I?" I whispered as we ducked when the escort detail and a photographer approached in search of her.

"Maybe the Tower," she said breezily and we started to laugh. "My God, I haven't had this much fun in ages!"

"A pleasure to be of service, ma'am!"

"I am in your debt."

"Not really."

"Here's payment."

She kissed me and without thinking, I returned the favor. I didn't expect to be kissed back, twice, or to have those kisses stir everything dying inside of me.

We slipped away up a flight of stairs and found a corridor of locked hotel rooms, but there was a bathroom available with a large, antique tub—one of those big-as-a-boat jobs with feet. I jumped in and pulled Penelope down on top of me.

I couldn't believe how easy this was and every indication led me to believe Penelope was enjoying this seduction. She was working her magic on me, too, and we were about to seal the deal when the shower curtain was yanked back and Chloe smiled down at us.

"Hold on, the bet was with me, Radcliffe!" she said.

"Then join us," Penelope offered as she struggled out of her gown and was helping me out of my tux. Chloe wasted no time and wrapped herself in a bath sheet before she slid down beside us.

I'd listened to other guys talk about these fantasies, or read about them, but this was real. Oh God, it was real. Two beautiful women were naked and grinding against me, giving pleasure and taking it. I was ready to explode and did just as the bathroom door flew open and a hotel security guard demanded to know what the hell was going on.

Fifteen minutes later we were dressed and in the custody of Buckingham Palace security personnel when the Music Director, Nigel Ernest, entered the crowded bathroom. We were struggling to keep our composure and dignity, but with the champagne and medication in me it was a lost cause. Chloe, however, managed to sober quickly and she tried to impress upon me the seriousness of the situation and what it meant for us.

The Music Director made a quick assessment with narrowed eyes and turned them on me. "Showing us how free love is done in San Francisco, Mr. Radcliffe?" he asked.

"My God, yes!" Penelope giggled. "And if we hadn't been interrupted…"

"Want to go another round, do you?" I suggested.

"Don't make it worse, Quinn. At least pretend to show some respect," Chloe whispered, nudging me.

"Or a little self-control," the Music Director hissed. He now trained his sights on Chloe. "Miss Carlisle, go sober up. We'll talk in the morning about your future with us."

"Oh now wait a minute!" I protested. "This was my idea—I seduced her."

"Not the best use of your talent."

I was going to say she wouldn't agree with him but Chloe shook her head and then punched me in the arm to shut me up. I waited until we were out in the corridor and one of the Buckingham Palace security officers escorted Penelope and Chloe down to the ballroom before making my defense argument.

"It was stupid. I know it; I don't usually act like this."

The Music Director held his hand up for silence. "The stories I heard and read would prove otherwise."

"They're just tabloid gossip, you can ask Miss Carlisle and anyone in the orchestra."

"I thought your judgment better than this, Quinn. In your own time and in your own living you can do what you want and with whomsoever you choose; but to carry on with such immaturity and indiscretion, the Benefactors and members of the Royal Family present and our very future in the balance," the Music Director growled with anger mounting and in a voice loud enough that people were starting to pay attention. "I'd throw you out on your ears in a heartbeat if it weren't for your father. Now make yourself scarce while I'm still in a good mood!"

What he'd said didn't register until he was halfway down the staircase.

"Wait!"

I hurled myself at him, blocking what he'd hoped was

a dignified and discreet exit.

"What about my father?" I demanded.

"Now isn't the time, Radcliffe," said the Music Director as he tried to get past but I held him back.

"What did he say to you? What's he got to do with tonight?"

The Music Director grimaced. "I owed him a favor and let's leave it at that. See you tomorrow. We'll discuss your apology and make a statement to the press then. Get some coffee in you and some sleep."

"No!" I shouted and that got everyone's attention. "Tell me what the hell this is all about!"

The Music Director walked over to the bar, gesturing at me to follow. He ordered two coffees and handed me one. After a thoughtful sip from his cup he said quietly "I received a phone call from your father saying that you were in a bit of mess with a girl at home; he was sure she was pregnant. There was also a problem with drugs and drinking. He said you needed to get out of the States to clear your head, as it were. He wanted to know if we would accommodate you."

"What? Those are fucking lies!"

"No matter; Professor Radcliffe said in no uncertain terms that he could make life difficult if we didn't reach an understanding on helping you with your career. One call led to another, and there you have it. Not exactly the golden child, are you?"

"I didn't ask for this! You're not being fair!"

"It doesn't matter. Your father threatened me and until tonight I thought playing along was a good idea. Goodbye, Quinn. Good night; tell your father he's run out of favors. You'll turn in your resignation after you've made your apology and we've met with the press."

The Music Director finished his coffee and turned to leave. I pushed my way through the ballroom to catch up with him and ignored the advice of people who cared to let it go, move on, sober up; I shook my head at a tearful

Chloe as I brushed past her.

"Quinn—don't! You'll make things worse," she begged.

"How can they be any worse?" I shouted back and pulled her off of me. "Leave me alone!"

The Music Director stopped midway on the Prince Consort Stairs leading down to the street when he heard my shout. How I made it down those many stairs without falling and breaking my neck was amazing. The adrenaline pumping through my system was doing a good job of clearing my head.

"You didn't hear me, Radcliffe?" the Music Director snapped.

"I heard," I panted in between gasps for breath. "Maybe you should listen to me. Yes, I was indiscreet— but don't we all have moments we'd rather forget? This was mine, and there won't be any more, I promise. I think my talent has been proven. I have the drive and the desire to be better than my peers—I've shown that. Whatever my father did and said—that isn't me. I had nothing to do with it. In fact, I almost didn't come here, but that is beside the point I'm trying to make."

Did I say that?

Did I actually make a stand and defend myself?

Oh God, the light was changing…maybe I shouldn't have…but I felt a strength I'd never experienced.

I looked down at the Music Director, hands spread in supplication. I even smiled.

"*Not what you did in 1975!*" my choir of voices, my muses, whispered.

"Get to it; I have another engagement."

"Don't judge me by what my father does. Let's just say tonight was a horrible mistake and get on."

"I believe I did say that in my own words. Good night, Radcliffe. Again, your resignation will be on my desk by the end of business tomorrow afternoon."

The conversation was over.

CHAPTER 17

THE POUNDING ON the door was like cannons firing. I shifted the pillow covering my face to be sure it wasn't an IRA attack somewhere in the neighborhood, or I'd fallen into the Battle of the Somme or the landing at Normandy, and then glanced at the alarm clock when it was obvious that all was clear. Ten-forty-five in the morning. I had nowhere to go and rolled over for another snooze. I was hung over and out of a job.

Still, I let the pounding continue until it reminded me of the soothing *lub-dub, lub-dub* of a mother's heartbeat.

Oh wait; my mother didn't have a heart.

The shouting started next. My name. I didn't have a name, not in the music world. I'd change my name. Make sure no one knew I was related to that bastard. Too bad I wasn't a real bastard, the result of my mother's indiscretion that led to a night of passion.

Oh wait. My mother had no emotion. Those fires had never been lit.

"...Oh dear, he's talking to himself. That's never good, is it?"

The voice was unfamiliar; the faces I recognized. Richard III was standing with arms crossed, Janis Joplin and Hildegard von Bingen were like sentries on either side of the bed and both shushed Jimi Hendrix when he entered the flat. The Proprietress was leaning over me now and raised my right eyelid with a thumb. "He's alive," she sniffed and then flicked my forehead.

"Ow! What was that for?" I whined, trying to bat her away.

"Something to think about other than your hangover."

I sat up, finding myself in my corner in The Shop.

"Fouled things up, didn't you?" Richard said.

"Wait, wait, wait…didn't I apologize? Didn't I try to set things to rights with the director?"

"You weren't supposed to try it there," Jimi sighed.

"Well, if not there…" I yawned, looking from face to face.

"Send him back," Hildegard sighed.

"Don't move me around like a damned piece in a chess game," I protested. "If I'm dead, let me be dead."

"Where's the fun in that?" the Proprietress asked.

"Quinn, darling," Hildegard interrupted her and added a glare at the Proprietress for good measure; "we are here because you are here. Angels won't get their wings, and bells won't ring, but we won't be able to go home until you get it done right."

I frowned and reached for the cup of coffee in front of me. "But…Hildegard, Richard, you were here for Alice, weren't you? Why didn't you leave already?"

"He's got a point," Thomas Wyatt said, joining our circle.

"Half-finished isn't wholly done," Hildegard said quietly.

"So many things left unsaid," Richard added.

"It's getting late."

The unfamiliar voice again. I looked around the others, but there wasn't a new face in the party. Then I looked outside. The Man in Blue was standing at the window. He smiled and raised a hand in greeting.

"Can't be good," sighed Thomas.

Everyone seemed to lose interest in me and went back to whatever they were doing before I came to entertain them. The Proprietress was noisily stamping books and organizing trinkets in their boxes. Hildegard tended her damn flowers and there was Richard with his damn *Times* crossword puzzle. I put a hand on the fret to Jimi's Stratocaster and shook my head when he started to play *Stairway to Heaven*.

"Someone's in a mood," Rafe said to Richard. He pushed my folio of music at me. "I've done as much as I could with this. Maybe you have, too?"

The pages were blank.

I looked up, bemused. "What happened to my work?"

"You finished that. There's more business left undone that needs attention," Rafe said kindly and patted my shoulder.

"Send me back, then."

"You have our blessing," the Proprietress spoke up. When I passed the counter she handed a gemstone to me, something like a pearl that had a mist swilling in its center and its entire surface glowed. "Pay close attention to that, dear boy."

He was still outside when I came into the street, this smiling, handsome man dressed all in navy blue, from turtleneck, to slacks, to full length overcoat and boots. His eyes were intriguing, and almost as dark blue as his clothing.

"Hello," I greeted.

"Quinn! Nice to finally meet you personally," he answered.

"You are…?"

"Michael Arcangelus."

I narrowed my eyes in suspicion. Where were the wings and halo? The blinding white garments and sparkle?

"You don't like the blue?" Michael queried. "I remember hearing that Alice had an idea for you like this."

"Her modern setting of Hamlet," I said absently, still studying the archangel.

"It goes without saying you're a tragic figure. Walk

with me?"

He pointed up the street towards a park near the bridge and I shrugged, following. We walked in silence, smiling at the occasional villager or mouthing a 'hello' when required. I expected some deference or awe, but no one seemed to pay attention to him, despite his beauty and commanding presence.

"Let's just sit," Michael suggested as we arrived at the park. He sat on the one bench available and picked up a twig that had fallen from the tree sheltering us. That in itself was unusual for nothing was ever out of place in the village, except me.

"What if Alice hadn't answered the phone?" he asked now, staring out into the street.

"It would have made no difference," I admitted after a time.

"Bravo! That's the first time you've been honest with yourself. Perhaps now is the time to stop punishing yourself over it."

"The time I wasted, the stupid things I said and did, it would have been a lot different for us," I said.

"Do you think so?"

"Why wouldn't it be? I wouldn't have wondered what if. I would have healed, she would have. No what ifs," I sighed.

Michael handed the twig to me and in doing so, it transformed into a conductor's baton. "What you're admitting, then, is you chose one love over another."

"I didn't say that. I said we would have healed and the wounds wouldn't have festered and always been there, a barrier between us, reminding us."

"There were other wounds—deeper, uglier."

"Those have nothing to do with Alice and me."

"Don't they?"

I wanted to argue but the glint of the sun on the beck caught all of my attention. I watched the waves of liquid sunlight shimmer and dance until I couldn't stand it any longer. "See you later," I said and scrambled up and over to the bridge.

"No doubt of that!" Michael called after me.

Once at the bank of the stream I knelt down and cupped my hands, letting the water glide between my fingers.

I took a drink and discovered it as sweet as ginger ale. The more I drank, the more contented I felt. I splashed my face and decided to dunk my head, for the afternoon was intolerably hot. When I came up for air I was in the bath in my flat the morning after the Savoy disaster. The pounding on the door turned out to be the pounding in my head from the worst hangover in months.

I might have stayed there in the bath all day until my skin shriveled and I looked like a dried apple or walnut shell, but there was only so much wallowing in soapy, self-pity a man could do. While I shaved and dressed I ignored the ringing telephone and the occasional knock on the door, the pleas from Chloe to come to my senses. A breakfast of leftover bangers and mash and the tail of the dog that bit my ass left me feeling no better. A cursory review of the want ads in the Times for musicians didn't help. Finally I picked up the phone and placed the call I'd been dreading.

"Hi...it's me. How've you been?"

That evening I was on plane for San Francisco. A day later, I was standing in the middle of my room at home in Berkeley, having returned to the castle. Nothing had been touched since I'd last been home, almost a year. It was as if they expected me to fail. To come running back home.

The strum across the fret of my guitar made a hollow echo, drifting out the open window, conjured a small cloud of dust to go up. The chord was a signal, for my mother knocked and came in with a stack of laundry to be put away. It was placed on the middle of the bed and she stared at it as if it would find its way into the correct drawers and shelves without any help.

"Thanks," I offered.

She looked startled as if surprised to hear anything from me. "What? For this? It was left in the laundry room and it's been there all this time," Mother said matter-of-factly. She went back to her meditation on the socks and tee shirts. "I'll have Cook make you something for dinner—you probably didn't have much to eat on that long flight."

"I'm only here for a short while," I said as she finally turned to leave. "I'll find a job and move out for good. It would be better for everyone."

"Pork loin roast? That's your favorite, isn't it?" she said going through the study and down the stairs.

Dinner for one was served in the formal dining room. A single setting of Wedgwood china, Waterford crystal and the best silver. A small vase of flowers was placed in the middle of the table and Cook had switched on the radio so that I could listen to light classics. No one noticed when I finished the roast, potatoes and asparagus and slipped out the front door.

A late spring moon was starting up the horizon as I walked down the hill, following the path to Southside, where I had a beer at LaVal's and then wandered across the Graduate Theological Union campus to Rose Street and kept walking until I reached her house.

There was light in the window and Harry's van was parked in front. The front door was open, screen closed to keep out bugs and other pests after a warm day. I wondered which one they'd think I was when I walked up the stairs and pressed the buzzer. A few minutes passed before Harry came to the screen with a bowl and spoon in hand, his dinner preparations interrupted.

"Quinn! My God! Come in, come in—Denny! Denny, you'll never guess…!" Harry exclaimed happily when he pushed the screen open for me to pass through. The scent of cooking, the smells of a family, wrapped me in nostalgia as I followed through to the living room. Harry shoved a pile of laundry off the sofa and tossed it on to the chair. My heart caught in my throat when I saw a familiar blouse, a sweater. "Here, sit. Are you in town to visit?"

"No, I left the orchestra, so I'm here until I figure out what want to do." I lied.

A door slammed upstairs and Dennis came down, rubbing a towel over his wet hair, the room now effused with bath products reminding me of another homecoming not so long ago.

"Hey! Look who's here! How are you?" Denny asked as we shared a guy-pat: three quick pats in a loose embrace.

"Fine, fine. Nothing's changed, I see," I chuckled, glancing around.

"It shows, does it? Don't mind me, I'm baking a cake," Harry said and made a tactful retreat back to the kitchen.

"How long are you in town?" Dennis wanted to know pulling up a chair to sit across from where I positioned myself on the sofa.

"Don't know—I left the orchestra. So I'll be looking for work. Alice home?" I asked, nodding towards a sweater, my favorite one, the one in beiges, blues and peach and brown. She'd knit that and a scarf the winter before we got together. I knew their story. I knew how soft it was. How soft with her wearing it.

"Just missed her," Dennis sighed.

"Oh."

"D'you want her number? Maybe she'd be happy to hear from you."

As much as I wanted to shout yes while I searched the cluttered end table with my eyes for a pen and scrap of paper, as much as I needed to talk to her, I shook my head. "I don't think that'd be a good idea. She's never returned my calls, or,"

"Oh," Dennis sighed, nodding. "I know that look. And the feeling behind it."

"She was mad for weeks," I commented.

"And you wouldn't be? Did you expect her to come running back into your arms and cover you with kisses?" Dennis scoffed.

"She never answered my letters."

"She moved on—maybe."

"I get it, Denny. I get it."

Dennis stood as I did and placed a hand on my arm. What did you expect, Quinn? It might be a good idea to leave things in the past and move on, too."

I swallowed the lump in my throat and said, "There's someone else, I guess."

"If there is, I don't know who he is. Honestly, knowing her schedule and knowing her, she doesn't have the time."

Nodding, I smiled and extended a hand that was grasped in brotherly handshake. "Good seeing you, Denny."

"And you."

"Let her know I stopped by?"

"Sure."

But he didn't.

CHAPTER 18

MY WALK BACK up the hill led me to The Shop. The Proprietress glanced from her busy work at the counter and nodded in the direction of my corner where Dennis sat in his bus uniform drinking coffee with Janis. Neither seemed to notice when I sat down and pulled my own cup closer, folding my hands around the warm bowl as if seeking warmth on a day that was anything but cold. Janis finally acknowledged my presence and moved away, muttering about finding better conversation in a cemetery.

It was Dennis and me. The Proprietress sighed something about flowers in the church and slammed the door behind her. We sipped from our mugs and said nothing until Dennis set his mug down and rubbed his face in weariness.

"Do you suppose she'd be fussing with a temple if you were Buddhist, a synagogue if you were Jewish?" he asked, looking directly at me.

"Most likely." Now I set my mug down near his and let it tap ceramic bowl to ceramic bowl. "You never said a thing to her," I accused.

"The time wasn't right. She was happy, excited about the future, getting her degree, the year off before grad school. I saw no point in throwing a monkey-wrench into the works."

"But you saw how things fell together."

"No, I didn't," he said softly. "Remember? Why do you think I'm here? The worst is yet to come—but you know that."

"I should be going."

"Take the five-thirty train. You'll make it."

I looked where Dennis now pointed and saw the sundial. Fifteen past five. I grabbed my things and ran, waving off the Proprietress, Richard, who had returned from wherever he'd been, and waved off the bouquet of flowers Hildegard shoved at me. I reached the train with moments to spare. An empty compartment was ready, and Jack Lemmon smiled as I negotiated the narrow corridor against a stream of jabbering, happy tourists to reach it and him.

"Afternoon, Mister Radcliffe," Jack Lemmon greeted and rocked on his heels as I dug in the messenger bag for the book of tickets. "I wasn't expecting you for some time to come."

"Some things need to be taken care of, don't they?" I replied cheerfully and sighed with relief when I found the tickets. I rifled through the booklet and was ready to hand an 'A' ticket over when he tapped the back. I flipped to the last tickets and pulled a deep purple rectangle from them. "I don't remember there being purple tickets—or with the letter 'G'."

"A dark ride, Mister Radcliffe; a seriously dark ride."

The compartment door shushed to a close and I was alone.

There was something comforting about the movement and sound of a train in motion. The gentle swaying of the car, the rhythmic clatter of the wheels riding along the tracks, the blur of landscapes and buildings as we sped by. I found a book in my messenger bag and pulled it out. Hardy's *Under the Greenwood Tree*. I smiled, knowing it was from Alice's extensive Hardy collection and flipped through pages, skimming the text until my eyes were heavy and I drifted off to sleep. How long I slept, I didn't know; I wasn't on the train when I woke, but the Underground, en route to The Royal Albert Hall. It was 1976, and I had returned to England.

I was returning to the orchestra.

Graham Sudley was pacing outside the entrance at the Prince Albert Steps when I crossed the street and started the climb. He heard my footfall and looked up, then broke into smiles.

"So it's true!" he exclaimed, pumping my hand in a nervous shake. "Well done, Radcliffe! Great to have you back!"

"Thanks—you look well for a concert master," I greeted, punching his shoulder.

"I had to kill some people for it," Graham joked.

"At least you didn't have to snog a royal for leverage in your negotiations," I fired back and winked when his face went gray. "It's been nineteen months Graham. I've had a good laugh about it several times. Now I hope to God I can win over the ones who didn't want me here in the first place."

"That old bastard Ernest never gave any of us a chance, did he? Cared more about how we held a cigarette or what scotch we drank. Wanted to believe what people told him without bothering to ask about the truth. Of course, when the truth came out about *him*…"

"Let the dead rest in peace," I commented and catching Graham's sly grin, added "I had nothing to with his untimely demise."

We started our stroll into the hall, and I was greeted with the familiar smells of floor wax, disinfectant and paper, all nostalgic and welcome. Heads turned and I exchanged welcomes and hellos, smiles, an occasional handshake. Chloe Carlisle ran up and threw herself into my arms.

"It's about time!" she cried. "You wouldn't believe how this place started buzzing when the news got around you'd been asked to return."

"You are a sight for sore eyes, Chloe!" I murmured in her hair. We stood at arm's length, taking the other in while Graham stood back and beamed. "Someday when I'm not doped up on cold medicine and half-naked in a bathtub, I'll tell you both the entire horror story of the negotiations."

We had reached the stage and it felt normal, as if nothing had changed, nothing had happened in the intervening year and I had never left. I took my place in the string section and nodded hello to two new cellists who considered me with wide, frightened eyes. I was the infamous Yank, Quinn Radcliffe, the prodigal cellist, returning to the fold after writing one hundred times on the blackboard that I would behave like a gentleman. I will not show up my betters, one hundred times.

And so began my rehabilitation. Over the next months I would prove myself ten times to a hundred times over, garnering a solo number on an album, solo concerts, and teaching master classes. The pivotal moment—everyone has a pivotal moment in their careers, don't they?—came when I was invited to conduct a rehearsal one afternoon.

Amidst a spattering of applause and a few derisive comments, some pats on the back, words of encouragement, I threaded my way to the podium and took the baton from Sir Edmund Howard, the Interim Conductor on loan to us from the London Symphony. He smiled and made a welcoming gesture to the podium and stepped down.

Before me was Beethoven's Ninth Symphony in D Minor, the second movement. An exciting and quick piece, the *Molto Vivace*. Running my hand through my hair as I studied the score, I nodded, nervous as hell, and glanced over at Graham who gave me a slight nod of encouragement.

Raising the baton, I lightly counted the meter and leaning forward a bit, on my toes, the strings took the cue and attacked in the opening measure. Within minutes it felt natural to stand before all of these musicians and take them through their paces, putting my own interpretation on this revered work of art, respectful of the composer at the same time, as trite as that might sound. What I was doing, as we would say years later, was owning it.

As the baton came down for the final measures I was drenched in sweat and shaking. For a second, and only that, when the last of the notes faded away, I stood quietly expecting something more. Applause maybe? A 'well done you,' perhaps? None of that came. You could hear crickets as I went back to my place and it was business as usual.

A week later I was called to Sir Edmund's office in the Royal Albert after a full day of rehearsal and preparations for our tour of the United Kingdom. Not in the best of moods, I threw a "What Now???" look at Chloe, Graham, Julian and Anna and told them to go on to the pub without me. Before I went downstairs to the office I cleaned up a bit, even put on the tie I'd discarded three hours before.

"Mr. Radcliffe, you got my note," Sir Edmund greeted when his secretary announced me and stepped out of the way. Sir Edmund was on his feet, a hand extended in greeting. We shook and he gestured to a chair. It was then I noticed Sir William, the Chairman of the Board of Governors and several benefactors.

"Your work at the podium last week was impressive," Sir Edmund began. "I've said as much to William and the rest of the Board of Governors."

I rubbed my hands against my knees, that nervous habit of mine, and hoped I wasn't sweating. What was this? This was inevitable; this was supposed to be. It led to the final movement. Why was I ready to faint?

Sir William said, "Edmund's time here wasn't supposed to be permanent and he's been invited to take the London Symphony on a tour of Asia, which, since the death of Ernest, leaves us in a pinch. He suggested we consider you."

"As student conductor, or interim?" I asked, my throat dry, my heart pounding in my throat so that I could barely breathe or speak. "I suppose I'm ready for that, Sir

William."

"Student? Oh no, Quinn! He suggested we bring you on as Music Director and Chief Conductor. We all agreed and there it is. We want you to assume your duties next month – it will give you time to settle in, set up your office, make a statement to the press."

And that was it. While I sat in stunned silence the men in the room congratulated me, pounded me on the back and someone put a champagne flute in my hand.

"But I haven't said yes," I stammered while another round of congratulations circulated.

"Don't tell me you're going to turn it down!" Sir Edmund laughed.

"No, no! God, no! It's just that I want to be sure it's the Board's decision."

"Quinn, your father has nothing to do with it. He doesn't even know about this move if that's what you're wondering," Sir William said quietly for my ears alone.

"If you think I'm ready,"

"More than enough. We saw the potential a year ago; there were some obstacles,"

"I know," I muttered, my face going red.

"Not that. Bloody Hell, if we put black marks against every member of the Orchestra who was guilty of a youthful indiscretion there'd be no one left in the Percussion and Brass Sections!"

I took a gulp of champagne and nodded, smiled lamely at Sir William and nodded again.

"This is one of the things I want most in my life," I replied.

One of my life's goals had been met. There was resistance from some orchestra members, but for the most part the decision was made and it was a political move to save a struggling symphony if it was anything.

And then in the early winter of 1978 my beloved Ellie died.

CHAPTER 19

1978 WOULD BE a year of memorable events in my life; the revelation that would be Scarborough, of course, but as in Alice's journey, my redemption and resurrection came from death.

I got the call at three in the afternoon when the Orchestra was in Bristol for a weekend of concerts. My secretary was waving frantically from backstage while I was running a rehearsal for the evening's performance. I knew it couldn't be good when she disappeared and came back with Sir William. "Take five, everyone," I announced and stepped down, crossing through the string section to where they waited.

"Missus Haddon, what's the matter?" I asked.

"Oh sir, sir, a Missus Pettigrew called. It's your grandmother Missus Radcliffe. She's gone to hospital–heart I think; she says it's not good."

"Book a seat on the next train north," I answered and everything was a blur after that, from boarding the train at Bristol Temple Meads to arriving in York some four hours later. A taxi took me to the hospital where I was met by nurse outside the intensive care unit.

"You're Mister Radcliffe, her grandson?" the nurse asked in that gentle, cautious tone one uses as the worst is about to happen, or has happened.

"Quinn. How is she?"

"She comes and goes; doesn't complain about much. She's asked for you."

"Thank you, Sister. Can I go in?" I nodded towards the heavy door with the tiny window.

"Of course, sir."

Before pushing on the door I asked, "How long?" I swallowed when she looked me straight in the eyes and put a hand on my forearm.

"Not very; I'm so sorry, sir."

It seemed that I'd lost my power of speech and all I could do was nod. Nod to say yes; nod to acknowledge understanding; nod to accept the inevitable.

"Here's a handsome fellow."

Ellie's whisper was cheerful enough and she patted the chair beside her as I came around the white curtains enclosing her bed. Leaning over, I kissed her cheek and then sat down, my coat dripping rain on the shiny linoleum floor, which she noticed right away and tried to laugh. "Matron will have words with you, Sweetheart; she had an orderly mop that floor twice this evening."

"Spilling your soup, again?" I teased, trying to be comfortable and act normal in this least comfortable and normal place.

"This time it was my blood."

I blanched and stared up at the machines beeping and ticking, the lights pulsing, all these unnatural things doing their best to fight nature Then I turned to face Ellie and saw that she was smiling. How was it possible a woman whose existence gave life and hope to everyone she encountered could not take some of that back and will her body to hold out and keeping running the race? In this she was so much like Alice.

She didn't look like someone dying. True, her face was paler but maybe that was the absence of cosmetics. Like Alice, like my mother, she didn't need them to look beautiful. Men still turned to get a look back or positively melted when she smiled. Soon all this strength, this beauty, this force of life, would be gone.

"How long have you known?" I asked.

"For some time, but I never paid it mind. There was too much to do, like dinners with my grandson at Snickelway."

"Where you can spill your soup on local nobility," I reminisced, putting on the brave face. I paused for a moment and shook my head. "You didn't say a word when I was in town for my birthday, Ellie."

"Darling, you knew it was going to happen sometime," she said, taking my hand. Her grasp was warm, but there was no strength.

"So much I want to say, Ellie, to share with you," I said, fighting tears.

"Don't we know each other so well that we know what it would be?"

"Ellie,"

"The shop and flat are yours. I don't want to leave it to your father or uncles. They never cared about it. Now you'll have a place to hide. Even better, come to terms and plan a real life."

If the sentiment had come from my parents it would have stung and been meant as an insult, but from Ellie it was her understanding that the little place in The Shambles was where no one could hurt me, touch my wounds, or take from me. I thought of that three days later as I stood in the churchyard and avoided the glare directed at me by my father across Ellie's grave and only looked at my mother once. I was heading in the direction of The Shambles with Chloe when I heard the shouts.

"Pretend we didn't hear that," I ordered Chloe, who was looking back at my parents advancing on us.

"For Chrissakes, Quinn, they're your parents," she hissed, "and today of all days."

"You know my history. C'mon."

"You once said you owed me—after the bath incident."

"Chloe, please."

"Payback time!"

"Why do you care?"

"I never got a chance to patch things up with my mum and dad. They died never knowing I forgave them.   Do you want to carry that around?"

"That would be nothing compared to what I already carry."

"Your mother looks hurt. Really."

"Just this once!" I growled and spun about to greet my parents with the sweetest and most insincere of smiles.

"Darling," Mother greeted, her lips barely touching my cheek. God forbid she'd show affection in public.

"Maestro," Father said, nodding.

"Quinn will do," I responded.

"And this is-?" he asked, nodding towards Chloe.

She stepped up and said "Chloe Carlisle—an honor, sir!" Chloe then pumped his hand a bit too strenuously. "Your staging of *La Boehme* was all we could talk about last year—I have friends that play for the opera orchestra in Swindon."

My father grinned and pulled his hand back none-too-gently. "I didn't know Swindon has an orchestra," he said.

"Dad," I sighed.

"A new girlfriend, Quinn? Hard to keep up with you. Haven't seen anything in the Pink Section or on the news lately," he dug.

"Grandma Ellie's gone—you can go home." My voice was even and low—a warning to most people.

"We were hoping you'd come back with us, Quinn," Mother started. "I know Eloise left the house and shop to you, but do you really want to live in York? You have the place in San Anselmo…"

"My work and life are in England for most of the year. Thanks, but I have no desire for a transatlantic commute."

"Not even for a few months out of the year, darling?" Mother pled. "We do miss you. I miss you."

"She's got you in noose, has she?" Father chuckled,

winking at Chloe.

"Now just a minute!" Chloe protested.

"Dad, Chloe and I are just friends," I sighed. "Look, I have to go—"

"She's living in New York now, or is it Rhode Island? I heard a rumor she was seeing a scientist or university professor from Brown. That's not too hard of a commute, is it?" Father said as he extended his hand. I ignored the hand.

"What are you getting at?" I demanded, even though I knew.

"If you broke up that relationship you wouldn't have Buckingham Palace to worry about."

With that, my father walked away pulling my mother along, Mother glancing back only once as they hurried back into the church.

"Everything you've told me about him is true. What a miserable bastard," Chloe sighed as she dug in her purse for a cigarette.

"Quinn!"

Chloe's hand on my arm prevented me from turning to face my father. We stood close and I feigned interest in her search. He was behind us and in earshot.

"Quinn, when you do see her at whatever hotel you meet up in, tell her I said no hard feelings and that I hope she's well."

My father's parting shot was a dirty blow.

CHAPTER 20

"WHY DOES HE do that?" Chloe insisted when we found a booth in a pub not far from the churchyard. I chose it because my father wouldn't be caught dead there.

"It doesn't need an explanation other than he's trying to get to me – do you want something to eat?"

"Whatever you're having is all right. And it got to you; that's pretty evident."

I ignored her look of concern and went to order food and drink and came back to find that look still stuck to her face. Sliding into the booth I grabbed her hand without a cigarette and planted a kiss on it. "I know you're concerned, Carlisle, and I love you for that, but I just have a problem letting go and so does my father."

"From what I could tell he likes to beat you over the head with it."

The food and drinks came after a few minutes of morose silence from me and Chloe exhaling cigarette smoke into the already dusky air of the pub.

"To Eloise Faithwaite Radcliffe."

We raised our glasses after my toast and drank, Chloe digging in to the sandwiches piled on a plate before us.

"So, Radcliffe," Chloe began a little while later, filling my glass from the pitcher, "The real question is this— would you go to the New York or Rhode Island to break up a relationship?"

"Leave it alone," I chuckled, hoping that I sounded lighthearted and callow.

Chloe took one of the chips from the greasy newspaper-lined basket and set it on the table before me. "There. There it is. I've left it alone."

My laughter was genuine now. "At least you know to let well enough alone. Cheers, Carlisle!"

"From what I can guess, your dad has unresolved issues in spades and you aren't just the prodigal son and heir, but his whipping boy."

"I'm being punished for being me and not him."

"The lament of every child."

"Y'know sometimes I feel like a real bastard, complaining and moaning about my dad and mom, especially when I consider all that they have given me compared to some of my friends, who had so little but seemed so…happy."

"No one's ever happy with their life," Chloe sighed. "Well, I am – now."

"Your father was a barrister, your mother a solicitor. I suppose it was a comfortable life in some way?"

"In a lot of ways. I didn't approve of their work—they represented the Crown in cases against the Irish Republican Army—and that made for a lot of interesting conversations at dinner in Suffolk," Chloe answered, her shoulders rising and dropping in a shrug.

"You're pro-IRA."

"Why don't we leave well enough alone? That was my last argument with them before I left for school. I never saw them after that."

"Deep seeded anger. I know that."

"They were killed by an IRA bomb."

Whatever smartass comment I was forming was left as a stupid thought and I drank the rest of the beer in silence.

"Going back to London?" Chloe asked as we left the pub at dusk.

"Rehearsals and the new recording for Angel. Tour

details, meetings. Music doesn't slow down for death," I commented.

"Walking me back to the hotel?" Chloe asked, nudging me playfully.

"I'm going back to my hotel."

"Doesn't Ellie have a flat over her shop? Your shop?"

"Ellie's shop. Not ready for that. I'm staying at The Golden Fleece. You?"

"A dive near the railway."

"You could stay with me. I could use the company," I offered.

Chloe stopped and spun about to face me. "As glorious as I know it would be, and I'm not flattering you, it's gospel truth, I've pretty much become exclusive."

"Lucky Julian," I said.

"Lucky Anna. We won't go into the details, but Julian talked too much and liked to keep score. So thanks all the same, Radcliffe."

"My friends don't stay in dives near railway stations. No sex. No cuddling, no making out. Just company, conversation, and maybe some gin. Could you turn that down?"

She couldn't. We sat up until dawn and in a state of sobriety talked about her parents, her childhood in Suffolk, how many times her heart had been broken and how good Anna was for her. Chloe knew all about Alice, Denny and Harry, and I talked about my surrogate family as if I was still a member of that fortunate clan. I never once spoke of life in the castle on Buena Vista Way in the privileged hills above Berkeley. We parted at Knightsbridge Station a few days later, returning to London on a cold January Sunday.

"See you tomorrow in rehearsal, Maestro," Chloe said in parting. Gone was the easy friendship and intimacy. We were conductor and musician now – a façade put up for the sake of professionalism and to keep the gossips at bay. In London I was the maestro, the loner, the serious young man with secrets.

"Thanks for coming to York. It made it all the more bearable, Miss Carlisle," I said as we shook hands.

"A word of advice, sir?" Chloe hinted.

"If you want,"

"I know you're not the type to break up a relationship, but try to find some happiness. At least call her and make a clean break and move on. See you."

That advice stayed with me every day after and on nights when I wanted to pick up the phone and didn't. It certainly was at the back of my mind when I returned to York in the summer that year to take care of business.

"Taking care of business?" laughed Edward IV when I walked from the train into the station and entered the Shop in the Village.

"Good to know nothing's changed," I responded, crossing over to my table. Richard III looked up from his crossword and nodded in greeting. Janis Joplin put down the issue of *Rolling Stone* that featured a cover article on me and glared before she took a sip from her mug.

"Tell me something, Maestro," the Proprietress said as she put away the ledger and came around her counter. She folded her arms across her chest, the ubiquitous handbag held against her like a shield. "We gave you the means and opportunity, we gave you clues, and yet here you are." When I didn't respond, she added, "Of what are you so afraid, sad little prince?"

"Don't call me that."

"Then don't act the part, dear boy."

"And don't call me that, either."

"Why? Because your father called you a dear boy?"

"I don't have to stay and listen to this—"

"But stay you will," Richard III interrupted. "You're here so long as you say nothing and do nothing, and you've been doing a lot of that. I would like to go home. I'm here as long as you are here. We all are here because you are here. Now grow a pair, Radcliffe, and do something."

The activity in the shop came to a standstill. Even the Proprietress paused. "Well done, Richard Plantagenet!" she whispered loudly.

"Then I'll do something. I'll go home."

Taking my jacket from Hildegard, I went back out into the street and found myself in The Shambles in front of Ellie's shop and it was the summer of 1978.

CHAPTER 21

I WAS HOME.

I welcomed the familiar scents of Ellie's shop as I pushed the door open with my suitcase and flight bag that subsequently were dropped on the door mat. I paused, waiting, expecting to see my grandmother come from the stocking room or past the curtain that led up the stairs to her flat. I expected a riot of psychedelic color, a cloud of Chanel Number Five and the sound of *Top of the Pops*. Of course those expectations weren't met. The hollow sound of my footsteps on the wooden floor echoed as I took a tour of the shop. Everything was as Ellie left it in January when she collapsed during the lunch hour and was taken to the hospital, except that a kind soul had draped the display cases and tables, probably the housekeeper, Mrs. Pettigrew. I wondered if I should go through the morning ritual and pull off the sheets and turn the sign on the door. I pulled off the sheets and in doing so unwrapped bright, colorful trinkets, gew-gaws, women's accessories, books, toys, bottles of perfume and knick-knacks.

Yes, we are open for business.

Just as I was going around the counter, I heard a door upstairs close. I went to the stairwell and saw a shadow in the sunlight streaming under the hall door.

"Hello? Missus Pettigrew?"

There was no response. A shuffling of feet, another door slam. I took a few cautious steps up and then a solid woman with her hair tied up in a bandana and wearing a sensible calico dress and sensible oxfords with elastic stockings came to the top of the stairs with a box of cat food in her arms.

"Sir, can we get rid of the cat now? It's made a mess of things in the sitting room and what it did to the lovely throw you brought back from California, well, I don't know," the woman groused.

"Missus Pettigrew, the convention is usually to say 'hello, how are you' but that will do," I teased, and bounded up to meet her and planted a kiss on her hairy upper lip. "I didn't see you at the funeral in January. Not your back again?"

Mrs. Pettigrew allowed a hug and pushed me away gently, leading the way into the flat. "Better than some," she sniffed, trying to look and act discomfited but I saw a gleam in her watery, aging eyes.

"Like my grandmum?"

"Oh now I didn't say that."

"Just yanking the chain, Missus Pettigrew. I am concerned about you, though. What will you do now that Ellie's gone? Do you have other clients?"

"Oh, I do all right, Young Radcliffe. I have the dean and the archbishop's, the lord mayor's house. It's enough. Might retire, seeing how Missus Radcliffe left me something by, a tidy sum."

"I wouldn't expect anything less of Ellie."

"What about you, world famous conductor?" she simpered as we went through to the tiny kitchen. Becket hissed and turned his back on me when I entered, waiting impatiently for the breakfast that Mrs. Pettigrew poured into a mixing bowl and set before him. The cat glanced up every now and then to make sure I wasn't going to take any of his kibble and only growled once when I filled the kettle and placed it on the stove.

"You didn't answer my question," Mrs. Pettigrew said, setting the table.

"I'm the world famous conductor!" I said proudly, but

with a tinge of sarcasm.

"What else? Haven't read anything in the papers, nor seen your handsome face on the covers of glossy magazines. Everything is fine then?"

"I miss Ellie."

"So do I, sir. What a good and decent woman she was. And she was so proud of you. She talked about you more than her sons. How Mister Andrew managed to get a fine young man like yourself, well, you were Missus Radcliffe's pride and joy."

"She was everything to me," I said softly, and took one of the shortbread squares off the plate and set it down. It was store-bought; not the rich, homemade cookies I had grown to love.

"And you were everything to her," Missus Pettigrew chirped. "She only had one regret, sir, that you never married."

"There's still time," I laughed.

"Surely there's a girl by now? What happened to that pretty girl?"

"There've been lots of pretty girls!"

Mrs. Pettigrew got up and went into the living room and then came back with a framed photograph that she set on the kitchen table. "Not like this one."

It was a photograph of us—Alice and me. I didn't know Ellie had framed it; it was sent in a Christmas card in a moment and time of extreme happiness.

"No, not like her," I said.

"Missus Radcliffe would look at that photograph for the longest time, sir, and say how she wished you'd bring her over. She used to say that one could tell how intelligent and clever a person was by the eyes and she said this young girl's eyes held so much life and cleverness by half."

"I guess compared to me," I jested.

"If you don't mind my saying so, Young Radcliffe, do your Ellie's memory proud and marry a girl that would love this shop and be twice the woman Ellie was, because that's what she wanted. I know. She told me."

We drank our tea in quiet after that and once Mrs. Pettigrew was reassured that I would take care of Becket and the shop, the cleaning woman moaned about her aching joints saying she had a long day ahead of her at the Minster Chapter House and disappeared into The Shambles.

The cat considered me suspiciously as I cleared away the dishes and did the washing up, his dark green eyes narrowed to slits as he followed me as I went down to the shop for my things and brought them back up to my bedroom, putting them on the bed where Becket usually held court. I left the bedroom with the cat sitting on top of the suitcase.

I was home.

This was my home.

I wandered around and took a mental inventory even though I knew every cobweb and corner of the flat and the how and why of how things were placed or purchased. Memories came attached with each china plate and tea towel, each Royal Doulton mug. It got to be too much and I went for the antique wardrobe in the living room. That was where Ellie kept the hard liquor.

"A bit early in the day, don't you think? Even for you?"

The unfamiliar voice was startling and I turned slowly from the wardrobe, sure that I was going to find myself either in the Shop or on a street in the Village, but no, I was still in The Shambles and no one was in the room with me but Becket the cat.

"I surprised at you, Tarquin. Of all the things you hate the most about your father, isn't it his drinking? And he's an angry drunk, isn't he? Whereas you are the happy drunk, am I right?"

Sonofabitch, the cat was talking to me.

Becket had daintily leapt from the floor to the coffee

table and curled up in his usual orange ball. He blinked, considering me, probably waiting for a response.

"Well?"

"Sorry – I don't talk to cats," I said, reaching for the Nolet's.

"Would you listen to me, then?"

Again, an unfamiliar voice. This time I was ready to shoo the cat out of the room and found myself face to face with twelfth-century Archbishop of Canterbury, Thomas Becket. Also known to some as that 'miserable priest.'

"Thomas a' Becket—"

"Thomas of London, to you!"

"—or Thomas Becket, archbishop of Canterbury murdered in his cathedral and someone whose ego is only a little less than Henry the Eighth's and whose arrogance and stubborn streak make mine look non-existent," I said as I poured some gin into a glass and carried it to the overstuffed chair that had been designated mine years ago. I invited His Holiness to sit, but Becket remained where he was.

"If you know that much, sir, then you know how ill it serves you to be so arrogant and stubborn," Becket answered.

"I know why she sent you. You want me to make amends so you can all go back to whatever you were doing in your afterlives before I made such a mess of my life," I snapped. "I'm still not ready."

"If not now, when?"

"When I know I won't hurt anyone, when I won't hurt Alice."

"How will you know if you don't try?"

"I'll just . . . know." I said, ready to take a drink, and then paused, adding, "Besides, who's done the real injury? Where do you think the fear comes from?"

Holy Shit, NOT what I had thought in 1978!

"You know what month and year it is. I hope that epiphany comes soon, Mister Radcliffe."

"It will come when it comes," I snarled and took a drink and winced. Alcohol at eight in the morning really wasn't a good idea. When I put the glass down only Becket the cat was with me, and he was still curled up on the coffee table. The cat mewed plaintively.

"Shut up," I said.

Becket stretched and then jumped lightly from the table and disappeared into the kitchen, leaving me to brood.

All I could think about was who the real injured party was in this sick, twisted triangle I've made of my life—or had been made for me. Yes, I had some serious thinking and decision making ahead.

"Well done, Radcliffe!" I heard Ralph Vaughan Williams' voice in my head.

I was pouring my gin down the kitchen drain when I noticed the photograph of Alice and me where Missus Pettigrew left it.

"All that promise," Whispered Richard III.

I would have dissolved into a vegetative state of self-pity and remorse, perhaps some self-evaluation, were it not for the knocking on the shop door. The photograph was left on the shelf behind the sales counter while I went to see who it was.

"Ah! I was wondering if you were open. I need a special kind of wedding present," a nervous-looking woman in an outrageous hat blurted out when I opened the door. I hedged a bit and she added, "I was told to come here by a friend in London? She said you have the most interesting things."

A moment passed and I smiled, saying, "Of course. Just getting a late start today. Come in, please."

The woman squealed something in 'shop talk,' a strange language only women spoke and seemed to understand. She squealed some more and sighed happily as I switched lights on so that the antiques and costly bric-a-brac were more visible. She spent a great while looking and talking to herself and finally decided on a Wedgwood teapot. When I had boxed and wrapped it, I glanced up and saw her smiling. "You look a perfect couple," she said, nodding at the photograph.

Money exchanged hands and I counted out change from the ancient register. "Good of you to say so," I said cheerfully and felt it, meant it. "My best wishes for the bride and groom from Eloise Radcliffe's."

The doorbell chimed happily as she left for the wedding and I smiled at the unexpected encounter, that smile and feeling of contentment staying with me as I raised the shades over the windows and propped open the door with the sword of Excalibur wedged in its stone. The noise and thumping of the composite stone curiosity brought shopkeepers to their doors and windows and I received some 'good mornings' and well wishes. I called greetings out and smiled, feeling good. Really good.

Becket joined me sometime after that, taking his place on the cushion next to the cash register, watching as always with his big green eyes narrowed in what I suppose was a feline look of suspicion while I swept the floor of dust, and rearranged some displays. Another customer arrived, and another, and then another. And several more. Soon it was six o'clock and I had made one hundred and seventy-eight pounds and fifty-three shillings, nine pence from sales to American tourists and locals, all of whom had wonderful things to say about the shop and Ellie. Like everyone else in The Shambles I locked up and would have gone upstairs for dinner—if there had been any food in the flat. I decided to go up to The Bitter End on the northern end of the street.

Merchants in the neighborhood stopped and asked how I was getting on, offering condolences for my loss and wondered if I would make York my home. I thought about that during a supper of fish and chips and was still ruminating on the possibility of commuting on the weekends from London when the plate was empty and the beer stein drained. I started back to Ellie's so I could prepare myself for the meeting with the solicitor in the morning, spend an evening making plans, and make a call that was long overdue.

As I was opening the door to leave The Bitter End, the late summer sun blinded me and I collided with a young woman.

"I'm sorry," I apologized, and then, "My God! Alice!"

CHAPTER 22

THERE SHE WAS, as wonderful and beautiful as ever. All I saw were the eyes and the mouth, that wonderful mouth as round as an 'o' as she tried to apologize for something not her fault.

Okay, Worshipfulness, anywhere but here. The Battle of Hastings, the night I totaled my father's car, Viet Nam during the Tet Offensive. Anywhere but here. Not this pain.

"Quinn! Wow, what are the odds...?" she stammered.

"Are you on vacation?"

"No, no, I'm working here through August."

"Working? Doing what?"

"I was invited to replace one of the faculty for the summer session," Alice said and I when leaned in and down to meet her gaze, she blushed and looked away. "Couldn't get anyone else on such short notice. Lecturer in Medieval Studies at The College of Ripon and York St. John. Sorry, rambling. That's your specialty."

"Not the University?" I asked. "I could see you in King's Manor at St. Mary's Abbey. It would be perfect. Didn't know they had medieval studies at Ripon York St. John, but what do I know?"

"Rambling?" she laughed.

"Yes, some things never change, do they? Just here for the summer, hunh?"

"Then I return home and..."

"And?"

"...and I figure out what the next chapter will be in this bad Jane Austen novel that is my life," she replied.

The pain I felt in my chest caught me off guard momentarily and I studied her face, which was closed up like a book.

No, why fault her for lying when you've been doing it all your life?

"So it's Doctor Martin, I guess?"

"Yes, Maestro. And you? Is the orchestra here for a concert?"

"No, taking some time off this week to take care of family business. My grandmother died a few months back and I've finally got the time and the courage to come up and deal with things. I'm here to take care of the flat and shop."

"Oh, Quinn! I'm so sorry. I know you were close."

"Pardon," a man said as he tried to squeeze his way around us. Muttering apologies, we stepped to the pavement to allow patrons access to the door and for a moment just stared at one another. The pain in my chest was coming in waves now and I wondered if this was how I died, or was going to die: a massive heart attack or a broken heart. There was so much I wanted to say—I needed to say.

"Alice,"

She looked up expectantly. "Yes?"

Why wouldn't the damn words come out of my mouth? I noticed movement across the street and saw the Proprietress sweeping the pavement.

"They won't come because it's not your hour," she called airily.

"Damn her!" I said out loud and caught myself.

"What?" Alice glanced behind her and saw what I saw: a broom up against a shop door.

"I should have called you," I blurted out. "I wanted to. Then I thought, no, she wouldn't want me to because I'd been such an asshole, then I got busy, things happened, my career and—"

"Quinn, it's forgotten."

"So, did you marry the guy?"

"Who? What guy?"

"The guy that interrupted our date."

"Adam? No, I think he's doing time somewhere. Most likely for assault and battery on someone else's boyfriend," she joked and did that beguiling thing women all over the world did when nervous or flirting, nervously pushed back her hair to avoid something, or to allow a better view of their face. In Alice's case, I never knew which, but I was glad she did it. I got to see that beauty I'd been dreaming about of late.

"You're worth a good fight. Or a beating in my case," I said. "Wow; y'know, I'm always saying the wrong things with you, Alice."

"As opposed to what you say to other girls?"

"Yeah—well, no, no—God! I did it again! What I mean to say, is, what I wanted to say that day wasn't what came out of my mouth."

"Ahhh…"

"Yeah, I couldn't imagine you with someone like that."

"Well my score card hasn't improved much," she mumbled.

"I'm sorry, what?" I asked knowing full well what she'd said.

"Nothing—I meant to say, I should have given you a break."

Hope!

"Listen, do you want a drink?" I pointed behind us at The Bitter End.

We went inside, taking a table in a corner and for the most part of an hour caught each other up on the major events of our lives—some of which were glossed over or not mentioned at all but were still there, unspoken words that hung over us. We came around to my career.

"Ask me what's on the new album," I said as we playfully fought for the last of the chips. Our fingers met and locked and I leaned in, her face close enough for a kiss. "Ask me, Alice!"

"What's on the next album, Quinn? *White Rabbit?*"

Our hands were still clasped when I leaned even closer and whispered, "Vaughan Williams. *Lark Ascending, Greensleeves*," then pausing for drama, but more to take in the scent of her perfume, of her, said, "*Fantasia on a Theme by Thomas Tallis.*"

Our lips were almost touching now.

"Really?" Alice whispered, genuinely surprised.

"No joke. I insisted."

"Really. Hunh. All these years…"

"I listen to it whenever I need inspiration, whenever I'm lonely."

"My friends say it's the most depressing music they've ever heard, and one guy—oh, it doesn't matter." I knew whom she meant and the pain lessened considerably as she smiled now. She added, "Think me crazy, but I thought it was about a relationship between two people when I last heard it."

Us!

"Let me guess—the shades of dark and light in the music, the drama?"

"Exactly! Scary. Scary in that you still know what I'm thinking at times. I've never thought it depressing, though."

"No it isn't. It's like a summer morning after a shower, or an evening. Everything is there—the light and dark, the changes in colors. I should take you to Scarborough to show you what I mean. Most of all, it brings back good memories."

"I think of it as a friend—I know it sounds maudlin or silly, but when I need to think, while I'm writing, I like the *Fantasia.*"

"What do you think about?"

"The usual—Dennis, his health, my parents, screwing up my life in so many different configurations, do-overs."

"I wonder if you think about me?"

"Yes."

My heart was pounding but it was lighter. She was smiling at me and I smiled back and we sat there for moments in this state.

"What about when you're happy?" I finally spoke.

"*Here Comes the Sun.*"

"*Purple Haze* when you're feeling silly?"

"That's just for go-go dancing. *White Rabbit* is for silly."

I was still leaning in, and wanted to kiss her. I tapped her nose playfully and said, "C'mon Grace, I'll walk you home."

"Grace…?"

"Grace Slick—Jefferson Airplane?"

"Damn!"

"How soon they forget," I teased.

"How I wish they would forget," Alice playfully groused, and rolled her eyes as she slid out of the booth and accepted the hand I offered. She kept hold of it as we strolled back to her place. Once in a while I'd glance down and study her lovely profile and she'd look up and smile. Not exactly the warm, loving, expression I'd experienced so many times before but something brittle, masked.

Might as well get it over with; you know what's coming . . .

"I didn't ask." I blurted out.

"What?"

"Maybe it's just—nope. Doesn't really matter."

"Ask!" she implored. "What?"

"I suppose you've got a couple of kids, an attorney for a husband or an English Professor from Cal," I said half in jest.

"None of the above."

"Really?" I did my best to sound incredulous and watched her for some telltale sign of a confession to be offered. "Wow. Go figure. Well, there's got to be someone."

"He'd like to think there was," Alice said.

"Serious, or…?"

"He'd like to think it was."

"I guess your work takes up most of your time," I said as we strolled along at a leisurely pace. I was in no hurry to see her home, and judging by the way she moved and reacted, didn't think she was either.

"Pretty much. But then, when am I not doing something to keep busy?"

"Do you still sketch, design?"

"Just for friends when they need a Renaissance Faire costume, or their kids need something for Halloween," she answered. "And you? Is there a lady?"

I paused in walk and thought. She let go of my hand and I knew what that meant. She'd figured it out. I sighed and then nodded. "She's a girl whose father donates a lot of money to the orchestra. We've been dating for a few months."

"Ah, sounds like an arranged marriage to keep the orchestra afloat."

"Pretty much."

"Do you sing to her, play songs to keep her smiling? Play games of Risk or read aloud from Tolkien and John Donne?"

"I follow her around to social events like the Ascot, show up for photos at nightclubs. Her father is a peer. She's . . . interesting."

"Does she have a soul or a heart?"

Inflicting pain, Alice? Jealous, I hope?

I started to laugh. "Believe me, I've been searching for them for months. If they existed, I think I would have found them by now!"

"Geez, I really stepped into it, didn't I?"

"No, no, of all the women I've been with, and there haven't been that many, so don't believe what the tabloids scream, you're the only one who really knows me. *Absolvo te*, Faery Princess. Besides, I'm pretty sure it's over."

"*What??*" Janis Joplin screeched in my ear. "Back up the truck, Chuck!"

Janis and I were walking up the high street of the village to the *Toad in the Hole* and once inside we joined Richard III and Thomas Becket at a table. The Proprietress brought drinks all around, each according to their taste and century. "Be very glad it isn't hemlock, Mister Radcliffe," she said.

"Why aren't you telling her the truth?" Thomas Becket wanted to know.

"Like you know anything about being faithful and loyal," I groused, taking a sniff of the gin and tonic before me just to be sure it wasn't hemlock.

"What's that got to do with Alice knowing what really made you leave?" Becket demanded. "How you expect absolution?"

"It's easier this way," I argued; "let her know there's another girl. It would be easier for her to understand."

"She's not stupid," Janis argued.

"Besides, it's one fat lie," Richard said.

"Only one of many," Becket added, and touched Richard's glass with his.

"You'd broken it off with Miss Atwell, hadn't you? Several months earlier? It was in all the papers," Richard stated.

"It only made the six o'clock news in the States. Briony Atwell didn't have the celebrity of other royals."

"Like the delicious Penelope?" Janis teased.

"Okay, Alice knew about that, but she doesn't need to know about Briony – yet,"

"Not unless you were hoping to get lucky. And what makes you sure she didn't already know? C'mon, Sad Little Prince. Do the right thing," Janis replied and taking my hand, pulled me out of the chair effortlessly. The others raised their drinks to my success. Janis pulled me along as we walked back out into the high street that slowly became a street in York, the bright sunlight and impossibly blue sky slowly dissolving into a summer's evening in Northern England and as Janis slipped away Alice took her place.

I spun around to face Alice, winking and walking backwards as I said, "Now, your guy. What's this guy got that I haven't?"

"A degree in archeology and a substantial stake in the dig going on at Petra, the chance to have a building named after him."

"An archeologist like Allan Quartermain in *King Solomon's Mines?* Remember that old movie with Stewart Granger and Deborah Kerr?"

"Sure—we saw it, what, three times? And I think Quartermain was an adventurer, not an archeologist. Handled snakes better than someone I know." She smiled at me sideways.

"Better than me? Hardly! Remember that giant garter snake we found in your sanctuary?"

"Yeah, that was pretty amazing, Quinn. I would have been more impressed if it had been real."

"How was I to know Harry put it there for an April Fool's joke?"

"I think he's finally over your ruining his best golf club on a fake reptile."

"That was a memorable spring break."

We shared the best of laughs over that, leaning into one another as we walked and laughed, remembering the shrieks and hysteria, especially the looks on Harry and Dennis' faces when they came downstairs and found me in my boxer shorts with Harry's golf club still in my hands as I thought to defend Alice from the snake.

As we paused for another traffic light, I draped an arm around her casually and said, "I'm pretty good with plastic creepy crawlers, aren't I? I suppose your archeologist would come swinging from the rafters with a machete or something."

"Not quite. He'd have a Sherpa drive him in an off-road vehicle and bring a bottle of scotch with an ice bucket, tongs and glasses. Actually, I prefer the strong, silent types who quietly tell guys to back off and then walk away; the kind that defend a lady's honor above all else and personal humiliation."

I smiled, remembering. "Did that a few times and will gladly do it again if the occasion calls for it."

"Good to know."

We walked in silence for a time, my arm still draped around her shoulders. I didn't remember her this thin; I did remember the scent and the warmth of her skin. "I guess you guys talk about Roman *sarcophagi* and *stele* at the end of the day?" I queried.

"Mostly. He works at Petra, though. Not many Roman nobility buried there."

"And you discuss your latest theatrical designs, or your latest book, research, how you unlock the mysteries of Italian city states and their governance."

"The love affair with Italy's been over for a while. Now it's the vagrancies of the Crusades, the Anglo-Saxons and the backlash against the Conquest."

"You'd debate whether England could have survived if Harold hadn't taken that arrow in the eye?"

"Nope. Just whatever was dug up at Petra, or his latest press conference, tour. Latest photo in *Time* or *Newsweek*. Whatever."

"You'd be his equal in so many things, Alice."

She stopped suddenly and I turned and raised my brows in question.

"He isn't. He's not my equal, you see. He's not you."

"I'm flattered."

"With you, I can just be Alice; be myself. I'm never on guard, never worrying about saying or doing the wrong things, never worried about offending extremely wealthy and class-conscious friends, colleagues and relatives."

We were at her flat. I stood on the sidewalk while

Alice walked up the stairs to turn the key in the lock. "And yet he's got a hold on you," I said matter-of-factly.

"One that I'm trying to untie, I guess, or figure out."

The door now open, she turned and gestured with the keys. "Do you want some coffee, a nightcap?"

"I wouldn't mind some honesty."

Our conversation from The Shambles to Gillygate had revealed much and not much. Alice told me half-truths that I saw came painfully as she eked out details about him. Still, it wasn't enough. She didn't seem surprised by the seriousness of my tone or how I stood at the bottom of the steps with hands in pockets—my confrontational stance, she called it.

"C'mon," she invited.

This would have been her home in Berkeley—the nouveau gothic touches and femininity, the vases of flowers and the clutter of books, papers, sketchbooks and art supplies, the typewriter on the kitchen table that one day would be replaced by a laptop attached to her hip. Photos of her family were everywhere. I was surprised to see a few of us together. The snow globe sat in a place of honor on the mantle. What I didn't see was photos of this mysterious archeologist she said looked like me and had an ancient family name that went back to the Mayflower, the man who wrapped her around his little finger.

"Nice digs," I commented.

"They are, aren't they? Do you want crumpets or scones?"

"Doesn't matter. You know I'll devour anything edible. Looks like you've settled in for a long haul."

"I'm still trying to decide whether or not to extend the contract. I like the work, the students, definitely like York, so I'm trying to work out a deal with Brown University to let me work here, or something."

I was interested in the deal and who was involved, but I didn't say a thing.

Maybe an excuse to stay away from the States as long as

possible?

"I'm here through the end of next week, then down to London—I told you that, didn't I?"

"To record the new album."

"The one dedicated to you."

"That's a huge honor, Quinn. You don't have to."

"It's a gift a long time coming."

I studied her now—noticing the tightness of her jaw, the line between her brows as she concentrated on the scones and crumpets. How her hands trembled. Was she afraid of me or the truth?

"I don't think he has a hold on you, Alice," I said softly after a time.

She glanced up, surprised.

"I think you're being strangled. Tell me if I'm wrong—or worse, if I'm right."

The toaster oven bell went off and gave Alice an excuse to retrieve the bakery goods and place them on a plate, find the jam and butter. She took her time measuring scoops of coffee as if it were a scientific experiment and I gently took her hand as she passed by me for the fourth or fifth time. Without looking at me, she said, "This isn't something I want to discuss with you right now."

"But you do want to discuss it?"

"It's been a long day and I'm tired, and seeing you again…"

"Understood."

Wordlessly she set the table with our coffee, scones and crumpets. I took a place at the table and then was on my feet. Alice glanced up, frowning.

"I should go."

"Well, at least we know where to find each other," Alice replied, shrugging.

"Right. See you around, Alice."

I kissed the top of her head before slipping quietly out the door.

CHAPTER 23

MY WALK FROM Gillygate back to The Shambles led me past other disappointments in my life and to The Shop where Michael Arcangelus waited for me.

"Buy you a cup of coffee? Pop Tart?" he greeted, opening the door for me.

"I hate Pop Tarts," I groused, brushing past him.

"What did you expect, Quinn? These things take time. Give her time to heal."

"I think there's a platitude or three you left out there."

"If you want her, woo her. Win her back," said Edward IV in passing.

"I'm not sure she wants me. She's got a boyfriend."

"I know what he's thinking," the Proprietress spoke up. "He's angry because she moved on."

Michael shook his head. "We know Alice, don't we? "Maybe it's convenient, just as your hiding from life is convenient for you."

"I can't explain it. I'm just not ready."

"Because if you were, you'd have to do or say something. Change, for example." Michael said. "Anger is easier to pacify when you feed it. To state the obvious, this little womb of our making that we crawl back into when handed disappointments of all kinds makes everything palatable. No one can touch us. We can exist without meaning and for as long as we desire."

Damn him for being so handsome and charming, for the navy on navy clothes! Damn him for always being right! On top of that, he was so distracting that you soon forgot you were angry.

"Well that's the whole point of our village, isn't it? We can exist without meaning for as long as we desire," Richard III said when he came in and took his place beside my table. "Forget your cares, your woes, how many times people have screwed you over, stuck in a knife and twisted it? How many loved ones you've betrayed and screwed over. That's what the village is all about. Just ask anyone."

"No one asked you," I snapped.

"Some of us become mentors, such as myself, and some become like Hubert."

"Hubert?" I asked now.

"Do you know the old gentleman that sits at the end of the lane on the oak stump? He talks to himself and has no friends. I suppose I should tell you why."

Richard sighed and focused on the *Times* crossword as I waited.

"And?" I demanded.

"He's alone for a reason. He liked it here in the Village. Now he wallows in self-pity, and who wants to put up with that all day? I could only take it for an hour, to say the truth."

"Hubert refuses to take the opportunities granted to him. One has only a short while to put things to rights." Edward IV explained.

"He grew complaisant; lazy. It was too comfortable," Richard added.

"Well you can't say that about me, can you?" I said. "You can't blame me for being stuck in this place."

"After so many chances the clock does run out and things get, as you would say, fucked-up," Michael interjected. "So I ask you, why would anyone squander a chance to put things to rights for all of *kairos* and *kronos*?"

"He does have a point," the Proprietress said while she arranged a new display of soda bottles on the coffee counter. "After all one goes through at home, why would anyone want to keep at it here? And you, master musician, have got to be one of the most clueless—"

"Not fair," Hildegard piped up, leveling her spoon like a weapon at the Proprietress. "Everyone is different. You've said so many times."

"My dear, all he has to do is one thing. That's all. How many chances has he had? How many times has he blown it? Well?" the Proprietress insisted, glaring at me.

"She does have a point," Michael sighed.

He snapped his fingers and I startled, finding myself sitting up in bed in my old room at Ellie's. The snapping sound was a blue jay pecking at the mullioned window across the room. I glared at the bird and threw myself back down, staring at the ceiling, watching the shadows of people and vehicles in the street as The Shambles woke up for another summer day.

My encounter with Alice was all I could think about while the solicitor told me I was inheriting a fortune; while I took a conference call with the orchestra board and another with Graham Sudley to plan the next week's schedules; while I strolled the walls of York.

More than a telephone call was overdue.

I waited a day and then showed up at the university late in the afternoon. A polite secretary showed me to a bench in the hallway outside Alice's classroom and I slid down beside two co-eds that simpered and blushed when I smiled and said hello. It was like waiting outside the principal's office, imagining the punishment to be meted out.

I will not break Alice's heart; I will never lie to her again; I will never withhold secrets—twenty times ten times a thousand on a blackboard...

An officious looking woman smiled down at me as she walked past briskly and went into the classroom. Moments later she came out with Alice on her heels, the woman pointing in my direction. Alice and I met halfway.

"I owe you an apology for the night before," I opened

and looking around, added, "Can we go somewhere to talk?"

Now I was getting the look—the one that warned to tread softly and carefully. Alice was nodding and smiling at people as they maneuvered around us, but not at me. At last she glanced up and said, "I'm finished for the day. Carry my books?"

"Do you want to grab something to eat?"

She turned on her heels and said, "If we're going to have this talk, I'd rather it be in private. We can have a proper dinner at my place, if you want."

"You *cook?* Since when?" I blurted.

Alice was trying hard not to laugh and she folded her arms. "Learned in Italy."

"Okay, then. Sure. Can we make a stop on the way to your place?"

The stop was Ellie's store. I set down Alice's things on the sales counter and went round to the cash register which I opened and I dug around in a drawer until I found what I was looking for. "Hah! I knew she kept them -- I met with the solicitors about the estate and some receipts were missing from accounting. Here they are." I held them up and saw that Alice was strolling around the store, awestruck.

"If you thought bringing me here would lessen the sting of my scorn," Alice began and paused, glancing around, added, "Well damn you, Radcliffe, you were right. And I hate it when you and Denny are right."

"Alice, I just want to apologize. I'm sorry. I guess there's nothing else to say about it."

"At least tell me what 'It' was about."

"You're with someone."

"It didn't stop you before." When I frowned she said, "That afternoon at LaVal's. When I was waiting for Will. You wanted to go out."

"Yeah, but that was a while ago. Honestly, I didn't know what you'd do, then or now."

"I'm here now."

I played with the currency for lack of something to say. Alice continued her tour of the shop and every now and then I heard a comment about some treasure or curio that grabbed her attention.

"I get the idea that this enormous wall or gate is between us and it's this guy," I began.

"I get to have friends, Quinn," she laughed nervously. "He doesn't begrudge me little things."

"Nice to know I'm a little thing."

"You know what I mean,"

"I don't."

"I mean I choose my own friends."

"Good to know."

"Sometimes you sound just like Dennis," Alice laughed.

"I'll take that as a compliment."

She stood at the full-length mirror now and tried on hats. She did have the face for hats. They made her more beguiling, more beautiful – if that was possible. The hat she chose was a large, floppy, beret of embroidered wool, a paisley pattern in different colors and one that Ellie would have chosen for her. "He knows I'm in York, but he doesn't know about our meeting up."

I hedged and then, "Is that something you'd want to tell him?"

"I won't listen to another lecture about my boyfriends or guys I'm seeing." Alice said, now trying on another hat, this time an early-twentieth century type with flowers on the brim. "No one ever is good enough. No one pleases him."

"I always thought he liked me," I said lightly and hoped I was hiding my feelings of disappointment.

"You were the only one he liked. He's got a photo of us on the mantle – one of the Christmases we had together. Every time I'm home he sighs, 'Now that was glad tidings!'"

"Is this the one?"

I held up the framed photograph of us and she was at the sales counter.

"You gave a copy to your grandmother? How sweet! My God, that must have been Christmas of 1969 – I remember wearing my hair like that, and the corduroy jumper," she laughed happily.

"Right before I ditched an audition and came here instead."

"That was the second emancipation proclamation, right? The first was the year before?"

We laughed easily and she continued her tour of the shop. "Is that when you bought the musical globe and the silver rose? When you came here in the early spring of '70?"

"Ellie gave them to me. I told her all about you. We went for a walk on the walls and she wanted to know what made me happy in my life, so I told her."

While I sorted change and pound notes, Alice continued to explore. She paused at a counter where perfumes and bath products were displayed next to a stack of cashmere scarves. "I understand why you love this place," she commented, "it's welcoming, comforting."

"That was Ellie. When she found the silver rose in an antique shop and when I saw it here, I thought of you and she offered it, somehow knowing it would be perfect for you and that it would please me to gift it. I wonder if you still have it."

Alice unbuttoned the top buttons of her cardigan and pulled the rose out, which I took and held for a moment, feeling both the smoothness and pattern of the rose and the warmth from her skin. I replaced it, keeping a finger on the center of the rose and felt her pulse, the rapid rise and fall of her breasts.

"I know what this means," I said at last. "At least, I hope I do."

I pulled her gently into my arms and kissed her; seven

years of longing and regret was in that kiss and I was glad for her own passionate response.

I wasn't surprised when she broke away, whispering, "I'm sorry! I shouldn't have..." and left the shop. The door slam echoed as I went back around the counter and closed the register. The 'No Sale' flag popped up.

That, also, came as no surprise.

CHAPTER 24

WE PLAYED A game of 'cat and mouse' for another day, each of us seeking the other out and accomplishing nothing, until Thursday of that week when Alice came to the shop at closing. She stood to one side as customers filed out, smiling and nodding politely as if she'd known them all her life. I smiled and sauntered over to lock the door and pull the shades.

"I owe you dinner. I was going to cook something for you," she said after a sterile 'Hello, how are you?'

"I haven't forgotten – your place? Let me finish here and grab a coat," I answered.

"I have a better idea – why not here, since we're here already?"

"Let me guess. There's no food at your place," I teased.

"I was going to go shopping, but I got a call from Denny, and then the department chair called from Brown and I got sucked into paperwork for the fall semester…"

"No need to apologize, Faery Princess; I'm sure there's a lot to do in your realm; a lot that needs your attention."

"I hope you're teasing me,"

"What do you think?"

"So that's a yes - wait, do you have food? You have a habit of keeping laboratory specimens in your fridge."

I wanted to ask how she knew that but kept silent.

"Enough for us and the cat."

"The cat?"

"You'll understand when you see him," I said over my shoulder as I went back to the counter for the sheets that draped the counters and display tables at night and started in the evening ritual.

"You don't have to apologize, Quinn," she blurted out. "For the kiss. I wanted you to kiss me."

I frowned. "Not that I was going to," I commented. "Apologize, that is. Since we got that out of the way, now maybe you'll tell me what I don't want to hear?"

Alice nodded but took her time responding. Taking a step backwards as I passed to cover a mannequin wearing medieval garb she sighed and said too quietly, "He wants to marry me, Quinn. He pushed for a wedding in August—this August. Dennis and Harry say it's a bad idea."

A dull pain started in my chest, the air escaping my lungs so that I thought I might suffocate. I knew all of this; why did it hurt me?

Because I brought it on. Because my decision led to hers.

She couldn't look at me, and when I gently turned her face towards mine, tears streamed down her cheeks.

"I was pregnant and he insisted we get married, do the right thing, for the sake of his family, for appearances. I was lonely and was tired of being alone. Then I lost the baby,"

"Alice! Oh my God, I'm sorry!"

I reached out instinctively to embrace her but she shook her head.

"Maybe it was a good thing. I don't know. Everything's been arranged, put in place, and I could be happy."

"You don't sound happy about the decision."

"I was at first, but I'm having second thoughts."

The pain in my chest started to subside. "Then why marry him?"

NOT, definitely NOT what I asked in 1978!

"Yes," she said.

"C'mon, woman. Make me supper."

Our walk through Ellie's shop and up the stairs to the flat became a light-shrouded climb up the hill from the Berkeley flatlands to the driveway of my home on Buena Vista Way, the floral wallpaper and my childhood artwork, my school photographs and framed reviews from newspapers, dissolved and reappeared as the trees and flowers of the hills overlooking San Francisco Bay. As usual, I glanced at the car port and relaxed when I saw the empty space. My mother was sitting in her little office listening to music and doing needlework when I found her.

"Darling! How was dinner at the Martins?" she asked. Mother's tone of voice made it seem like an invitation to an English country house weekend.

"Fine – fun. It always is," I answered. "Harry made this casserole that you make – the *Timballe alla Ferrara*, the Italian shepherd's pie with the pasta and sausages? I mentioned it to Alice once and I guess she told Harry."

"I haven't made that in a while," said Mother. "Shall I make it on Sunday?"

"Sure, if you want,"

"How is Alice?"

"Perfect, as always. What are you making?" I leaned forward to see the needlework – it was a re-creation of a medieval tapestry and the figures, a man and woman holding hands under a flowering tree, had started to take form from the pale blue outline of an illustration.

"It's a plate from the *Codex Manesse*," Mother said brightly, holding up the linen in its hoop. "I suppose your Alice would know all about that work?"

"She's not my Alice, she's Alice with a mind of her own, a soul, and a heart."

"First love," my mother chuckled. I failed to see the humor in that.

"Were you ever in love?" I sniped.

She looked up at me with those enormous brown eyes

and the flawless, perfect expression of 'Whatever-do-you-mean?' with perfectly shaped brows slanted upwards into question marks.

"What kind of question is that?" she laughed. "Of course! I married Andrew, didn't I?"

"I learned that it was a shotgun marriage. Dad had to marry you because he got you pregnant and my grandfather Faithwaite forced him," I said nonchalantly.

Mother stopped in mid-stitch—of course she would in this circumstance—and frowned, studying her work for imperfection. The embroidery wasn't the imperfection I was talking about.

"Your grandmother again," Mother sighed. "She has an imagination. I suppose that's where you get it."

"Ellie doesn't lie to me. She said you met Dad at a cocktail party in London after his first *La Traviata* and he started flirting and after a few dates it got ugly. That would explain some things I've always wondered about," I said quietly. I now reached over and took her hands. She resisted at first, but I was surprised by how her fingers curled around mine and grasped tightly. For the first time I felt warmth there.

"Why does this concern you, Darling?" she whispered. "It was a long time ago, and we learn to live with the choices we make."

"That's the psychiatrist talking, not a woman in love, or a mother wanting better for her son," I answered.

"In time I grew comfortable with Andrew and it's been a good marriage in many respects. You, for example. We've helped each other's careers in some way. It's a good partnership."

"Where is love? Passion? Don't you want that?"

"If I thought marriage is all about that and nothing else, then I'd be very naive. Again, Quinn, why do you ask?"

"Because when I'm over at Alice's, I see Denny and Harry—two men, yeah, and it's supposed to be wrong—

but you pick up on the love and happiness, their relationship and how good it is and it comes down to Alice."

"Ah, the romantic 'poor but happy' notion," she said.

"But true. I want our family to be like that."

"We have our own happiness. Christmas, for one,"

"Crap!" I stated.

"If you've come here to start an argument, Quinn, I won't have it. That's a trait from the Radcliffes I wish you'd never inherited."

She tried pull away, but I held fast. Something I didn't remember from that afternoon of 1970.

"Mother, Mom. Leave him. It's not good for you; for us. We can be a family somewhere else."

"And where would that be? York? Living with Ellie? No, I don't think so, Darling. Things will change; you'll see. Once you have a position in an orchestra your father will be happy again, his old self."

"To hell with that! You can't put everything in that basket and put all the responsibility on me!" I shouted.

"One day you'll understand. Sometimes we have to make sacrifices in order to live a meaningful life. Sometimes it's one's happiness."

"Is that the kind of psychological crap you sell to your patients?"

"That is my own belief, coming from my own experience."

"Physician heal thyself," I quoted from Hippocrates. "Leave him, Mother. He's destroying us. You don't have to settle."

"Sometimes, that's all you have."

Her quiet response ended the conversation. It was a conversation I remembered as I found myself back in the Shop and staring down not at my mother's perfect, flawless, hands with the heavy gold wedding band shackling her, but at the red and gold journal the Proprietress set before me on the velvet cushion. From the ubiquitous handbag she removed a sheet of gold foil stars of all sizes and took one the largest and placed it in the middle of a page that was already decorated with smaller stars.

"That's impressive," I commented.

"No dear boy, that's improvement. You still have a ways to go."

"Would it kill her to say 'well done' or congratulations?" I asked myself as I passed the coffee bar and took the steaming mug of French Roast that Janis Joplin offered.

"Probably," said Janis. "I'm surprised it bothers you," she said.

"Considering the loving neglect Jane Radcliffe served up with her *Timballe alla Ferrara*," Ralph Vaughan Williams joined in.

"You're talking about my mother!" I protested.

"We're talking about the woman who gave birth to you and left you with nannies and babysitters," Jane Austen commented and she made a notation in her manuscript, saying aloud, "'The young man was of prodigious talent and excelled in physical beauty and charm, the attributes any heroine of a novel would find worthy. His compassion was exceeding for a man of his times, at times it would be his downfall. Yet another imperfection was that he sought the same in those he loved and was always disappointed to the point of depression when he found them lacking.'"

"Not quite Mr. Darcy," said Richard III.

"I don't want to be Mr. Darcy," I answered.

"What you need to be is yourself," Hildegard von Bingen spoke up. She placed a bouquet of flowers on the table before me – the white and yellow flowers that I'd come to associate with Alice. Inhaling their fresh, evocative, scent, I was now back in The Shambles at the door to the flat with the bouquet of flowers in one hand and a bottle of Valpolicella in the other while I fumbled for the lock. Alice rescued me.

That was an understatement if ever there was one . . .

"That was quick. Did you get the wine?" Alice greeted as she opened the door. "How pretty!"

"For the table. I saw them and thought they'd be perfect," I replied, handing over the bouquet.

"Well, I found some things on the shelves and in the fridge, so I whipped something up – I'm hoping it will be a surprise," Alice said as she went back into the kitchen and returned to the living room with the flowers in a pottery jug, two glasses and a corkscrew.

"The fact that you can cook is a surprise."

Alice screwed up her face in a silly smile as she handed over the corkscrew and said, "Make yourself useful."

We were sitting opposite one another in the living room, I in my chair and Alice in Ellie's enjoying conversation and our wine when Becket appeared from one of the bedrooms. He yawned, stretched and purred when Alice bent down to greet him calling him the cutest, fattest, most loveable cat in the world. The cat turned to butter and lolled on the carpet, taking in the attention. I must admit I was a little jealous. Finally, she let the cat alone and looked around, beaming.

"Now why would you ever want to leave this place?" she asked.

"It's my version of Never Land," I said. "Some people have bottles of scotch they crawl into, and I have this place where I never have to be any older than twelve, I guess. And now it's mine."

"I know some people who could testify to the scotch experience," I heard Alice say as she excused herself to check on the meal that was smelling delicious and intriguing. I held my tongue, for when it came to comfort from twelve-year old single malt or gin I had taken more than my share.

"I don't want to make that mistake," I whispered as if to myself and smiled sheepishly when Alice looked back, a puzzled look on her face. "Can't wait for this surprise," I said.

Dinner was a surprise: it was the casserole of sausages, peppers, tomatoes and filled pasta like ravioli, baked in a savory crust in a deep dish. The *Timballe alla Ferrara*. That meal, my favorite dish and my favorite person, would be my *agape*, my love feast, and where everything began to make sense. The one mystery was how closed Alice had become, the sadness that was just there on the surface but seemed to bind her.

Strangely, Alice's news didn't weigh as heavily on me as I thought it might. Of course it wouldn't. I knew the eventual outcome.

I persuaded Alice to share the bottle of wine and the evening was wonderful and bittersweet; we talked about everything, laughed, and shared memories, all but the most important subject that was a dead elephant in the middle of the room. That didn't come up until I took her to the city walls.

"When in August?" I blurted out.

"The twenty-sixth."

"Well," I sighed, taking her hand as we climbed the stairs from Bootham Bar, "You're not married yet."

"Is that an offer of infidelity, Maestro?" Her quiet expression and dark eyes told me it was anything but a joke.

"No; I think that would make us both miserable," I answered. "Let's call it friendship for now."

"Oh, just as bad for a woman to hear as for a man," Alice laughed. "But if it's all that's on the table, well then." She pivoted and looked towards the north and then suddenly, "Why aren't you married?"

"Who'd want me?" I laughed, shaking my head.

"What do you mean? I mean, look at you. You were gorgeous nine years ago, but now…"

"There was only one girl I ever loved."

"Your cello Petula," Alice said and when she gave me

a goofy, sideways grin we laughed. "A secret I'll take to my grave."

Among others! Tell me the truth, Alice!

"There's another. You know her pretty well. She's got a heart and a soul. A sense of humor. She's smart, beautiful, with a smile that takes your breath away and eyes that are so incredible. And she's still all that."

"I know what happened to her; I just wish I knew what happened to that boy. Did he grow up and just forget, or was it something else?"

"I was stupid. I was given choices; no, I was forced into making decisions with ultimatums."

"Why didn't you fight?"

"I wish I could tell you why. I actually did fight for a while but things happened. There was also a degree of shame."

"I know."

"What?"

The light started to change and I waited for the jettison back to the Village or another moment in my time. Meeting her glance for only a moment I said, "What do you know? About my parents? Me?"

"I heard the argument, Quinn."

"Pardon?"

"When you told your parents we wanted to marry. I heard the argument you had with your parents. It was hard not to."

"I thought…"

"And I waited at the library. When you didn't show up I assumed you didn't want me. Then you came by that winter day and I knew it was over. When we got together later, we never talked about it. I guessed it was too painful a subject to broach. It was for me."

"I guess," I said after a time.

We walked silently back to her flat in Gillygate.

"Well, this is me," Alice sighed as she unlocked the door and hesitated with the catch.

"Thanks for dinner – I had no idea."

"I like to surprise people with my unknown talents. Like coffee."

"Oh no, I've had your coffee. Dennis said he uses it kill the weeds in his rose bushes," I teased, giving her a wink.

"Then I won't invite you in," she purred, "and you'll be sorry you missed out."

"I'll make it up to you. Come to Scarborough with me this weekend," I said of a sudden.

She spun round, frowning. "What?"

"I want to show you something—there's the castle, the cliffs. I think you'd like it and frankly, I could use some time away with a friend just to relax."

"I don't know… you won't come in for coffee…" she jested now.

"Strictly honorable. Two friends from school—no strings. Maybe some soul searching, true confessions, lemon meringue pie." She was still fidgeting with the catch, pressing the lever up and down so that it groaned and squeaked until it became annoying and I took her hand. "Who's your oldest friend besides Denny?"

She smiled. "That would be you."

"What's wrong with spending time with a friend? If you're worried about what the neighbors would say, and your fiancé seeing it on the news, well, your neighbors don't live on my street in Scarborough and the news teams only come around when a part of the cliff falls into the sea. When will we get this chance again? You'll be back in the States and married, living your cozy academic life," I said brightly and too quickly. "I'll be spending summers at Saint Tropez with my latest supermodel girlfriend and longing for the days when I could talk to an intelligent woman—*Ow!* What was that for?"

Alice had punched me in the arm playfully and was laughing. "Beautiful women aren't stupid," she stated.

"You should know," I said, planting a kiss on her

cheek. She moved slightly as if offering her lips and I hedged, backed away from the opportunity. "Think about it? You know where to find me." I said good night and started back to The Shambles.

She was still standing on the doorstep when I looked back, watching me. The battle was half-won, I thought as I continued on my way, but I soon discovered that I wasn't walking back to Ellie's shop and flat, but down the corridor to my dressing room at Lincoln Center on Opening Night of the Orchestra's American tour in August of 1979, a year later.

Oh God…

"Why the long face?" Richard III asked falling in step with me. He took the clipboard from Mrs. Haddon running at my side and signed documents for me as they were presented, handed over stacks of sheet music, grabbed bouquets of flowers being delivered and passed them to Mrs. Haddon who didn't seem to notice or miss a beat.

"I don't want to be here!" I hissed back. "We could have avoided all this!"

"So you say; you have to be here and you know it. Now, put on a good show."

Richard was gone as quickly as he appeared and I continued towards the dressing room. People moved out of the way as I passed. I had my grim determination, game day face on.

"…there's a guy outside who says he's the son of a politician running for President, a senator from Rhode Island," I heard a roadie say to Graham.

"So?" Graham asked impatiently.

"His mother is some heiress who gave a lot of the cash to put the tour together. They want to know if Mister Radcliffe is interested in coming to a party at Le Cirque after. Lots of money in the crowd—donations promised, something like that."

"Christ! If I had a penny farthing every bloody time

some bloody rich mother wanted her son or daughter to meet Quinn…"

"You'd own Hampton Court," I interrupted, turning on the roadie with a dazzling smile. "The guy's name?"

"Donovan…something."

Trist. I didn't say the name aloud.

They watched me, waiting, and I shrugged. "Sure. Why not? Haven't been to Le Cirque in a while. A society maven and her middle-aged gay son, probably. Their connections may help us raise more money for the new headquarters in London." The dig at Alice's mysterious archeologist had me smiling on the way to the dressing room, which was now impeded by Chloe Carlisle.

"Maestro, you have a guest waiting for you in your dressing room," she giggled.

Surely not Alice! The way Chloe was giggling and leading the way made me wonder. The combination of fear and anticipation turned to delight when I opened the door and saw Jordan Gregson, my friend from Oxford, sitting on the sofa and helping himself to the fruit basket.

"Hey! Why didn't you tell me you'd be in town? When did you get in?" I exclaimed as we shook hands and then offered 'guy pats' on the back.

"You're not the only sex symbol with an American tour," Jordan said, winking at Chloe, who had linked her arm through mine in her friendly, sisterly way. "Who's this delightful young lady, Radcliffe? I tried to get her number but she's keeping silent. Please don't tell me this is the girl in that photograph of you making out on the beach in Cannes. I'd be heartbroken."

"Chloe Carlisle. Violin. Your heart is safe, Mr. Gregson. You don't have tits or a vagina," said Chloe cheekily as she blew me a kiss on the way out of the dressing room.

"She's into girls," I replied to the unasked question.

"Ah. Hang out with the rival team and it keeps the ladies at bay because they think you're together, and let's face it, Radcliffe, you don't want to bother."

"When did you become such a prick?" I laughed.

"Since my divorce, apparently. Believe me, I understand the attraction to stay single in this business."

I dismissed the comment and started rifling through the scores piled on an end table near the sofa. "Staying for the concert, I hope, or just here to get a drink after?" I called over my shoulder.

"I can stay; I can hang out backstage."

"How 'bout stage center? You being here just gave me a great idea. I've got a number I want to do," I said, and handed him a score. When Jordan's brows creased as he flipped through the music, I added, "Alice is here tonight."

CHAPTER 25

SHE WAS THERE—somewhere in the house.

She was all I could think about while Graham was warming up the orchestra. While Jordan paced, looking a bit nervous for an internationally-known singer who'd crossed over from classical to pop and wound up an idol, complete with screaming girls and a fan club. While my heart pounded and I wondered if I was doing the right thing.

I was putting my career on the line for a hunch. Wishful thinking.

Guilt.

"It's just a song," I teased, checking my hair and white tie, brushing lint from a sleeve, making sure my voice was even and didn't betray my nervousness.

"Right. For my next show I'll have you do *Stairway to Heaven* on that cello of yours."

"You don't think I could do it?"

"Bloody hell, you'd do it, wouldn't you?" Jordan laughed, taking a pull from a glass of water. "But this song? Honestly, mate, I don't think it's been done like this before."

"I don't know why you're nervous," I insisted, turning to the mirror again and checking my hair one last time. "It won't be your head in a noose if it falls apart."

"Then why do it?"

I shrugged. "Because I love her. I always have; I always will."

A knock on the door and the stage manager poked his head around. "Excuse me, sir; a Doctor Trist is outside—he's that senator's son and would like a word with you before you go on?"

I glanced at the clock and frowned. "Ten minutes, that's all."

The stage manager saluted me with a nod and disappeared, returning seconds later with Donovan Trist, Ph.D., archeologist and lecturer at Brown University. This much I knew about him. I wasn't prepared for what came next.

He walked into the room like he owned it and stopped a few feet short of me, hand extended in greeting. I was staring at my older, shorter, less muscular brother. Even Jordan saw the resemblance, for he stared at my doppelganger and said "What the fuck?"

"Maestro Radcliffe, thank you for seeing me on such short notice—I'm Donovan Trist, my parents are Senator and Arielle Trist of Rhode Island," Trist gushed. "Mother's been a benefactor of the arts for decades." His voice was as oily and smooth as the disingenuous smile being offered.

"Call me Quinn," I said, shaking his hand. "What can I do for you?"

I knew what he wanted; I also knew what I wanted to do to him.

"It's my wedding anniversary."

"Congratulations, how many?"

"Just a year. Anyway, I've brought my wife, and she's from Berkeley—you may have gone to high school with her—in fact, I think you did."

"Name?"

"Alice Martin."

I nodded and tried not to smile. "Yeah, I remember her. Does she want an autograph, or anything?"

Jordan made a sputtering sound like he was choking in his water.

"Could I bring her backstage after the show? Just to say hi, maybe get a picture—oh, and we've arranged a reception for you at Le Cirque, if you're interested."

I glanced at Jordan who was shaking his head. "I don't know how busy it will be after the concert," I started and then added, "I might be able to fit in the reception. Not so sure about afterwards, backstage."

"Oh."

I'd knocked the wind out of his sails.

The lights flickered, a bell, and then, "Mister Radcliffe, ten minutes, please," the disembodied voice warned over the loudspeaker.

Trist pumped my hand again and then glad-handed the stage manager as if he'd done him a favor, talking about his dig at Petra all the way out.

"That was fun," I said to Jordan as we followed moments later. We nodded and wove through a cannonade of strobe flashes and the steady white eye of a local public television station's cameras *en route* to the stage, my vision trained not on the path before me, nor the assistant leading us to the elevator, but Doctor Donovan Trist, archeologist and lecturer at Brown University, who was a few feet ahead, still acting as if he owned the room and everyone in it. He continued to glad-hand and greet like the walk to the boxes was a political campaign stump until a stunning blonde stepped in his path.

"Wait a minute," I hissed at Jordan and paused facing Trist as I made a pretense of going over the score in Jordan's hand. Jordan nudged me and I put my finger to my lips and jerked my chin in Trist's direction.

"What are you doing here?" I heard Trist growl, pulling the woman into the shadows.

"You should return calls once in a while," she purred back. I booked the room, just like you asked."

"Not this weekend!"

"You said this weekend!"

"Oh for Chrissakes, my wife is here tonight!"

"Really? Good! I've always wanted to meet Saint Anne, or Alice, or whatever her name is."

"You can't be here!"

"I bought a ticket, who says I can't? Besides, I wanted to give you this."

That was one sloppy, noisy kiss echoing down the corridor. It was all I needed and I tapped Jordan, signaling that our last-minute huddle was over. "Nice meeting you, Mr. Trist," I called out and winked when we passed, Trist and his honey still wrapped around each other like a pretzel. I started singing lyrics from a Beatles tune.

"You're gonna lose that girl, yes, yes, you're gonna lose that girl."

Trist looked like he was going to have a stroke—too bad he didn't.

"Boy, now that was fun," I said to Jordan when we got into the elevator. By the time we reached backstage the moment of elation had passed and it was time to go to work.

I seldom looked at faces in the audience when I came out to the podium in the glare of a spotlight but that night I did look up and I smiled when I heard the screams from the ladies in the balcony and the applause that followed it. Orchestra members were glancing at one another in amusement for the serious, dark, Quinn Radcliffe was actually smiling and acknowledging his fans.

But I didn't see Alice.

The orchestra had never been better as far as I was concerned and it came as a surprise when during intermission I announced the special encore number and got nods of approval and even wistful sighs from the women.

"Who're you trying to impress, Maestro?" called out one of the trumpeters, which encouraged others to tease and the chant of *"Who? Who?"* started.

"A friend," I admitted and received one of those sympathetic *'awws'* and a few claps on the back. "I've had the music placed on your stands and Graham will conduct this number."

Intermission came to an end and I spent a moment alone in the dressing room, waiting for the call. When it came, I took a breath and went up, managed to get through *Lark Ascending, Greensleeves* and the *English Folk Song Suite*. The curtain calls started and finally I nodded to the stage manager, Graham, and Jordan, who gave me a 'good luck' punch on the shoulder in passing. The applause was starting to die down when we took our places on stage and waited for the curtain to go up. I turned in the glare of the spotlight from the podium and raised my hands for silence.

"I've invited a friend to join us this evening—Jordan Gregson," I announced.

Jordan came out to an ovation that broke ear drums. We laughed and waited for calm before I stepped off the podium and handed my baton to Graham. This brought whispers and murmurs of speculation. Stagehands brought my cello and a chair and placed it stage right of Jordan at the piano.

Again I waited until the house was silent, and then said quietly, "You may recognize this song—it's a special one, and for a special friend from home."

Jordan began on the piano—measures from Nino Rota's music from *Romeo & Juliet*, which I picked up on the cello, and then, Jordan sang *A Time for Us* in Italian, *Un Giorno Per Noi*, accompanied by the Orchestra. My solo came at the middle. I closed my eyes and concentrated on every note, remembering that day in Scarborough when I first played it; in my mind's eye I saw the shadows cast by the daylight on the floor, the bow as it went back and forth in scales and *arpeggios*, the silhouette Alice cast as she listened in rapt attention and how we came together in that moment and at that time. It had been a spiritual bonding as well as physical, for later I would make love to her and she would reciprocate and it was something neither of us would forget.

The applause and cheering startled me back to the present—or that particular present—and Jordan picked up the melody and finished the song, holding the last note as I offered another *arpeggio* to end the number.

And it was then I saw her. Not the stunning voluptuous blonde I'd seen Trist kissing, but Alice. She was the only one seated while people were on their feet and applauding and cheering. Trist was bending over her solicitously and then she disappeared. I wouldn't see her again until he pushed his way backstage and pointed her out in the crush of staff, musicians, and friends wanting to congratulate us and while I was being interviewed for the late news broadcasts.

"Quinn!" Trist shouted, elbowing towards me and grinning like we were old friends. The cameras naturally turned on him for people started whispering his name and moved aside.

"Doctor Trist, hello; I'm tied up right now."

"Not too busy to say hello to your high school sweetheart?" he chuckled and it had the effect he wanted: whispering, conjecture, and all eyes on the beautiful woman standing in a corner looking like she wanted to be any- where but there.

Our eyes locked—a cliché if there ever was one—but yes, all I could see was Alice and her sad smile. Trist was nudging me in her direction and babbling about his mother Arielle when I was intercepted by Lincoln Center's director, who begged a few minutes of my time for a photo op. I looked back and she was gone but once the photographers had what they wanted I made excuses and sprinted towards the main entrance to the Grand Stairs.

"Alice! Alice, wait!"

They were waiting for their car when I scrambled down the staircase two steps at a time and pulled myself together in a dignified halt right before them.

"Maestro!" Trist greeted, a hand outstretched. I took

it, but my eyes were for Alice. "Alice…Alice, my mother told me about Denny. I'm so sorry."

"Thanks. He did ask about you in the last weeks," she said.

"We were on the road, and there was a recording session, all the usual nonsense. But I was home a month after, and Harry said you'd moved back east for good."

The tension was more than palpable as I waited for a reply. Alice glanced at Trist and said, "Donovan had to get back to the dig at Petra and I had lectures, so we couldn't stay in Berkeley for very long. I wish I'd known you were in town; we could have met for drinks, isn't that right, Donovan?"

"I've been wanting to meet this mysterious friend Dennis and Harry always talked about. Little did I know he'd be a famous musician," Donovan's accompanying laugh was forced and brittle.

"Why don't we pick this conversation up at Le Cirque?" I said of a sudden, and asked, smiling at Alice, "Do you want to come? I know Doctor Trist spent a fortune on food and drink. Wouldn't want it to go to waste."

"Angel?" Donovan asked, turning to look at Alice.

Aha! Now I knew why she hated being called 'angel.'

She took her time to respond—again—and finally, "It's been a long night, and I haven't been feeling well," she apologized. "Donovan, you should go. I can take the car back to the hotel." Then she looked up at me and I saw the tears. "Sorry. It's nothing personal."

"No worries," I whispered. I wanted more than anything to take her in my arms and kiss her. "I really am sorry. It's been a while, hasn't it?"

I wanted to make a joke about one of her favorite movies, *Brief Encounter*, but decided against it. Besides, Trist was smiling triumphantly as if he had won a quarrel or debate. "Shall we go?" he asked.

"I have to get my things," I said, and turned away as

Trist gave Alice a perfunctory kiss on the brow, as if she was a favorite niece rather than his wife. He was following, trying to keep up with me as I went back to the Center, hurrying past the photographers and orchestra staffers who had materialized in their search for me.

"Thank you, Quinn," Trist said, that annoying happy laugh in his voice, the newscaster's tone.

"Always happy to oblige my fans and the public," I responded, and then paused to let him catch up. When he did I threw an arm about his shoulders familiarly for the photographers and Trist enjoyed it as the strobes and flashes went off. I leaned in and said low, "I saw you. I know you saw me. Hurt Alice and I will come after you."

We took separate taxis to the restaurant.

My cab took me straight to the village.

The ovation I received made me smile. Hildegard came forward and presented me with a bouquet of mixed flowers with colors that seemed to glow and throw off ribbons of light like the reflections from stained glass windows. When Janis ran to me for a kiss, I respectfully declined.

"Well done, you!" Rafe greeted, pumping my hand until I had to let go for fear it would drop off. I was pounded on the back, showered with more bouquets and given a plate of Pop Tarts as I made my way to the counter where the Proprietress waited. She slid her glasses up her nose with the middle finger and cleared her throat as she took my box down from the shelf and opened it to reveal a silver rose with all of its petals but one, which lay on the velvet-covered bottom. When I reached for it she slapped my hand.

"Mind what you touch, sir!" she barked. "The battle's half-done, half-won."

The book came out next and she plastered a medium-sized blue star in the middle of a blank page. I protested. "You have to admit I showed a bit more courage than in the past. Blue? Seriously? Even silver would be better."

"You can only avoid the inevitable for so long. Have your tea and be on your way. Time's running out."

She snapped her fingers and pointed at my table. The Shop returned to its quiet, normal state with customers coming in and going, served with cold efficiency and speed. Only my companions remained as I sipped my tea and stared at nothing. Michael took the seat opposite me and helped himself to the Pop Tarts.

"I understand the attraction to these," he mumbled in between bites. "So. You're feeling smug, aren't you?"

"Not exactly. A sense of accomplishment, maybe."

"It's one victory, Quinn. That's all it is," Michael said and pushed the plate towards me. "Want the last one? No?" He took the Pop Tart and finished it before speaking again. "Remember that dream you used to have as a boy? The one where you were riding a bike on a country road in Yorkshire and there was a door in the middle of the road that you couldn't get around?"

"I remember that. I had it a few nights ago—rather, whenever it was that I last slept. No matter what I did, the door was in the way and I couldn't go any farther. It was blocking the way. I'd always wake up yelling about the door."

"Time to open the door, Quinn," Richard spoke up as he worked on the crossword, never taking his eyes from the page. "What's a five-letter word for *martyr*?"

"Saint?" I ventured.

Michael shook his head. "You're far from that. But you're on the right track." He leaned back in his chair and studied his coat sleeve, plucking a speck of silver lint from the fabric and blew it away. I expected something to happen but to my amazement, there was nothing except my corner in the shop and no one else but Michael.

"Now, say to me what you haven't said to anyone," he said.

I couldn't take my eyes from his face, especially his eyes. Around him there seemed to be a shower of light, silver and pulsing like a heartbeat, yet soothing. I felt like I was falling into one of the episodes that came with my headaches, the times when dizziness made me nauseous and a watery light blinded me until I would black out. I didn't want that to happen in front of Michael and I relaxed a bit, breathing slowly, until I realized the silver light was the flash of lightning in the skies over York during that summer of 1978. I had just answered the telephone when the storm began.

"Hello, Darling! You're home," Mother exclaimed from her side of the Atlantic.

"What's up, Mom?" I asked as cheerfully as I could.

"Your father heard that the Orchestra is coming to the United States next year – something one of his students read in a trade magazine. You must be so excited, Darling! I just called to see how you were doing and to hear about it," she chirped.

"To find out why I didn't tell you," I answered. A clap of thunder like a tympani roll and another branch of lightning caught my attention. No, it was a real storm; there was no sign of Her Worshipfulness or any of her minions. I could continue. I was ready.

"You might have dropped a line so we didn't have to hear the news second hand. I can't tell you how disappointed he was when you didn't tell us. Tarquin, are you still so angry?"

"I thought I made myself clear when Ellie died. I want him to stay away and if you insist on staying with him or condoning his actions then you might as well stay away, too."

"Emotional blackmail. I wonder where you learned how to do that?"

"Shouldn't be hard to guess. I have to run – I'm taking a friend to Scarborough for the weekend."

"How lovely! Good for you!" My mother's mood changed instantly. "Is it that darling girl we met at the funeral? The violinist?" Mother sounded hopeful.

I hedged. "Old friend from better days. You've met her a couple of times," I hinted. Why hide it?

"I haven't met most of your girlfriends, and you haven't got many friends, so—Dear Lord! Not Alice!"

"We're going to talk, take care of old business. I'm going to tell Alice everything so she knows it wasn't just me."

"And what if she talks? Says something to that brother of hers? It will be all over town!"

"You didn't hear? She's marrying some rich college professor at the end of summer. She's not so vindictive as to make your lives miserable because she can. Alice has a lot more compassion and integrity than you give her credit for."

"What can I say or do to make you reconsider? Show some of that compassion and integrity you say Alice has because I know you have it in spades. I beg you to reconsider. Please."

"Stop prying. See you around, Mom."

After I hung up I glanced out the window and noticed patches of bright blue sky in between the storm clouds starting to drift south. Great allegory if ever there was, as Ellie would have said.

Ellie would have been proud, I thought happily as I grabbed my overnight case and keys and headed for the door. I even gave Becket a scratch behind the ears and for once the stupid cat didn't growl or try to bite my hand off.

Things were improving.

CHAPTER 26

THE GENTLE ROLLING of the train was soothing, but not as soothing as Alice sleeping in my arms.

We'd found an empty compartment on the train and kept it to ourselves. I shut the doors and rather than sit beside Alice, I sat on bench opposite hers next to the enormous bouquet of silver roses that I'd picked up on the spur of the moment because it felt right. Everything felt right.

"There's room here," Alice said, patting the cushion on her left. "You never know if those flowers are going to multiply like Triffids or Tribbles over night."

"I'll take my chances. I love looking at your eyes when we talk," I answered. "Besides, I can take on killer plants as well as plastic snakes."

Alice leaned close and whispered, "Better lock the door just in case you wind up in your boxers!"

Jumping up, I leapt to the compartment door and locked it then sat down with my elbows on my knees, chin in my palms, expectantly, like a child waiting for a treat. I didn't get a snow cone, or a gum drop, or even a kiss, but Alice's musical laughter and a bright smile, perhaps the brightest I'd ever seen and that was enough.

"You always know the right things to do and say," she laughed.

"It's easy to do when the woman is so beautiful," I said.

"You're teasing me, right?"

"No, just speaking the truth. And you've always been truthful with me, Alice Rose."

A wistful smile crossed her lips now and the brightness faded. She tried another smile and dismissed my comment with a forced giggle and a shake of her head. Then Alice fumbled around in her bag and pulled out a mirrored compact, opening it to check her face, or hide that perfect face from me.

"It's perfect. You're perfect," I said. "You're beautiful." When she didn't respond, I asked, "What's wrong?" I leaned forward to take her hands.

Alice shrugged. "Some of my Catholic guilt has resurfaced."

"Meaning...?"

"We're both in relationships and yet, here we are."

"Two longtime friends spending time together, not legally bound to others...maybe bound to each other by a promise made not so long ago."

"Yet we broke it, and may break it again."

I leaned back and exhaled a sigh. "Well, we can turn around at Scarborough if that's what you really want."

"No. The trouble is I don't know what I want. I thought I did."

"You're not alone there. Let's use this time to figure things out."

"Maybe I want, or I'm expecting, something more than you're willing or able to give," she confessed.

"You don't know what's being offered," I jested lightly.

I slid across the compartment and held Alice in my arms like I had on our first date. Leaning back against the armrest, I stretched out over the seat and brought her with me so that she was snuggled in my arms with her head on my breast. "My beautiful Alice, one thing you must know is that you will always have my love. Always."

My faery princess drifted off to sleep then, and I relaxed, listening to her kitten snores.

"Not a bad start, this." Ralph Vaughan Williams' voice and presence weren't unsettling. I opened my eyes to see Rafe and Richard III smiling at us from the opposite bench.

"Not at all," Richard added.

"Did you bring any stars for my notebook?" I teased. "This gives me at least a silver, don't you think?"

"At least," Rafe answered and Richard nodded.

"No advice? Sarcasm? Irony?"

"It will be difficult enough, dear boy. You'll know what to do," said Rafe. "And hopefully the right things to say."

I motioned with my head towards the compartment door and they were gone. Again, the gentle rocking of the car as we rode east to Scarborough made me content and lulled me to sleep. I suppose it was the stillness that woke me. Alice was still by my side, but we were in her bed in the sanctuary and it was the late spring of 1970. My eyes focused on the screen blocking the stairwell to the kitchen. The five medieval ladies painted on the screen were watching me, probably with disapproval, for I'd come back to Alice's house after everyone was asleep and made love to my love for only the second time and it was amazing, no, incredible, no, glorious! Judging by the light, it was about six in the morning and a Sunday.

I pulled Alice closer and the effect on me was instantaneous, both in love and longing. Because we were still strangers to one another in this respect, I took my time and just held her in my arms, loving the feel of her velvety skin. I knew that that was such a cliché, but she really did feel like the most expensive velvet and silk. Her scent was incredible and sensual and I breathed it in as I planted kissed on her neck and breasts, hoping to wake her so that we could make love one more time before I slipped away and no one knew we'd slept together. It would be one of many secrets binding us.

The telephone ringing upstairs was merely a

distraction at first, and I tried to ignore it as Alice finally woke and wrapped her arms around me as we kissed and our tension and longing grew, as she threw off the covers and we were unencumbered by the blankets.

"You are so beautiful," I whispered between kisses and as my hands explored the wonderful contours, the softness of her body.

"...No, he left around midnight," Dennis said from the kitchen phone.

Alice and I froze and looked at one another in horror.

"I hardly think he's here, Professor; Alice knows the rules," Dennis continued. "...you can come over and search under her bed if you'd like . . . yes, I was being sarcastic . . . hang on a minute . . . Alice! Alice, are you awake? Alice, is Quinn down there – and if he is he better not be!"

We both flew from the bed when we heard Dennis' footsteps and Alice was throwing my clothes and shoes at me as I slipped out the garden door and dressed behind a rosebush. I'd never look at rosebushes the same again. As I slipped out of the yard I made sure the neighbors didn't see and pulled up the collar of the windbreaker and hunched down as the milkman passed by making his rounds.

I walked further up Rose Street and made a right at Oxford, which would have been out of the ordinary for a walk home. It take long to notice that the late summer sunrise was paler than usual and a chill was in the air. When I reached to zip up the windbreaker against the unexpected cool morning, it was my winter coat I was clutching against an eastern breeze. I was walking downtown and carrying a school bag and enough money for two plane tickets to England.

Anxiety and anticipation roiled together in the pit of my stomach, sweat rose on my forehead and upper lip as I realized it was winter of 1972.

Almost forty-eight hours had passed since the

confrontation in my father's study when I announced my intention to marry Alice. That didn't go as expected; I was foolish to think my parents would receive the news as well as Denny and Harry. That fear was confirmed when I noticed Edward IV ticketing cars on Center Street. He nodded as I walked by.

The plan was to meet at the Berkeley Library in the newspaper room. From there we'd take the bus to San Francisco and find our way to the airport.

No one was around — it was still Christmas vacation and a weekday. The clerk at the checkout desk smiled as I walked by trying to look inconspicuous by digging around in the school bag as I passed through to the reading room and fiction stacks to the newspaper room. Yet another scholar looking for a pencil, a slide rule, in my case, courage. I ducked into the alcove and threw myself into one of the smelly over-stuffed chairs and grabbed The Chronicle. The paper rattled as my hands shook. Twice I thought I saw Alice and was twice disappointed.

"He's over there, Sir. In the newspaper alcove."

Stupid fucking desk clerk! She was pointing in my direction and smiling at my father, who wasn't. Slumping down in the chair or hiding behind the newspaper did no good. He was glaring down at me.

"Don't say a word, Tarquin," Father quietly ordered. "Get your things and come with me now."

"I'm of age in the U.K. So just back away, Dad," I warned in an equally quiet and terse voice.

"Let's see how that works for you when you're living in a flophouse or on the streets, because that's where you'll be if you keep up with this juvenile game. Now come along and not another word!"

"What? If I don't you'll beat some sense into me?"

A librarian came over and threw metaphorical daggers at me from behind her bifocals. "I'm going to ask you to leave if you won't keep your voices down."

"This man is threatening me, Ma'am," I said.

"You little bastard!" Father growled. He turned to the librarian. "This is my son - you know this younger generation; no respect, no moral values." The delivery was perfect - smooth, calm, full of charm. Not to mention the famous Radcliffe dimpled smile and devastating good looks.

"That's enough! Both of you - out! Before I call the police," the librarian ordered.

I was doomed - a dead man. Grabbing my stuff, I sprinted back down the stairs to the street and started east towards the high school. With any luck I'd lose him and duck somewhere to wait and go back to meet Alice. With any luck . . .

"What are you playing at, Quinn?" Father snapped. I felt his hand on my shoulder and shrugged it off.

"Why can't you leave me alone? Why do you need to control every damn thing in my life?" I yelled. People were looking, pausing, but I didn't care. Out of the corner of my eye I saw Andersen rolling up in the Bentley and for a moment I thought I'd get a break – if I could jump in and tell Andersen to floor it.

No such luck.

My father had grabbed my arm and twisted it behind my back. I refused to cry out for the pain it caused. We stood on the sidewalk up against the Bentley.

"I can break your arm, Tarquin," Father whispered menacingly. "It's all I need to do to ruin a career – that or a telephone call to those who matter. Now get in the car!"

People were starting to gather – the usual gawking and whispering – and Andersen was giving me the 'it's all you can do to save yourself look,' that glance that was two parts pity, one part anger (if that was possible). I extricated myself and fell into the back seat of the Bentley holding the school bag against me as a shield. One of my bows was on the floor and I grabbed it. I could use it as a weapon.

We took off just as a police cruiser circled back and

Andersen did as told when my father instructed him to roll down the window so that he could talk to the officer.

"A family dispute – runaway adolescent. We're perfectly fine," Father cheerfully volunteered.

The officer glanced back at me. "Son?" he asked.

"Fine," I muttered. "Difference of opinion." I looked over at the officer as we drove off, remembering the badge number and name, the face.

The ride home was quiet. Andersen didn't bother to ask me for my things as I got out of the car. He disappeared to the servants' quarters and left me to walk into the house with my father close behind.

"I found him," Father announced as Mother came out of the living room into the hallway. Mother was hiding her emotions well. It was easy to guess by the bland, pale, perfect face and the perfectly-applied crimson lipstick on the prim mouth. Even so, I took a step forward.

"Mom, you understand, don't you?"

I don't remember what she said. All I remember is my father's fist on my face and falling...

I came to on the train heading towards Scarborough.

CHAPTER 27

THE TRAIN WAS slowing down and after the initial moment of panic subsided, after I realized what this reality was, I relaxed and kissed the top of Alice's head. I took in the scent of her perfume and hair and swallowed tears of gratefulness. It was around midnight and we had arrived at Scarborough. I was certain redemption was not far away.

"Alice, we're here,"

She sat up and immediately fussed with her hair, swiped fingers under her eyes to remove mascara smudges that I thought gave her a sultry, smoldering look.

"Are we staying in a railway hotel?" she asked, looking around at the buildings nearby when we disembarked and took our bags to the taxi stand outside the station.

"Nope, somewhere better: my house."

"Your house?"

"I have a little house facing the south bay – it's in the shadow of the ruins of the castle –"

"Castle?" she squealed with delight. "You live near Scarborough Castle??"

"I take it you like that idea?" I laughed as I waved down a taxi and we piled in with our bags.

"Do you own this one?" she teased.

"I wish!"

The last time I'd brought a woman to the house for the weekend it had been a disaster, so much that I started to feel the anxiety when we pulled up. It wasn't really much — an ancient row house with a few amenities, its flaws covered with new paint and window boxes of flowers...

"It's lovely!"

Alice's exclamation dispelled any fears. She sat on the bottom step while I sorted out our luggage and paid the fare and when the taxi drove off I sat beside her.

"Well, this is me," I said.

"Lucky you!"

"I guess you're glad you came after all."

She leaned forward and put her chin on the top of my head in an awkward display of affection and I felt a kiss not long after.

"Forgive me?" she whispered.

"For what?" the chuckle was not derisive.

"For failing to see the good in coming to Scarborough and for being afraid."

"You're not the only one."

I lifted Alice from the stair with a gentle tug on her hand and we climbed the stairs. For the first time I counted them. *One, two, three*, I wouldn't be climbing back to the Village, *four, five, six*, I needed to be there in Scarborough, seven, eight, I had set my mind to the reason for being there, *nine, ten*, a clock somewhere chimed the half hour and *the time had come*.

We were at the door and I unlocked it and stepped aside as far as I could without falling off the porch to let Alice in, switched on the lights so that she could see the little English row house with its overstuffed furniture, the low, oak-beamed ceiling and mullioned windows set with deep sills and seats.

"Won't be a moment," I said and went down to get our things. Back in the house I found Alice in the living room, studying the bookcase set into the wall.

"How many of these have you read?" she asked, throwing a smile in my direction.

"Three, including yours," I admitted. "I just put them

on the shelf to impress people."

"You're joking, right?" Alice laughed.

"Not about reading your book."

Alice leaned into the shelves and after a moment pulled out a well-worn copy of her first book, a history of medieval Italy. "You read my work." Not a question, but a statement.

"Why wouldn't I?" I asked, joining her at the bookcase. "I remember how you used to talk about wanting to write if you couldn't design costumes. For someone like me who only knows about Dante and Petrarch from college classes it was a great introduction."

She replaced the book on the shelf and shook her head. "I was miserable when I wrote it. Life wasn't all that I'd hoped it would be. Bad choices, bad moments. I guess Italy reminded me of bad times. Then while in the middle of research on another paper I discovered late Anglo Saxon England and it drew me in."

I tapped her nose playfully and said, "You champion the doomed. No wonder Richard likes you so much."

Oh my God, what had I done??

There was a rumble of thunder outside and an eerie purple glow was spreading across the horizon when I looked out the window to see if it really was a summer thunderstorm or Her Worshipfulness' bad temper. Seeing Richard III and Jimi Hendrix down in the lane below, I knew I was in for it. In unison they drew their index fingers across their throats. When I turned back, the Proprietress was standing in the middle of the room, arms folded and tapping a heel on the floor.

"You've made a mess of things," she snapped.

"I didn't say it on purpose," I defended myself. "It just . . . slipped. It's the truth, isn't it?"

"Yes," said Richard when he joined us. "I'm glad you recognized that. But you have made a mess of things. Now all you can do is tell the truth. You know where we'll be."

Richard jerked his head towards the door and the Proprietress expelled a sigh and followed. Alice was frowning at me now and I remembered that look from the party in Berkeley back in '75.

"You look tired," I said, trying to diffuse the situation.

Fortunately for me she smiled; never mind that it belied her state of mind, for it was a weary attempt and now Alice tried to stifle a yawn. "I didn't realize how hard I've been driving myself until we got off the train," she admitted.

"This weekend is for relaxing, having fun, some serious conversation and renewing a very special acquaintance."

Alice glanced at me. "I could go for that—with some honesty." When I didn't respond she added, "Do you have a spare bedroom, or do we play roschambo for the sofa here?"

"There's a bed in my study, a pull out. It's the attic. Do faery princesses sleep in attics?"

"Cinderella does, and those royal tarts that get locked up due to circumstance and evil intent," she responded, winking mischievously. "Let's see."

Alice went for the narrow and angular staircase and glanced up, as if expecting something or someone.

"Something wrong?"

Now she turned slowly and looked at me suspiciously. "How do you know about Richard?"

"Maybe I heard about him from my mother or Denny. You took a trip to England on the last year of your doctorate, didn't you?"

"So?"

"I heard the name dropped in a conversation and assumed he was a boyfriend."

Her eyes blazed for a moment and then she nodded slowly, her suspicious gaze still locked on me. "I wish Denny's mouth wasn't so big," Alice sighed as she began the climb.

I caught a flash of lightning reflected in a photograph of Ellie and me that hung on the wall and saw the Proprietress, who winked and asked, "Who's lying *now?*"

"Want a night cap?" I called up and retraced my path to the living room bar to avoid further conversation.

"A glass of wine or an ale, if you have them?" Alice called back, and then, "Quinn! This is incredible!"

I laughed and said, "Yeah, I should have cleaned up the room, but the decision to come over was a last minute thing – and you know I'm a slob."

Grabbing two bottles of Old Peculier I took the stairs two at a time and would have gone straight up to the attic if I hadn't seen Alice in the master bedroom. I back tracked and paused in the doorway, admiring her moonlit silhouette. She was standing on the balcony and taking in the view of the massive ruins of the keep of Scarborough Castle.

She turned and smiled, waved a hand at the panorama before us. "Incredible!"

"Wait 'til you see it tomorrow," I said.

"I was just thinking that. What made you think to buy a house here of all places?" Alice asked.

"I came here with the orchestra for an annual musical festival back in seventy-five and I fell love with the town. Once I had enough money saved, I bought this house as a vacation home, a place to be with my music, my thoughts – get away from it all."

We drank our Old Peculiers in silence, neither looking at the other, neither daring to speak. Once in a while, she'd ask about something on the horizon and I responded in monosyllabic tones.

"Well," Alice sighed, moving away. "I can't wait for tomorrow. I'm sorry, Quinn, but I'm dead on my feet. I'll take the attic. It goes with the territory, y'know? Faery Princess trapped in her ivory tower waiting for the prince to rescue her? Hapless victim of love?" Now she laughed and shook her head. "Wow, that's the alcohol talking.

Well, g'night," She bussed my chin with a kiss and started for the door.

"Hold on. If I promise to behave myself, would you stay with me here tonight?" I asked, a little too desperately, I might add. "Stay with me, Alice?"

She nodded and uttered something softly as I went past to get our luggage. I could have sworn it was the word, 'Always.'

And so we slept until the sun rose on a wet summer morning. I was the first to wake and glanced over at my sleeping beauty. How I wanted to make love to her, my eyes following every curve of her incredible body, from the perfectly round face to her shapely legs knowing how soft and warm she'd be, how welcoming...

A thunder clap and strobe of lightning reminded me that that was no ordinary summer storm outside, so I kissed Alice's brow and slid out of bed to shower and shave.

Alice had managed to brew a pot of coffee and made omelets and French toast for breakfast when I at last came downstairs.

"The domestic surprises never end," I teased as I entered the kitchen.

"And neither does your humor," was her droll reply. "I thought I was wrung out, but you must be exhausted from the touring," Alice mentioned, taking the cup of coffee I poured and offered. "You fell asleep the moment your head hit the pillow."

"I've got a lot on my mind right now," I answered truthfully, tapping her nose in a playful way. "And you should know that's the first restful sleep I've had in ages. Thank you."

"For what?"

"For saying yes and coming with me to Scarborough. Just knowing you were beside me, Faery Princess—it meant a lot."

I brought our meal to the table and slid in beside her

at the little nook under the mullioned windows and nudged Alice playfully. "Forgot you were left-handed. Elbow wars at the table, just like the good old days."

"We can't play catch with the toast, though; need dinner rolls for that," she said, reaching for the toast.

"Who cleaned up after that Thanksgiving dinner, I wonder?"

"I think it was Harry? I know whoever it was wasn't happy."

"Every family dinner should have elbow fights and table wars. Harry can cook, and his desserts are legendary as far as I'm concerned. The way they always kept piling on the food and saying, 'Eat, eat!' I could have sworn you were Italian. We should visit the castle today. You don't mind going in the rain to see it? I want you to see it, and the view. It's incredible," I said helping myself to toast and eggs, poured another round of coffee.

"Sure, why not?"

The tone of her voice surprised me. I'd been rattling on happily about the good old days and hadn't noticed the change in her mood. When our eyes met I noticed the tears trailing down her face and the sad smile. I immediately was contrite and leaned over for a hug. "Oh God, Alice! I've upset you."

"No, no, it isn't you. It's knowing I can't stay here forever even though it's all I want, and that things will change between us," she sobbed into my shoulder.

Outside there was a clap of thunder that rolled for the longest time and the sky grew darker. I ignored it and held Alice even closer. "Maybe things will change for the better," I whispered, kissing her cheek. "Of course, no one knows, but I'm hoping." Again, there was a clap of thunder that shook the house and the sky lit up with the bluish tinge of lightning. Alice clung even tighter. "Let's not worry about things we can't control. Right now I just want to spend a few days being with you, showing you this place I love, reacquainting ourselves."

"Sorry," she sniffed.

"Don't be. Remember, we're here to figure things out. It's bound to be bumpy. The path to that place is pretty steep and rocky."

Alice moved away and frowned, watched as I finished breakfast. I looked over with brows raised in amused question.

"*What?*" I chuckled now.

"Nothing. Are you sure we can see the castle in this?" she gestured towards the buckets of rain pouring down and splashing on the windows, lightning ripping through the dark clouds.

"This? It'll clear up soon."

Alice sniffed back the last of her tears and asked, "Wouldn't happen to have a Risk game handy, would you?"

"Left it at my London flat. But I have something better in mind."

"What could be better than my losing another game of Risk to you?" Alice teased, taking the last bit of sausage from my plate and popping it into her mouth.

"You'll find out. I'll clear this away and do the dishes while you settle in, then you'll get your surprise. Hopefully after that the weather will cooperate with my plans."

She looked at me skeptically but after a last sip of coffee she slid out of the nook went upstairs to shower.

Once the kitchen had been put to rights I read the morning paper and listened the comfortable mantra of the rain outside, the shower upstairs in the bathroom, then tended to the mail, organized the books and papers in the living room that I'd left where they sat the last time I was in Scarborough, made sure the obscenely-large bouquet I'd given Alice last night was in a proper vase and set in a place of honor.

Alice was sitting on the bed and lacing up her boots when I came up to the bedroom moments later. I noticed that she was studying the photographs on the dresser and some of her artwork on the walls, the personal touches to my vacation home. She rose and picked up a framed photograph of us. The snapshot of taken the Christmas of 1972 right before the break-up. There we were, Alice, Dennis, Harry and me, sitting on the backyard steps and we each wore a scarf that Dennis had knitted. She set it down carefully and now picked up a photo of Ellie and me on the walls of York.

"Whenever you're ready," I said, knocking.

"Oh! Hey!" Alice greeted, seemingly embarrassed by being caught. She pointed at our photograph. "Do you still have that scarf?"

"Yes, it's in London. Still have yours?"

"Everything Denny's made for me I wear – mostly because he'd make a comment if I didn't." she chuckled, "It's nice to see that photo again. That was a happy time."

"I think of it as my family portrait," I said, dusting off the frame with a gentle finger.

"No pictures of your parents, or other friends," Alice hinted.

"Only the people and family I care about."

"Your grandmother was beautiful – I see where you get those dimples and smile," Alice remarked, pointing to Ellie.

"Well, I didn't get all of her looks," I laughed self-consciously.

"From what you told me you got her spirit and sensitivity. The will to survive at all odds."

"Sure," I answered darkly. The moment was charged with tension and Alice waited for me to respond, but I didn't and wouldn't. She moved slightly as if to touch my hand and let hers fall to her side.

"What's this surprise?" she asked brightly.

I came out of my reverie and said, "Follow me, milady."

We raced downstairs to the little study off the living room where an upright piano and my cello nearly filled the space. I led Alice to the overstuffed loveseat and kissing the top of her head moved to the cello.

"This is a special song, for a very special friend," I said and began to play Nino Rota's love theme from *Romeo and Juliet* – the popular version known as *A Time for Us*. I sang in a bari-tenor voice, the familiar verses not in English but Italian. After the chorus I improvised a solo of the theme and added arpeggios and chords that were lush and spine-tingling. When I finished, I leaned back in the chair and closed my eyes, exhausted. Moments passed before I looked over and saw Alice smiling.

"I hope you liked it," I said, my eyes tearing up. I reached for her and Alice melted in my arms. "That was for you, Alice."

"You are a dangerous romantic," Alice laughed. "That any man would offer something so, so, romantic!"

"Hasn't done me any good. Just ask Lady Briony Atwell or the countless disastrous relationships the tabloids report," I commented. "And just look where we are."

Alice made an exasperated sound and held me tighter and I remembered our first time together, how she nestled against much in the same way as now. I smiled at the memory and singing *Here Comes the Sun* and Alice joined in. "Hey!" I exclaimed in mid-verse, pointing at the window. "Here comes the sun!"

It was time to go. Everything would change and yet be bound by what we said and did that afternoon.

CHAPTER 28

WE CLIMBED TO the ruins of Scarborough Castle that afternoon, politely refusing the assistance of a national park docent who appeared out of nowhere when we paid our admittance price and went through the gate, though Alice persuaded the woman to take our picture with the late afternoon sun burnishing our faces and the castle throwing shadows in the background.

"Here, this is what I want to show you."

I led Alice to the eastern tip of the promontory where the castle stood facing the North Sea. Below us was the shore and to the north, the flat darkness of the moors. Patches of green were speckled with whitewashed towns and villages along the horizon. Alice turned slowly to take it all in: the waves rolling and crashing on the beach, the vast, empty horizon to the east where the Netherlands lay, to Denmark and Germany, to the fishing boats and touring yachts bobbing in the harbor as waves slapped against them, as well as the daffodils and gillyflowers, white roses in clumps near the foot of the donjon, the cliffs of Scarborough and the town nestled above, around and upon them, the clusters of houses along the quay and around the approach to the castle itself. The wind picked up as we walked higher still and turned to face the sea and let the wind gently buffet us. It swirled about in her hair and around us, made the fabric of her dress dance. She pulled her sweater closer for warmth and smiled at all this beauty. Waves crashed below and gulls cried as they soared and dove, circled and lit on the traceries of the castle donjon. The air was crisp and sharp with the tang of the sea, the damp earth after a rain.

"I have been here many times in my dreams," Alice said.

"Remember what you said?" I asked when I wrapped her in an embrace. "'A meadow, or a moor at sunrise, or walking across the moors, standing on a cliff, looking out to sea...' Every time I come here, and that's a lot, I think of what you said, and of you, especially you."

"You said I'd be part of the picture," she whispered.

"You are; you always are."

"Then tell me what this shadow is hanging over us; what it is that you're holding back, dying to tell me but can't."

I leaned in and put my chin on Alice's shoulder, holding her tighter now, as if to prevent her from escaping. "I've been dreading this," I said at last. "But I'm not ready to watch you walk away forever."

"Oh God, you're married or engaged to that princess or countess or lady, or whoever she is," Alice blurted out and looked like she was indeed ready to run, but I held her firmly.

"No! It's not that."

Alice turned in my arms. "Then what is it? You're not dying of cancer or something?"

"Not that, either. First confession: I lied to you, Alice. About Briony. We aren't dating any more. Briony Atwell and I, well, it was a political thing for the orchestra. I broke it off. It was a sham, anyway."

"Were you trying to make me jealous?"

"Pretty much. Actually, I don't know what I was doing. I was jealous of your archeologist."

"Would you please stop calling him my archeologist? I don't own him and he certainly doesn't have rights to me."

"But you're getting married in a few weeks, aren't you?"

"Haven't made up my mind."

"Well, think about going through with it."

"So this is the final brush off? How many times am I going to put myself through this?" Alice demanded and I held up my hand for silence.

"Second confession," I interrupted. I looked around and motioning towards a park bench near the Visitors Center and the outer curtain of the castle precincts, led me there. "I haven't been telling you the truth about a lot of things. Let's sit here." I sat close and took Alice's hand and for the longest time said nothing.

"*What are you waiting for?*" I heard Janis Joplin whisper. I glanced around but saw no one save the tourists and docents.

"The stories about me, well, some of them, were true. I won't get into the whole story now because they're in the past and the only person I hurt was myself. But I wanted you to know. I ruined every chance I had with the orchestra to get back at my parents. I wanted to show them that I was a regular guy, with regular interests, not some damn musical prodigy. More than anything, I wanted to ruin my father's career because that was my life, you know. *My* life, *my* accomplishments, *my* talent, were my father's. Fortunately, I atoned for those sins and I am where I am because someone had faith in me."

A lump was forming in my throat. I paused and then, "You know what my life was like, growing up – what with my parents, everything. "My father controlled everything, from when I got up in the morning and what breakfast I ate, to who my friends were. I was pretty much forced into everything I did – except the attempt at ice hockey. Everything I wanted was taken away one by one until the only thing I loved was the music and the cello. I was able to lose myself and get away from everything that hurt."

"I always felt bad because I couldn't help you."

"You did. You weren't so much a faery princess as an angel – my guardian angel."

"Please don't call me an angel – I'm far from that!"

"You are! Don't you see, Alice? You kept me sane and when we were together I had strength."

"Why didn't you stand up to him? We might be married today if you had."

"You've got every right to resent me for that," I sighed as I let go of her hand and moved away just a bit.

"I'm sorry. I've been holding that in for years," she confessed.

"And I blew some pretty good opportunities to set things right with you."

"Well, that goes both ways, doesn't it?"

"Even so, I'm one fucked up guy. You have to know that. If we had gotten married, God knows what might have happened. It might not have lasted a year. And it's all because of my father, I know that now."

"Quinn, you don't need,"

"Alice, he was a monster. He did things to me…"

"Don't tell me, please, I can guess. It will only make me sick to my stomach."

I nodded. "It went as far as my mother, too. This wasn't something we shared with our friends and neighbors. We didn't talk about it then. We don't today. If only I had had the courage."

I broke down, then. I didn't care that we were in public. I leaned into my hands and let the tears come, the angry, wretched sobs escape. Alice grabbed me and held on for dear life, whispering endearments and promising safety. "Quinn, no matter what, no matter, I love you. I always will," she whispered. "I just wish I could have helped. I wish I had known. Denny and I always thought there was something wrong, but Harry said to leave it alone. We're as bad as your parents and I am so sorry."

"No! You don't take the blame for something you had no control of, or really knew about. He's the monster. My father is the guilty party here," I growled and moved away. After a moment while I summoned more courage, I watched gulls soaring over the ruins and followed the path of one with sunlight on its wings expecting to be carried off to The Village. Instead, I found myself looking at Alice lit by the setting sun and looking even more beautiful as she studied my face.

"Okay," she whispered. "Just know we loved you then and now and we were worried about you."

"Fair enough."

"It surely explains some things," Alice ventured.

"It broke me, destroyed me. Now I'm so confused about who and what I am, Alice. My father taught me that what he did was normal. I was confused and ashamed. I saw how other parents acted with their kids, and there was Dennis and you. The love was so obvious and it was there. I wanted that kind of family, a place where I felt safe. Ever since I can remember, my father used me."

I paused and Alice drew me into her arms again. I leaned against her and desperately tried to stay composed. She kissed me gently and touched my face. The warmth of her hand was healing and loving.

Drawing a breath, I continued. "That Christmas when I proposed and my parents and I argued about what I wanted for us, for you and me, was the worst. When I got home from your place, I unlocked the gun my mother kept in her study and thought about killing myself. Then I found my father and threatened him. He turned it around and threatened you, said he knew people who could ruin you and Dennis, because, he said, homosexuals shouldn't be taking care of children, especially young girls. He said he knew authorities who could plant evidence and make it look like Denny and Harry molested you or had you pimping for them, and have them thrown in jail – I'm probably shocking you with this, aren't I?"

She shook her head no but the anger and pain were so evident in her luminous eyes that suddenly went dark.

"I got the worst beating of my life when he followed me to the library. I went home and listened to their threats and all the reasons why I should follow their advice. It was either or. One way or the highway. I was so afraid. All I could think about was getting away from them so I could plan the future, start a new life. So I got on that plane as my parents demanded and I regretted it. Pretty soon, I started to forget and got lost in my studies and my work—but there wasn't a day I didn't think about you. I wanted to pick up the phone but I thought by then you wouldn't care. Or you'd hate me. And I figured if I didn't find out, didn't know, I'd been happier. I didn't want to know. But I did. Does that make sense?"

"It does and doesn't. I do know what you mean. Ignorance is bliss. We always have our dreams, right? In our dreams we're with the people we love. I'm sure that's why people write romances and love songs. I know that's over simplifying a difficult, ugly reality, but,"

"No, you're right. It' all true. Especially what I just said." I leaned in and kissed her gently, saying, "Thank you. I've been holding that in for so long. You are the only person I've told."

"Haven't you told your mother?"

"Why tell her? She knew then. She plays a denial game even now. I've told her I'm going to speak up. You know, I've always felt so ashamed, so different. And then I met you – I'd always been attracted to you, ever since we came from England when I was ten. I never knew what to say to you or how to act, but you had such a beautiful smile and your large eyes, your gentleness. I could lose myself and my shame just being around you. Then I knew all I had to do was say, 'Hey! Alice.'"

"And I waited outside my locker, hoping you'd come by and say hello and glance back. My friends would melt every time you walked by."

"Here's another confession. At first I wanted to be with you just to annoy my father and to show him I was a regular guy, normal, I guess. Oh, it did piss him off, believe me, he didn't like it one bit. Then after we started meeting up by accident in the hallways, or when you'd stop by the music room at lunch to do the choir score filing, and when we went on our first date, I knew that wasn't the real reason. It was because I loved you. I couldn't wait to see you every day, and when we made love…"

I stopped there and took her face in my hands, offering what I believed was the most loving and passionate of our kisses.

"I need your forgiveness, Alice."

"You have it."

"But I'm afraid I'm going to hurt you again. I want to be with you for the rest of our lives. I've never given up hope, but I need to figure myself out. I need to take care of my anger and my pain and I can't expect you to take on the burden. I need time."

"How much do you want, Quinn?"

"I don't know. That's why you should go ahead and marry him if that's what you want. I can deal with it."

"And if I don't?"

"The time isn't right. Not yet. I've got to get my life in order. I'm going to get some help. And then there's dealing with my father and making him accountable."

"You know that I will always, always. Be there for you no matter what. When you've sorted out things, let me know. I'll come to you and we'll take it from there." Alice stood and offered her hand and I gladly took it.

"I've always loved you. I love you, Alice. I'm sorry that I hurt you so much."

It came easily, that.

We walked towards the gate leading down into Scarborough. Back at the house while we made dinner she said casually, "It's decided then."

"Pretty much."

"So we're going to be one of those couples that meets once a year, maybe twice, to catch each other up, exchange photos of the kids and dogs, send Christmas cards. Stand by and hold the other's hand when the youngest child is sick and the spouse is out of town," Alice said quietly as she chopped vegetables.

"Don't friends do that?"

"I suppose they do."

"But is that what we really are talking about, Quinn?"

"It must be because that's what makes sense right now."

"Funny, but I thought you'd be more in to the 'same time next year' thing."

I took a sip of wine and then a bite of the vegetables and shrugged. "Looks like you do believe all the tabloid garbage."

"Actually no; I'm rationalizing, Quinn. If I knew you believed in that or wanted that it would make everything easier."

Raising my glass I said, "Here's a thought – no, a promise. If, in a year, you decide it's not what you want, well, you know where to find me."

She didn't clink her glass to mine but I drank anyway and when I lowered the glass, I was in The Village and Michael was seated with me at the table in the Shop. He poured two cups of tea and pushed one towards me.

"She wasn't married at the time," Michael commented, "and so after dinner, after wine and sharing conversation, after serenading her, you made love to her hoping she'd change her mind."

"It wasn't the first or last time I used sex to try to win a woman over. You don't need to remind me."

"Why didn't you offer to marry her? She just might have said yes."

I turned on him. "I was afraid of turning into my father. I was afraid of hurting Alice the way my father hurt my mother because that was all I knew at the time. He destroyed my mother's spirit and I could not do that, I would never do that to Alice. I wanted it to end. I had to make it end."

"You tried and failed. I remember. The night at the

hotel in New York."

"Unfortunately there weren't enough pills in the bottle. You saw what he did."

"Every time."

"And you did nothing."

"You don't pray to God for ponies and winning lottery tickets, or getting a high mark on a term paper. You ask for the way to go. You made a good start with Alice and Jane but now it's time to end the drama, don't you think?"

I took a sip of tea and was about to ask how he came up with that but never got the chance. When I put down the cup it was on the coffee table in my suite at the Plaza, back in New York, back in August of 1979 the night of the concert.

A bottle of prescription pills was in one hand, a glass of scotch in the other. Staring down into the bottle, I frowned when I saw there were only three capsules. You didn't commit suicide with three Valium. Still, I swallowed one and chased it with some scotch. With any luck it would take away the pain of seeing Alice that evening.

"I hate this," I leaned back on the sofa and shouted, "Enough! I've had enough! Send me home or to hell if there's a choice!"

I paused, hearing drunken giggling off in the distance; that echoing, ethereal sound meant to accompany dark spirits.

"I know you can hear me, dammit!"

The laughter continued, increasing in volume and chill factor.

I curled up in the fetal position and stopped my ears with my fingers and shut my eyes tight—it worked when I was a little boy—to get through the spell, to hide from the demons I thought were around me. My head was spinning and the sofa teetered as if it were being lifted off the floor, rocking and swaying. The trembling started just as I sat up and made for the darkness of the bedroom.

With any hope, I would slip into a deep sleep afterwards, like all the times before, and not remember much. Maybe I would finally die. I fell on to the bed and tried to relax, waiting for the end.

Unfortunately it wouldn't happen that night.

Someone was at the door and refused to go away. I heard the voices and a key in the lock. What was going on? I staggered out to the living room of the suite and found my father, the hotel concierge and a bell hop looking around.

"What are you doing here?" I barked at my father.

"Our apologies, Mr. Radcliffe—you didn't answer, and Philip here saw you come up after the concert," the concierge babbled as my father came forward, relief on his face.

"Thank you, Mister Stevens; we'll be all right. Looks like the maestro was celebrating his successful opening night. For your trouble..." Father passed a twenty to the bell hop who, nodding, smiled and followed the apologetic concierge out before I could get his attention. More than anything I did not want to be alone with my father.

The door closed and we stared each other down.

"Another night of sulking and drinking? Whoring?" Father opened. Of course he'd start the conversation—or in our case, quarrel.

"I didn't ask you here; you can leave." I only got as far as the sofa and slumped down. Damn me for a fool, the pills were starting to take effect. I reached for the coffee on the table and with a shaking hand poured a cup and drank not caring how burning hot it was. I had to be sober for this. I could not show weakness.

"You might have told us you were coming to New York," Father opened.

"Stop stalking me!" I bellowed.

"Stalking you?" he laughed, incredulous. "Stalking you? I'm your father!"

"We had this conversation months ago, Dad. I told

you and Mother to stay away. I don't want you around me."

He walked over to the bar—of course—and poured two drinks, handing one to me, which I knocked out of his hand. He watched the expensive bar glass shatter against the coffee table with distaste. What bothered him more, the waste of scotch or Waterford crystal? Certainly not the waste of a spirit or dream. Nor did he waste his own drink. Taking a sip, he eyed me carefully.

"When will you let it go? There is so much more available to you now, Quinn. All these years of work, sacrifice; surely it's sunk in?" Father said quietly and smoothly. He reached out to touch my face and I knocked it away, too. "She's just a girl. Christ, how many have you had since her? How many boys, I wonder? How many royals? That story won't die!"

As he laughed to himself and took another drink I slammed him into the wall and held him by the throat, watching him turn purple and red, wondering if I should tighten my grip and watch him take his last breath.

"Did it ever occur to you that I wasn't grieving over a lost love? Yes, I love Alice. But what would you know about love? You know a lot about abuse and control—I've always wondered who it was before me, and after. What little boys did you molest and scare? How many wives did you beat into silence? The perfect gentleman with the perfect career, wife and son. You live comfortably in a castle, but for how long?"

I shoved him away and headed back to the bedroom where hidden under the Gideon's Bible and hotel stationery in the nightstand was a gun I'd carried for several years.

"All families have skeletons, Quinn," he called after me. "I bet we could find where your secrets are buried." He started to laugh, that annoying high-pitched braying. "What would you do if I let some stories leak to the press? You wouldn't be the golden child for long! No more

Sexiest-Man-Alive stories, no more covers on Time and People, the Rolling Stone!"

My father was in the bedroom now and I turned with the gun trained on his chest.

"I won't use this if you for once say you're sorry, get some help, and divorce Mother. Get the hell out of our lives!"

"You're threatening me again?" he laughed. "You never carry through with threats or promises."

"Say it!"

"You make a lot of noise, Quinn, just like when you used to shag Alice—you didn't think I heard? I knew?"

I fired the gun into the bolster, the bullet tearing the silk cover and releasing feathers and down into the air. My father, cringing, straightened up when he realized he was still whole and though he didn't make a move, his face blanched white when I placed the muzzle to my head and pulled the trigger. He actually looked disappointed that there were no bullets left in the chamber and I was still alive, still standing before him in that flurry of down. Moments later a knock on the door, rather pounding, as we stared each other down again, and the concierge returned with hotel security. They looked at my father, who for once wasn't offering that disingenuous smile and charm, then at me. The gun was placed on the bed and I stepped away with raised hands. The Security Officer glanced at the bed and reached for the gun, looking straight at my father as if he would bother with the truth.

"Sorry; I'm drunk," I admitted. "Had too much to drink—and other stuff. I'll pay for the damage."

"Mister Radcliffe, you don't look well," he said.

"I'm fine," my father and I answered in unison.

"I was speaking to the younger Mister Radcliffe," the officer replied, glaring at Father. "Sir?" he said, a hint of concern there.

"Like I said, I had too much to drink. Should have learned a long time ago not to celebrate alone…wasn't the best of evenings,"

"Not the best of evenings?" Father spoke up. "Eleven curtain calls, that love song with the pop star, the press all over you—"

"Not the best of evenings." I reiterated. I shrugged, and then, "God, I'm such an asshole." Now I turned to the concierge. "A favor. If you would keep this out of the press? In exchange for my custom, of course."

The concierge cleared his throat. "Whatever happened here, Maestro, is none of the hotel's concern. Just make sure you give a report to the proper authorities."

"Thanks. I have every intention of doing so," I replied, looking straight at my father. To him I said, "You should go with them. Now." The order was quiet and forceful. Everyone in the room would know who was to blame for the disturbance of my peace.

He took a step forward as if to hug me and I backed away, hands up to ward him off.

"Quinn, I'm sorry. Sorry for everything. Please, son, you have to understand the pressure I was under."

"Acknowledged, Professor. But not accepted." I walked across the suite and opened the door. "Get out. Now."

Not what I had said or done as I watched my father follow them out into the hall and disappear into an elevator. I didn't consider the evening a victory until I heard the bell and saw the doors close.

He was finally out of my life.

CHAPTER 29

"COFFEE, SIR?" the bell hop offered when he returned with a member of Housekeeping to clean up the mess I'd made.

I hung up the telephone receiver and flushed with a shade of scarlet to go with the look of guilt on my face. "Yeah, sure. Yeah," I answered. He poured a cup and motioned to the cream and sugar, but I shook my head and took the cup handed over, settling into the sofa. He watched me drink and I commented, "I've done my bad boy thing for the night. Do whatever you're here to do and I'll stay out of your way." The bell hop nodded but kept watching me all the same. I ignored both of them while they puttered around the suite, straightening up things, clearing away the dinner tray and empty scotch bottle, replacing the damaged bolster with a new one, one I suspected without a bullet hole or the stink of cordite and burnt linen. When after fifteen minutes had passed they finished their work and I passed twenties to each, thanking them for their trouble.

The most logical thing to do now was sleep, but I sat there waiting for a train to appear and take me back to The Village, or the unexpected arrival of one of my mentors to talk me through this momentous occasion and perhaps tell me everything I'd done wrong that evening, but this did not happen. I fell asleep like a normal person.

Maybe this acid trip, or whatever it was, was really over for there were no detours, no side trips on trains or buses through the Yorkshire dales or to strange little village shops as we continued the American tour into that autumn. The reviews were good and I started to relax, especially when there were cameras around and interviews to be given. The newspapers and talk shows all wanted to know about the mysterious friend to whom I had dedicated a romantic ballad. *People* Magazine screamed that I was off the market—frankly, I didn't know I was on it, or had a shelf life – and soon I was being asked to make guest appearances with orchestras in Europe and the United States. No one in the orchestra or on the Board of Directors seemed to complain about my notoriety because it brought revenue and for the moment, job security. *The Times* of London offered a feature article about "The Redemption of Tarquin Radcliffe" at Christmas that year. I was a cautionary tale, a Dickensian character come to life. There was life, it seemed, after acclaim. Classical music was hip, thanks to me.

I wondered if that would have been the case had my life been different. If I was truly happy.

One thing was for certain: I was learning to be happy and in that state I returned to England. I was still wary, though, expecting to be propelled back to The Shop and given a talking to, scolded for my behavior, or given unwanted advice.

Again, that didn't happen.

As soon as I arrived in London life was filled with rehearsals and meetings, sitting in on auditions, planning concerts. My friends Chloe Carlisle and Graham Sudley met me for dinner and drinks and brought me home for holidays and birthdays, for I had no intention of going to Berkeley any time soon. I was the bachelor friend with nowhere to go, even though I had a family and a home. I wasn't ready to share that part of my life with them.

"You'd rather stay here than be in California for Christmas?" Chloe demanded a second time while we relaxed over drinks after our annual Christmas program at the Royal Albert.

"You've never been in California for Christmas. There's nothing remotely Christmas-y about green grass and trees, sunshine and blue skies," I answered.

"Horrors!" Chloe gasped.

"You're mocking me."

"I'm disgusted with you," she teased, and more softly, "I guess it really is bad, then?"

"My father was fired from the university and the opera company when word got out that I pressed charges against him. My mother isn't talking to me."

"Nothing like a mother standing by her child," Graham spoke up.

"It wasn't good. It wasn't what I expected would happen," I admitted. "Especially when he confessed everything in order to cut a deal and they let him out on bail."

"What about a trial?" Chloe asked. "They're not just going to let him go free, are they?"

"Sometime in April. My mother and I fought for hours about it. She just doesn't see, or want to see the reality of what happened. I didn't—I don't want him preying on others," I said and finished my ale to avoid having to say another thing.

"I'd be happy to be there for you, Quinn," she offered.

"And me. Don't blame you for not wanting to go home, mate," Graham offered and poured another round of ales.

"I do have a home, you know. In York. Here in London. And Scarborough."

It was then I got the idea and it was decided our Christmas revels, such as they were, would be held at the house in Scarborough. Plans were quickly made and by Sunday of Christmas week, I was in the north and getting ready for the next day's Christmas Eve dinner party. Chloe and Anna took care of the food and drink and were at the shops while I managed to organize the house.

While I was re-shelving books in their case I found the record album.

The copy of Vaughan Williams' *Fantasia on a Theme* by *Thomas Tallis* with *The Lark Ascending, Dives and Lazarus* and the *Fantasy on Greensleeves* was wedged against a dictionary and encyclopedia volumes on the topmost shelf and a fine shower of dust came with it when I pulled it out, sliding the vinyl record carefully from the sleeve and turning it over in my hands. There on the label she'd carefully penned 'Quinn Gave This to Alice!' In lieu of a class ring, which I didn't have, or a pin, I gave her music when I asked her to be my steady girl. I smiled, remembering the way her eyes lit up when she unwrapped this gift and how she said she didn't need a ring to tell the world that we were a couple and we loved each other. She gave me proof of that later on a May afternoon.

Oh, what an afternoon that was ...

More than a year had passed since Alice returned the album after our weekend in Scarborough.

"Here's the sign. Return it and I'll know we'll both have a lot to talk about."

My eyes widened at the sight of the album. "I gave this to you...you're sure about this? Everything?"

"It gives me, us, hope."

Without second guessing, without debilitating anxiety, with no fear, I carefully wrote a note and slipped it into the album sleeve and wrapped the record in unexciting brown paper, addressed it to one Dr. Alice Martin in Providence, Rhode Island.

I ran in to Chloe and Anna as they returned with the food and what looked like enough wine and spirits for a castle cellar.

"I have to post something," I explained on my way out.

That sense of accomplishment, that elation in knowing I'd done something right, stayed with me on the walk back to the house, during the successful Christmas Eve dinner party where friends kept remarking how happy I looked and jokingly demanded to know what was wrong, what had happened. I didn't share what I hoped would be a life-changing, a happy, life-changing event and wore an enigmatic smile until the last guest left.

"What are you about?" Chloe asked while we did the washing up.

"About six foot four if I'm not slouching," came the clever response.

"Come on, then."

"Looking forward to my future happiness. That's all."

That was easier said than done especially when I read in the morning paper a story about a horrific automobile accident involving archeologist Donovan Trist, the only son and heir of presidential hopeful Senator Martin Trist. The euphoria evaporated when I read further and discovered Trist the younger had been driving drunk and people were killed in a head-on collision. It was a miracle, Senator Trist was quoted as saying, that his son and daughter-in-law survived. Unfortunately, they lost their unborn child.

I flew from the house and sprinted all the way to the Post Office. It was Christmas Day, but surely no packages would have gone out the night before, nor would they today. As luck would have it, Mr. Blanding the post master was arriving just as I did. He took the pipe out of his mouth and nodded 'hello,' staring at me quizzically. Then I couldn't get a word in edgewise.

"Happy Christmas, Mister Radcliffe! I did enjoy the concert on television last night. Going to make that an annual thing, I hope? Expecting something from the States? Come in; I was going to check for Missus Erickson – she's waiting for something from Surrey," the postmaster went on while I tried to catch my breath and then use it to tell him my purpose.

"A square package – the one I brought yesterday

afternoon – did the post go out?" I sputtered and gasped.

"Ah no. I hope you didn't want that to go last night?" You did bring it past the deadline, sorry to say," he apologized as he finished fiddling with the lock and opened the door.

"Can I have it back?"

*Not, definitely **not**, what I remembered doing that Christmas!*

"Of course. Just a minute,"

After ridiculously long minutes while Mr. Blanding shuffled around looking for the package and regaling me with stories about past holidays in Scarborough, the album was back in my possession and I went home to put it back up on the shelf and stood in the middle of the living room staring at the floor, trying to decide what to do.

First, it was time to make some calls on the pretext of it being Christmas Day. But the hour – I was eight hours ahead of them and I would have to wait, and wait I did until five o'clock that evening.

The first call was unsuccessful. No one was at the Martin residence in Berkeley. No doubt Harry was on his way to the east coast to be with Alice.

Alice!

My mind reeled with images and sounds, wondering what she'd gone through and how she could have survived.

I grabbed my wallet and dug through receipts, snapshots, credit cards and foil-sealed condoms for a business card she'd given me and dialed the office number. What the hell was I doing? It was Christmas morning there; no one would be at the university. The next number was the house phone.

The call was picked up on the first ring and a tired-voiced man answered.

"Hello, this is Quinn Radcliffe of Berkeley; I'm calling to ask about Missus Trist – Doctor Martin," I said. "I heard about the accident, and so…"

"One moment for Missus Trist," the man said,

mechanical and colorless in tone and delivery.

Could it be that Alice hadn't been injured, that the newspaper report got it wrong? I waited and hoped.

"This is Arielle Trist," a woman announced herself. "To whom do you wish to speak?" The voice was New England, upper crust, full of pretentiousness. All that came from eleven carefully-minced words.

"I'm Quinn Radcliffe, from Berkeley – a friend of Alice Martin's," I introduced myself when I found the courage to speak.

A long pause and then: "Yes, I know who you are, Maestro Radcliffe. What do you want?"

"I read in this morning's paper about the accident—"

"Well, that's been blown up out of proportion, I can assure you," she sighed.

"Alice is alright?"

"I hardly think that's your business."

"Look, I'm a friend,"

"I know who you are. Your calling here won't change things."

"I just want to speak with Alice to make sure she's okay. I don't see why that's a problem."

Again there was a pause. "What do you think they were arguing about when the car skidded on black ice?" she snapped. "I'll let my son know you called and he'll decide whether it would be in Alice's best interest to speak to you."

It was my turn to pause. "And how is he?"

"Remarkably well considering," she said in a lighter tone. "We do have a guardian angel."

"Tell him I called, then. He can call at 44, 01723, 861066. Oh. Happy Christmas."

"For some."

Staring at the humming receiver didn't change things, either. I turned on the news with the hope of more information, which was silly - no one in the United Kingdom gave a rat's ass about an American politician or his family unless their name was Kennedy.

I was ready to join Chloe and Anna for Christmas dinner at their hotel when my phone rang, throwing coat and keys on the hallway floor in my haste to grab the call.

"Hello!" I shouted.

"Quinn Radcliffe? Donovan Trist."

"Yeah, hi. It's been what, four months?"

"About that long, I guess. You called about Alice."

"How is she? Is Harry with her?"

"Harry? Oh no; Harry's with his family. Trip to Hong Kong, I think. We weren't expecting him out this year."

"Well does he know?"

"We haven't been able to get a hold of him."

"So...Alice?"

"Still in the hospital."

"It's bad isn't?" I was feeling sick to my stomach.

"It's been three days and she's still out. If she makes it through the night she's got a fighting chance."

"I'm coming over. I can be there sometime tomorrow your time,"

"Stay there. We'll let you know if anything changes and if she wants to see anyone. I don't think your showing up here like a knight in shining armor will help anyone. It will certainly feed the rumor mill."

"For Chrissakes, you don't think-?"

"Stay away. We don't need any more bad press. Not with the campaign and everything else going on."

"Good to know you've got your priorities straight, Donovan."

"You're a real bastard, Radcliffe," he growled.

"Let me know about Alice—one way or another."

It was my turn to let the dial tone hum.

"Fuck him," Chloe stated when I arrived at the hotel and told her what had happened. "Not only get up on a bloody horse but bring something sharp and pointy to skewer him with!"

"Like your wit?" Anna said, shaking her head.

"She's my oldest friend," I said. "It kills me that I can't help her, or be with her."

"She's Alice and you're in love with her," Chloe stated. After dinner we'll sort you out and get you on a plane to New York."

And so it happened.

CHAPTER 30

IF ANYONE KEPT score of the reckless things I did, it would have been Her Worshipfulness. Yet, when I walked home from dinner with Chloe and Anna and entered not my house at Scarborough but the Shop in the Village, she didn't look up from her note-taking, nor throw a scathing invective in my direction.

"See what happens when you grow a pair, Maestro?" the Proprietress said as I went past. The tone was almost sympathetic.

I glanced at Jimi Hendrix and Janis Joplin for an indication of what was going on and they both shrugged. Richard III stopped me as I made ready to take my place at the table in the corner.

"Not quite yet. Give this to her for me?"

He presented a large silver helium balloon in the shape of the *Rosa Alba* tied up with silver ribbons. Looking over the top of the bobbing and weaving rose, I saw a nurse smiling at me. I was in a New York hospital wing on a snowy December afternoon, the chill and tang of the winter air still with me.

"You must be Mr. Radcliffe," she greeted, taking my extended hand. "The others just left. I'll let you have five minutes and that's all."

"Thank you," I whispered as she opened the door to the room where, pale and still, Alice lay hooked up to machines and was swaddled in bandages. The nurse took the balloon, tied it to the headboard and pulled out the chair by the bed and I sat much as I did when I visited Ellie in hospital: bundled up in my overcoat with hands in pockets and hunched over on a chair waiting for the worst.

Had I changed everything by this latest impulse? I was getting used to the repercussions that came from rash decisions but what if there was no bail out for anyone this time?

And so I sat and watched the closed eyelids on the face of the woman I loved beyond reason, waited for that flicker of life that always happened when the hero arrived on the scene.

There was no movement save the steady, slow, rise and fall of Alice's chest, the even beeps and lights from the machines keeping her alive.

I leaned in and whispered, "I love you, Alice Rose!"

When I turned to leave, I was face to face with Donovan. We took silent measure of each other and said nothing, did nothing.

The press were in the lobby with Senator Trist and his ex-wife and current spouse when I took the elevator down. Once more I said and did nothing confronting the enemy but I felt Arielle Trist's cold eyes boring through me as I slipped away to the hotel.

The phone was ringing in my suite when I arrived and I paused by the door, listening to the timed bells. Years of conditioning made me dread the sound, for it would always be my father calling with his usual barbs and insults, the feigned sincerity. Not this time, for there was a restraining order in place and under no circumstance was he to contact me or be within fifty feet of me.

"Quinn Radcliffe."

"Hi, it's me."

"Chloe!"

"I just wanted to know if Alice is going to make it and if you're okay."

"'I don't know' is the answer to both questions, Carlisle. But thanks for asking. Say, isn't it past your bedtime?"

I settled into the chair and loosened my tie, kicked my shoes off and sighed rather loudly.

"Never mind me. Anna and I went to a party at Heaven – just getting home if you must know."

"I did this once before," I said.

"What, care about someone you love? That doesn't surprise me."

"Take a transatlantic flight to butt in where I don't belong."

"I disagree. I bet she's glad you're there."

"She's in a coma; I don't know if she even realized I was in the room with her. To make things even more melodramatic, I ran into her husband."

"Ooooo! Was there a stand-off in the hallway? Did a doctor have to pull you apart and keep you from murdering one another?"

"Chloe…"

"It would have been bloody romantic, Radcliffe!"

"It would have been bloody stupid and bloody awful for everyone."

"What will you do now?"

"I don't know. I haven't thought that far."

I honestly didn't.

Morning found me still in New York, waiting. Then everything happened so quickly that by the time I was back in Yorkshire, I wondered if I'd been gone at all.

The urge to call the hospital was with me when I woke that next day. The network morning news shows had no mention of the accident and I suspected that because Donovan Trist was up and walking about no one thought his wife's survival important enough even for a sign-off report much less a lead-in story.

"The priorities of some people have never failed to amaze me," Richard III said as I set aside the *New York Times* and reached for the coffee he was offering at my table in The Shop. I nodded in agreement and greeting. It was then I noticed how the light had changed. There were actually clouds in the usually-clear, stunningly bright skies over The Village.

"A storm is coming," I said to myself.

"It's nothing you haven't weathered before, little prince," Janis Joplin said as she sidled up and planted a kiss on my cheek. "So? Have you figured it out? What two wrongs eventually make a right?"

I smiled over at her and said, "Love and contrition. Funny how easy it is, but how difficult."

"And so many who don't get it."

"And not just for myself, or Alice."

It was another of those clichés, but as soon as I uttered the truth, a miniscule ray of sunlight shot through the gathering clouds and landed on the table where The Proprietress set down my box. It was opened and there before me were the rose and the opal gemstone. The rose was complete with petals and leaves and stem, the opal now glowed with different pulsating shades of red light.

"Complete love," Hildegarde von Bingen said and she offered a kiss. The warmth of the kiss, the touch, carried me to Berkeley in that winter of 1979 and the lips were not those of a remarkable eleventh century woman, but my mother as we met at the San Francisco Airport several days later.

"Darling," she murmured as we greeted one another and it was all that was said on the ride to my little house in San Anselmo. I stole surreptitious glances at her as she drove and noticed that her hair was up in an untidy knot, she work a minimum of makeup and casual attire, which was a cashmere cardigan over a blouse with slacks. This was a new look, a change from the matched pearls and Chanel suits to which I'd grown accustomed.

I opened the negotiations as soon as we were in the kitchen and I had a pot of coffee brewing, our take-out from the R&J Lounge, the scent of chow mein, pork fried rice and sweet and sour pork replacing the closed-up house smells. Mother assumed the role as hostess and set the table, using the placemats found in Ellie's shop—the ones with the Jack of Spades and the Queen of Hearts—and trying to match the cutlery from the assortment thrown in a drawer. She went as far as clipping the last camellia from the bush in the yard and placed it on the table.

"Thank you for picking me up," I said as I accepted the plate of food from my mother.

"It's no problem at all," she said, smiling. "I was glad to get your message. It's been too long. I thought you'd call Harry. He's such a gentle man and so delightful."

"You met Harry? I mean, other than when you and Dad came to Alice's house that night?"

"I was invited to Alice's birthday party a few years ago and I went. I now understand what you found so attractive in that family, and Dennis' passing was just so unfair. Pass the soy sauce, please?"

"You know why I'm here, don't you?"

"Oh, any number of things; the holidays, vacation time needed to be spent."

"Alice is in a coma in a New York hospital."

"What!"

"I guess you didn't see or hear the news."

"No, I've purposefully ignored it for reasons both you and I know."

"She and her husband were in a car accident – it can't be proved, but it's rumored he was driving drunk. He's okay, but Alice…"

Mother reached over and took my hands in hers. For the first time in many years I noticed the absence of bruising or cuts on her arms, how firm the grasp was.

"What can I do to help?" she asked.

"You can start by accepting my apology," I replied and when she gave me a quizzical frown, added, "For what I did to Father. For going to the authorities, for threatening him with the gun. For putting this chasm between us,

Mom."

"Do you think—Quinn, I understand why you did it and I do not hold it against you. You took steps that I was too cowardly to take. I was too ashamed to face you, because I couldn't, I was never able to protect my son. That morning at the hearing when you sat there so calm and quiet while your father carried on, and how you looked at him eye to eye…Quinn, I was never so proud of you."

"It's my place and my promise to keep you safe," I answered. "I may have blown it with Alice, but I will never let you down again and at least that's something I'll accomplish that comes to good."

We clung to each other and wept, my mother the first to break away and reach for a tissue or something to wipe her tears. Rather than make her more self-conscious as she blew her nose and dabbed at her eyes, I sat down and started digging in before the food got cold.

"Where is he now?" I said after a time. "At home, listening to Wagner?"

"If he's listening to Wagner, it would be in his room at the Hotel Durant."

I stared incredulously at the woman smiling at me now. "You threw him out?"

"It was that or leaving The Cloisters, and you'll remember whose money purchased the castle."

"Well done!" I clinked my glass to hers.

"As much as the place brings unhappy memories now and then, I do love it for all its peculiarities and I'm sure the same may be said for you, Quinn."

Pausing in mid-bite, I nodded and said after a moment, "Alice. It's where we shared our first kiss, where…"

"Your lovely Alice," Mother sighed.

"She's not mine," I answered.

"So you say, but you did fly across the Atlantic to her hospital bed."

The comment was teasing and the truth.

"I felt I had to come – not just because of my feelings, but because there's no one else for her. Harry and his family are somewhere in Asia right now. She needs someone from home."

"She needs you."

"I'd like that to be true."

"How do you know she doesn't?"

My answer was a shrug. There were some thoughts and actions I felt couldn't be shared with my mother. Though I knew the ending, I didn't want to tempt fate to work against me – or The Proprietress.

We stayed up for most of the night talking and reacquainting ourselves and the next day we stood out on the sidewalk saying goodbyes while a fine mist of rain fell and the temperature dropped.

"Are you going back to New York before returning to England?" Mother asked while she looked for the car keys in her bag.

"Only if you can sneak me into the hospital room," I said and winked. "I was told to stay away and that I wasn't needed or wanted."

"I can come with you," Mother responded. "Quinn, I could come with you for moral support. What hospital?

"Mercy Presbyterian in Manhattan."

"Ah! I know some well-placed doctors on staff. So if you have no objections, I might go with you."

"Even if you have to break up a fight between her husband and me?"

"Let's hope it doesn't come to that."

It didn't.

Our subsequent trip to New York was the beginning of our healing, my mother's and mine, and when I returned to England a week later a new decade was before me and for the first time in a very long while I had a sense of hope.

No sooner than I was in Scarborough than I took the

record album once again to the post office. This time I'd made the deadline and handed it over to Mr. Blanding, watched it go into a Royal Mail pouch.

Now to wait and I would wait in Scarborough where it all became clear and all made sense.

"Well done!"

I turned at the sound of Michael's voice. He was sitting in the chair by the cold hearth, sipping a cup of tea and helping himself to a caddy of tea cakes and breads, Becket purring contentedly on his lap. Michael offered tea; Becket hissed.

"No, 'why didn't you do it earlier?' No, 'glad you grew a pair, Radcliffe'?" I asked, sitting opposite him.

"Why? You did try it earlier—just wasn't the time."

"Is this it? Can I go back to my life as it was? I know how the story ends."

Michael shrugged. "That would depend on what your life was."

The Earl Grey was aromatic and soothing and I inhaled the fragrance while the cup warmed my hands. "My life was quiet. I was thinking of retiring," I said between sips. I paused a moment, and took another sip. "I was mourning Alice; she recovered from that accident and the latest illness, of course, but not long after...I'm regretting things I should have said and done, things done and left undone." The words came out quietly, sad. "After all we'd been through, that I should have..."

"Finish your tea and then finish your thought," Michael said. He rose and placed a hand on my shoulder.

A warmth began to spread through every pore and vessel, every hair and I felt the urge to cry out, to sob; but instead the warmth grew until I was surrounded by the brilliant sun and sky of The Village. The air was fresh with the scent of white flowers and I heard birdsong as I found myself on the bridge again. Alice was standing at its foot near the church.

CHAPTER 31

AS I WALKED towards her in one of those slow-motion attitudes one suffers in dreams, the people in the village started to dissolve—yes, dissolve—into white flowers that showered down like gentle rain. Slowly shapes changed from buildings and flora to swirls of soft, colored light; and just as deliberately the scenery melted and blended into more color and took shape as Rose Street in Berkeley and finally as Alice's house on a mild spring evening at twilight, one of those nights that still held the warmth of the sun on the pavement and the air full of nostalgic scents.

Harry answered the door on the first bell and without hesitation embraced me. "Quinn. God, it's been too long—and just in time!" I felt my throat constrict and the tears start to pool when he stepped back to get a look at me, smiling and shaking his head. "You look fantastic! Come in, come in!" The screen door was pushed aside to let me in and I nearly tripped over the luggage blocking the narrow hallway. Harry grinned when I looked at him. "Last night." Sensing my anticipation, he added, "She'll be back in a while - had to take Sammie to the vet's. It was time, you know – he hadn't been feeling so hot. So she went for a walk after dinner."

"Poor little dog. Poor Alice!" I whispered, knowing how much she loved Sammie, the last link to her mother.

"She's handling it well. But why wouldn't she? She's Alice Martin!"

"Him?" I spat the word out. "Did he come with her?"

"No. She left him. Didn't you know?" Harry glanced

at me suspiciously while leading the way inside.

"No, I didn't," I admitted and I wasn't lying.

"If you say so," he said, and pointed to the living room. "Make yourself comfortable; I'll get some coffee for us – unless you drink tea now?"

"No, coffee's fine."

"Alice made it!" he called over his shoulder.

"No problem. I was going to stay up all night anyway, working on the program for next season and take some calls from London."

"Coffee it is."

Once more I looked around and once more noticed, smiling, that everything had been left as if nothing had happened or changed over the years. As if Dennis hadn't died a painful and wasting death or Alice hadn't given in to a marriage of convenience that turned into her personal hell because of me. Because I told her to wait for me. The only changes were the framed album covers for the Orchestra's Vaughan Williams and Beethoven recordings sitting on the mantle.

Harry brought in a coffee tray and plate of cookies and I sat in my usual place at the end of the sofa.

"Alice?" I ventured, holding up one of the misshapen lumps that sported butterscotch chips and pecans.

"She didn't burn them this time," said Harry.

"You got the albums," I said, pointing to the covers with my mug.

"You were Denny's pride and joy—after me, of course." Harry said. Good to know the wry humor hadn't disappeared.

I hesitated, not wanting to ask the most obvious question and said, "When?"

"Hmm?" Harry finished his cookie. "When what? When did you became the pride and joy of this household?"

"When did she leave him?"

"A few weeks ago. He's been calling non-stop. Pays

more attention to her now than when they were dating and married and when she was in that damn hospital bed – thanks for getting word to me, by the way. I would have never known. Oh, by the way, you're a fraud and a home wrecker," Harry said with a wink.

"I object to the home wrecker allegation."

"You did keep showing up at the hospital," Harry replied as he tipped his mug towards mine. "Good move."

"Thanks, and as for being a fraud: I think the last year has erased that from my book of sins?" Again, I motioned to the two album covers. "Two Grammys each! Doctor Donovan Trist has what, a building named after him?"

"Doctor Donovan Trist. Silly bastard with a stupid name. I say good riddance to that ass! Do you know he's blaming you for his father's poor showing in the primaries? I guess everyone's overlooked the drunk driving conviction and the fact that Trist was seen around Cabo San Lucas with a blonde half his age while Alice was still in the hospital."

I shrugged and took another cookie, dipping it into the coffee. "Wonder if it was the girl he was making out with at my opening in New York last year? Money talks and sins walk."

Harry's eyes bugged for a moment. "Really? I didn't know. Did Alice…?"

"If she did, it's another reason why she's better than all of us."

"Well, it could get ugly, especially after that business with your father and his arrest, trial."

"Who do you think blew the whistle?"

"Out of the frying pan and into the fire? But don't take Alice with you."

"She can decide. I made a promise to Alice that I'd take care of things, and I meant it."

"Promise kept and paid in full."

Just the sound of her voice made my insides somersault and my heart pound. I looked up and smiled at

Alice, who stood holding the room-dividing tapestry in one hand. She was thinner, pale, but given all that she'd been through, that was understandable. The eyes and smile, however, were radiant.

"I got the album," she said. And then, "You look amazing."

"You are amazing," I whispered.

Then she was in my arms and we kissed and clung between whispered endearments. "You got the note inside the album sleeve?" I asked breathlessly.

"Yes," she said, kissing me again.

"And that's a yes?"

"I should hope so!"

"We need to celebrate some good news for a change," Harry spoke up as he removed himself from the living room and hurried into the kitchen while Alice and I shared the sweetest of reunions.

Harry cleared his throat to announce himself and we turned. Alice burst into laughter for there on a silver platter were orange-frosted Hostess cupcakes, the ones I loved, with three flutes of champagne.

"How about a celebratory dinner?" he suggested. "You've got news to share, I suppose?"

"The best and I'd like to invite someone if you wouldn't mind," I said between bites.

"Why don't you two go get this someone while I throw something together worthy of big announcements?" Harry offered, and handled Alice her shawl of cloud and twilight colors. I draped it around her shoulders as I had done while we were at the castle in Scarborough but this time there was no underlying sadness. She squeezed my hand and kissed it as we hurried down the porch stairs to the street and turned left, going up toward the hills.

"You know of course that we can't really do anything until my divorce is final," Alice said.

"Of course; but that won't prevent us from making plans, right? Proper proposal, bridal shower, et cetera?"

"Gives us something wonderful to look forward to," she replied and reached up on tiptoes to kiss my cheek. We held hands and walked in silence for a while until she said of a sudden, "Let me guess. We're going to see your mother and invite her to join us for dinner."

"Yes, I've healed some wounds."

"I'm glad. You both deserve happiness."

"*You* deserve happiness!"

"I guess this is our happily ever after?"

"Soon."

At a moment of triumph and happiness, that was all I could muster. Even that left me skeptical.

"Why?" Ralph Vaughan Williams as my stroll home with Alice asked became a walk through The Village. "Is this not the outcome for which you and Alice longed?"

"The battle with Trist, my father's trial. It was hard to think of our happiness, our future, when there was so much adversity," I said. "I waited for it to be taken away."

"Wasn't it?"

"No more questions," I insisted. "Let me have my life with Alice."

"Of course. But be careful what you do with it, Quinn," he warned and with a pat on the back he was gone and The Village literally dissolved before my eyes and became the sunset over the South Bay in Scarborough where I stood a month after we made our promise.

I thought it was too good to be true, fretted and worried as Alice sent word of the divorce proceedings and her life. Waited for dark clouds to loom overhead, waited for visits from the muses and mentors in The Village to set me to rights, to make me see the error of my ways and mistakes but they were gone from my life, and Alice wasn't. She was with me when I was in London for work, or touring with the orchestra, on my weekends in York and Scarborough, whether in person or in spirit, she was my last thought before sleeping, my first upon waking.

The next year was busy with plans, preparations, and

trips back and forth across the Atlantic while we waited.

And waited. Trist wasn't going to go quietly. Still, I was patient and hopeful.

When Alice finally called with the news we'd longed to hear, Harry and I put a plan in action.

The call came at the end of the day while I was finishing up in the Royal Albert office. No sooner had I expressed my love and happiness to Alice than I pressed the hook and waited for the hum of a dial tone and made another call.

"Hi, Harry. It's me. Did you get the news?"

"Hey Quinn! No, but I'm assuming it's good."

"Yes, and remember that idea you and I talked about when I was in Berkeley last spring?"

"Yeah – oh *yeah*! Want me to call Jane?"

"No, I can do that. Think we can pull it off?"

"I don't see why not. I'll make the calls."

"Good, you have the numbers, right?"

"Saved them in my planner."

"So...let me look at the calendar," I said as I threw open the appointment book and flipped a few pages. "I have the perfect date open. Here, block this out."

Everything was set in motion and when I arrived in California in May that year on the night we'd chosen, my mother and Harry had already been at work.

"I don't understand," Andersen said as we set the table in the formal dining room at my mother's house and Mother and Harry hurried back and forth with aromatic dishes and bottles of champagne. "Doctor Martin already knows you're getting married, sir."

"This is something to make it extra special," Harry replied. "For a very special young woman."

"Everything ready upstairs?" I asked.

"Fix your tie," Harry said, twirling his finger at my neck.

"You'd think after wearing a tux for most of my life I'd know..." I muttered and Mother stepped in to help.

"God, I'm nervous!"

"You have nothing to worry about. There. I've always thought you looked your best in a tuxedo," Mother said and admired her work. "She'll find you irresistible."

"He looks delicious," Harry replied and handed me a box of matches. "Lights and fire now."

I was lighting the candelabra and Mother stoking the fireplace in the dining room when precisely at six o'clock Alice arrived.

"Everyone in the living room now!" Harry ordered, shoving Andersen, Mother and me out of the room and he went to answer the doorbell.

"Harry! What are you doing here?" I heard her laugh; "Is this a family dinner?"

"Of a sort. Here, let's take your things. Now, follow me," he replied.

We were posed like an English Country Hunting Party around the fireplace in the living room. Mother was seated in the Queen Anne chair looking elegant, Andersen standing behind her holding a tray of hors d'oeuvres and Harry leaned against the mantle with a gin and tonic. I was standing in the middle of the room holding two flutes of champagne when Alice appeared.

"Remember when I invited Harry and Dennis to come to dinner?" I greeted after a kiss hello and in response to her questioning smile.

As soon as we were settled on the sofa, I gently tapped my glass. Everyone looked up expectantly, especially Alice, perhaps waiting for a toast, and as soon as the bell-like ring faded music filled the space, the voices of twenty-four men in song, members of the Cal Men's Glee Club, as they encircled us in the gallery above the living room and sang *Tros y Garreg*, the Welsh folk song she'd sung when we met by chance on the high school auditorium stage back in 1968. At the second verse, they came down the staircase two by two and presented Alice with a white rose.

I could only see Alice—the luminous, beautiful eyes as

they misted with tears, the radiant smile and beauty that was only hers.

The Glee Club finished their serenade and stood back as I slid to one knee and took Alice's hands.

"Alice my Faery Princess, will you do me the incredible honor of becoming my wife?" I whispered huskily.

Harry handed the ring box to me and I presented the engagement ring – a band of diamonds and rubies in white gold.

Alice's tearful, happy, acceptance was heard only by me as the Glee Club sang an encore of the last verse and everyone cheered.

But that was not the end of our faery tale.

Our day finally arrived months later.

I woke alone in the house at Scarborough as if it were any other day. But it wasn't. I went downstairs and saw that my Faery Princess had been there during the night, for a small Christmas tree stood by the fireplace and a birthday cake sat on the end table. Today was my birthday and she was giving me the best present of all.

A knock on the door about noon told me it was time, but I'd been ready for hours. I put aside the cello and went down to greet Jordan, Chloe, Anna and Graham, who flashed smiles, showered me with confetti and stepped aside to let me greet the local and international press as they took photos and followed us on the leisurely stroll to the castle.

My mother met us at the appointed place and kissed my cheek, wished me well. We'd only been there a minute and were greeting guests and well-wishers when a limousine drew up and Alice stepped out with Harry. Mother took the train of my bride's incredible dress as she walked over the castle grounds to where I waited. Alice wore an ivory lace gown and carried white flowers, wore a crown of silver roses over a diaphanous veil.

She was amazing.

I saw in her eyes the girl I'd fallen in love with a decade ago, the woman I'd loved and lost, the friend that stood by me in the worst of times.

I took Alice's hand and kissed it when we met and we walked arm in arm to where the vicar waited at the cliff overlooking the sea and our friends and those we called family gathered around us as we exchanged our wedding vows.

That moment of extraordinary love, of healing, bound us in the years we shared—almost thirty of them—and it was still with me when, so many years after she left our world, we met again on the bridge in The Village.

I learned that hearts broken do mend, because the love overflowing from them mends all.

Not Quite the End ....

Acknowledgments

As with the first edition of "Scarborough," thanks is offered to my friend and legal community colleague, Tamora, for giving me the idea of writing this story from the boy's point of view – and for the paper sword and the introduction to coffee. To Sandra, my friend, confidante, artistic enabler.

I give thanks for my colleague in writing, Molly, who gave me honest, helpful criticism for this story.

Finally, there's one last person to which I express my gratitude.

Thanks.

About the Author

A NATIVE of the San Francisco Bay Area, Ellen L. Ekstrom makes her home in Berkeley, California with her family. She serves as the parish deacon for The Episcopal Church of the Good Shepherd, and along with ministry, she enjoys knitting, cycling, a good book and good company. Ms. Ekstrom's growing library of work includes *The Legacy, Armor of Light, Ascalon, A Knight on Horseback,* The *Midwinter Sonata* Series, which includes the companion novels *Tallis' Third Tune* and *Scarborough,* and, writing as Caitlin Luke Quinn, *St. Edmund Wood.*

Coming soon: the third book in the *Midwinter Sonata* series, *The Shambles*; the sequel to *Armor of Light, Ascalon,* and the Whyte Rose & Violet, Scribes edition of *The Legacy,* a story of fourteenth century Florence and Tuscany.

Made in the USA
Charleston, SC
19 December 2014